Witch's Folly

~ BOOK ONE ~

OLIVER'S ANTIQUES

Vincenza Di Martino

Witch's Folly:
Oliver's Antiques

Vincenza Di Martino

RhetAskew   Publishing
United States of America

Cover Illustration
& Interior Design

© 2021 – Flitterbow Productions
And RhetAskew Publishing

ISBN-13: 978-1-949-39865-6

*this story is dedicated
to my late sister Angela,
whom I miss dearly,*

*and to my husband Travis —
the hero of my own story*

PROLOGUE

NIGHT FELL ON THE heavy hearts in the sleepy inn, none heavier than the restless woman occupying the only room on the third floor.

She paced, still wearing her scorched dress from earlier in the day. Her trembling fingers pressed to her forehead, trying to relieve the headache that was cousin to the ripping pain through her chest. Unlike the headache, this pain sought permanent residence in the new hollows within her soul. A pain so ravenous and raw it held her tight, a prisoner to her mind and body; the worse sort, leaving invisible scars that would reopen and fester before closing again. Dampness clung to her like moss to rock, a film of slick unease across her skin in the wake of the day's monumental shock.

Gone. The word reared its wretched, smiling face in her mind. Mocking, until her balled fists ached to hit the walls, as if capable of destroying the vermin once and for all. But there was no escape from herself.

She'd chosen her path. She could not deny the truths in her soul, her thoughts being all the armor she had against the darkness of the world looming over. Everyone was gone. The rain and ashes mingled—her past, a thing of faded screams.

Life astonished her with the things that could change in a matter of hours. She recalled the happiness she felt before it all happened. Remembering, down to the last second, before the door flung open and her world crashed around her.

A soft rapping came from this new door, freezing her to the floorboards. She dared not make a single sound. Silence, then a click. Her breathing hitched as the knob turned and the door creaked open. A man popped his head inside her room, cautious yet curious. He cleared his throat, alarmed by her wide eyes and lack of words.

"Excuse me, miss," he stepped half inside, "I just thought I'd check in on you. See if you're alright."

"Why?" her dusty voice asked.

"Well, you've been pacing for hours and—"

"How would you know I was pacing?" she asked in alarm.

"I could hear your footsteps 'cause my room is below yours. You've been going on for a good two hours now, so I figured you're restless." He spoke as if dealing with a skittish animal.

She didn't care for his tone, and a strange anger flared inside her. "How dare you waltz into my room, speaking to me like this? What business is it of yours—my pacing?" she spat at the uninvited visitor, her fury causing him to step back out of the door.

"I didn't mean to offend. I was just trying to be neighborly—"

"Black Hells, if I wanted some prying neighbor to pity me I'd—" she raised her voice, cutting him off. He held his hands out in defense.

"I wasn't comin' to pity you. Just trying to be pleasant and shut you up so I could sleep. Figured if you insisted on keeping me up, least you could do was talk to me. But looks like I'll be in the bar with all of that. Don't need some woman tellin' me to piss off." He paused, shaking his head. "You kiss your mother with that mouth? Good night, and good luck to ya."

This time he stepped out the door, shutting it behind him with a solid thud.

A knot of guilt settled in her stomach. With a heavy sigh for her irrational behavior, Orianna flung the door back open.

"Wait!" she called to the stranger who hadn't made it far. "I'm sorry to have disturbed you. I guess I am restless."

He remained silent, and she sensed the overwhelming emotions seeping up inside her again. The impending immobilization was welcome, allowing her to feel without distraction.

"Please don't go," she spoke with more calm. "Look, I'm a pain in the ass, but I'm also alone. And...I can't stand to be alone with myself right now." Tears pricked her eyes and nose as she felt the weight of truth of what she said. "So would you mind coming back in? I'm sorry for keeping you up."

He continued to stare in stubborn silence. "Well?"

"Well, what?" she asked. "What else do you want?"

"What ever happened to please?" He stood, waiting, and she noticed his considerable height. "Are you going step aside so I can come in?"

"Yes, yes of course," she said, waving for him to come in.

She gave him a skeptical once-over, then crossed to the fireplace. He seemed decent enough, and she could not argue that it was the least she could do after her incessant pacing kept him awake. In due course, she figured, he would see how wrong he was for caring and be on his way. He entered and closed the door behind him, waiting, in case she changed her mind and threw him out on his ear. He carried a white sack, and she eyed it.

"Mind if I sit?" he said, taking a seat by the window. "Maybe you should give sitting a try. It's a lot quieter, you know."

"I suppose so," she said, thankful for the reprieve as the twitchy tiredness in her legs sang. It felt good to rest.

Another silence stretched, and she decided she would not be the one to break it. She had made nice with him, and it was his turn to keep it going.

"I know you don't know me, but I heard about what happened to you today. Wanted to say how sorry I am for your losses." He rested the sack on his lap.

"Thank you, but again I'm not looking for anyone to feel sorry for me." She gazed out the window as the falling rain pattered against the glass. "I don't deserve it, anyway, no matter what it is you heard."

"That's not true. You can't blame yourself for something you couldn't see coming." He craned his head to catch her eyes. When she met them, she felt as if he could see into her soul. She was shocked by the appeal; all of the rawness, tucked beneath the surface, was suddenly on display to his eyes alone.

"It doesn't matter, they're gone. I—" she choked, relaxing a fraction with the touch of a warm hand on hers. She turned her attention back to the stranger beside her, who continued to stare. His face brimmed with kindness and something else she couldn't put her finger on.

"No," he said in a gentle tone, "a million times, no. Tragedies don't come with warnings or else they wouldn't happen. This isn't your fault."

Her eyes welled up, and a single tear rolled down her cheek. She began to crack, the anger breaking through her walls. He reached to brush it from her face, and to his surprise, she let him. His touch was an elixir, helping the cold grief in her veins dissipate. Every inch of her had been so impassive to all things, unfazed by the others thanks to the bitterness she wore as armor. She hadn't realized how cold she'd become until now, as he touched her.

"I brought you a few things. Now I know you're a stubborn one, but I won't take no for an answer so don't bother." He rummaged through the sack, handing her a white nightgown. It wasn't fancy, but it looked warm and thick and clean. "I took a guess at your size. I'm sorry if it doesn't fit well."

She took it with a skeptical frown, but the softness of the fabric made her realize for the first time how dirty and uncomfortable her current clothes were—the only clothes she had left. Her mouth tried to form a rebuttal but couldn't find one. "Thank you."

The stranger's face brightened a little. "No need to thank me. I also brought you some other things. Wasn't entirely sure what you woman need on a daily basis, but I tried my best. Thought you'd need some food, and I was a bit hungry too." He handed over the sack.

She opened it and saw it contained a brush, an apple, a package of dry sausage and cheese, perfume, and a small leather coin purse. Her pride rattled in her chest.

"Thank you, but I can't accept this. It's too much. I can't." With a firm hand, she gave it back to him and tried not to make eye contact, but he wouldn't take it.

"I said I won't take no for an answer. Can't tell me you're not hungry." He cocked an eyebrow. "Innkeeper said you haven't touched a thing since you got here."

Annoyance flickered inside her at the fact that he had been more right than wrong in his assumptions. "Only if you have some of it with me, and I'm paying you back someday for all of this. I'm not a charity case, you know."

Her offer took him by surprise, and he had to admit he liked her fire. "Okay, fair enough—but only if you change out of those clothes." He thought of it as banter, but when her face darkened with unspoken accusations of his intentions, he was quick to speak up. "No, no, no! I only meant for you to slip into something more comfortable. No, that's not right either. Ugh, I'm not lookin' for any of *that.* I'm just being polite."

She gave him a hard look before trusting her gut that he was telling the truth. "Very well," she sighed, taking the gown and walking over to the changing curtain. "Turn your head," she prompted, and he obliged with a grin.

"Can't blame me for peeking. I'm still a man." He chuckled under his breath.

She made haste changing. As she walked back to where he was sitting, she was shocked to notice his head was still turned away; he had kept his eyes averted whole time. Her skin felt lighter, appreciative of the gesture. Settling back in her seat, she waited for him to turn back around. It took her tapping his shoulder until he did; this made her deem him as respectable.

"Looks like it fits well," he said, proud of himself.

"It does."

"Good." He fished around in his pocket, pulling out a small knife to cut a piece of the dry sausage. The smile he offered was disarming. "Here, ladies first."

She nibbled at the pieces he gave her. "Thank you. I'm sorry I didn't catch your name. Who are you?"

"Oh, forgive me. Here I barge into your room and not introduce myself. I'm Zavier."

A small smile crossed her lips, a peculiar sensation after the stress of the day. "Nice to meet you, Zavier. I'm Orianna."

He eased the tension by sharing stories of growing up in North Country and how he came to live here. Their conversations circled round and round, filled with the usual things people say to get to know one another, but it wasn't strained like most first meetings. Getting to know someone often felt forced, yet one continued out of politeness. Instead, their talking reminded her of home. Somewhere, deep down, they knew each other as if they were lost embers of the same flame, searching the damp night for one another. He was soul food, his kind presence a balm to her chapped spirit.

"Where did she go?" he asked, stroking her hair as she laid back with her head on his chest. "The little girl?"

"I don't know. But she is somewhere safe." She closed her eyes as his caress eased her closer to sleep. "She is far, far away from me. But that's the best thing for her right now, even if it's not the best thing for me."

CHAPTER ONE

PEOPLE ASSOCIATE FAMILY WITH belonging, a membership confirmed by marriage or birth; but for Gemma, it meant understanding who she was—her identity. She sat on the bed, knees to her chest, staring at the white box on the desk. It loomed, mocking her sudden wave of cowardice, warning her to stay as far away as possible. She'd waited her entire life to obtain any shred of knowledge she could about her parents; but now, being so close to it paralyzed her.

She watched as the rain streamed down the glass, washing away the residue of days past to leave a clean pane that dissolved her trepidation. Windows always reflected the day's events, past and present; after a storm, they were made new. She turned back to the desk. This was her storm.

Gemma climbed off the bed, walked to her desk, and picked up the DNA kit. It weighed next to nothing compared to how heavy it laid on her mind. When she was about to tear the plastic from the box, the doorknob turned. A sliver of panic shot through her, causing her to drop the box and kick it under the desk as her mother's face appeared in the doorway.

"Gemma, why aren't you ready yet?"

"Sorry, I just don't have anything to wear." Gemma lied, heart pounding.

"That's not possible. Hurry up, and meet me downstairs."

Gemma let out a sigh of relief as her mother closed the door. She hadn't told her mother about the DNA kit, worried that her active search for her biological family would upset her. She grew up knowing she was adopted, a fact that stoked the fires of her imagination. She'd dreamed of ridiculous scenarios throughout her younger life, ranging from her parents being astronauts lost in space to royalty from far-off lands who'd somehow misplaced her. After graduating high school, about to embark on her college career, her imaginative ideas boiled down like tree sap to simpler hopes—that they were good, or at least not thieves or drug dealers. She craved meeting ordinary parents with complicated pasts, who had stayed alive long enough for her to know who they were.

She grabbed her jacket and headed out, giving the white box one last look before shutting the door.

* * *

THE WORLD WHIZZED BY in a blur of color from the car window. They passed families in restaurant windows, children stomping puddles in tall yellow boots, people sharing umbrellas. The rain pelted against the windshield in wide splatters.

Gemma and her mother had been driving around most of the day, going from antique shop to antique shop looking for "just the right thing" to spruce up their summer home, since it was becoming their permanent residence. While Gemma didn't mind putting up with the shopping and idle chatter, they were going on their sixth hour of it and her feet were soaked from the rain. An internal groan rippled through her as they weren't getting any closer to finding whatever the perfect thing was, if such a thing even existed.

"This one looks nice!" Her mother chimed as she pulled into the driveway, splashing through deep puddles and not waiting for Gemma's opinion.

Gemma let out a heavy sigh.

"Oh, come on! This is fun! This will be the last one, I promise. It looks so charming. Grab your umbrella." She opened her umbrella, jumping from the car and waiting for her daughter.

Gemma squinted at the charcoal-gray building with its ancient ambiance. The rain lent the place a more haunting appearance.

"If by charming you mean creepy, then yes."

Gemma climbed out of the car, feet heavy with obligation as she took cover from the rain. An old iron sign hung about the door, "Oliver's Antiques"—a name that struck her as peculiar, for some reason. The building wasn't huge but big enough to occupy her mother for a while. Built with weathered bricks, the two-level shop appeared to have been there for ages. Two diamond-latticed windows further showcased its age, draped in heavy red velvet curtains that were antiques themselves. But Gemma couldn't remember passing it before in all the years of vacationing in Lake Fort.

Her mother struggled to open the hefty maple door, which seemed reasonable; it was constructed of thick, solid wood that had to have weighed more than Gemma. The artisan iron scrollwork added to the weight. When the door at last gave way, her mother stepped inside—out of breath, with quick feet forging ahead faster than Gemma expected. The door swung back and Gemma hurried to catch it. If it shut all the way, opening it again would take much of her effort. The door nudged her from behind, impatient to push her inside. She looked back in scorn at the brief assault.

Gemma couldn't help but think of all of the things she'd rather be doing instead of breathing in more ancestral dander. Her mother, however, was already engrossed in some strange old thing. Coming to terms with her fate, she plodded deeper into the shop, knowing the sooner she got in the sooner they could go home.

The longer she looked, the more she started to like the shop. The lower half of the walls were weathered wood, the upper half being battered gray sheets of crinkled wallpaper. It looked more fragile than real, and something warned her not to touch. There were stone accents in the corners and strange wooden hangings between the ceiling and wall. Shelving ran along the walls, scattered in uneven patterns and holding odd objects. Despite its obvious old age, everything in the shop was spotless without a speck of dust, rust, or dirt.

"Can I help you with anything, ladies?" a woman asked, standing with great posture and clear authority—in charge, but younger than her manner implied.

"Oh, just browsing, thank you," her mother said.

The shop had a unique assortment of antique and medieval pieces. Gemma turned to face the shopkeeper, surprised to find her staring straight back. The lady dragged her eyes away before smoothing her blouse and clearing her throat.

"No problem. Let me know if I can help."

The shopkeeper's gaze lingered on Gemma before she disappeared behind the counter. Once Gemma and her mother moved past the counter, she took a moment to peer back at them, her heart pulling from the inside down into her stomach and thought: *It can't be.*

Gemma had a strange feeling about the shopkeeper, but she couldn't quiet put her finger to it. As she pondered, she noticed everything looked museum worthy—from knightly armors, to decorative swords, to ambiguous leather books. She picked up one of the swords with its silver, jeweled hilt that appeared a relic from King Arthur or some other fairy tale.

"Mom, look at—" she turned in excitement, frowning to see her mother wasn't nearby, and set it back down.

The store smelled of old things: a mingling of dust, matured wood, and moth balls. Its contents were a collage of oddities, peppered with strange furniture.

And there was the quiet. The same one found in libraries where tight-faced elderly biddies offered scowling glares, a tangible thing able to crack from a loud voice. It held an eeriness trapped inside that wandered with her throughout the store, causing the hair on her arms to stand on end.

On an aged wooden table, she came across a silver necklace with a pink crystal hanging from it. It wasn't her style, but it had a certain appeal. She put on the necklace, admiring it in the jagged mirror on the wall. To her surprise, she loved it. The braided chain hung at the perfect length, and the crystal caught the light in a sparkle that seemed to glow. Gemma carried it with her as she browsed.

An old-fashioned hearth stood against the back wall, made of brown and gray stones in a style she'd only seen in movies. Unlike the rest of the shop, it was covered in thick dust and cobwebs. A selection of candles sat on the mantle, an old mirror poised above with a hand-carved frame; it was a picturesque sight. To the left of the fireplace was a tennis-ball-sized bulge sticking out through the dust and webs. A swipe of her hand revealed a round, golden crystal and above it, a small wooden plaque read: "Only the fire-touched gain entry."

She placed her hand on the crystal to examine its rough texture when, without warning, it began to glow. A groan slipped out from the hearth as Gemma took an uneasy step back, unsure what was happening. In a bright flash of heat, the hearth lit and shifted down the wall to reveal a darkened room.

Struck with nervous disbelief but equal curiosity, she stepped inside to see the outline of candles scattered around the room. She squinted as she walked inside, gasping as they flickered to life and dispelled the darkness. Their sudden self-combustion made her more nervous than before. The light revealed a desk with some paper, ink and quill, and a book with a blank cover. Gemma approached the book; the closer she got, the more the cover quivered until words formed on the leather.

"What do you think you're doing?" the shopkeeper asked from behind her.

Gemma spun around in a panic to face the scowling woman. "I'm sorry. I didn't mean to open it. It just happened."

"What do you mean 'it just happened?' How did you open this room? Tell me everything that happened until this point," she said, jabbing a finger before beginning to pace.

"I dusted the crystal after reading the sign and—"

"You read the sign?" the lady asked, baffled.

"Yeah, but what does it mean by, 'Only the fire-touched gain entry?'"

"First, how did you light all of these candles? I'm more interested in how that happened."

"I didn't."

"That's it? *POOF!* They all lit up just like that?" The woman's face became exasperated, as if she was in another argument that Gemma couldn't hear.

Gemma nodded, a little put off by the shopkeeper's odd behavior. It was all getting too strange, half-convincing her that she suffered from some borderline personality disorder.

"Fascinating..."

"Am I in trouble or something? What is this place?" She held her arms out to the room.

"What?" The shopkeeper waved her off. "What's your name, girl? Where are you from?"

"Ashley. I'm from out of town," Gemma stammered, instinctively lying for fear of whatever trouble the brusque shopkeeper might offer.

"Ashley." A faint smile crossed the shopkeeper's face, as if she were amused.

"You never answered me. What is this place? And what's with the creepy sign?"

"This is my room, and that *creepy* sign is none of your business—not right now, anyway. Come."

The lady turned around, took a deep breath, and gently blew—snuffing the candles all at once, quick as they'd been lit. With one flick of her finger, the dust and webs covered it all up again.

Gemma stared in disbelief. "What? Who are you?"

"Orianna Oliver. I'm the owner of this shop." She stood firm and tall as if staking her claim through posture.

"How did you do that?"

"Magic."

Gemma snorted, "There's no such thing as magic."

Orianna turned quick on her heels. "Bite your tongue, girl! Don't disgrace the craft and abilities you are apparently clueless about."

"What ability? You're crazy. I'm out of here." Gemma turned around, fists balled, ready to storm out.

"How did you read it?" Orianna asked.

Gemma turned back. "What?"

"The sign. How did you read the sign written in an ancient language?"

Upon second glance, the wooden sign was composed not of letters but jagged runes she'd never seen before; her mouth ran dry.

"And how did you light all of my candles?"

"I-I didn't do anything," she stammered. "They just...lit on their own."

"Did they? Or did you need the light, and they ignited?"

"I mean, it was dark. But I couldn't have done that. Like I said, they just lit."

"Whatever you say, Gemma." Orianna headed for the desk.

"Wait, how did you know my real name?" she asked, face scrunched in confusion.

Orianna paused with her back turned, contemplating her answer.

"One doesn't forget family."

"You're family now?" Gemma's voice cracked. "That's impossible."

Turning back, Orianna threw her hands on her hips— annoyed by the sudden and unnecessary attitude sent her way. "Oh? How would you know that? You're adopted, aren't you? Don't know any of your biological family, right? Or where you came from?"

Before Gemma could say anything back, her mother came along behind her.

"Look what I found," she said, holding up the painting like a trophy. "It will look great in our living room! Did you find anything you liked?"

"I think so, but I'll wait a bit to buy it." Gemma thumbed the crystal in her palm, its smooth texture soothing her.

"Opportunities never remain stagnant. How much for the painting?"

"I can let it go for $75." Orianna attempted a warm smile. "Let's go up front and get you cashed out."

"Great!"

Orianna played a good charade that she was neutral about the situation; believable, with her blasé attitude. For Gemma, however, the world she thought she knew tilted off its axis. She watched in hazy silence as her mother made the transaction. Orianna bagged the painting up and tried to make idle conversation as if she were a different person than the woman who put the hearth back to its original state with nothing more than a flick of her finger.

"My card, in case you want to come back." Orianna slid a black business card with silver writing across the checkout desk. Her mother gathered up the painting and bounced toward the door, leaving Gemma to take the card. She stood a moment, turning the card over in her hand to admire its design.

Orianna smiled at Gemma and her puzzled expression. "Do come back. But please, don't wait too long."

"What's too long?"

"Before it's too late." There was a pained look in Orianna's eyes this time, replacing the gusto they'd held seconds ago.

Gemma nodded in wordless reply, feeling sorry for her. She turned to leave but realized she had the necklace clutched in her hand and hadn't paid for it. "Oh, I'm so sorry, the necklace. I—"

Orianna put up her hand. "No charge for that. It's yours, anyway."

Gemma clutched the crystal, thanking her and walking out the door.

CHAPTER TWO

"**DON'T YOU AGREE, GEMMA**? Gemma? Hello?"

"Oh, sorry. What did you say?" She had been fiddling with the pink crystal, absorbed in her own thoughts.

"I said that shop was fun, and we should go back sometime," her mother said in mock slowness.

"Yeah, it was okay. A bunch of old stuff, as usual," Gemma said, fighting to stay in the real world and out of her head.

"I guess, but what a steal for that painting! It's quite beautiful and so vintage." She trilled on until she noticed Gemma's glazed expression. "Are you okay, honey? You seem distracted."

"Huh? Oh yeah, I'm fine, just tired. Let's go hang that painting."

Gemma exited the car, hoping for a distraction from Orianna's nonsense. At the door, the knob twisted before she touched it. Startled, Gemma jerked away and stared at the knob.

"Aren't you going to go inside?" her mother asked, confused.

Gemma pushed past the door, heading straight to her room.

"I'm going to start dinner. Would you like to help me?" her mother called up the stairs but was answered by the slam of Gemma's door. She pondered her daughter's curious behavior as she set the painting on the couch. She settled on it just being teenage moodiness before resigning herself to a night of solo cooking.

* * *

DINNER WOULDN'T HAVE BEEN so bad if the saltshaker hadn't slid off the table as she reached for it. Her mother, of course, was oblivious. Nor did she comment when Gemma excused herself soon after.

Gemma always found therapy in washing dishes...until she noticed the soap bubbles floating out of the sink and moving with a mind of their own. She tried her best to continue washing, but a shadow formed above her head as she rinsed the last plate. She looked up, staring at a ringed cluster of bubbles swirling in a perfect circle. They fell from their formation at her gasp, popping on their way down.

She faked a yawn once the kitchen was clean, disappearing back into her room. Gemma turned to shut the bedroom door, but it shut on its own without her even touching it.

"I'm getting really sick of this shit," she cursed through clenched teeth.

Gemma spotted her basket full of clean clothes that needed folding. What could be more normal than the tedious act of folding laundry? She reached for a shirt inside the basket and began. Three garments in, a pair of pants jerked themselves from her hand. She grabbed again, and they threw themselves in the opposite direction. Her face heated when another pair of pants dodged her a few times until she knocked the basket off the bed, sending the clothes tumbling across the floor.

She fell onto her bed in a fit of frustration, happy they were strewn about in disarray, then covered her head with a pillow. Her life would never be the same, forcing her to uncover the mysteries surrounding her adoption and parentage.

Later that night, her mother opened the door to Gemma's room, and found her sitting on her bed clutching her pillow and appearing low-spirited.

"Honey, what's wrong?"

Gemma considered how to best reply. "Mom, what do you know about my birth parents?"

"No one knew much about them. In fact, they didn't have any next of kin, either." She took a seat on the bed next to her, placing an arm over her shoulder. "From my understanding, you were in the system until you were three months old. Then one day, we all became a family, and I've never been happier." The biggest of smiles pulled at her mother's mouth, and Gemma couldn't help but smile back. A mother's love truly was the cure for all things. For a tick in time, Gemma forgot her problems.

"Thanks, Mom."

"I'm sorry I don't have more information for you, sweetheart. What made you think about this?"

Gemma thought about whether she should tell her mother about Orianna and what she witnessed at the shop. Desperate for someone to talk to, but a voice inside her fought against it. Her mother had enough to worry about.

"No particular reason."

"If you say so." She looked at the clock. "Well, it's getting late. I'll see you in the morning. Love you, good night." Her mother leaned forward and kissed on the head before retiring to her room.

Gemma stayed up, pondering. There were still so many holes to her story, enough to make magic more believable. Orianna seemed to know her and maybe had information about her past. She adjusted the necklace and admired the crystal's unique shade of pink. It glowed, but this time it wasn't a trick of the light.

She eyed a candle sitting next to the window. A second attempt might prove it hadn't been her, that she was a normal person. She concentrated on the wick as she willed it to light. A flame sputtered and sparked from the candle, jarring her concentration, but no flames arose like before. Her stomach turned to ice water. It was settled. She would go back to Oliver's Antiques in the morning to speak with Orianna.

CHAPTER THREE

BARLOW WALKED HOME AS the sun began its descent. He enjoyed his long day of picking herbs in the large garden. His cultivation powers were legendary, able to grow anything; his skills were precise for optimal potencies. Folk came often for his effective remedies, ranging from pest killers to tea leaves to cooking herbs. Alcohol drew bigger crowds, and his various mixtures of beer brought in most of his profits. A good beer and solid sleep could cure most anything, in his opinion.

A shiver ran down his spine. Once he was inside, he locked the door behind him. Something felt strange; the air was different, stiller than usual with a staleness about it—which was odd, since he'd left the windows open. Common practice of his profession to let out the vapors of cooked potions. The farmer down the road requested a poison he could use on some furry pests eating his crops. Barlow agreed and made a potent herbal cocktail, so deadly the vapors themselves were not safe until cooked boiling hot. The open windows kept him safe from a variety of poisonous deaths.

Paranoia set in as an impromptu breeze swept through the room, leaving icy gooseflesh across his arms. He stilled, scanning for any abnormalities, but everything was as it should've been. This was certainly due to his rebellious need for order that bordered on sickness. The crash of a shutter stole his breath, and he jumped. *Just the wind, you craggy old fool,* he reprimanded as he walked to the window, securing the shutter.

"I must have gotten too close to those poisons. Probably what's causing my paranoia. Or this business itself has finally turned my mind."

"Perhaps..."

Every hair on his body stood on end at the unexpected voice. A swirl of black smoke appeared in the middle of the floor, leaving a snarling woman standing in its place.

"Or perhaps you're just getting old now, Barlow." She narrowed her eyes at the potions master.

"Hilda—but how?" he asked, terror splayed across his face.

In a flash, too fast for his eyes, she stood mere inches from him.

"Glad to see you remember me, darling. It has been oh so long. Did you think I'd forgotten you?" A cruel smile curved her lips as she ran a finger down his chest, burning through the shirt to flesh. He yelped in pain. "It's hard to forget someone who tried to kill you. How unfortunate for you that your efforts clearly failed. Here I stand, as young and vivacious as I've ever been." She gestured, showcasing a lush body.

"I don't deny what I did. It was for the greater good. You were so consumed by greed—by hatred—that you were no longer my benevolent wife." He pleaded, "I tried to save you, pull you out of the darkness, but you wouldn't listen to reason. You shouldn't even be alive, not after the poison you drank." Barlow's bewilderment clung like sweat to his face. He had mixed her a pungent poison that should have worked; yet she stood in front of him, clothed in younger flesh.

"Silence!" she screamed. "I did not come here for your lies, Barlow. I came here on business."

"What business could you possibly have other than revenge?"

"You underestimate me. I would never seek you out solely for something as petty as revenge." She backed away. "I've joined Leo's army. After all, he's the reason I'm still alive. I owe him my loyalty. I'm here on his behalf to aid in executing his plans. I require ingredients for a certain potion. Here, look it over." She tossed the note at him.

Barlow read the list, mortified at its contents. "These are very dark ingredients, Hilda. I don't possess any of these herbs. You know that I don't dabble in this sort of magic. It's not one to take lightly, by any means."

"Tsk, tsk, don't sell yourself so short, Barlow. You're the most experienced potions master around. Who else, other than you, could cultivate these ingredients with such potency? Pity to waste it all on beer and impotency potions. Join Leo's cause, and come back to me," she breathed into his ear. "Lose yourself in the power of it all. Do this, and you'll be renowned."

He closed his eyes, lost in her touch. This was not something he could do, it was wrong. He missed his wife, losing himself in the thoughts of having her back again, but she'd become a vile thing. A tool in the arsenal of the most immoral character that Goblidet and its surrounding cities ever had the misfortune of housing.

"No. Hilda, this is insane. You know my feelings on Leo and his radicals. I would never involve myself in mixing these ingredients. They're far too dark, and much evil rests in their roots." Barlow did his best to stand tall and unnerved against the thing wearing his wife's skin.

"You will do it! Don't be a fool, Barlow! There are worse things than going against your morals," she spat at him again, closer this time. She slowed her last sentence to saturate him in dread. "You will, or else."

"Never!" He crumpled the paper and threw it to the floor. She stalked closer. He tried to back away, but she followed.

"Never say never, darling. I have my ways." She dragged another finger across his chest, and he screamed in pain. "Where were your morals when you tried to take my life?"

He tried to strike, but every time he made contact with her skin his own burned.

Every door and window slammed shut, sealing them both inside—cold as a tomb. The evil in Hilda's eyes told Barlow that the chances of him making it out of alive was as thin as frost. The woman he once loved had been replaced by this depraved creature. His screams echoed against the walls of his home as her every touch seared his skin. The wooden floor thickened, soaking up his blood.

CHAPTER FOUR

GEMMA PAUSED IN FRONT of Oliver's Antiques, having nowhere else to go. Everything about her life lay beyond inches of concrete and brick, close enough for her to touch. Once the answers were released, there was no going back.

Squaring her shoulders, Gemma pushed the heavy door and peeked inside but Orianna wasn't at the desk. Searching further into the store, passing boxes of new antiques, the shop seemed to have expanded. She wondered how deep she'd have to look until she rounded a corner and found Orianna on a small ladder dusting a tall shelf.

A large smile crossed the raven-haired woman's lips. "I had a feeling you'd be back. What can I do for you?"

"How did you know it was me?"

"Like I said, it was a feeling. Also, there's a mirror over there that allows me to see who comes in."

Gemma's face fell, embarrassed. "Oh right, that makes sense."

"Not everything is magic." She grinned. "What's brought you in today, Gemma?"

"I have some questions that need answering."

"Ha! I'd be disappointed if you didn't." Orianna swooped down from the ladder. "We have a lot of ground to cover. Walk with me." She strode through the store, dusting away as the ladder followed her, dragging itself along the floor like an obedient puppy.

Gemma's mind stirred, unsure what to make of the pet ladder. "You mentioned we were family. Who are you to me?"

"Ah, an easy one. I like those. Your mother was my sister, making me your aunt. Next question." She picked up a tiny bottle with an old-fashioned sprayer attached, sniffed it, and sprayed herself.

"What happened to my parents?"

The question fell, dropping like an anvil of silence to the floor. Orianna paused, mid-dusting. Gemma watched the stiffness increase along the woman's shoulders.

"Let's skip that for now."

"I guess that's fair." A sinking feeling made its home in the pit of her stomach; the question must have held an unpleasant answer. "Weird things happened since I left the shop yesterday. Why is that?"

She examined a skull with a knowing eye before cleaning it with utmost respect. "Hmm, what kind of weird things are you talking about?"

Gemma grimaced at the skull. "Like doorknobs moving without me grabbing them, levitating bubbles, clothes with a mind of their own, and a candle sparking in my room after I only looked at it. Those kinds of weird things."

"Sounds like your powers are fighting to make an appearance. That's great news!" A smile cracked Orianna's face. "Did the candle ignite or just spark?"

"Just sparked."

Orianna pursed her lips in mild disappointment.

"Are you saying I'm a witch?"

"Of course you're a witch. You're certainly not of the fae." Orianna snorted.

Quiet slathered the air as Orianna looked back to see Gemma's feeble look, an expression that hit hard. As she drew in a deep breath, Orianna stepped down from the ladder and put her hand on Gemma's shoulder.

"How about we sit a spell and talk about this?" Orianna forced a grin, but it didn't fit right. "Come, I'll make us some tea."

Orianna walked her to the back of the store, cleared the hearth, and lit the fire. She motioned her over to a table and chairs, tucked away by a wall that hadn't been there yesterday. Gemma sat down, watching as Orianna placed a kettle of water above the fire, her act and form radiating comfort.

"Aren't you worried someone might come in?"

"Not particularly."

With a wave of her hand, the front curtains closed, the sign flipped, and a curt click sounded from the door—all while Orianna settled into her seat.

"Now where did we leave off? Right, your mother being a witch. Let's hold off on questions about your parents for now. It's a hard subject, but we will get there. I promise."

"I understand." But understanding did not make her any less disappointed. "So are we good witches or bad ones?" A ridiculous question but she felt it was valid.

Orianna laughed. "We're good witches, I can assure you of that much. There has never been a witch or wizard in our family that was malicious, a fact we're proud of. We're also one of the more powerful bloodlines in the land we hail from."

"Where's that? Where are you from?" Gemma leaned in, crossed arms on the table.

" *We* are from a different realm. You're from there, too, you know. It's where you were born. Our home is within a magical realm at the edge of Goblidet Center. It's full of magic folk like ourselves and creature's unknown to this world." A memory flitted across Orianna's face. "We'll have to go sometime so you can see your homeland yourself."

"That would be incredible." Gemma said, surprised she meant it; but she was sincere, feeling drawn already to this land she'd never heard of until today.

"Tell me about the spark." Orianna leaned back in her chair.

"I have a candle in my room and was curious if I could recreate what happened here, but it only sparked. I mean, I was concentrating for it to spark so I guess it was my own doing, but I didn't *really* do anything."

"That's wonderful!"

Gemma became frustrated, unable to see the wonderful in her failed experiment. "Is it, though? Is it really?" She folded her hands on the table, businesslike. "Why is it happening? Why now? I've never heard about spontaneous firepower being a side effect of antiquing."

"And *there* is the Oliver spirit!" Orianna chortled.

"The Oliver spirit?"

"That's our last name, your true last name—and yes, it's a good thing. It means your powers are coming to the surface, coming up for air. That crystal around your neck is yours. It's been yours since birth, and there is a reason for that. That magical stone helps you channel your powers when you desire to use them. It is essential until your powers learn to come on their own. You seem to follow in the family footsteps, too, with your fire ability."

The kettle whistled, and Orianna returned to the fireplace.

"So what are we—arsonists?"

Orianna set the cast-iron teakettle on the table and summoned two fluted teacups with matching pink flowers.

"Not exactly, we just have a strong affinity for fire. If you practice, they will become stronger and there are things that we may need to do together someday. We should work on that as soon as possible."

"Like what?"

"It's complicated. Sugar?" Orianna offered after adding a spoonful to her own cup.

"Yes, please."

Gemma spooned some sugar into her teacup and waited. An awkward silence grew and shaped itself between them as they both sipped their tea, one waiting for the other to speak first—a standoff.

"What's wrong?"

A pained smile cracked on her face as she looked down at her tea and took a deep breath, as if to allow herself to feel the happiness. When Orianna looked up again she glowed with family love.

"All of these years...I never thought I'd see you again."

"All these years? Were we together before?"

"Yes. I was there when you were born, right until you weren't with me anymore. I never left you for long. Neither did your mother and father until their untimely passing. It's such a long story, you and I, your mother and father." Orianna paused, twirling the small spoon on her saucer. "Are you sure you're ready to know?"

"Yes, of course I am. What happened? Why didn't you keep me after they died?" Her sharp tone unearthed a sadness that lingered, buried deep within.

"I did. I tried to keep you, but you were almost taken from me. It was clear you weren't safe, and it broke my heart. You were like my own." She paused, unable to go on with her thoughts. She wiped a tear from her eye before continuing. "Here, I'll show you."

Orianna slipped the tear into her teacup and slid the cup over towards Gemma. The tea swirled inside the cup as an image appeared.

Orianna playing with baby Gemma, smiling and happy together. Flashing to a scene of black fog surrounding her crib. Orianna storming in just as the fog crept up to Gemma inside the crib. A flash of light and fire. Orianna carrying Gemma away as a house blazed behind them, standing in the woods as a black hole opened in front of them, and they disappeared together.

The images faded as the tea stilled. Gemma brushed away her own tears as she looked up at Orianna, noticing the worry aging her face. She wanted to keep her, save her from whatever that thing was in the memory. A cold piece of her heart warmed at the thought that she was a wanted child.

"Oh Gemma, don't cry. I'm sorry, I should have waited to show you that." Orianna touched Gemma's arm.

"You didn't want to give me up. All these years I wondered if I was just an unwanted child, some sort of burden, but I wasn't. That just feels good to know." Gemma gushed as she wiped back more tears. "What was that thing? Where did we go? What happ—"

"The black fog. It is an extension of a very dark sorcerer, a type of hand that does most of his bidding. It's composed of the souls he claimed from deals. His goals, at the time, were power and control...and to inflict pain." Gemma could feel the anger hanging on her words.

"He was trying to kill me?"

"Yes. It was then that I realized you weren't safe in our world—or, even in my care, in my own home."

"Why didn't we stay together here then?"

"I planned to—"

A loud rumble shook the shop as a man fell from the hearth, face first onto the floor. He stood, covered in soot and coughing up dusty clouds as he brushed himself off.

"Tobler! What in Black Hells are you doing here?"

"Just thought I'd drop in," he said with a crooked grin, followed by more coughing.

"Always making an entrance." Orianna glared at him. "Why did you come here? You know my portal potions are off limits."

"I know that's why I attempted my own potions." Tobler coughed again. "Zavier sent me to bring you back. There's been a disturbance."

Orianna made it to her feet. "Well, don't talk about it here, for Ophelia's sake. We don't want to endanger two worlds. Did anyone see you?"

"No one saw me. Oh," he said, noticing Gemma sitting at the table, "didn't realize you had company. I'm Tobler, who might you be?" He offered his hand.

"I'm Gemma." She put her hand out.

Tobler bowed, turning her hand over, and kissed the back—leaving a patch of soot in its wake.

"Very nice to meet you, Gemma," he said with a sly twinkle about his eyes.

Gemma blushed roses. Orianna swiftly kicked him from behind.

"She's my niece, you fool. Watch yourself, or I'll carry your thumbs in my purse." She scolded Tobler before smiling at Gemma. "Are you coming, dear?"

"T-to the other realm? Right now?"

"Yes. I'd like to show you where you're from, but it can wait if you're not ready."

Tobler stared, confused. "Wait? But—h-oh"

"Go grab my potions in the office, boy," she commanded.

He did as he was told with a strong measure of reluctance.

"Pay no mind to him. Like I said: you can wait if you'd like, or you can come with us now. The choice is yours."

Gemma froze at the thought of leaving the only world she'd known to see where she belonged. Belonged. The word tasted sweet in her mouth, tipping her decision. If she didn't go now, then when? Why wait?

Gemma stood, thankful her feet weren't as unsteady as her insides. "I want to go."

Orianna smiled.

"How do you plan on doing that? The days don't exactly pass the same between the realms," Tobler asked, skeptical.

"Simple. I'll just slow it down."

"But that's forb—" His words were cut off by a cuff from Orianna as she took the vial of potion from him.

"Thank you, Tobler. Now stand back, the two of you, while I open the portal."

Gemma and Tobler obeyed as Orianna walked up to the hearth. Muttering a few words as she rolled the vial between her palms, it glowed a vibrant blue; then she tossed the vial inside of the hearth. There was the shattering of glass, blinding white light, and the hearth opened into a swirling black vortex.

"That would have made getting here a lot easier than trying to brew up my own vials." Tobler snorted.

"I don't like to be disturbed while I'm here, but you could have also asked." Orianna slung back. "Okay, Tobler: you go first."

Orianna moved to the table where a hefty hourglass sat. Placing a finger in the center of a brass cog, she cursed then flipped it over—blood magic, not exactly an approved practice. Black sand flowed as specs of white light dripped to the bottom: graveyard dirt, the hearts of dead stars, and ground bone. A rippling sensation fluttered through the air, turning it sluggish. She put a finger to her mouth to hide the blood.

"Zavier wouldn't approve, you know," Tobler whispered in Orianna's ear.

"Then he can deal with me—or you could keep your yap shut, since this is none of your business." A glare hardened Orianna's face as she spoke to him.

Tobler slogged through the portal, but not before giving Gemma a flirtatious wink. Orianna huffed, crossing her arms over her chest.

"Okay, dear, your turn."

Skittish, Gemma slowing walked through in a tingling flash. The atmosphere was different. She looked up to a chandelier hanging from the ceiling, glancing at the old black and white pictures hanging on the walls. The weathered wood floor creaked beneath her feet as she stepped closer to study the people in the photographs. There was a shimmer of light as Orianna crossed over the portal.

"Ah, it's good to be home," Orianna said, taking a deep breath as she left the room. "Are you coming, Gemma?"

"Right behind you," she said, still amazed but determined to learn more.

CHAPTER FIVE

GEMMA WALKED DOWN THE creaky staircase into a sitting room warmed by a crackling fire; the hearth looking eerily familiar to the one in the shop. A tall man with black hair and a longer black beard walked over to Orianna, enveloping her in a firm embrace.

"I missed you, you know. Where have you been?" he asked.

"I missed you, too. I have someone for you to meet." Orianna took his hand, looking proud as a mother duck. "Gemma this is your uncle, Zavier. Zavier, this is our niece, Gemma."

"You found her," Zavier whispered with awe. "So nice to meet you, Gemma. We've been looking for you." He shook her hand, losing it in his own bear-like grip before enveloping her in a hug.

"Nice to meet you, too?" Gemma stammered, taken off guard by the statement.

"Zavier has helped me try to track you down."

"Yes, it took longer than we thought but makes your homecoming even happier. However, I'm more your *almost* uncle than a proper uncle," Zavier said, teasing Orianna, but there seemed to be a bigger issue that hung over both the looks and words.

Orianna cleared her throat. "This is true. He is almost your uncle."

Gemma was puzzled at the odd phrasing. Before she could ask more, another voice piped up.

"Yeah, she's been stiffing him for the walk to the alter."

Thump!

Orianna cuffed him upside the head. "Watch your tongue, Tobler! And who said you could eat that?"

Tobler gave a guilty smile, holding a half-eaten apple. "Oh, come on! I didn't think you'd mind me staying for dinner." He winked at her, clearly trying to get back into her good graces.

"Hmph! Well, considering this is *technically* your home, I guess you could stay. I need wood for the fire, so make yourself useful. You and Gemma can go fetch it. In the meantime, I will start dinner. You don't mind do you, Gemma?"

"No, that's fine," she said a little too quickly.

Tobler wore a smug smile, walking out the door behind her.

"Don't be too long!" Orianna called after them.

"They'll be fine, Orianna. You shouldn't worry so much." Zavier said.

"How do you know about how worried I am?" She protested, her hands on her hips.

Zavier put his arms around her waist, pulling her close. "Because I know you better than most. You're a worrier. You get that crease right there," he said, tracing a finger from her forehead and down the bridge of her nose.

Orianna smiled. "I guess you might know me a little."

"Mhmm," he bent to kiss her, "so they'll be gone a while?" He raised an eyebrow as he squeezed her hips.

Orianna gave a dramatic gasp, "Not long enough for that! Goodness Zavier, behave yourself."

"You never minded my misbehaving before," he chuckled.

Orianna walked to the kitchen as Zavier followed, giving her rump a fun pinch. She giggled, swatting him with a dainty hand.

He was a bear of a man with a true heart, and Orianna loved how he made her feel small and safe.

* * *

GEMMA HAD NEVER SEEN so many shades of green or breathed air as clean beneath such a vivid blue sky. She concentrated in silence, listening to the scurry of animals within the undergrowth. A squirrel-like creature ran over her feet and up the nearby tree, then sat and nibbled something between its paws. Birds sang off in the distance, floating on the air, their song clear as bells in a church tower. Every step introduced a fascination between the lush land and its denizens.

"So you're the lost niece." Tobler said, breaking the silence.

"I guess so, except I had no idea I was lost."

"Well, what are your thoughts so far?" He gestured with both hands to their surroundings. "Must feel unreal, having only spent your time in The Echo."

"Why do you call it that?"

"Because that's its name," Tobler teased. "It's like when you yell out and your voice bounces back. It sounds like you, except it's not. They're similar places, but they don't work the same."

Gemma considered his explanation. "I guess that make sense."

"Is it common where you're from to answer a question with a question?"

"Oh right, sorry. It's a lot to absorb all at once. One day, I'm an ordinary person wondering why she was given away, and then I'm not. Some crazy lady tells me I have magical powers and a family who's been looking for me. Before I know it, I'm standing in a strange place I never thought existed."

Her thoughts were tumbling out much faster than she anticipated. She never liked people who had verbal vomit, leaving no door shut to the public. Tobler was a complete stranger, yet she felt compelled to get everything out in a sudden burst.

Tobler absorbed what she said, word by word, digesting them whole. "That's understandable—normal, even—but I can't be positive since I've never met anyone who came from the Echo to the Magic Realm." He shrugged before continuing. "I think you'll come to like it, though, if you give it a chance. This realm is full of opportunities for newcomers and old timers. We're a decent enough people, always giving a splash behind our ears."

She felt something swoon inside of her at the sight of his disarming smile. "We'll just have to see where time takes us—me."

"Not a bad idea. Give yourself time to get used to it all," he chuckled as if he was holding a dirty secret.

They had only just met him, but there was a warmth radiating from him. Tobler had a spirit of calm about him, carefree, as if he had all of the answers to life hidden in a deep pocket. Gemma shook herself, realizing that she had been staring. He caught her in the act, a sneaky glint in his eyes.

"So, do you have powers too?" The worlds left a strange residue in her mouth.

"Yes, I too can conjure up magic and spells," he said, his smile stopping at her glare. "I'm not always the best at it, as you witnessed in Orianna's shop earlier with my graceful tumble to the floor."

Gemma giggled, remembering the shock and his handsome features smothered in soot.

"But I can read minds," he added, and her giggles ceased.

"Oh?" She floundered, desperate to remember her thoughts.

37

"No, not really! I'm only teasing. I have a keen sense for emotions, though—so almost like reading minds. It's my affinity. Reading emotions can be bad enough. I would never want to know people's thoughts behind them."

"Do you feel them, too?" Gemma asked, plagued with curiosity now that she knew her thoughts were safe.

He picked up more wood. "I can feel and manipulate emotions. There is a moral line that comes with manipulating. It has its moments, not that I've found many."

He was rambling. He never rambled. He was always in control of himself, but she made him feel clumsy. "I've never had to explain it. It's harder than I expected."

"No, it's okay, I see what you're getting at. You must have a strong sense of morality to contain a power that persuasive." Gemma watched a pale bluebird dart by, chasing another winged creature. Her open interest illuminated her face, making his heart skip.

"So what about you?"

"What about me?"

"What powers have manifested in you? I imagine something big and imposing with you being an Oliver." He tried to stop the corners of his mouth from turning, feeling the scurry inside her whirl.

"Oh, it's only been fire and some moving objects. I don't have much else."

"Only fire and moving things?" He snickered. "Those aren't exactly light affinities to have running in your veins. Seems that you've acquired your family's fire ability. That'll come in handy."

"What do you mean 'come in handy?'" she asked, beguiled by the sweat sliding down his face.

"Nothing. It's a practical ability, lighting fires and stuff. Never know when you'll need a match—which you clearly won't have need for." He tried to cover his tracks, knowing he'd said too much.

"I guess so, especially for lighting candles. I like those." She felt her mind warp at the thought of using her newfound magic again.

Tobler nodded back towards the house.

Arms full, they walked and chatted about odd things and common interests. Thankful, he turned the conversation over to a more normal discussion, not pelting her with more. He was glad she had relaxed. It gave him time to thumb through her feelings and learn the curves of her smile. Tobler took time to notice the flecks in her eyes when the sun touched her face, warming something inside him that had been wrapped too long in a cold familiarity which he ignored. A stirring of his own had begun, and he didn't want it to stop.

Gemma stumbled over on a rock, falling forward as wood flew from her grip. Before she could hit the ground, Tobler caught her.

"Whoa, you okay? That would have been a nasty fall," he said, helping her to her feet.

"Yeah, just clumsy. Some things never change." She touched his arms, enjoying the feel of the muscles flexing. "I guess your other powers are speed and strength?"

"Not even close compared to Zavier. You'd swear that man is half ogre if you saw what he can lift."

They both felt a surge of awareness, electric to the touch, prickling over their skin. Their proximity teetered on embarrassment as her hands still gripped his muscular forearms and his hands still clasped her waist. Awkward and reluctant, they stepped back from each other as silence hung in the air between them, blobby and uneven.

"Here, let me help you." He bent down to gather the wood.

"Thanks, but I can—"

Something dark caught Gemma's attention, like a shadow from the corner of her eye. When she turned her head, there was nothing there.

"What's wrong?" Tobler asked, feeling her unease.

"Thought I saw something."

Tobler took a look around; although he didn't see anything, he wasn't convinced she hadn't. A feverish chill ran up his spine, proving the emptiness hadn't been so empty seconds ago. "We should probably get back before Orianna comes looking for us."

This time, the silence remained unbroken.

Gemma thought about the peculiar feeling that crossed her skin when Tobler touched her, unlike anything she had ever felt. Making her skin prickle and hair stand on end in a way that felt more exhilarating than frightening—like a hand reaching inside, a secretive touch. Her blood sang out, like a bell being struck.

Orianna prepped as Zavier stood by and watched, smoking his pipe. The thin smoke scented the air with notes of black cherries and dark tobacco, creating an ambiance which warmed the corners of Gemma's mind and heart. This was the first time she could describe a house as feeling welcoming. She sensed it in every stitch of the curtains adorning the windows and in the blankets laying on the couches. Every wooden floorboard was etched by the weathered hands of time, proving there was much life that had run through the house—ghosts of past celebrations and potential for more in the future. The stone hearth pulled it all together, comfort crackling with its flames that took away any dampness or drafts that resided in the old home.

"You can put that over there." Zavier gestured with his pipe.

She had never seen such an intensity, or strong sentiment, before from a single look. Her heart beat a silent hope.

"It's not polite to stare, you know. It's not smiled upon," Tobler said in a teasing whisper, too close to her again.

Gemma jumped, unaware that she had been gawking. She turned red and continued to pile the wood in her arms.

"I'm sorry. I was only teasing. No need to be embarrassed." She didn't want to move away from his hand, but Tobler forced himself to let go.

"I'm not," she stated, her cheeks burning hotter.

Tobler stifled a laugh. "If you say so." He gave her time for her cheeks to return to their natural color. "I'm not trying to make you uncomfortable, but you don't need to worry so much."

"What?" She was perplexed by what he meant.

"I can sense what you're feeling, remember? You have a longing, a worry, a hope. If I was a betting man, I'd say it's for what you're seeing in that kitchen. It'll come for you in its own time, not a second sooner."

The words made him seem older, far too wise to come from a young man's heart. His rueful smile confirmed her thoughts.

"You'd be surprised what's revealed by the emotions we try to suppress. I tried not to focus in on you, but your emotions are pretty forceful."

It seemed a dangerous thing for him to be able to read her emotions, making her feel vulnerable. A sliver of excitement cut through the rawness of it, releasing a rush she'd never experienced before. Before he could respond, Orianna was a bucket of cold water on their flirtations.

"Dinner will be ready soon. Could you help me set the table, Gemma? We can sharpen your skills."

"Sounds great."

Gemma worried about the first impression she was making. Flirting with a guy she just met, in a place she didn't know well, seemed like a display of poor judgment on her part.

Beside the kitchen sat an old farmhouse table. Its bare top revealed a lifetime of family suppers and breakfasts, each engrained into the dark wood. Gemma walked to the cabinet to fetch the plates.

"Oh no, dear. We're going to do this a little different than you're used to, but you can leave the door open," Orianna said, waving Gemma to her side.

Gemma kicked herself; of course she wouldn't use her hands.

"Now, move the plates from the cabinet to the table with your powers. It's all about thought and will. Take a deep breath." Orianna closed her eyes, sucking in a deep breath through her nose then exhaling slowly through her mouth. "Just clear your mind and concentrate."

"That's it?"

"That's it. Give it a try."

Gemma closed her eyes, trying to mimic Orianna's breathing technique; she squinted in concentration, envisioning the plates moving from the cabinet. She opened one eye to see if she had done anything, sighing at the unmoved plates. She looked back to Orianna for assistance.

"Perhaps you're more of a visual learner?" Orianna shrugged back. "Try keeping your eyes open and don't squint, dear. That never works. You'll just give yourself crow's feet."

"That's alright, she can always just rub some of your old maid's cream on 'em, right Orianna?" Tobler teased, barely able to stifle a chuckle.

With a graceful flick of her wrist, a fork shot across the room and just missed Tobler's shoulder. It made him jump, but it was Orianna's slow backward glance which chilled him into silence.

"Give it another try, Gemma."

Keeping both eyes open, hoping to not make a fool of herself, Gemma focused on the plate; she willed it to move, and it began to shake. She moved her eyes, hoping the plate would follow. It moved along in a shaking pattern—up and down, on its way—but it fell short of the table, breaking on the floor.

Gemma gasped, her hands at her mouth, "I'm so sorry!"

"That's okay, dear. I expected you'd at least break one." She motioned over the plate, causing it to reassemble itself and jump onto the table. "Try again," Orianna reassured, gesturing to the cabinet.

Relieved, Gemma tried again but her efforts frustrated her as the next plates met the same fate. This time, three fell at once. She tried again, making it at last over the table, but they crashed onto the tabletop, shattering. A new scrape appeared on the table, showing she too left her mark on the home. Gemma covered her eyes in disappointment, skin damp from exertion.

She didn't seem to be any sort of magic savant. She worried after her failed efforts that Orianna would give up, tired of her mistakes. Knots built in her stomach at the thought of never touching magic again and being banished to the Echo for good.

"It's okay, dear," Orianna said, putting the plates back together. "Good progress, nonetheless. I have one more thing for you to try."

"Are you sure? I just seem to break things," Gemma said, defeat clear in her voice.

"Don't be silly! We all started somewhere. None of us came out of the womb wielding magic perfectly." She placed two candles onto the table. "All you have to do is concentrate and light the candles."

Gemma looked at the candlesticks, determination gleaming in her eyes, and willed them to light. All of a sudden a burst of hot, white light came from both the candlesticks and the hearth—all of them jumping together.

"Oh Tobler, you're on fire!"

Tobler looked down, alarmed to discover she'd set his pants on fire. With a quick move, he began smacking it out.

"Dammit, that's hot!"

After a few *whops* from his large hand, Zavier helped smack it out before Tobler was burned too badly. Silence filtered through the room in thick waves. Tobler and Zavier stood, wide-eyed with amazement at the intensity of Gemma's fire show; both appeared almost afraid of her.

Pride swelled in Orianna's chest, but it did not touch her eyes. No, they reflected an unknown sadness, a loss glinting then dying in the black orbs.

"That was amazing! Simply amazing," Orianna said, embracing Gemma in a firm hug. "I haven't ever seen such intensity. Not even your mother was that powerful." Orianna gave her an encouraging wink.

"You're right, considering that took significantly less effort than levitating the plates." she said, patting herself on the back.

"We Oliver witches have been able to bend fire to our will for centuries. You will need a little guidance. Take care not to roast poor Tobler—although that *was* hilarious." Orianna laughed before composing herself. "Okay, time to eat. Everyone take your seats."

Tobler sat beside Gemma with some caution, yet not scared enough to give her a wink. "That was impressive—dangerous, but still impressive. Looks like you'll be one powerful witch, even more so once you gain more control, I bet."

Orianna watched, moving to disrupt the intimate moment, but Zavier stopped her. He was not blind to what was happening, either. He placed a hand on hers and gave a reassuring squeeze, queuing her to let it go. Zavier saw nothing wrong with Tobler and Gemma's getting to know each other, and she trusted his judgment.

Tobler and Gemma continued with some idle chatter and flirting when Orianna remembered something.

"Zavier," she whispered, "what was the disturbance that made you send Tobler to get me? I assume it wasn't hunger."

"It's a long story. Do you remember Barlow?" He tried to jog her memory while keeping his voice down.

"Yes, what about him?"

"He's been murdered. Tortured to death by, we assume, his late wife due to the brutality of it. She joined Leo's group a few months ago and seemed to want something from him. Trashed the entire shop looking for it."

"Impossible! She's dead!" The color drained from her face.

"Apparently, she's not dead-dead. Something must have brought her back from the verge, and she topped that phenomenon by killing her husband."

"That's terrible! What was she looking for?" The hushed rage in her voice was hard to control, and her voice grew louder.

"Shhh!" Zavier looked over at Tobler and Gemma, both still not paying any attention to them. "Whatever it was, she didn't find it. We didn't find anything missing other than poor Barlow's eyes. Scratched them right out of his head, the crazy beast."

"Who is this 'we?'"

"Tobler and I went to pick up some potions for the horses and found him, dead and mangled on the floor of his own house." Zavier read the look on Orianna's face. "He won't say anything, Orianna. The boy gave me his word."

"He better not!"

"Shhh, don't get so excited. But you should tell her sooner than later, since it seems Leo and his army are looking for something. We need to prepare—"

"What's all the whispering about, you two?" Tobler interjected.

"Nothing for innocent ears to hear," Zavier said with a sly wink.

Tobler held up his hands in protest, dropping the subject.

CHAPTER SIX

ALL TOO SOON, IT was time for her to leave. Orianna was already upstairs getting the portal ready as Gemma lingered near the hearth. She gazed into the flickering fire which sent a crackle through her soul, a warming sensation that bonded her to the flames. The longer she looked, the more relaxed she became, but a sudden, hot tingling formed in her palm. She discovered a tiny fire burning there. Something in the window made her lose concentration, a quick blur darting away yet grabbing Gemma's attention. She, however, wasn't the only one who noticed.

"So, how was the first day of your new life?" Tobler asked.

"It's been pretty interesting. I might like it here."

Tobler stepped closer. "I'm happy to hear that. Does that mean you'll be back?"

Gemma enjoyed her time with her newfound family, but she didn't want to overstay her welcome. "Guess you'll just have to wait and see," she teased with a wink.

"Orianna and I would like that," Zavier interrupted, crooning as he gave her a hug. "I know she's missed you very much, and I'd like to get the chance to know my niece."

"Thank you, *Uncle* Zavier." She smiled wide at him. "It's so much to take in, but it feels so good to be here. It feels like...home." After the word left her mouth, she felt childish for loving a place she didn't know, but something inside of her awakened.

"Good," he said, appearing almost like a father. "You come here anytime you like. Orianna will show you how to use the portal, and when you're ready, she'll give you easier access if you ever need it."

"I'd like that."

A sudden sadness overtook her. She'd be going back to the world she shared with her adopted mother.

"Here, I'll walk you up the stairs," Tobler interrupted her thoughts, feeling the shift in her emotions. They took their time ascending the stairs as Zavier moved to the kitchen. "What's wrong?"

Gemma contemplated an excuse, but it was a moot point. She didn't want to keep secrets from him. "I'm just not sure what to tell my mother. Is it allowed for me to tell her things about this realm?"

"Ah, that is a sticky situation. The Echo folks aren't supposed to know about our realm, but—"

"But what?" Orianna asked, catching the tail end of their conversation.

"I wanted to ask you what I could say to my, um..." She had a hard time saying the word to Orianna.

"Your mother," she finished her sentence. The word felt strange, given its context, but it was a reality that needed no introduction. "You can say it, Gemma. She still is technically your mother, since she did raise you. Unfortunately, we can't tell her anything. It's imperative that our worlds not collide with one another. I'm sorry, but that's how it has to be."

"That's okay. I'll figure something out with her." It was more of a relief as she didn't know how to explain what had happened, short of saying she fell through a rabbit hole like Alice and was transported to a land of tea parties and acid trips.

"We'll come up with a plan a together dear, don't worry. Will you be coming back tomorrow?" Orianna asked, unable hiding her hopes that Gemma would say yes.

Gemma's thoughts leaped with joy. Goblidet was the new beginning she needed, the adventure she'd craved; it all felt tailored to her. She needed Orianna's help with controlling her powers and stole a peek at Tobler from the corner of her eye. "Yeah, I think I'd like that. That's okay, isn't it?"

Orianna smiled and hugged her close. "Of course it is. You will always have a place here with us." Orianna opened her eyes, still embracing Gemma, and noticed Tobler making a "victory" gesture. She cocked an eyebrow at him, stopping him cold. "Okay then, time to show you how portals work."

Orianna approached the arched wall. "First rule in magic is to clear you mind. You must think clearly to be effective. Imagine where you want to go, see it in your mind's eye. Then," she pulled another vial from her pocket, "toss this at your target, and there it is." Orianna tossed the vial at the wall, causing a flash of light and the swirling vortex to reappear.

"Is it really as easy as you make it look?"

"Well," she chuckled, "yes and no. Practice in anything makes an expert, and it will come to you faster that way. Okay, now: I'll step through, and you follow. Nothing more to it. Tobler, please let Zavier know I'll be back soon." In a swift step, Orianna vanished.

Gemma turned to Tobler, who watched from the sidelines, glad that her aunt gave them a moment alone. "Well, guess it's time for me to go back home? Geez, that sounds so weird."

"Why is that?" he asked, interest piqued.

"I've only spent a day here—a few hours, actually—but this feels more like my home than where I've spent of my whole life." She crossed her arms, adding, "A sense of belonging I thought I knew but didn't. That must sound crazy, falling in love with a place I've only been in for a few hours." His potential opinion weighed on her, but she couldn't figure out what that meant. She took a step closer.

"I don't think you're crazy at all. When you love something, or someone, it doesn't have to make sense. It's all based on emotion and instinct. If you feel this place is your home, then it must be true. Love, in any of its many forms, isn't supposed to make sense because it is not ruled by logic."

And there it was again, the disarming smile that made her breath catch in her throat. She was at a loss for words as a smooth silence tangled them closer. The sensory overload resurfaced.

Orianna popped her head through the portal, bursting the moment. "Coming, dear? It's getting late on this side. Tobler? I thought I sent you to give a message to Zavier. Go on, now, and tell him." She disappeared again.

"I should get going. She seems to be getting a little impatient."

"You'll get used to that." His joke made Gemma laugh, a sound that he was starting to enjoy.

"Thanks, Tobler." She walked towards the portal.

"No problem. Anything for a friend, right? See you tomorrow?"

"Yeah, I'll be back tomorrow. Goodnight." In a sweep of light, she disappeared as the portal closed.

"Goodnight," he whispered. Tobler descended the stairs, whistling. Perhaps he and Zavier had something to discuss, after all.

* * *

BACK IN THE ANTIQUE shop, Gemma sensed a shift in the atmosphere. The air seemed thicker and heavier than it had back in Goblidet Center. There was also a difference in color, she realized. Things on this side were duller and faint, as opposed to Goblidet where everything carried its own pulse. Outside the window, the sun tinted the sky as it started to set.

"How can that be?"

"What?"

"How is it still light out? Is Goblidet a different time zone?"

"Goblidet is a different *world* which doesn't allow time to align in any particular way. It took a little manipulating, but I managed to get you back as promised."

"Magic," Gemma said, full of whimsy, "I'll never get used to it."

"It has its dark sides and carries more responsibilities than you could imagine. We can talk about that tomorrow when you come back. It'll be good to give you a night, at least, to digest all you've done today." Orianna walked behind her desk, rummaged through drawers, and retrieved a set of keys.

"You can drive a car?" Gemma's eyes widened, shocked at the thought.

"Of course! What were you expecting—a broomstick?" Orianna chuckled, opening the door and heading outside. "How else would I get around? Come on, before you're late."

When Gemma stepped outside, her mouth dropped at the sight of a red sports car at the curb. Orianna strode gracefully to the driver side door.

"Gemma, dear, it's not polite to stare and we really must get a move on." Giving her a wink, she got in.

She climbed in and buckled her seat belt just in time for Orianna to punch the gas, pushing them against their seats, before letting off the pedal. Gemma warned her aunt about cops and getting pulled over, but Orianna waved it off saying she'd charmed herself out of dozens of such situations. Soon the laughs wore down since neither of them wanted to part ways, even for the brief period of time facing them. With every turn and mile, it felt harder to say goodbye.

"So, I had a thought," Orianna said as she stared off at the road. "We can tell your mother that I've offered you a job in my shop for the summer. That'll give you an excuse to come in and use the portal as often as you choose. Does that sound feasible?"

"It's actually very believable."

"If you want more time to stay in Goblidet, we can always rework visits for whatever time suits you." After the first ten years of searching, Orianna realized there would need to be a balance struck if she found Gemma and beat back her selfish reservations. "As much as I love having you with me, I don't want you to feel trapped. If at any point you want less of this, I won't be upset. Just say the word, and I'll understand."

"Thanks, but I'd like to spend as much time as I can with you." She squeezed her aunt's hand. "There is still so much I want to learn."

Orianna squeezed back, and all sadness erased from her face. "And I cannot wait to teach you."

The conversation left Gemma lighter, as if a weight had been lifted. Near her mother's house, a thought struck. "What should I call you?"

Orianna thought for a moment. "Well, I am still your aunt—that's never changed. If you want, call me Aunt Orianna. Or, if that's too odd right now, you can try Orianna."

"Aunt Orianna sounds nice. Never had an aunt before."

"Your parents don't have siblings?"

"No, both my adopted parents were an only child. They're not close with their extended family or parents either, so we've never associated with them."

"That's unfortunate," Orianna said, pulling into the driveway, "Family is a wonderful thing. I know that was a lot for one day, but sometimes it's better to dive in headfirst."

"It was, but I liked it. What time can I come back tomorrow?"

"Any time you want, Gemma. How's midmorning sound? I'll be at the shop by whatever time you get there. We have a lot of ground to cover still." She pulled a silver skeleton key away from the keyring. "Here, take this. It's the key to the shop entrance. I want you to have full access to it and the portal." She laid it in the palm of Gemma's hand and closed it.

Overwhelmed by the gesture, Gemma hugged Orianna tight. "Thank you so much."

Orianna squeezed back harder until she saw someone stir within the house. "You better get going. Looks like your mom is waiting," Gemma still hadn't let go and Orianna didn't want to either, as tears stung her eyes. "Now, dear, I can't do long goodbyes. I'll see you tomorrow."

"See you tomorrow." Gemma reluctantly got out of the car and watched as Orianna drove away.

She walked up the steps, her head full of new wonders. She reached for the knob but stopped, figuring now was as good a time as any to practice. She held her hand level with the knob, willing it to turn and come to her. It jiggled, half turning, then stopped. She took a deep breath and tried again; this time, it flew open and almost smacked her in the head.

"Well, I guess that's progress—dangerous, but progress."

"Is that you, Gemma?" her mother called from within.

"Yeah, Mom, I'm home." *Kind of,* she thought, immediately feeling guilty.

"You were gone awhile today. What did you do?" She maneuvered around the kitchen, pausing to stir a pot on the stove.

Gemma shrugged. "Nothing really, just looked around that old shop."

"Did you find anything new?" she asked, coming to the doorway and drying her hands.

"I got a job, that's definitely new."

"A job? I thought you weren't looking for one this summer with you going to college and all?"

"Eh, changed my mind. I thought some extra money would be nice. That lady from the antique shop, Orianna, offered me a position today. She needs an extra hand to help this summer. It seemed like an interesting job, so I took her up on her offer. I start tomorrow."

It was an odd feeling, lying to her mother. They had always had an open line of communication, but she understood the necessity of not revealing the whole truth. College had been the furthest thing from her mind, cast to the wayside at the thought of picking up her life where it left off in Goblidet. Life was changing, making the Echo shift into the past as a new path materialized.

"Gemma?" Her mother waved a hand in front of her face. "Are you still in there?"

Gemma snapped from her thoughts, coming back to where she stood in the house. "Yeah sorry, just zoned out. You know, contemplating college and all."

"That's fine, dear. Let's set the table and eat."

A rueful smile crept on Gemma's face at the thought of the last table she tried to set. At least this time there wouldn't be any broken plates or pants catching fire.

They sat down for dinner. Her mother had taken time to prepare a special roast turkey dinner with all of the fixings. Everything was laid out in the china her mother kept for holidays and served on her best tablecloth.

"Are we expecting anyone?" Gemma asked, surprised at all the food and the fancy décor.

"No, silly, it's just us. Why do you ask?" she said, matter-of-fact, placing a napkin on her lap as if this was the normal dinner setting.

"No reason. There is just so much food," she paused, "And it looks delicious. Thanks, Mom."

"Anytime, sweetheart. Let's eat before it gets cold." She scooped a dollop of green bean casserole onto Gemma's plate. Gemma flinched as a splash of cream splattered onto her face.

Gemma was horribly stuffed from Orianna's dinner but pretended to be starving, not wanting to deny her mother the sharing of a meal she worked so hard on. She could tell her mother had a rough day, probably from talking to her father. While others ate away their stress, her mother cooked it away, making everyone else but herself put on the pounds.

"Hey Mom, want to watch one of those old movies after dinner?" she asked, breathing between bites as her stomach stretched.

"I thought you didn't like those?"

"I like them. Just have to be in the right mood."

Her mother smiled, and Gemma sensed her spirits lifting. "That does sound nice. I'll dig one up once we're done eating."

Gemma took a deep breath, bracing herself for another bite. She was thankful for the time differences between realms so she could spend time with her mom but wished her stomach would reset itself after crossing the threshold.

They laughed and sat up talking until her mother grew tired. She kissed her goodnight, and they retired to their bedrooms.

Once alone Gemma practiced her levitation, searching for something that wasn't breakable. She spotted a pencil—perfect. She focused and picked it up into the air, but it soon fell onto the desk. A few more attempts, then the pencil rolled onto the floor; it would take more effort to move since it was at a lower distance. She felt a difference in how the magic worked. In The Echo, it was sluggish. The air was thick, a viscous fluid she had to swim through with greater effort.

Soon she picked it up, letting it float before spinning in the air. She pushed the pencil farther, then willed it towards her direction. It trembled, faster, until it shot toward her head. She ducked just in time, and it crashed—point-first—into the wall. She pulled hard on the end to retrieve it, surprised at the strength it required. It left a good-sized hole in the wall, concluding her practice for one day.

She curled up into bed, pulled the covers over, and willed the light switch to turn off. With the sound of the soft click, she smiled; finally, a solution for forgetting to shut off the light.

CHAPTER SEVEN

ORIANNA RETURNED TO HER antique shop, happy to see all was as she had left it. She loved the little dwelling she'd created. Her heart was full now that she found Gemma after many painful years of fearful searching. She was happy the family who adopted Gemma had cared for her, a concern weighing on her after seeing how heartless this realm could be.

She grabbed another vial from her pocket and repeated the portal opening spell. In a flash of light and a whirl of wind, she was back in her warm home. She inherited it after both of her parents were lost, and it became her hideaway from a world she wasn't ready to face. For the better side of a year after meeting Zavier, he had been the only one that had visited her. Over time, he became more welcomed; then, he was always there. When work called him away, Orianna grew to hate the chill emptiness left in his wake. He, not the house, had become home to her.

When the time came for him to choose whether to reenlist in The Guard, Orianna—with all of her womanly charm—persuaded Zavier to stay and make a life with her. Engagement followed soon after, and their lives harmonized. He supported and aided in Orianna's search, his compassion another quality that made her love him so much.

Downstairs, Zavier and Tobler awaited her by the fire. Cautiously, she scanned their faces as she walked closer, not liking what she found.

"What's wrong?"

Zavier looked at Tobler, whose expression grew guarded. "Come on now, you can't be afraid of her forever." He nudged his shoulder. "Just tell her what you told me."

"Tell me what?" Orianna's eyes narrowed at Tobler, full of reproach, and crossed her arms. The longer he stayed quiet, her angst stacked, making her more agitated.

Tobler swallowed and mustered up some courage to face his fear, Orianna. "Today, when we were in the woods, I saw a wisp of black smoke." He wrung his hands as he waited for Orianna's face to shift. "Perhaps it was nothing, but I thought I'd bring it to your attention."

Orianna paled. "She only just got here! How could they know already?" She whipped her gaze to Zavier, thick with disbelief.

Zavier held up a hand as if calming the oncoming calamity. "Now hold on. We still aren't sure, but he must have recruited more Eyes since we last left him."

The Eyes. If they had seen Gemma and her affinity for fire, there was no doubt they would try to claim her. Orianna's anxieties calmed, a swell of comfort taking its place... Wait, that wasn't right. She glared at Tobler, her face twisted in anger as she stepped closer.

"Don't meddle with my emotions, Tobler!" she snarled. "We've spoken about this, and I've strictly forbidden you. Leave it be!"

"Well, dammit, Orianna, reel it in then! I'm only trying to help you. I can't help that your pain runs so deep that it seeks others to share with," Tobler snapped at her with venom, her barbed emotions bringing out the worst in him.

"I said leave it be!" Her face came within inches of his. "My pain is mine and mine alone. It is mine to feel as my reminder."

"It doesn't have to be that way," he pleaded.

Orianna's face fell into a frown, all of her bottled anger losing its potency. "It's all I have left of Charlotte. The last moments I stood with her, the last breaths she breathed...so do not touch the pain. This *is* the way it must be."

Tobler's face fell into defeat. He cared about Orianna. She and Zavier were the only family he could remember. He wished she would let him help. Tobler moved to speak again, but Zavier put a hand on his shoulder. Orianna was pacing. Zavier knew to give her some time to shake off the foul mood trying to swallow her.

Orianna slowed to a stop, putting her hands on her hips staring off into the fire. "Are you sure of what you saw? Could it have just been your mind playing tricks? A shadow of a bird flying overhead?"

Tobler gathered his thoughts. "I'm not sure. I want to believe it was a trick of nature, but the look on Gemma's face... I don't mean to upset you, Orianna, I just wanted to let you know, in case it was a bad omen—for her safety, if nothing else."

He watched the gears turn in Orianna's mind, almost hearing them. He did not interrupt her process, reluctant to add to her frustrations. Tobler had been the one to see it, anyway, so he waited. After her working silence, she stopped and faced them— more collected this time.

"Thank you for bringing this to our attention." The light on her face dimmed. "It means a lot to me that you're trying to look out for Gemma."

Zavier breathed a sigh of relief as the tension faded from the room. Tobler cracked a weak smile, thankful she hadn't been too rough with him. Orianna wasn't one to have a bark worse than her bite. The bite was way worse.

"I know how much she means to you. You've searched long and hard for her, and I want her safe as well. I like her, she's a nice girl."

"I'm always watching you, young man, and don't you forget it."

"Alright, you two. It's late, and we better get off to bed if we're going to figure any of this out tomorrow," Zavier interjected, fatigued by the day and conversation.

Tobler shrugged. "Am I still welcome?"

"Of course. There are fresh linens on your bed and keep it neat."

Tobler would sometimes spend time away to center himself, and Orianna always kept the room ready for him. As much as the little urchin bothered her at times, he was still young. She didn't mind taking care of him, be it a warm bed or a hot meal, whatever he needed—within reason, of course. He was practically her orphan, too.

"Thank you. See you both in the morning." Tobler headed up the stairs.

"Alright, now you. Time for bed," Zavier said, scooping Orianna up in his arms. He carried her upstairs to their room, his lips to hers and her arms around his neck. He was her haven from the monsters of the world.

Tobler lay in bed, listening for their door to close. His thoughts threw themselves against the inside his skull. He thought about the dreadful possibilities of The Eyes watching them—or worse, looking for Gemma. Leo's army hiding in the shadows, creeping up on them, dismantling the peace in their lives. Gemma didn't need them warping her outlook on the new world that she found.

An image of her smile pushed into his mind, inspiring one of his own. Her big dark eyes, captivating and deep... His heart raced the more he thought about her. The hair on his arms stood on end as he remembered the sensation when they touched. Could it just be an odd tangle of emotions from him and her?

Fear and fondness battled in a fierce whirlwind within his mind, colliding with brute force. Tobler closed his eyes, struggling to summon sleep and bring the dawn of a new day.

CHAPTER EIGHT

IN A CLOUD OF black smoke, Hilda appeared in front of the stone castle. It had a crumbling façade but remained a beautiful sight—tightly guarded by dark magic. As she entered the main door and headed to the gathering room, the voices of the other followers grew louder. Seated at the large table, her confidants anxiously awaited her report. Some squirmed in their seats while others resembled statues, each a cluster of nerves in their own way—all except their master. He sat at the head of the table in black robes, poised and calm as an untouched pool, waiting. But when his eyes held Hilda's, his expression hardened.

"Ah Hilda, you've returned. Tell me what news you bring us?" He drank from a glass goblet. The contents left his lips tinged redder than wine.

"It is her, Master. The girl *is* back in Goblidet."

A cascade of whispers hissed around the table, ricocheting through the dark room in a rolling cloud of white noise.

"Enough!" he growled, choking the noise into silence. "You're sure of this? It is definitely her? We can't afford any delusions."

"Yes, I'm positive it's her. The senseless bitch brought her back here, to her own house—no protections." Triumphant in her boasting, Hilda puffed up in pride as she waited for her reward.

His face was deadpan. "No need for name calling and insults, Hilda. We aren't children. You address the woman plainly or not at all."

The face of the red head seated beside him fell slightly at the chastising words, and Hilda's face tightened.

"I'm sorry, My Lord, it won't happen again."

"Well?" Seriousness burned across his expression.

"Well what, my lord?" Hilda appeared puzzled, panic seeping into her face.

"Where is she?"

The whispers halted in throats all around the table.

"I do not have her with me," she stammered, her voice on the verge of breaking.

"And why is that?" He pushed away from the table, chair scraping. "The orders were to bring her here, to the castle, to me. Were they not? Why don't you have her with you?" He strolled towards her.

"She wasn't alone! It would have been a suicide mission!" Desperation soaked her voice.

"Then you are clearly not dedicated to the cause." He turned his back to her.

Hilda fell hard to her knees, clutching the ends of his cloak, "No, but I am! I've proven myself dedicated to the cause. I spilled blood for you, killed my husband for you when he failed to comply. Let me prove than I am worthier!"

He turned back with the grimness of a reaper. "Not. Good. Enough."

Terror filled Hilda's eyes as her mouth formed to release a scream, but before she could cry out, it was too late.

Leo put his hand palm out, releasing a terrible black fog. The foul shadow stream wrapped itself around her face, traveling down the rest of her body, constricting and turning. Her body contorted inhumanly before she was nothing, the skin peeling back and the muscles stiffening. The black shapeless thing returned to Leo's palm, disappearing into his skin as he walked back to the head of the table.

"Let that be a lesson to anyone who disobeys my orders. Insubordination will not be tolerated. Now, be gone from my sight. I will summon you all again when there's a need. Until then, I want tabs kept on our new visitor." Leo's revulsion was clear, the scolding reinforcing his followers' obedience. "I won't require the girl right now, but I insist on learning more. Be vigilant about not being seen, and report back to me when summoned."

More whispers echoed from their mouths as they stood and filed out, all but the red head. She sat in her chair—stewing, balled fists on the table—staring at the pile of bone ash on the floor. Shooting up from her seat, she trudged down the hallway as irritation raged inside her. Upon coming to an old arched door, she burst through and caught Leo off-guard as he stood at the window. A storm gathered itself outside.

"It's impolite not to knock before entering someone else's room, Griselda. Surely you know that." He faced her, taking off his robe.

"What was the meaning of that?" she demanded, slamming the door.

"The meaning of what?" His expression remained unmoved.

"You know what! Hilda was one of our—your—most loyal servants! She killed her own husband to prove her devotion, and you disintegrated her! Why?" Crossing her arms, furious, she stormed halfway across the room.

"You know very well why, my dear. She did kill Barlow, and I rewarded her for that by inviting her within my ranks. I gave her back her life. My biggest gift!" Having raised his voice, he centered the calm back into himself. "She disobeyed an order, the most important order I ever gave—defying the only order that matters. It's that simple. Unfortunately, she happened to be a friend of yours. I can't appear soft of heart, ever—especially not now." He closed some of the gap between them while rolling up his sleeves.

"Was it her disobedience or her insult against Orianna that angered you to annihilation?"

"Is that what you think?" His sharp eyes stared her down, as if needing to assert dominance.

"Of course I do! It's obvious after all those years you still have feelings for her." She mirrored his expression as a small tempest ripped through the room, disappearing as quickly as it came; outside, the maelstrom deepened.

Leo smiled, closing the gap between them. "Oh my spirited love, jealousy becomes you. That is all rumor and gossip. How could I have any desires for Orianna when I have a rare beauty like you by my side?"

He ran his hands from her shoulders, down her arms, and spanned her waist. He was as charming and seductive as he was brutal and dangerous, an intoxicating combination that Griselda couldn't resist. She reciprocated his affectionate embraces.

"I got a little carried away—"

He pulled her against him, pressing a finger to her lips. "Enough talking."

He kissed her hard with vigorous lust. They became nothing but animals, succumbing to primal desires. Griselda's jealousy vanished with Leo's every touch and kiss, surrendering to his wickedness.

The night grew darker with no moon to brighten the castle, swallowing them both. Their dastardly deeds to come scowled in the shadows, eager to unleash their black wings and fly.

CHAPTER NINE

ORIANNA'S EYES FLUTTERED OPEN as she awoke, uncomfortably warm. Zavier's body heat was to blame, his arms wrapped around her waist as he held her close. The house stood in stillness in the twinkling seconds before the dawn. A sliver of sunlight slid across the floor and past the curtains, a golden sign of new beginnings.

She loved these early hours. The time when the world was unmoving, full to the brim with quiet, an overflow of static peace. Thoughts grew more tangible when the body was at rest. She planned the day in her head but soon faltered. Gemma was in trouble, and she didn't know what to make of it.

"Relax, my love. What is troubling you?" Zavier groggily questioned.

Orianna stroked his arm. "What makes you think I'm troubled?"

"Your body gives you away." He kissed her temple. "Now, what's on your mind so early this morning?"

"I'm just trying to plan for Gemma's safety. What if Tobler's suspicions are true?" She turned to Zavier with glassy eyes. "What if—" the words caught in her throat, choking her.

"Nothing will happen to her. She is safe here, and we will not let anything happen. We should try to find out if that's what it was, first, but we will take necessary precautions." His large hand caressed her. "You won't lose her again. It'll be okay."

Her mind uncoiled, a sigh escaping. "I will try not to worry as much, at least, not until we know for sure. There are some charms and spells I can use to safeguard the house, just in case. No harm in taking precautions, as you said."

"Right, a few charms will help a lot. When will we be expecting young Gemma again?" Zavier stretched, then got up and began to dress.

"She'll be coming by the shop sometime this morning. I'll meet her and bring her back. I can have her open the portal for practice." Orianna grabbed a black dress from the chair, slipping it on gracefully.

"Opening the portal herself? Isn't that a bit advanced?"

"It is a little quick," she ran a brush through her hair, "but she needs to learn. Her powers are strong, and she needs to control them. Did you forget about the blaze of fire last night?"

"Ah, yes. That was almost a blistering issue. Luckily, we put out Tobler's arse before he roasted too bad," he chuckled. "She certainly is an Oliver woman, huh? Fires of Hell flowing through your veins."

Orianna swatted him playfully as Zavier moved behind her, twining his arms around her waist. "She possesses the family affinity for fire, if that's what you mean. She's much more powerful than I ever could have imagined, possibly the most powerful yet to be born. That makes her a target."

"I know, but don't forget you're not alone in this." He kissed her cheek, then added an impish demand. "Now where's my breakfast, woman?"

She looked at him pointedly. He gave her a playful swat, laughed, and ran downstairs. He was right, as much as she hated to admit it. Protecting Gemma was something she wouldn't be able to do alone; it would take all of them, possibly more, to keep her safe if Leo had rebuilt an army. She found herself lost in a whirlwind of consequences if they failed, but she shook them away like pesky black flies. She would see Gemma again today, and that was all that mattered.

Orianna gathered her thoughts as she straightened her dress and walked downstairs to face the day. Zavier sat at the table, eating his breakfast, with Tobler perched at the stove cooking.

"Good morning, Orianna." Tobler tried to make himself useful around the house in any way he could, an unspoken tradeoff for staying with them.

"Good morning," she poured herself some coffee. "Sleep well?"

"As good as can be expected. What would you like for breakfast?" He tossed some eggs about in the pan waiting for her answer.

"I actually need to be quick, so whatever you are making is fine. I have to meet Gemma at the shop." A moan of happiness escaped her lips at her first sip of coffee. "Ah, the true elixir of life."

"Hmm, I see." A clever expression on his face. "Returning so soon, huh? She must like it here or something."

"Yes, that is possible. Bit early to tell, I suppose."

Tobler dished up her eggs as she thanked him between sips of coffee. Orianna scarfed them down, ready to leave by the time Tobler sat down with his own plate. She kissed Zavier goodbye and headed to make more portal vials. Zavier sat across from Tobler, finishing the last morsels on his plate, when he noticed something different.

"You're awfully chipper this morning." He gave him an incredulous look. "What's crawled into you?"

Tobler exchanged his grin for a more stoic countenance. "No more than usual."

"Come now, Tobler, don't insult me." He gnawed at the last piece of bacon. "What's on your mind?"

Tobler chewed, giving himself time to gauge Zavier. "Tell me," he shifted in his seat, "what was it like when you met Orianna?"

"I'm not a woman, Tobler, I can't remember that far." Zavier scratched at his beard. "Happy, I guess, but not without some frustration. There isn't a good way to describe it other than I liked how I felt when I was around her...the headstrong woman. Why?"

"Hm, no reason." Tobler avoided eye contact, rearranging his eggs.

"Oh, boy." Zavier ran a hand over his face. "You're in troubled waters, my friend."

"You don't know what you're talking about, you old buzzard."

Zavier cleared his throat in annoyance at the insult.

"Sir," Tobler added, choking down his eggs.

"If I didn't know any better, I'd guess something—or more, someone—has caught your eye. Perhaps a certain new face? Hm? Or a niece?" Zavier gave him a teasing look.

Tobler snorted. "Don't be ridiculous! I don't even know her."

Zavier grunted in disagreement. Zavier was the closest thing Tobler had to a father, and they both tended to act the traditional parts, but there was also a friendship.

"I see you're sitting fine today." A good-humored chuckle boomed from his chest.

Tobler narrowed his eyes, "My ass is fine! She didn't burn me...that much."

"Just remember to behave yourself. If Orianna senses any funny business—or, worse, you break the girl's heart—not even I will be strong enough to save you from her wrath."

"Let's not chisel my headstone just yet. Besides, these things don't just happen overnight."

"What doesn't happen overnight?"

Tobler dropped his fork and almost choked at the sound of Gemma's voice.

"Nothing, you know. Plants." He kicked himself; it wasn't like him to not be light on his feet.

Zavier looked at him as if he were the town idiot.

"Plants?" she asked, confused.

"Well, yeah, plants. I, um, enjoy spending time in the garden," he smiled nervously, "fresh air and sunshine and all."

"We don't have—" Zavier was cut off by the swift kick Tobler delivered to his shin, "Yes, the garden. Just started it last week."

"Right." Gemma took a seat next to Tobler.

There was a slight pause in the sinking conversation, and the smell of her perfume was intoxicating. Tobler didn't usually care for floral scents on a woman, but this suited her well.

"So, how was your night?" Tobler stated nonchalantly.

"It was weird, unnatural to have so much time back. How about yours?"

"Uneventful, I gue—"

"Would you like some breakfast, Gemma?" Orianna interjected.

"No thank you. I'm fine." Her stomach spoke up in a loud growl.

"It sounds like someone disagrees with you. Go grab a plate, and get some food in you." Orianna gestured to the cabinet.

Embarrassed by her body's open betrayal, she did as she was told. With a motion of her finger she opened the cabinet door, levitated her plate carefully until it landed in her hand with a tremble. She beamed at Orianna, who nodded in approval.

Orianna sat down next to Zavier. He put his hand over hers before giving the tip of her finger a suspicious look.

"Time Blocking," he heaved a sigh, but his words were quiet. "You know that's not permitted." He shot a sharp look at her.

"I've only done it in small doses, a few hours. That's not so bad."

"You weren't supposed to do that anymore, and you were to destroy the hourglass." His tone soft as to not alarm anymore.

"I couldn't destroy it. No matter how hard I tried, it just won't explode or melt or break in any way. It seems to be indestructible," she claimed, the truth of it written on her face. "I'm sorry. I know Time Blocking is prohibited, but how else was I to get her back in a timely manner?"

"I understand that, but that doesn't mean others will. I assume you had the sense not to do it again." Zavier kept his voice hushed, resigned her stubbornness.

Orianna fidgeted. "Yes, of course."

His eyes widened, his whisper hissing with agitation. "Orianna!"

"Don't you take that tone with me!" Her whisper rose, matching his severity. "You would do that same to spend more time with someone you loved. No one will ever know."

"Regardless of your intentions, you can't be doing this. It's unethical to stop time anywhere, for any reason—you know that. It's a dark art."

"But I've never stopped time. Just slowed it down a little."

Zavier gave her a stern look, the kind that said she lost the argument.

"All right, all right! I won't do it again," she said with a pout.

Satisfied, Zavier resigned from the argument as they brought their attention back to the table.

Tobler and Gemma were enjoying some small talk amongst themselves, focused on each other so much that they appeared to have forgotten they weren't alone. There was something easy and natural about their interaction. Orianna noticed the gleam in their eyes, recognizing their dreaminess from memories of her own years ago—new enough, neither of them noticed it themselves yet. The tender threads of their lives were soon to be changed by one another.

Orianna understood those feelings well, but she wasn't ready for Gemma to be consumed by thoughts of love. In her mind, she was still the baby she'd lost all those years ago. Worry slipped in—not about her growing up too fast, but of the heartaches that could lie ahead if Tobler wasn't her true love. A broken heart was difficult to mend, leaving invisible scars stunting one's ability to love. Orianna's own experiences crawled to the surface. Poor Zavier, she was lucky to have found a soulmate like him, her kismet. But with the good came memories of the bad...

"What's wrong?" Zavier put a hand on her knee, pulling her out of her mind.

"Do you see what's happening between them?" Her unease was thin, but visible.

Zavier nodded, "I do. It wouldn't be so terrible, now would it? He's a good boy."

She hesitated, wondering when they would notice. "No, long as it's pure and true."

He gave her hand a reassuring squeeze. "No, my love, it won't be like that for her. You do not live the same lives. Tobler is nothing like—"

"Aunt Orianna, what do we have planned for today?" Gemma noticed something off about her aunt's expression. "Is there something wrong?"

Orianna blinked, distracted as if climbing out of a thick thought. "Nothing, dear. Um, let's see."

"I believe you wanted to work on securing the perimeter, right?" His verbal nudge cleared her mental fogginess, the possibility of danger pulled her together.

"Yes, that's what it was. I'm going to teach you about charms and their uses."

Gemma tilted her head, curious. "Perimeter charms?"

Tobler opened his mouth to say something, but Orianna's voice came out instead.

"I'll explain that to you as we go." She stood, as if physically taking control of the situation.

He waited for them to leave the room, sure she was out of earshot, before he spoke up. Tobler leaned toward Zavier. "Why is she securing the perimeter?"

Zavier lit his pipe, giving it a thoughtful puff. "Don't you remember our talk last night? Orianna is a bit shaken up and wants to take some precautionary measures." He gave a half shrug. "It'll make her feel better and shouldn't hurt anything."

"Hmph," Tobler replied, a little put off by her decision; but he chose to let it go. "Hopefully, it was nothing. How far do you will she'll go?"

"What do *you* think?" He snorted at the obvious answer.

Tobler nodded, realizing what a stupid question he'd asked. Of course, the place would be armed to the teeth with charms and spells.

Orianna and Gemma walked down the hallway, stopping in front of a heavy black door that looked dungeon-worthy. The handle and hinges were made of an equally black iron. Gemma wonder what Orianna's fascination with iron was. When Orianna opened the door, Gemma stared at the room— awestruck by the lovely sight.

The room was filled with bottles of various colors, shapes, and sizes. Upon the opposite wall hung four sheathed daggers made of silver, gold, stone, and a white substance she didn't recognize. A stone counter lay ahead, in the similar style of a bar. A cabinet sat beneath with dozens of drawers of different sizes alongside shelves gleaming with utensils, tools, clear stopped bottles, and more.

The most attractive part of the room was the large silver cauldron hanging in the center, a ring of coals beneath yearning to be burned. The base boasted simple, raised scrollwork forming a design that stretched all around its middle. Gemma reach out with her hand, as if it were calling to her.

"Ah ah!" Orianna rebuked with a pointed finger. "No touching! Not until you've had more training."

Gemma recoiled as if she'd been slapped. "Sorry, it's just so pretty."

Orianna smiled, circling the cauldron and running a hand around the mouth. "That it is. One of my prized possessions. Your mother Charlotte and I spent lots of time around it, mixing up all kinds of trouble." She smiled true as a memory wrapped around her. "And now it's time you and I put it to good use."

Gemma smiled, eyes twinkling with curiosity. "What kinds of trouble?" She'd been so focused digesting the fact that magic was real that she'd lost sight of finding out who her parents were, and here was an opportunity to learn more.

"Oh, all kinds of child's play! Honey potions, charms, fever elixirs—all perfectly harmless, of course." A childlike giggle played at the edges of her voice, a chime in the air, light as a fleeting feather.

Orianna wore a smile that Gemma could tell didn't occur often. It made her look so young and lighthearted, a lost reflection from eons ago. Orianna shared more cherished memories, stories she had kept closer to her heart than precious gems. Gemma listened with open ears, hanging on every word like an awestruck child, laughing until their sides ached and tears dabbled at their eyes. Gemma learned of her mother's good nature, wild spirit, and how she wasn't much different from her—almost the clichéd spitting image.

Gemma had never understood familial warmth. Her adopted mother was warm and loving, but she'd always felt different from her. Her adopted father was a cold man who'd never been much of a father. He stuck around until she was ten, then became buried in his work at the firm; they didn't see him very much those years following. Separating after two years of his "working" absence from their home, her parents had divorced a year after that. It left a hole in Gemma's life, but in time, she realized they were better off. She wished him luck with his new family and the biological children he'd always wanted.

CHAPTER TEN

BEING IN THE WORKROOM with Orianna, learning about her biological mother, laughing, and hearing old family stories was a new joy she'd never felt. She felt like she belonged the second she'd crossed the portal, delighting in the shared similarities between the three Oliver women.

"So you and my mother were very close, then?" Gemma managed to get out through a laugh, wiping her cheeks.

"Yes, very much so," Orianna said, her smile a twist of happiness and lament. "Even after she married Ross—your father, of course—we grew even closer."

Gemma felt lighter knowing she came from a close-knit family, but she still had so many questions.

The air shifted around them. Orianna's expression fell, despite the happy memories reflected in Gemma's face. The weight of her niece's inevitable question settled, burdening the air between them. Orianna took a deep breath to find the courage to continue.

"Aunt O?" Gemma fiddled with a sage leaf between her fingers.

"Aunt O?" Orianna questioned back, more to herself than to Gemma.

"Well, your name is kind of long so I shortened it—unless you don't like it?"

"No, no, I like." Orianna looked away, focused on a floor plank. "What was your question, Gemma?"

"What happened to my parents? How did they die?"

There it was. The question Gemma most wanted to know. What happened to her loving family that had been so close? The question that no one was ready to answer, but it was a vital piece of information she craved.

Orianna remained silent, wearing an iced-over expression. Gemma shuddered, sensing her heart turn colder.

"I'm sorry—"

Orianna held up her hand, halting Gemma's words.

"It's okay. We can talk about this. It won't be easy, but these things never are." She steadied herself; even after all those years, it was still hard. "Put simply, they were murdered. There was a threat to the realm and your parents stood against it, on the side of light and ethics. When they heard that evil was coming to their doorstep, they held firm. They probably would have had a fighting chance if they had been in the same place when it happened." She took another breath.

"I mentioned Leo to you before? He visited your parent's house when your mother was off shopping with you. Leo offered your father a great deal of wealth and power to join him, but Ross was an honorable man and wealthy in his own right. He denied him, and Leo killed him where he stood—no one knows the full details. Your mother brought you home to find him dead in the hallway; strangled, his windpipe crushed, with deep lacerations around his neck. The pain ripped her apart, leaving no time to grieve. She fled with you to my house, terrified he'd come for her next. It was her Leo wanted an alliance with, because of her powers and mine. Your father was an accessory, having no affinity powers. If we just had more time to prepare...if we'd known she'd been followed. One of The Eyes trailed her and saw her heading my way, then leaked word to Leo."

"What are The Eyes?" Gemma interrupted.

"Not what, who. The Eyes are a dedicated group of Leo's followers. They make pacts with demons, giving pieces of their souls in exchange for dark cloaking abilities. Letting them turn to wisps to travel quickly and spy on the unlucky souls Leo wants tabs on. Some say they are the most heartless creatures, typically nonaffinity witches. He keeps the powerful ones closer to him."

"Creatures? They aren't people?" Gemma was trying hard to keep up.

"Not anymore. Once the witch or wizard makes a pact with a demon, their humanity is torn away. They become creatures of evil and carry out Leo's bidding. He made a deal with his own soul to a higher-ranking entity, from what I understand. No one is quite sure which one, but some say it's a demon more wicked than the Devil himself."

Orianna shifted in her seat to finish the story. "He came for us sooner than we hoped. He sensed you were in your crib upstairs. Your mother read the look in his eyes, knew he would go after you...but we never understood why. She struggled against him, trying to keep him from getting near you. I tried to stop him, but your mother made me leave so that I would get to you first. I ran upstairs as he attacked me. I hurled a fireball at him, but he deflected it, setting the house on fire. I succeeded in burning him, but the flames spread to the ceiling under you room. I made it to your cradle just before it became engulfed. I still have nightmares of the what ifs. I fought very hard for you, and we lost so many that day: your grandfather and grandmother, your mother... I almost lost my life, as well, keeping your location a secret."

Orianna quieted as tears dropped from her eyes. Gemma was pale with shock. The horror had been more than she could bite off. She wasn't sure what part of the story hurt her worse:

her parent's death, or the visible suffering her aunt still carried. Grief hung between them, heavy and ragged.

"I'm sorry, Gemma."

The door creaked open as Tobler stuck his head through. "Is everything alright in here?" he asked, face set on edge.

"Yes, why? What brought you up here?" Orianna snapped in surprise.

"Just stopping by." He turned to Gemma, who wiped her eyes with her shirtsleeve. "Are you okay?"

"Yeah, I'm okay," she said, stifling a tear. "Why do you ask?"

"Just checking. Thought it rude not to ask you, too."

Orianna stared at Tobler and saw what he was trying to conceal. Concern, not for her, but for Gemma. She didn't realize it'd gone so far. There must have been a strong bond forming between them if her emotions were audible to him from such a distance.

Tobler blushed slightly, as if sensing the conclusion she'd drawn. "Yes. I was worried that—well, doesn't matter. I see now that all is fine. I'll be getting back downstairs now."

Gemma watched him carefully as he closed the door behind him. "Is that a bad thing? That he can feel my emotions like that. Does it mean I'm unhinged?"

"He's just very gifted, is all." Orianna brushed it off. It wasn't her place to tell her what it meant.

She forced a smile, making her way over to a corner of the room. Up on a pedestal was the leather-bound book that she recognized from her first visit to the antique shop, the one that started to shift and change the longer she looked at it. Orianna flipped through the pages, displaying frustration as each turn failed to reveal what she needed.

"Is something wrong?"

"Ugh! No just trying to find this damn spell..." She flipped faster.

Questions played at the corners of her mouth, but it just seemed too ridiculous. "Don't you have a table of contents or magic Google or something?"

"No," the word escaped her as an exasperated sigh. "Sadly, this old thing pre-dates any of that. Sometimes we aren't the most brilliant—even with magic. Our values are too different, or no one thought to make such a thing."

"Couldn't we just make a spell to pull it up faster? Or conjure up the internet?"

Orianna's scowl soon gave way to surprise, "That's actually not a bad idea. I'm sure we could figure something out."

"We're going to make the internet?"

"What? No! We can't make the internet." She gave her a flummoxed look, "We're going to create a spell to find other spells faster."

"Oh. Well, isn't it just a bunch of rhyming words strung together?" Gemma shrugged.

"No, spells are more in depth. They need the right words and follow the three C's: clear, concise, and creative. Your intentions must also be abundantly obvious."

"That doesn't seem too hard."

"Let's give it a try."

Orianna closed her eyes and muttered a string of words under her breath. The pages flipped violently, like beating wings as a wind rustled through. Orianna appeared mystical, fluttering black tresses from her hair and clothes like a character from a storybook Gemma read in school. There was a quick surge of energy that ran over her body, a heady mix of summer and winter clashing on a battlefield.

The flipping abruptly stopped to a page titled "Perimeter Charms" until the book slammed itself on Orianna's finger. She pulled it back with a yelp, grasping her finger after forgetting the book's heaviness. Orianna shot Gemma a pointed look, cutting off her near hysterical laughter.

"Well, we tried it. At least I saw what page it was on before it closed," she said, thumbing back to the correct page. "Page 1098."

"What happened? Why did it close itself?" Gemma asked.

"Oh, it's just a stubborn book!" she chastised, as if it could hear her. "He's pretty set in his ways. Guess that's what happens when you're over 1000 years old."

Gemma felt put off hearing the book spoken of as if it were a breathing creature and watched it suspiciously, wondering if it could hear them.

"Ah ha! Here it is! I will call out the ingredients, and you bring them over to me. Everything is labeled and lined up in alphabetical order, so you shouldn't have much trouble."

Gemma nodded, preparing for her task.

"Willow blossom, dragon's blood, beast fang, blue fairy hair, oil of troll, and seed powder."

Orianna made a shooing motion with her hand as Gemma rushed to the shelves. One by one, she picked the respective bottles and jars off the shelf and lined them up on the counter.

"Perfect! Looks like we have plenty of each to make about thirteen charms. That should do the trick. Now, Gemma, it's very important while making anything that you add the ingredients in the exact order that they're listed. If you don't follow the order, you won't get anything but smoke and ash, understood?"

Gemma nodded, watching as Orianna meticulously open each bottle, carefully pinching and pouring each ingredient into the cauldron. The concoction moved and changed its appearance. Orianna grabbed the red bottle of dragon's blood, dripping it in with precision.

"Is that real?" she stammered, hoping she didn't sound too silly.

"Is what real?" Orianna cocked her head. Gemma had been so quiet that she forgot she was even there.

"The dragon's blood. Is it real, or is it just a cool name?"

Orianna raised an eyebrow at her. "Why in Ophelia's name would we name something what it isn't?"

"Symbolism, I guess?"

"You won't find anything like that in this realm, I'm afraid. Everything is what it says it is, no getting around it. This *is* real dragons' blood. Grab me that bottle of sea water, would you, dear?"

While Gemma's back was turned, Orianna stuck her finger with a pin and dripped a few drops of blood into the cauldron, careful not to be seen.

"Wow! What are they like? Are they always guarding treasure or distressed princesses like the fairytales?" Gemma's shock faded into curiosity, making her look like a wide-eyed child listening to a bedtime story.

"Well, depends on your idea of treasure, I supposed. Dragons are faithful creatures, but they differ from dragon to dragon. They are all very protective—be it of gold, a family, gateways, sometimes entire towns. As far as the princess part goes, not so much anymore. They stopped that service eons ago, much too risky. They couldn't tell the difference between the good or the bad, killing anyone who came to their keeps or getting killed themselves." She walked over to the wall, grabbed a long gold spoon, and began stirring.

"So they aren't evil then?" Gemma peeked inside the cauldron, watching as the mixture swirled and changed color from gold to gray. A mesmerizing sight, like they'd captured a storm of their own.

"Not all humans are evil. Dragons follow the same premise. The dragons have had their share of bad eggs, but most of them are good souls who need some extra loving. You might want to stand back a bit, it'll start smoking soon."

Gemma took heed as smoke and sparks rose from the cauldron, brushing against the high ceiling. Gray and black clouds billowed; an unfamiliar fragrance wafted through the room, disappearing back into the cauldron. Orianna shrunk the pot to a more manageable level and reached in to withdraw a crystal-like stone. One by one, she laid them on the counter to cool, each being a different color with a unique set of jagged edges.

"They're so pretty. What do we do with them now?"

"Now, we bury six around the house. Then, we place the other six onto the outside walls of the house. The thirteenth goes on the roof."

With a wave of her hand, all of the bottles closed and levitated back to their places on the shelves; the utensils cleaned themselves and moved back to where they hung on the walls. Orianna moved towards the door, stopping short as she remembered something.

"Gemma, grab me two bottles from the shelf please. Raven bones and ground Gildor feathers for our next project. Then please shut the door."

She shook the black bottle, a shudder crawling down her spine at the rattle of bones against thin glass. Trying not to think about it, she ran out the door; the slam echoed back with muffled curses from her aunt. When she got to the bottom of the stairs, the conversations halted and left paranoia in its wake.

"I have the things you asked for." Gemma said with her best smile, handing the bottles to Orianna, unsure why everyone was staring at her.

"Black Hells, Orianna! Shadow glyphs too?" Tobler complained, exasperated.

"Watch your tone with me, boy! I'll do as I damn well see fit!" Her eyes were wild, a scowl snarling on her face; but when she turned to Gemma, her features softened. "Thank you, dear."

"You're welcome?" Gemma felt uneasy at Orianna's sudden Jekyll and Hyde impersonation.

"Now then, Tobler, start digging holes for the ground charms. Zavier, you'll secure charms into the walls and roof. Gemma, you and I will mark the windows with glyphs." Everyone stood unmoving, looking to one another for objections. "Did I stutter?" She placed her hands on her hips expectantly until the men dispersed. "Come Gemma, I'll teach you what to do."

Gemma followed. "Aunt O, what's a shadow glyph?"

Orianna stopped at one of the closed windows. "A glyph is a particular symbol that conducts a specific magic. A shadow glyph is just one of many tools at our disposal. It casts a shadow against the place that it marks."

She opened the bottles, pulling out a raven bone, dipped it into the Gildor feathers and smudged a symbol on the pane. "This protects against spies and the like. It allows us to see out, but no one can see in." When she finished, she laid the bone on the windowsill and it vanished into the wood. "Good for peeping neighbors, too. Let's go to the next window and have you try it out."

Gemma took the bottle as she watched a dark tint form over the window. "Do I just start drawing?"

"There is a process to it. Dip the bone in the ground feathers," Orianna instructed.

With a cringe Gemma grabbed one of the raven bones, tipping the second bottle to reach in easier. "Okay, I'm ready."

"It's already dead, dear, it can't bite you anymore," she encouraged. "You give it a try. Remember, it has to incorporate every aspect."

"What will happen if I forget something?"

"Then it won't work. Glyphs must be precise, down to the last detail. They don't need to be in the same places, but have to be placed where the design isn't compromised."

"Got it."

The pair went from window to window, diligently marking them with glyphs. Orianna taught her the various combinations she might use and where to place the bones to be sure they'd vanished as intended. Gemma took in what she could, but her head spun from the overload of information and her aunt's meticulousness. With so much to be learned, Gemma could feel her appetite for magic turning into a pit.

CHAPTER ELEVEN

TOBLER LEANED ON HIS shovel, but with his lack of attention, the shovel slipped. He fell into the hole he was digging.

"Oh," Gemma tried to suppress the oncoming snicker. "Are you alright?"

"Of course I am. I meant to do that." He shook his head, trying to reclaim his composure while wondering if he hit his head on the way down.

"Yes, because it's important to sample the dirt before burying the charms." Orianna teased, extending a hand to help him up. "You sure you're not hurt?"

"Just injured my pride, no real damage." He looked at the windows with their thick layer of shadow. "I see you've done well with the glyphs. Can't see anything inside, not even the glow of the fire."

"Can't take any chances," Gemma chimed.

Tobler chuckled. "Oh no, you've been hanging around your aunt too much. After Zavier and I finish this, we'll be the most protected home in the entire realm. You'll have nothing to fear, except spiders—but no witch, wizard, sorcerer, evil or what not. I'm always here to help, too, of course."

He winked at her and her cheeks flushed pink, making her wonder if that would happen every time he winked at her. Tobler's abilities to read her every emotion made her feel like a piece of fresh glass, clean and transparent—even more reason to blush.

"Glad you can dig a hole and bury things. Now, where is Zavier?"

"He's on the roof securing the last charm. It's giving him quiet a time though."

"Hmm, better go help him. Come, Gemma, we'll help him fix it to the roof."

"All the way up there?" The thought of it made her dizzy and her stomach flipped.

"Of course all the way up, silly. It's the top, we have to protect us against attacks from all angles." Orianna turned, setting off for the roof.

"Actually, can I borrow her a moment? I've hit a rock here, and I could really use her levitation to move it," Tobler pleaded.

Orianna paused, her face full of skepticism. She eyed him like a child asking to be left alone with a fresh batch of cookies.

"I could work around it and risk not putting them far enough down, but they might be detectable then," he said.

Panic flashed across Orianna's face at the possibility of her barriers being undermined. Tobler sensed the anxiety spike through her confidence, churning inside her—an emotional shift only he could detect. Despite her ability to remain impassive, anyone could crack. If it were tangible to the eye, it would've looked like the striking of a crisp line across a frozen pond, or the first fracture along a pristine pane of glass. But for Tobler, it was as vivid as a sunset, the breaking of a thought.

Orianna straightened, pushing back her shoulders and stiffening. "I guess you probably should do that. Good idea, Tobler. Do you mind, Gemma? It would give you a chance to practice."

"No, that sounds grea—uh, I mean, ah okay. I would have loved to have helped you and Uncle Zavier, but you're right. I can use the practice." She feigned disappointment, trying her best to appear remorseful, until Orianna walked off. When she was far enough away and out of earshot, she released her sigh of relief.

"Feel better?" Tobler grinned.

She slumped against the house, more at ease. "Yes, thanks."

"Anytime. But you should tell her that you're afraid of heights, at some point. She might keep trying to get you up into high places if you don't," he cautioned.

"Yeah, I'll probably mention it to her whenever it comes up again. Nice excuse about a rock being in your way. I almost believed you. You're rather light on your feet, huh?" she said, feeling the rough wood under her hands, causing her to wonder how old the home really was.

"Oh no, I wasn't kidding. There really is a rock in my way. Would you mind giving it a nudge?" He gestured to the hole he was digging, and she saw the sizable rock in question.

"Oh! Sure, of course!"

She scrambled over to help him. He took a step back to give her some room—and for his own safety. Gemma took a deep breath, clearing her mind as she planted her feet on the ground and raised her hand above the rock. She concentrated on moving the rock. The dirt around it shook, but the rock itself wouldn't budge. With a disgusted grunt, she tried again; again, the dirt shook but nothing happened.

Tobler peered at the rock to see if the issues was supernatural or just nature in its stubbornness, but Gemma never budged. He knocked at the edge of the rock with his shovel. On the third tap, it shot up from the ground, just missing his head. The rock landed hard on the ground behind him, cratering the earth beneath it.

"I swear woman you're aiming to kill me!" Tobler said, half teasing and half scared.

"I'm so sorry!" she said, unsure whether he was serious. "If I do though, just know I didn't mean it."

"That's comforting to know," he chuckled. "Thanks for the help, anyway." He threw in the last charm and shoveled dirt to cover it up, happy to be rid of them.

"How do those work, anyway? They're just silly little rock things."

"Those silly little rock works like a shield and barrier. The ones in the ground make it so that nobody can cross their line to the house. The charms in the walls deflect any magic aimed at the house. The same goes for the charm on the roof. Add that all to what you two did inside, this place is locked up tighter than a toad's ass."

"That does sound a bit excessive." She gestured to his dirty, streaked brow and soiled clothes.

Looking down, he became painfully aware of his disheveled appearance, running his hands over clothes attempting to fix them. With the back of his hand, he nonchalantly tried to wipe the dirt from his head only to make it worse.

"All because I'm here..." she trailed off, staring at her feet.

Tobler looked at her, surprised to see she was clearly the more embarrassed of the two despite his transformation into some sort of soil creature.

"Oh no, it's nothing, really. It's all worth it," he cringed at the innuendo, "if The Eyes are out there. They're a nasty bunch, from what I've heard."

"I've heard, too."

Tobler felt her worry and self-consciousness as they walked to the back of the house.

"Sorry that you got roped into all of this," she gestured about. "You know, Aunt Orianna's crazy overprotectiveness and all. I'm sure you had better things to do today."

"Nonsense, like I said it was nothing. I didn't have anything going on today, anyway." In his mind, he tried to puzzle out the real reason for her apology, whether it was really his time she was concerned about or the fact she didn't feel worth the trouble. "What were you before you met Orianna and fell into all of this?" He made an exaggerated gestured at the house, happy to see it made her crack a tiny smile—so small, but it made him feel brighter.

"You mean what did I want to do?" Gemma shrugged. "I had some plans, but nothing earth shattering." She thought for a second longer about her former goals, realizing they were more in shades of gray than the vivid hues offered in this new world. "Actually, everything before now seems pretty boring."

Walking inside the house, Gemma relaxed—more at home here than her other home. She never thought she'd be one for rustic style, but it made her feel good, cozier than any expensive home her adopted parents used to live in. Recalling those spaces now, they all seemed cold and empty.

Tobler sat at the kitchen table. "I'm sure I can spare a few minutes to hear about it."

His willingness to listen surprised Gemma. "Well, I was accepted to a college far from home—or, at least, what I thought was home."

He waited for her to continue, assuming there would've been more to her story.

"That's the extent of it."

Tobler nodded. "Oh, that sounds nice enough. What did you want to study there?"

His undivided attention settled on her—watching, but in a pleasant way. She felt important. It wasn't as if her family hadn't loved her—there was no question of that—but no one actually listened to her. She was always the one doing the listening.

"Nothing stood out, so I decided to pursue a degree in Liberal Arts." She paused, realizing she hadn't thought about it again since she got accepted. Time was slowly ticking away for her in that regard, followed by how boring she must sound to him.

"So," he inquired, clearing her mind of worry, "why go at all, then?"

"What?" She stared at him.

"Why go? Why not leave your options open?" He leaned back, tipping the chair onto two legs.

"It's just better to go, anyway, if you're accepted somewhere. Take a few classes and see how it goes."

"Oh, okay. Is there any cost for the classes?"

"Well, yeah. You pay per semester and for books and stuff."

"Paying for classes is reasonable, but your books? That seems a bit rash. They must give you some sort of reduction on attendance if you're 'trying out a few things,' right?" he questioned, pondering over the charges of an education.

"Yeah. Buying the books is inconvenient, but that's just how it is over there. And no, we don't get any tuition differential for not know what we want to do. You still have to pay the usual sum like everyone else," Gemma said, frowning as she realized through their talk how the idea seemed even more unfair and costly.

Tobler mulled the ideas over and winced as if he were in pain. "And you do this again because...?"

"It's what you do: go to school, graduate, go to college, get a degree, find a job, get married, have kids. Steps of life, you know. Always thought I'd just figure it out once I got there." Gemma wondered if she made sense to him, for she was beginning to doubt those standards now.

The ideas floated around her, thinner than book pages and weighing less than sparrows. She was lost on the thought, picking at some dirt under her nails. When she glanced back to see he hadn't taken his eyes off her, she abandoned his gaze to stare out the window—a much-needed distraction from both him and this strange new mix of emotion.

"Hmm." Tobler picked at a loose splinter on the table to give her a break. He could tell their talk was affecting her.

Her eyes shot back to him with her brow furrowed, "Hmm? What do you mean, hmm?"

"Nothing, nothing, just sounds like you're settling is all. Making life-altering decisions when you don't know much of anything by the sounds of it." he said in a casual tone, unconsciously shaking his leg.

"Excuse me? Settling? What makes you think *that*?" She couldn't keep her irritation off her face nor the hardness from her eyes.

He froze still in his seat, mid-pick at another splinter, as he realized he'd offended her. Tobler more often than not found himself in situations exactly like this, where his mouth worked faster than his brain, leaving the two with a significant distance to catch up. He watched Gemma's creased expression darken to a glower. He had to come up with something to say, feeling thicker than tree sap in mid-frost.

"Well," he swallowed and decided to just be honest, "what would you call taking what life gives to you because you're doing what's expected of you? I mean, knowing what you want for the entirety of your life is a journey, not something you pick up like that." He snapped his fingers and smiled in an attempt to find friendlier ground, repressing the instinct to soothe her which might piss her off if she caught on.

Gemma considered it. She spoke slowly, choosing her words with care so as not to admit defeat. "I'd call that getting by until something better comes along."

The words felt wrong, but she was nothing if not stubborn. Her efforts were futile, of course, because he saw it. It passed on her face—only a second, but he noticed it going—a flicker of awareness. He perked up a little from his guarded position, feeling some of the air returning to his lungs.

"But does it stir up your soul?" He frowned on his last words. Stir up your soul?—he sounded like some half-cracked cave dweller who'd been feeding off of the moon. He chided himself for being too flowery, even as he'd spat the vernacular vomit. He rubbed a hand over his eyes for a moment, squeezing them shut.

"Well, no, I guess it doesn't." Her voice sounded small, but immediately stopped his inner torture. "I never knew anything else existed before, I..." She pursed her lips and rested her head on her hand.

He let the silence coat the air between them, knowing that it wasn't a thing of awkwardness but a thoughtful suspension. Anticipation grew, partly from him and partly from her, making him puzzle at what she'd do next.

"It's different now, after coming here. Is it possible your plans might change course? Goblidet has a lot to offer a young, talented witch—especially if you're smart and hone your craft."

She nodded. "I'm at square one again. I'm not sure what I'd do here. Orianna and I haven't exactly discussed my staying in this realm longer than a day, never mind what I could do here for a lifetime."

"I'd imagine about the same as your old one, though I don't know much about The Echo." He grinned. "More opportunity to use your abilities here since you really weren't sure where you wanted to head in your old life. That should make the choice a little easier."

Everything he said made sense to her. This was her true home and the only place she could use her abilities. There was no place for her back across the portal, no true connections other than her mom.

"Okay, you might have a point. I'll have to give it some thought—at least until the end of the summer so I can pull out of college if I choose. Maybe that's why I've never made up my mind about my future." She didn't mean to say the latter out loud, a silent thought voicing itself regardless of her wishes.

"You mean like fate?" Tobler asked simply.

His face wasn't readable. She had been disappointed before by a belief in fate, thanks to her adoptive parents; but to Gemma, fate always felt like something real, something that could be touched and sought.

Tobler's blue eyes rested on her face, delving into her soul and making her squirm.

"Yeah, don't you believe in fate?" She attempted to mimic his same intensity but felt very foolish doing so. She noticed the corners of his mouth repressed a smile.

"I do. I'm just surprised you do. Didn't think that was something that your realm believed."

"Depends on who you ask. What about around here? Do you all religiously believe in fate or something like it?"

"Fate has its place here, but it's mostly the old folks and their tales."

"Like what?"

"It's used more for—"

Orianna and Zavier walked through the door. "Okay, everything is perfect. Locked up tight as I can get it."

"Black Damn, if I could ever finish a sentence—let alone a conversation—around here," Tobler grumbled, low enough that only Gemma heard him. She almost burst out laughing, but quickly pulled it back.

"Which means it's a fortress." Zavier's exasperation barely hid his attempt at sounding supportive.

"There is reason to my madness, Zavier. You don't need to understand it. You just need to trust it." She gave him a smile so lovely it broke his frustrated shell.

"So, what do we do now?" Gemma asked. "Do we need to put up more protection spells?"

Tobler's eyes widened at her words, his face twisting with distress. He motioned dramatically for her to stop before she could ask any more question. By the time Gemma understood, it was too late.

"Well..." Orianna turned, a finger to her chin as she thought.

Tobler frowned at Gemma, who mouthed an apology as a fit of laughter crept up on her.

"You were the child that would remind their father of missed chores, weren't you?" he whispered to her.

Gemma almost couldn't keep herself together any longer, until she noticed Zavier looked about at his wit's end, as well, and grew more serious.

Zavier closed his eyes, taking a deep breath to calm himself as Orianna's face lit up with a new idea. "No! No, no, that will be enough." He gave her a stern look. "The house is safe. Anything more and we would suffocate. But good question,

Gemma. It is always good to make sure you've finished a task before setting off."

All except for Orianna relaxed at this. Instead, she crossed her arms and pouted. She was being overprotective, but after everything, it had become her nature.

"What else is there to Goblidet, then?" Gemma chimed in, trying to steer the conversation into more pleasant waters.

"Well, the house is getting rather bare in the cupboards. We should take a trip into town for food and supplies." Orianna grabbed a pad of paper and a quill, walking from cupboard to cupboard jotting down a list.

"Come on, Tobler. We should ready the horses, make ourselves busy before someone finds other jobs for us to do. I could use more pipe tobacco, anyway." Zavier plodded out the door with Tobler in tow, not anxious to stick around.

"Horses? You mean, we can't just open a portal to travel to town?" Gemma was confused at this medieval method of transportation.

Orianna chuckled at Gemma's bafflement while scribbling away on her pad. "No, dear. Portals should only be used for realm travel. It becomes more difficult—messy, even—with closer ranges. For all else, we have to travel the old-fashioned way. But I see your point. You would imagine by now that someone would've invented something more precise. Maybe we'd just zap ourselves places, but sometimes it's just better to not abuse magic."

"Ah right, magic can only work for certain things...makes sense." Gemma turned to head outside to catch up to Zavier and Tobler, but Orianna caught her at the door.

"Oh Gemma, wait! You can't go like that. Come with me, we'll get you into some different clothes so you blend in."

Orianna let go of her quill and headed up stairs. Gemma walked cautiously past the still-writing quill and pad, both floating in midair before rushing after Orianna.

Upstairs, Gemma walked down a shallow hall and followed the sound of soft thumps and muttering behind a weathered door. The door creaked open to a bedroom in a sea strewn with dresses, as if a fierce wind ripped out the wardrobe's contents. Gemma never saw anything so messy in her entire life. Orianna was still at the wardrobe, tossing garb after garb out until—in a triumphant exclamation—she held up a simple, tan dress.

"Perfect! Here try this on." She hurled the dress to Gemma. "Don't worry if it doesn't fit just right. It's only temporary until we get you some clothes. Come downstairs when you're dressed."

Gemma snatched it as Orianna walked out, shutting the door with a solid thud. She held it at arm's length; it was of plain design with no frills. It seemed nice enough, but as she looked around the room of scattered dresses, it appeared dull in comparison. Beggars couldn't be chooser, she supposed. She shucked off her clothes, slipping the dress on and standing in front of the tall mirror.

It didn't look bad on her, but it didn't fit the way she'd liked; baggy in the top half, a little snug at her hips, and a touch too long. She didn't dwell long with the new world awaiting, slowing down only when she reached the stairs. She was klutzy, no sense in showing it off.

When she got downstairs, the kitchen was empty. She hurried outside, a little worried they'd left without her. Once she was out the door, she saw Zavier and Orianna sitting leisurely atop a wagon with Tobler in the back of the cart.

"There you are! My, that was fast." Orianna looked her up and down, "That doesn't look half bad. Needs some help, but it'll do for now until we get you to a shop. Let's go, lots to do today."

"Here, let me help you up," Tobler said, standing and offering his hand to her.

The times were truly medieval around here. In a dress, she wanted to avoid flashing unsuspecting townsfolk so she accepted the help.

Taking his outstretched hand, he hoisted her up and something tingled in their palms. It was there again. The strange, but calming, electricity from before. Gemma's every nerve ending stood at attention, like gooseflesh *underneath* her skin.

They both froze a few seconds, caught off guard. Tobler cleared his throat after making sure she was in, then sat down. Gemma followed suit, sitting across from him.

"Everyone in? Here we go." Zavier lifted the reins, muttered to the horses, and off they went.

* * *

GEMMA ENJOYED THE RIDE, leaning back to rest her head on her hands. The world seemed to move slower from where she sat, smoother than she'd imagined. The click of the horse's hooves against the ground along with the creaks of the wood made for a peaceful tune, opposed to the rumbling engines of cars and busses. The dirt road was well-traveled, with the occasional bump of a rock here and there. The whole experience was like an old timer's lullaby, crooning away at her. If it wasn't for the fact that it was the slowest mode of transportation, she would travel no other way.

The world around her was tranquil, hypnotic to watch it shuffle past. A beautiful countryside scattered beyond, displaying aged trees and rolling meadows of grass and hay. It graced her nose with the smell of cut grass, fresh air, blue skies;

if sunshine had a scent, it would've joined the rest. Birds chirped out their tiny songs overhead and in the trees—not in annoying constant chimes but in a sporadic symphony. Although she was a stranger in a foreign place, the peaceful atmosphere felt like home.

Gemma turned her head slightly and caught Tobler staring at her. He had a strange look on his face, one indicating that the sight of her puzzled him. When she returned his scrutiny, he turned away. It made her wonder what he was looking at. Had her deodorant given out, forcing him downwind? Subtly she sniffed herself just in case, but she didn't stink—although the dress did smell slightly stale. Perhaps there was some of her breakfast on her face, or worse yet a bug on her cheek. She brushed her face gently but felt nothing. A wave of self-consciousness washed over her, and she fought to suppress it down, telling herself it didn't matter.

The wagon drove under an overhanging branch, jostling it until some fruit fell at her feet. Gemma picked up the round, bright orange-like fruit with a strange, scaled pattern on only half of it. She brought it up to her nose. It smelled like honey.

"That a clover pear. I believe they're in season about this time," Tobler said.

"Is it edible?"

"Sure, of course it is. It's pretty popular around here. Tastes like—I don't know—clover pear. Orianna makes a good pie out of them on occasion."

Gemma lifted the fruit to her mouth.

"I don't know if—"

Before he could finish, she took a big bite out of the clover pear. After a couple of chews her mouth twisted into an unpleasant pucker, and she spit it out over the side of the wagon.

"UGH! You liar, it tastes horrible!" She spit again from the awful taste. "Honey? What kind of honey do you eat? Sour, bitter, just gross." The fruit stuck to the roof of her mouth causing her to spit again until it was all out.

Tobler couldn't contain himself. "Well, I *was* trying to warn you that one wasn't ripe enough. Honestly, do you always put strange things in your mouth before anyone can tell you about it?" He burst with laughter, his hands at his stomach. "Should have seen your face!" He pointed at her as tears streamed down his cheeks.

"Well, you should've spoken faster, tried to stop me, or opened with the fact that it isn't ripe first before telling me how great it tastes."

"You're right. You're right," he said, coming down from his laughter and wiped his face. "I'm sorry. Next time I'll give you the bad news first." He composed himself, resisting the urge to quirk up into a smile, but that would get him laughing again. "So how was it?"

"More sour than a lemon, and it made my mouth sticky."

After that, they road for a while until they came to a sign announcing their arrival to the Goblidet Market. Zavier pulled the horses over. Outside stood a dusty old man wielding a pitchfork. He abandoned his chore and approached, but he didn't say a word when he reached the wagon.

"You got room for them?" Zavier motioned to the horses.

The old man chewed, appraising the size of the horses. "Ya, I reckon I got room for these two. How long?"

"A couple of hours, depending on the ladies today." He nodded in Orianna's direction and she swatted his arm.

"A'ight, deal. Copper vellum each. Hay and water, an extra copper." The old man held out a leathery hand.

Zavier snorted at the cost, digging deep into his pocket then pressing four copper coins in the old man's hand. In another dusty walk back to the barn, the old man disappeared and hollered at someone else inside.

"Tobler, help him bring them in. I want to make sure he doesn't skimp on the hay for that price. Come and find us afterwards." Zavier said.

Tobler nodded and jumped out of the wagon. Gemma looked over the side; it wasn't far down, but it was enough to make her question her feet.

Tobler walked back to her. "Almost forgot my manners," He once again stretched out a hand to her, a slight bow in his form. "My lady."

Gemma giggled. "What storybook did you fall out of?"

She took his hand and placed a foot on the high step. Leaning her weight and holding onto him, she swung her other foot over but it caught the top of the wood, causing her weight to shift off-balance and slip. Tobler moved in closer, catching her both arms wrapped firm around her. She was mere inches from his face, a proximity which stunned them both. The overwhelming feelings flooded back in a dizzying rush.

"Oh! I'm so sorry. I'm not very good on my feet." Gemma moved back a step as her cheeks flushed an innocent red.

"It's alright. That wouldn't have been a pleasant fall the way you were heading." He smiled but stopped when he felt a warmth creep through his chest. He cleared his throat quickly. "I better get the horses inside. You should probably catch up to Orianna." He pointed in her direction. "Looks like she's waiting for you."

"Aren't you coming?"

"Yeah. Don't worry, I'll catch up to you guys soon. Why? Miss me already?" he said, half teasing and half flirting.

Gemma snorted indelicately. "You're joking, right?" Cockiness didn't sit well with her, and she wasn't sure if he was kidding.

She hurried off toward an expectant Orianna with an eye roll. As they headed toward the square, Tobler felt a strange flitter, but he brushed it away and headed in to rest the horses.

CHAPTER TWELVE

ORIANNA LINKED ARMS WITH Gemma as they walked along the dirt road to the market. "I think you'll like Goblidet Market. There are lots of shops selling clothes, ingredients, potions, and various foods. But remember, all places have their sour eggs. Keep a watchful eye out. You can never be too careful."

"Okay, Aunt O. I'll do my best to be mindful, but why are we walking? Why didn't we just ride into town?"

"It can get crowded fast so the town ruled to not allow transportation inside. It's much easier to keep the horses at a checkpoint instead of navigating a clogged street. It helps to keep order," Zavier explained.

"Ah, like a parking lot?"

"Yeah, something like that." Orianna answered.

After they walked a short while, they came to the mouth of the town where the street broadened into different paths. Before them laid a bustling city, streets lined with shops shouldered against each other. Every shop held a piece of unique charm in both design and an array of color. It was a long and curving lane, making her wonder how anyone navigated through the many streets and alleyways.

"Probably best to just keep to the main street. Side streets can get confusing, and you should avoid alleys all together." Orianna warned.

"If I got lost, couldn't I just ask for directions? Are the locals not friendly?"

"You could, but like I said before, every town has its bad areas. If you happen to ask the wrong person, and they suspect you've gone astray, they could try to rob you or just be nasty. Best to keep away from strangers."

"But that means everyone here." Something about Orianna's words didn't settle well with Gemma. She forgot to consider the dangers of her new life.

"For now. In time, that won't be the case. We have a long list ahead of us." Orianna pulled out the notepad and quill from her pocket. She flipped it open to the first page, running a long finger down the scribbles, "I need more supplies for my workroom so we better head to the Floating Toad."

"You two go. I'm going to Jamison's store for more pipe tobacco. Might do some bullshitting while I'm there." He kissed Orianna quickly and headed off in the opposite direction.

"Ready? We should hurry before all of the fresh herbs are gone." Orianna took Gemma by the hand, letting go of the notepad and dragging her off to do her bidding. Gemma was about to catch the notepad as it fell but—to her surprise—it followed them in midair like a pet bird.

"What *is* that thing?" Gemma pointed at the floating pad.

"Oh, that's Flip—my charmed stationary. She's quite handy. I used to always forget my lists at home. Never again, though, since Zavier got me Flip as a birthday gift. Poor thing, we're going too fast for her. Let's slow down." She smiled widely as they came to a green storefront with a hanging wooden sign. "Ah, we're here."

They stepped in and the thick smell of incense swept across her face. She had never cared much for the potent odor, barely suppressing a cough when a sweet-faced woman came up to them.

"Orianna, darling! How are you?" The woman embraced Orianna in a tight, quick squeeze. She was just a touch shorter than Orianna, with a lean and muscular build. Her dress was dyed a gentle green, contrasting nicely against her mocha skin.

"Hello, Maggie. I'm well. How are you, my dear old friend?" Orianna held Maggie at arm's length.

"Hey now!" Maggie raised a finger to her. "Easy with the 'o' word."

"I'm sorry. Forgive me. You don't look a day over 25," she said with a wink.

"Damn straight, I don't." Maggie chuckled. "Anyway, I'm fine. Business is doing well, so I can't complain much. Well now, who's this here?" Maggie turned her attention to Gemma, noticing her for the first time.

"Hi, I'm—" Gemma's introduction was cut short by Orianna's shushing.

"Maggie, can we talk in private? The three of us. There's something of grave importance we should discuss."

"Follow me."

Maggie lead them to a scarlet curtain behind the counter. As she ushered them through, she checked the entrance to be sure that no one was watching them. Once satisfied, Maggie stepped through herself, weaving her hand where the two curtains met and muttering something Gemma couldn't quiet hear.

"There—no one can enter, and no one can hear us now. However, I can only muffle so much with the curtain. What's going on? Are you a girl in trouble, honey?" Maggie put a concerned hand on Gemma's arms.

"No! No, no nothing like that. I need you to keep this between the three of us. Maggie, it's a big secret. I'm trusting you." Orianna's eyes grew serious.

"You know you can trust me with anything, Orianna. Now, what's going on here?" Maggie's face held an abundance of curiosity as she eyed Gemma, a distrusting gleam shining back at her.

"Take a good look at her. Who do you see?" Orianna nodded towards Gemma, urging her forward.

Maggie took a moment, observing Gemma as if she were a complex painting. She began circling, looking her up and down, until it finally hit her with a gasp.

"She looks like Charlotte...your niece, little Gemma!" Maggie pulled Gemma tightly against her in a hug that about took her breath away. Gemma made a few suffocation noises before Maggie let her go. "Oh child, it's been so long! I haven't seen you since you were swaddled up to your mother's bosom. My, have you grown. What else is going on, Orianna? How did you find her?"

"Got lucky, for the most part. We have reason to believe Leo is resurging. Recruiting more Eyes and watching us again."

"After all of this time?" Her hands flew to her mouth, shocked by the notion. "Are you sure? We should alert the High Authority. Get some—"

"We aren't sure. It could be something, it could be nothing. But it's not a chance I feel good about taking." Orianna whispered. "This must stay between us."

Maggie looked her square in the eyes, then gave a stoic nod. "I understand. You have my sworn alliance, Orianna, you know that by now. Locked of tongue, I promise."

Their faces turned grim with the weight of secrecy and a silent communication that unnerved Gemma. But something else crept up Gemma's throat. It had kept itself at bay while crossing the portal, curbed by her enthusiasm for magic and strange things that moved beyond her understanding. No, those other events sparked a natural curiosity and excitement, but witnessing the strained conversation between Orianna and Maggie rioted a chilling fear.

"Am I some kind of secret?" Her smile faded like a ghost at sunrise.

"No, of course you're not. This is your home, too. You're meant to be here." Maggie reassured her.

"That's right, this place is your home. Leo and those other radical bastards of his—" She choked off the angry sentence, then continued once she took a deep breath. "This, none of this, is your fault. You aren't a dirty secret. I just need to keep you safe. It's better no one knows for a while. It might jar a few things, understand?" Orianna spoke with urgency, seriousness dripping from each word.

Gemma nodded beneath her aunt's fiery gaze, but truth was, she didn't understand—not really.

"Okay, good. When we're out in public, we can't use your real name. Our family line is pretty well known, and we needn't raise any eyebrows just yet. We'll call you Ashley—should be simple enough remember. Be mindful to answer to it for we can't have anyone suspicious. Your story is that you're Zavier's younger cousin from the North Country, got it?"

"I'll try to remember, but does Uncle Zavier know that?"

"Yes, we worked it out on the way into town today. He's aware."

Maggie asked, "What will you do if people find out who she is?"

Orianna found the subject easier to avoid than to think about. "We will cross that road if we have to. I can't worry about it now. If we don't get back out there, people will wonder."

"Of course, come." Maggie unsealed the doorway, and they all stepped through. "Name whatever it is you need. I'm sure I have it." She gestured around the well-stocked shop, loaded with glass bottles, jars, and boxes.

Orianna ripped a sheet from the notepad, and another piece of paper materialized in its place. Gemma rubbed her eyes, hardly believing what she saw. She handed it to Maggie. "Here are the things I'll need, all ripened."

Maggie put on a pair of pointed half-moon glasses and skimmed the list, then looked back at Orianna. "Quite the list— an expensive one, too."

Orianna let out a sigh that turned into a smile. "It's going to be a very expensive day."

"Good thing you qualify for the family discount." Maggie grinned, making it clear the two were as thick as thieves.

As they continued sorting through Orianna's list, the ladies watched as Gemma wandered about the shop, marveling at the random things on the shelves and in the drawers; she looked every bit the curious witch. They reminisced on their youth and causing a fuss for their parents.

Maggie whispered to Orianna, "He's back? You're sure of this?"

"Honestly? I'm not sure, Maggie. I truly hope not. I want to bring her back home, but if her life is in danger, I can't. If I don't protect her now, then the time I lost would have been for naught." Remorse covered her face as she watched the inquisitive Gemma meander. "I've missed her so much. I don't know if I can bear her leaving like that again." Orianna's voice fell, choking up at the end as grief darkened her memories.

Maggie rubbed a reassuring hand on her friend's arm, then gathered the supplies neatly into a bag. "Don't be a stranger now. Come back soon. I've missed seeing your face. Stop hiding it from me." Maggie looked over at Gemma. "That goes for you too, miss! It's been dogs ages since I saw you. Don't be a stranger. You are always welcome here."

"We'll be back soon, Maggie. Goodbye for a little while." Orianna bid farewell to her friend as they exited the Floating Toad, realizing how much she needed to have an old friend in her life again.

"Okay, where to now?" Gemma asked, dragging Orianna back from her thoughts. She noticed her aunt would get lost in these far-off looks, and from the frowns they generated, she thought it'd be better to pull her out of her own head.

"I'm not sure what you'd like to see? We're here for you to get a feel for the place, don't forget."

"Everything, really, but I have no idea where to start, either."

With that, they walked. Gemma's eyes filled with glittering curiosity as she attempted to take in everything all at once. There were odd-named stores with strange wares in their windows, each with a different color palette that surprisingly blended well with the surroundings. Large windows loomed up, guarded by different styles of iron lattices. They passed magic folk of all shape and sizes dressed in a variety of common clothes and robes, matching or not. Creatures that ran about the side streets, the likes of which she'd never seen before.

Orianna watched Gemma, happy to see her back in the place she belonged, the world she shared with her sister. The town held much of their family history, and now it wouldn't end with them.

"We'll have plenty of time to get to everything, eventually. I'm sure you'd like something more your style and size. I know just the place."

They walked, arm in arm, until they were outside a shop with a black and silver front—The Dainty Pincushion.

"They really are colorful with their names here." Gemma muttered to herself as they stepped through the door.

"Your mom and I used to come here to do some shopping." Orianna reminisced as she touched some of the clothes. "Marlin is a friend of the family. He's owned this place since we were kids. He's a marvel with numbers, sizes, and prices." Orianna practically dragged her up to the counter, excited while ringing the small brass bell.

They waited a good minute before Orianna rang the bell again, finding it odd that he hadn't shown up. Orianna was about to ring a third time, and began walking behind the counter, until a shorter woman about Orianna's age appeared. Her corn-blonde hair was pulled back into an intricate braid. She had flawless pink skin and high cheekbones—expressionless until she saw Orianna. Her lips pinched, her eyes narrowed, and the tarnished bell cracked beneath her hand. The warmth of remembrance drained from the room, replaced by a cold tension.

"Orianna." Disdain was clear in the woman's impersonal tone.

"Jane? Well, it's a good thing Marlin didn't go into the mirror business, or else your face would scare them into pieces." Orianna huffed, a hand at her hip as she leaned on the counter.

"So clever," Jane said dryly, "What happened? Got too fat for the wedding? Or did Zavier finally come to his senses and see you for the sniveling wench you are?" She crossed her arms, matching Orianna's countenance of unpleasantness.

"You rotten, old b—"

Gemma cleared her throat, giving her a hard nudge to remind Orianna that a scene wasn't the best of ideas. The women glowered at one another as the air thickened with palpable hostility and loathing.

Orianna crossed her arms, doing a horrible job of trying to not look put off. "What *are* you doing here anyway? Where's Marlin?"

"Marlin got called away for a while. Family matters, so he said." Jane said, crossing her arms in the same gesture; the two of them appeared like bratty school children.

"Nonsense. Why wouldn't he say anything to us?"

"It was about *real* family matters, nothing that would concern you. He has me running things here until he returns."

"Why you?" she eyed Jane speculatively. "Certainly wasn't for your warmth and charm. You're not even that close to him."

"I needed a job. Extra coin in your pocket can be hard to come by. I can read a damn tape measure and know my way around a needle. But of course, I don't need to justify myself to the likes of *you,* now do I." Jane's gaze finally wondered from Orianna as she took notice of Gemma. "And who are you?" She snorted with disgust. "The hired help?"

"Hired help?" Gemma shot back, unsure why she was being dragged into their petty issues.

"You worthless—" Orianna spat as her temper boiled over.

Jane could talk to her however she wanted, but she wouldn't tolerate the same treatment towards Gemma. Then it hit her; this wasn't supposed to be Gemma. Their cover would be blown if she let her wrath fly completely unchecked. Orianna took a breath and smoothed out her dress.

"No, she happens to be Zavier's relation from the North Country—not that it's any of your business."

Orianna held open the door for Gemma and then stepped out herself, but not before the door hit her in the ass—with some help.

"Bitch," she said, glancing back inside at a smug Jane. "Sorry, dear. As I said before, not everyone is friendly here."

"What was her problem?"

"Jane? Oh, her and I don't have the best past. She's always been a foul old wench. That part wasn't entirely my fault...about as sweet as a cat stuck in a water barrel. Not to worry, we'll find somewhere else to go." She smiled then looked around to get her bearings. "The Golden Needle is just a short walk from here. Fitting name for the amount of gold you'll drop for their clothes, but the quality is excellent."

"I don't want to put you out, Aunt O. If it's going to be too expensive, we can just wait for Marlin to get back."

"Sweet girl, you are never putting me out. I missed my chances to spoil you all these years, and I'll be damned if I let that little gnat ruin our day."

Soon, they came to a store painted a bright apple-red with a front made entirely of glass. On the door—in perfect script, accompanied by an animated needle and thread design—were gold letters reading "The Golden Needle." Two elegant dresses, suspended in midair, slowly turned to showcase themselves.

"There you are." Zavier walked up to Orianna, placing his hands on her waist and giving her a chaste kiss. "You find what you needed?"

"No, we had a bit of an unpleasant interruption."

"I have something that requires your opinion. Mind if I steal her away for a moment, cousin?" he asked Gemma with a wink.

"Not at all." Gemma shrugged.

"Zavier, I can't. She doesn't know anyone here." Orianna scoffed. "You're sweet, dear, but I can stay here with you."

"She'll be alright, Orianna. I don't expect the dresses to swallow her whole. It will only be a few minutes."

"I'll be right back, dear. You go in and start looking around." Orianna said, trailing off as Zavier ushered her away.

Gemma smiled and shook her head. Time alone felt good, allowing her to gain a true feel of her surroundings. She figured as long as she didn't take any trinkets from strangers, she'd be fine.

CHAPTER THIRTEEN

GEMMA MARVELED AT THE vast selection, shocked to see more dresses floating along the ceiling; this would be a long trip. As she browsed, nothing seemed to catch her eye. The shopkeeper came over, but the overwhelming babbling made her anxious. After a few minutes, the shopkeeper seemed put off by her lack of knowledge and left Gemma to her own devices. She turned to another dress, startled to find Tobler at her side.

"Tobler? What—"

Without saying a word, he grabbed a long lady's jacket from the counter and wrapped her in it. Immediately, he pushed her toward a fitting room until she abruptly stopped in outrage.

"What do you think you're doing?" She looked at him as if he were a crazed animal.

"Shhh!" he hissed, jaggedly pointing at the hem of her disappearing dress.

She gasped at the sight of her exposed ankles, then legs, and hurried herself to the fitting room. By the time she got in there, she was stark naked under the dress coat—aside from her undergarments, which managed to stay intact. Tobler leaned against the fitting room door, letting out a relieved breath. It was short lived; the shopkeeper emerged from the back room, giving him a disappointed look. She'd missed all of it and glared at him with an accusation.

Tobler smiled his most charming of smiles. "My, uh, lady friend is in here trying on a coat and wanted me to make sure no one would come in. However, she seems to have forgotten to take a dress in with her. Any suggestions?"

"Well, any idea what the lady likes? She was indecisive earlier." She crossed her arms, being cordial but clearly not buying his innocence one bit.

He gazed around the shop quickly until something caught his eye. "That dress there. It would probably go well with her, um...well, it might just be nice."

"20 gold vellum." The shopkeeper's voice was firm.

"For a bundle of fabric and thread?" He didn't bother to hide his shock, but the two boys outside that were trying to vanish Gemma's dress caught his eyes. He plopped a stack of coin in her hand. "She's going to need some help." He hastened out the door.

Outside he grabbed the rude little tricksters by their ears and verbally thrashed them for the prank they'd tried to pull. After making sure they were sorry, he pushed them and watched in case they darted into an alley behind the building to do it again. Satisfied, Tobler brushed himself off and reentered the shop.

Standing outside the dressing room was a woman in a stylish crimson dress with black lace trim. Her hair, black as a night with no moon, flowed down almost to her elbow. The dress complemented her, and she wore it well. Certainly, not the other way around. It fit her perfectly, clinging to every curve of her body like a second skin. She was the most striking creature he'd ever seen, and he had seen his fair share of women. It wasn't until she turned to look at him that he realized it was Gemma. Sure, when he first met her, he thought she was beautiful; but in the crimson dress, with her hair down, his heart almost broke. The dress was worth every gold piece he paid to see her in it.

And there it was again. The feeling that consumed him before and he couldn't begin to understand. Was it truly a feeling of his own? He checked around him to see there weren't any other customers in sight. Just him, her, and the dress maker.

The shopkeeper giggled, leaning over to Gemma's ear. "Well, well, well, looks like someone likes what he sees." She gave Tobler a wink, making him aware of his open mouth.

Gemma smiled and turned her attention back to the seamstress. "The dress is absolutely gorgeous, Theena. How much do I owe you for it?"

"Oh, nothing dear. It's already been paid for. The dress coat, too." She nodded in Tobler's direction.

"Thank you, but that's far too generous." She walked closer, her brow furrowing "I'll find a way to pay you back, or Orianna could spot me in the meantime. How much was it?"

Tobler puzzled at her. "No, don't be silly. It was just a little coin burning a hole in my pocket. I really didn't have any use for it anyhow. No big deal." He noticed her shoulders lowered, a bit of tension leaving. She opened her mouth to begin a rebuttal, but he stopped her. "Thank you for your great work, Theena. It fits her perfectly. Have a nice day." He turned to leave, leading Gemma by the elbow toward the door.

"Have a nice day, and come back soon!" Theena called while they exited.

A group of young gentlemen, elegantly dressed, passed The Golden Needle. One turned to Gemma and nodded a polite "good afternoon," but Tobler felt his intentions were anything but polite. After the man passed, he brushed off his emotions and tried to relax—until he caught the eye of a man across the street, gawking, his intentions worse than the other one. Tobler threw a hard glare in the man's direction, causing him to walk into a different store.

He turned to Gemma. "Here," he offered her his arm, "walk with me?"

She hesitated before taking his arm, waiting for the telltale feeling that was a constant factor with them; instead of pulling away, they endured it.

"How did you manage to shake off Orianna? She's been on you like a falcon on a mouse since she found you."

"You noticed that, too," she giggled. "Zavier pulled her away for a moment. She said she'd be back soon. I was only supposed to get measured while I waited for her. Thank you, again, for your help back there. If it wasn't for you, I'd still be naked and penniless in that dressing room—not to mention humiliated."

"Aah, it was nothing, don't worry about it. Just glad I caught them before you had more showing than some bare legs—not the way you want to be remembered around here. I fear our world hasn't exactly given you a good first impression." He gave her a repentant look, sorry for all that had happened.

"Oh, you mean the prank those boys played. That's no reason to write off an entire realm," she snickered.

"Well, that and a crazed sorcerer out and about who isn't your family's biggest fan."

"Ah, almost forgotten that." Her face fell a little, remembering the probable danger. "You do that to me, it seems—make me forget the bad things." The words came out on their own.

"I'm glad to hear that."

"Are you messing with my moods?" The thought hadn't occurred to her before, and her stomach started to turn.

"What? Of course not! How could you—"

Tobler's outrage was plain as sunlight. First interesting girl he'd met in a long time and now she might have the wrong idea about him. He took a deep breath, reminding himself that

Gemma did not understand how what she said could offend him.

"I'd never manipulate your emotions, Gemma." He stopped her in their walk, arms still locked. He turned to her, seriousness engraved on his face; all he had to do was make her understand. "It's completely unethical and an abuse of my powers to do something like that. It might not seem like much, but my powers with emotion are no joke. Many believe it's one of the most dangerous gifts. That's why nobody knows. I hold myself to a higher standard. I'd never use it on you, unless you asked me to." His tone was hushed, and she could see this was important to him. "Do you understand?" He tried to loosen his tight expression.

"Yes, I understand. I'm sorry."

"It's okay, you didn't know. I'm just glad you understand," he said, setting the pace for their walk again.

"You have to call me Ashley," she blurted out and he looked at her oddly. "Orianna doesn't want anyone to know who I am. It's a recent development, I guess. You know, the old cliché, the plot thickens sort of thing."

"Crazy Orianna. I suspected that may happen sometime. Ashley? Hmm, doesn't really suit you, but it'll do. I mean, I figured Orianna to be protective, but this is the glaze on the sweet cakes. Can't say I completely disagree with her. It isn't a horrible idea until we know for sure."

"Tobler? Can I ask you something?" she hesitated. This realm was new to her and she obviously wasn't familiar with the appropriate questions. She didn't want to upset him again.

"Of course. No need to ask permission."

"Why is your power such a responsibility? Why is it so dangerous?" She watched his face go blank. He didn't look offended, but his friendly smile vanished faster than she had expected.

"I'm afraid I'd need some time to explain that to you. At a different time, though. Our conversations seem to get interrupted often. A less public place would be preferable."

"Okay, I can understand that." She sensed a seed of worry sprouting but did her best to push it down so Tobler didn't pick up on it.

He felt the flicker but it vanished, so he opted not to pursue it.

"So, where would you like to go?"

Gemma shrugged, "I don't know, what is there?"

"We could look at the perfumery. Sightsee? Anything you want."

"Did you say perfume? Now that sounds like my kind of shop." Her bright smile stole him. "How far is it?'"

"Not too far. Follow me, it's just around the corner here." He liked her playful tone, a breath of fresh air from what he was used to.

Around the corner, the storefront was a shade of dark green—an earthy feel, enhanced by a variety of hanging plants in the windows. A large branch with a vine of flowers, which looked to have grown from the eave, read "Phlox and Thistle." Inside was an eye-catching disarray of plants, stands, and shelves full of tiny jars and colorful bottles of all sizes, each more creatively designed than the next. Even better, it smelled clean instead of like a flooded herb garden.

"Welcome to Phlox and Thistle. Is there anything I can help you with?"

A tall willowy woman with green and brown hair appeared out of thin air. Her face was pretty with high cheekbones and a perfect dainty nose. The air around her smelled of patchouli with a faint note of tobacco. She wore a white blossom tucked in her hair, except Gemma couldn't tell if it was carefully placed or growing from her head. Her suspicion was reinforced when she noticed the blossom linked to a line of fuzzy green moss trailing down the side of her neck.

"Good afternoon, Zinnia. Just browsing, but do you have any suggestions? My friend here is new to the area so I'm just showing her around to the *best* shops, don't you know." He gave her a smooth wink, making red roses bloom in Zinnia's cheeks.

"Well then, good thing you came today. I just put up a few bottles of my new fragrances I concocted this morning." Zinnia walked to a shelf and took down a blue circular bottle decorated in flowers. "This one is a mix of hydrangea petals and honey-flower oil." She uncapped the bottle and handed it to Gemma, "Give it a whiff."

Gemma put her nose to it, taking a shallow sniff. It smelled exactly like hydrangeas straight from a warm garden and another pleasant smell that she didn't know; that must have been the honey flower. "Wow, that smells remarkable...like nothing I've ever experienced." She smelled it again, practically giddy.

"Oh?" Zinnia was pleased. "If you like that one, try this one. Come." She crossed the store to a clear glass table and picked up a cylindrical green bottle. "Try this one. It's more delicate than the last, made of fresh rain, a bit of fall leaf extract, and fresh grass." This time when she handed it to Gemma, she did not remove the stopper.

Gemma took it, curious at a tapping of sorts coming from inside the bottle. She held the bottle to eye level, surprised at what she saw. Inside was a strange swirl near the stopper. Something dripped from it, making a quiet patter against the glass. Her eyes widened; it was a tiny storm cloud raining inside the bottle. "How did you...?"

Zinnia bubbled at Gemma's amazement, palms together and up to her mouth, almost dancing with excitement. "Can't reveal all of my tricks now. It's a family secret. Now go on and smell it."

Gemma uncorked the bottle with a pop and a wisp of fragrance swept her nose. It was unmistakably the smell of a rainstorm and fresh grass, two of her favorites. "This is perfume? I love it."

"Yes, or you can burn it on a silver plate and let the scent fill a room. I'm glad you enjoy it. Tell you what: that one has been selling so well, I'll let you have it on the house. A welcome gift from our corner of the world."

"Oh no, I couldn't do that," she protested.

"Nonsense. I'll be greatly offended if you don't accept. Please, keep it." Zinnia closed Gemma's hand around the bottle.

"Thank you so much, Zinnia."

"You're very welcome. What's a small gift between friends? Did you see anything else that caught your eye?"

Gemma took a look around the shop until her eyes fell upon a bottle on a high shelf. It was shaped like a diamond with silver etching at each corner, black as the night sky with no moon or stars. The stopper twinkled in the light as if it was coated in diamond dust. "What's that one up there?" She pointed.

Zinnia turned to look where Gemma was pointing, "Ha, your lady has good taste Tobler—expensive, but good." She walked toward the corner of the shop.

"My lady?" He panicked at the accusation, "It seems you have the wrong idea, Zinnia."

Zinnia ignored his foolish grumble, letting out a small melodic whistle as she held out her hand. In a matter of seconds, a small gray and white owl swooped in; it flew high to the shelf, grabbed the bottle, and dropped it in Zinnia's hand before settling onto her shoulder. She gentle patted the owl on the head, praising his good deed.

"Where did he come from?" Gemma looked around for a cage or perch. How could she had missed him? He was an adorable creature.

"This is Scops. He lives everywhere and anywhere that he chooses, but he likes to stay close to me. He usually perches out on the sign, must have been hungry." The bird nuzzled her neck, and she complied by stroking him head to wing. Her attention returned as the vial began to glow silver. "Oh yes, now this here," she held it up, "this is one of my most rare creations. I've worked very hard to make the ingredients and even harder to draw the scent. Moon's breath made of moonflowers and light from the rising moon. It's the most expensive scent in my shop and can only be made by my hands. Here, only lift the top slightly and sniff—it is potent. Be very careful; if you drop it, I will have to charge you." Zinnia slowly offered it to Gemma as it continued to glow.

Gemma took it gingerly, holding tight as she lifted the stopper as instructed; it was a powerful smell, so pure she smelled the starry sky and moon alongside sweet florals. "That's incredible, I could never describe it any other way. Thank you." Very carefully Gemma pressed it into Zinnia's hand.

"You're very welcome." Zinnia gently passed it back to the Scops, who put it in its proper place. "Now then, I must leave you to help some other customers. Nice to meet you, Not Tobler's Lady, and please come by again. I hope you enjoy your visit to Goblidet Market. 'Til next time." She left to help an older woman squinting at a couple of jars on a stand near the back of the shop.

"I like her. Is she a witch?"

"She is very nice, one of the most peaceful witches I know," he said as he held the door open for her.

"So she is a witch?"

"Yes, sort of. Zinnia is her own creature—a Lady of the Forest, actually. That's why she looks like that. She's one with nature, literally."

Stepping out the door, Gemma placed her finger over the bottle and tipped it upside down quickly, then dabbed her neck and wrists. The scent mingled nicely with the natural oils on her skin, smelling better than it had in the shop. Tobler caught the scent in the breeze. "Is that the same perfume? Smells good on you."

She smiled and sniffed her wrist, marveling at the difference as she took his arm again. "I love perfume. It's one of my favorite things."

She felt something pull at her from down a dim street that resembled an alley—and a shady one, at that. It wasn't clean like the rest of the streets; this was lit by rows of torches lining either side of the path to reveal grimy, cracked cobblestones. She stopped, stretching her neck to get a better look at where it twisted, but her view was blocked. The alley was slightly crowded by a few out-of-place witches in ragged, dirty clothing with snarled faces, contrasting others dressed in fine black garments with faces that would've been the envy of any mirror. A woman stepped from the shadows, locking eyes with Gemma. Her eyes were a mesmerizing pale blue that almost blended in with the whites, but a snobbish pretense spoiled the face framed in flowy platinum locks. Gemma felt a pull toward the woman in the form of gooseflesh and curiosity.

"What's down there?" she said, about to take a step toward it, when Tobler stopped her.

"You don't wanna go down there. That's Ophelia Black Street," he pulled her closer to him, breaking her eye contact with the pale-eyed woman; her eyes glazed over in a trance like state. "If you're looking to start some trouble or dabble in Black Magic, that's where you go. After that, it's all downhill and harder to come back from, depending how deep you're in." He could see the fog of confusion leave Gemma's face, and he started to lead her away. "Trust when I say it's not for you. Would leave a worse impression than if you ran naked down the street."

The woman was gone by the time she looked back. "But Goblidet looks like such a nice place. Why would they have a street that caters to Black Magic? I know you all warned of shady people, but that seems pretty serious."

"Every place has its bad parts, yes, and there really isn't a way for us to contain it. Rule breakers simply don't follow the rules." Tobler checked around them before continuing on. "Orianna wouldn't like me for this, so don't say anything, but Black Magic has its place. It isn't on the ethical side, but it can be useful. There is a chance of it tainting a soul, but if you're careful, that's not a problem."

"How can that be? If something is bad, it's bad, no getting around it." She was taken aback, appalled at the thought of evil having a place, let alone a purpose.

"Magic isn't only black and white, as many believe. Some poisonous plants, when used wisely, can be helpful in medicines. Or if you need to counter a hex, then better to go to the source. Again, I'm not saying it's always good. Most of the time it's bad but sometimes necessary. Remember that's just between you and me, though." Small traces of worry peppered his face. He didn't want her to get the wrong idea about him but felt it important for her to hear.

His idea ricocheted in her mind against all she knew of good and evil. "I won't tell anyone. I don't know if I agree just yet, but I see what you're saying."

"I'm sorry if I upset you." Tobler felt the shift in her emotions and was concerned by what he felt.

"Oh no, Tobler, it was nothing." She bit her lip wondering if she should mention it. "Well actually, I felt something back there when we passed the alley."

"When freaky pale eyes looked at you? That doesn't surprise me. She creeped me out, too."

"Not exactly. I mean, yes, she was creepy. But before she showed up, I felt a sort of pull. Something inside me wanted to wander the alley, as if it called to me. What does that mean?"

Tobler thought a moment, "Well, I'd say it's probably normal to be tempted by things we don't know. Curiosity is life. It's the battle of good and evil inside us all the time."

Fear flooded her.

"Are you worried that you might have a bad streak in you? Because you felt an urge to go?" He stopped, turning to her. "Gemma," he whispered, "that isn't what makes you bad. I have a knack for these things, comes with my ability." He took her hand in reassurance, "I haven't felt anything suspicious about you since we met. Whatever it was, that urge or desire, it wasn't anything to do with evil. Okay?"

Gemma felt some relief at his words. This fight between good and evil inside her was something all magical people dealt with. If people were pulled to either end, black or white, then what of the people who fell into the gray?

"There you are!" Orianna called from behind them. "I've been looking for you. Almost didn't recognize you, dear. Where did you get that dress?" She admired Gemma's attire at arm's length.

"Oh, we had some trouble at the Golden Needle. But lucky for me, Tobler happened to be nearby and saved me a lot of embarrassment."

Worry poured over Orianna's brow, "Trouble? What kind of trouble? Tobler, what happened?" She turned her attention, looking to him for answers.

"Nothing serious, just the Orison boys playing around with incantations they didn't know enough about. They somehow made her dress disappear, but I realized what was going on before it got to risky. Got her covered up and gave the boys a talking to." Tobler said swiftly.

"Did you see anything?" Orianna narrowed her eyes at him.

"Of course not! She was well covered up before then!"

"You paid for the dress?"

"Yeah, picked it out myself. Thought it would complement her, uh," he looked Gemma up and down a second, "face. Complements her face."

"It certainly does. She looks stunning. Granted, not the low profile look I was hoping for as I'm sure most of the men have noticed you." Orianna said with reproach at the ogling men who passed. "Sure, they're all just admiring her *face*."

"No, don't be silly, Aunt O. I couldn't turn an eye, let alone a head."

"Don't underestimate yourself, dear. Just because you're not looking doesn't mean others aren't. The rabbit might not see him but the fox watches, nonetheless." Orianna warned with a raised finger then took a few steps forward, freezing when she looked down the dark alley. She turned to Gemma and Tobler, "You didn't take her down there, did you?" Orianna's stare became icy and serious, daggers poised in her eyes.

"No, don't be crazy Orianna. I would never take her there, it's not safe. She doesn't need that kind of exposure." Tobler's anger at her accusation was clear in his voice.

Orianna stared at him, looking for any trace of a lie until she was satisfied. She continued to walk, and they fell into step behind Zavier.

"Thanks for not saying anything. I'm sorry she got on you like that. What was up with *that* anyway?" Gemma apologized softly.

"Don't mention it. I'm used to Orianna's suspicions, but I can explain that later." He shrugged.

It bothered him that, after all these years, Orianna thought him capable of such reckless behavior. Her reservations against him formed the moment his empathic abilities became known. Zavier had taken his abilities as they were, without prejudice, treating him as a son. Orianna's judgment wavered, at best, but that was for another time.

Looking as they walked, Gemma became enamored by a pair of witches standing three feet tall with a keen resemblance to elves. As she stared in astonishment, she heard them arguing about how the other had apparently been turned an incredible shade of purple, and how it was all the non-purple one's fault. Now she had really seen it all, she figured—purple, elf-like people had to be the last of it. She was so engrossed by the strange pair that she ran smack into what felt like a brick wall, but upon looking, it was just Zavier.

"Oh! I'm so sorry. I wasn't paying attention," she said, rubbing her pained shoulder. He felt more like a solid mass than a regular human.

Zavier gave a deep chuckle, "It's alright. I didn't feel a thing, really. Are you okay? Hurt your shoulder, did you?"

"Oh no, it's fine, just surprised me is all." She put on her best nonchalant face, and he bought it, walking through the doorway. They stood in front of an all-white building with white latticed windows. The sign was clean and simple, reading "Apothecary." The building was almost boring, compared to the other shops.

"Hmmm." Tobler said, a hand to his chin.

"What are you hmmm-ing at me for?" Gemma asked defensively.

"Just that, I thought you were just acting clumsy around me, but I guess you really just don't have good use of your feet."

"Shut up," she said, hitting him on the shoulder.

"Ow!" He laughed at her frustration as she glared, walking through the door.

Once inside, the apothecary was much like the outside: simple, unadorned, and very white. It appeared nearly empty, aside from a smattering of white shelves on each wall and some tall, built-in cabinets behind the long glass counter. The only colors came from the blue, red, black, and clear bottles behind the glass doors of the cabinet and on the shelves. It was not enough to fill the vast space, leaving it feeling hollow as a bone without marrow. Orianna picked up a bell from the counter, rang it, and waited as a redheaded man in a black robe with a well-trimmed beard walked out from behind a white curtain.

"Why hello Orianna! How have you been?" The man greeted her with a cheerful demeanor.

"I'm well, Finn, and you? Doesn't seem too busy in here today." She looked around the empty store.

"I'm as good as can be. Yes, I'm afraid I haven't had a whole lot of business today, which is good and bad. I'm glad people aren't riddled with illness, but it would be nice to have a customer or two coming in." He sighed, then turned to acknowledge the others. "What brings you in today? Brought the whole family? How goes it, Zavier?"

"It goes fair enough," Zavier answered, then turned his back; conversation didn't seem high on his list.

"Yeah, I guess you could say it's a small field trip, stocking up on standard elixirs and tonics." She handed him a list from the enchanted pad.

Finn took the paper in his slender hands, glancing over it. "Mmhm, I see, quite the list you have here. I'm sure I can muster up all of it for you. Quinn!" he yelled toward the back of the apothecary. There was a faint sound of footsteps and a young man stepped forward, dressed in a white shirt and brown pants. His face was devilishly handsome, adorned with bright green eyes and pitch-black hair. "Quinn, go and grab these bottles while I jar up the rest in the back." Finn handed him the paper.

Wordless, the apothecary master's apprentice looked over the list and started gathering it up. Quinn had an air of arrogance about him that Tobler didn't need his Empath powers to see, and he muttered under his breath.

"The last two could take more effort. Was there anything else you needed to get done? Did you want to come back?" Finn asked.

"Do we have the time, Zavier?"

"There are a few more things we should settle before leaving, although we shouldn't leave too late."

"Let's do that then. You two don't mind staying until Finn is done?" Orianna asked Gemma and Tobler.

"I guess we could," Gemma stated, more as a question as she turned to Tobler. "Would you mind staying here with me?"

"I don't mind so long as you're paying." He wasn't fond of the thought of leaving her alone in a place she didn't know, especially with Quinn around.

Orianna sighed, handing him a few coins. "We should be back soon, but just in case we aren't, meet us at the beginning of the path to the horses. No side trips," she emphasized.

"Yes, ma'am," he said, rolling his eyes.

Zavier pulled Orianna toward the door to stop her worrying. The two waited at the counter, watching the assistant. Quinn was on the ladder when they turned back around, grabbing some items and placing them in a brown sack. Gemma, starting to become bored, wandered over to the shelf to see what types of things an apothecary sold. Tobler began some searching, as well, to chip away the time. She found fungal powders, wart busters, and rash creams—nothing too terribly interesting but something to look at, nonetheless. She examined clusters of tightly packed jars, studying their contents.

"Find what you're lookin' for?"

The sudden closeness of the unfamiliar voice made her jump. She spun around to find Quinn, just near enough to make her feel that he was too close. "What? No, not really looking, just browsing."

"Sorry, I didn't mean to frighten you. You sure about that?" His voice was smooth and warm as liquid honey. Combined with his dramatic green eyes, it made Gemma feel flustered.

"Yes, pretty sure. Why do you ask?"

"It's just that, well, usually when someone wanders over to our aphrodisiac collection," he leaned in closer to whisper the last part, "it's not by accident." He nodded slyly to the jars in front of her.

Once Gemma caught the gist of what he was saying, she flushed a violent red. Embarrassment overtook her, and she gasped while reading some of the labels. "I assure you that's not what I had in mind."

"Ah, forgive me. I didn't mean to make you uncomfortable. Come to think of it, I haven't seen you around before. Where do you hail from?" He leaned against the windowsill, and she watched as the muscles in his forearm flexed at his weight.

"Um," she caught herself staring, a minor sweat beading her brow beneath his sharp stare, "North Country, I'm from the North Country. Just visiting, though...enjoying some change in scenery."

He smiled at her fidgeting. "I see, and how is it? The scenery, I mean." He crossed his arms, adding, "See anything you like?"

Tobler eyed Quinn from across the room, not liking what he picked up. He wouldn't interfere without a sign from Gemma, but the protective pull he felt toward her made that difficult. It threw him off his guard. Then he was flooded with the need to ensure Quinn didn't push too far, but he couldn't barge in. Gemma had to want him to step in. Who she spent her time with was her choice, but that wouldn't stop him from watching out for her. Anything to prove that she wasn't okay with their interaction would do: a shift in emotion to distress, a look, a gesture, whistle, anything.

In the meantime, he would watch the ridiculous show Quinn was making of himself; flaunting like a dull-colored peacock, trying to prove that his tail span was bigger. Tobler rolled his eyes, patiently waiting for any suggestion of her need. Then there it was, Gemma shifting her weight, trying her best to seem casual, and sending him a look that was off.

"Um, well, the town is lovely." Her voice was sweet, except he felt the unease building inside her. When he met her eyes again, he took it for his signal and walked across the room.

"Find what you need?" He glanced over at Quinn, whose eyes narrowed as if he'd kicked his dog. "Everything okay here?" His attention returned to Gemma, searching her face as Quinn's anger roiled off of him, hot as iron in a forge. Gemma tried her best to give a reflexive shrug, but her eyes told him differently. "I found the face cream you've been talking about back there. Not that you need it, but it's over there." Tobler nodded to the shelf across the room.

"Oh, you found it! Thank goodness, excuse me." Gemma left the two, happy to be out from under Quinn's probing eyes.

Though she couldn't see it, his eyes followed her; within proximity of Quinn, Tobler easily felt the lustful intentions rolling off him in waves. Tobler's expression turned to disgust. Sure, the other men they passed earlier found her attractive, and their minds drifted to questionable places; but Quinn was not the same as them. No, his mind was darker—much darker—and it twisted differently than the rest. It was more than wondering; he was dwelling, obsessing, on what was beneath her dress. His emotions grew harsh and visceral, which made the hair on the back of Tobler's neck stand up. Tobler's expression darkened; ethics be damned, he aimed to do something about it.

"Don't you have more tonics to grab or something? A job you're supposed to be doing?" he asked, disgust thick in his voice.

Quinn turned his attention on Tobler, his smug face unamused at the disturbance of his thoughts. "What's it to you what I do?"

"That's none of your concern, other than I have no tolerance for men like you."

"Men like me, huh?" He crossed his arms.

"Perverted bastards. You know, the kind that leaves a greasy trail wherever they go." Tobler stepped closer to Quinn, keeping his voice low so Gemma wouldn't hear. "The kind that can't keep their paws off woman who don't want them."

A cocky half smile turned up on Quinn's face, "What's wrong? Jealous? Worried she'll like me better?"

"You?" Tobler snorted. "Please."

"Oh, I see now. You're afraid I'll show her what a real man can do, huh?" Depraved arrogance dripped from his smile. "You can watch, if you want, so you can learn a thing or two. We could make some quick vellum." He placed a hand on Tobler's shoulder. "A little tumble between friends?"

Tobler's blood boiled in his veins as the words fell from Quinn's mouth; for the first time, he fought the overwhelming urge to use his powers for harm. He could turn this sorry bastard into a heap on the floor by just manipulating his mind: pain, depression, suicide. Wouldn't take much with how weak-minded Quinn was. It took everything inside of him to gain control and swallow his anger back down.

"If you don't take your hand off of me, you'll be pulling back a bloody stump. You don't want to mess with me." His baleful expression was enough to make Quinn pull back. "You leave her alone. If I hear of her having even just a hair out of place, I'll rip off your head and shit down your throat."

Tobler had no use for fighting, but if that's what it took, he'd turn Quinn's world upside down. To Tobler's surprise Quinn backed down, wordlessly resuming his task of retrieving medicines from the shelves.

Satisfied, Tobler walked back to Gemma who was pawing at this bottle and that bottle just to look busy. She continued until Tobler stood beside her.

"Is he gone?" she asked, avoiding eye contact.

"Sort of. He's going back to doing his job, anyway." He put his hands in his pockets, following her lead.

"Good," she finally turned her face to him, "I thought he'd never leave."

"I would have interfered sooner, but I wasn't sure if you'd want me to," he said as he met her eyes.

"No, I wanted you to interfere. You came just at the right time."

"What was he doing?" he asked, bracing himself.

She paused, playing back the things he said, wondering how harmless flirting transformed into a knot in her stomach. "I just had a bad feeling about him. Something wasn't right, and my gut was telling me bad things. Now that I say it out loud, it just sounds ridiculous." She looked down, self-conscious.

"No. I know what he was feeling, and you weren't wrong. You've got good instincts, Gemma. If something doesn't feel right, it's not. Trust your gut. You don't have to explain yourself to anyone, understand?" Tobler tilted his head down, trying to catch her eye.

"Thank you," she said, gazing up at him.

"Anytime."

Finn came through the curtain and started putting more jars and bottles into the sack. "Okay, kids. It's all ready now for ya. I trust Orianna left you guys some money?" he said cocking an eyebrow in their direction and wiping his hands on a damp cloth.

Tobler reluctantly torn his attention away from Gemma to Finn. "That she did." He put the stack of coins down on the counter and waited patiently as Finn counted them.

"Yup, it's all here. Mind you, be wary with that bag now. If some of those jars clack together and break, you could have a big problem on your hands—could eat right through the bag," Finn warned, scratching at his beard.

Gemma eyed the bag incredulously. "Will it eat away at flesh? How would we clean it up?"

"Well, depending on what gets knocked together in there, it can be highly corrosive to human flesh. No good remedy for such a mess as that. Best leave it where it lays for a few days and not touch it."

Gemma's eyes widened, trying to think what the hell could be in that bag Orianna would need. Just over Finn's shoulder she caught Quinn gawking at her again, the intensity twisting something in the pit of her gut. Tobler felt it flood strongly over him. She wasn't holding back, and the anxiety Quinn stoked in her almost made him sick.

"Don't worry, we will be alright." Tobler said rigidly, his eyes boring into Quinn which broke his focus on Gemma. He led Gemma out with a hand on her back.

"Take care, Tobler, and um...Tobler's lady friend."

No one saw the scowl Quinn wore as he watched the two of them leave. He wasn't one to be told no, and his mind dwelled on dark things as the apothecary master called him for aid. It wasn't over.

CHAPTER FOURTEEN

"I'M SORRY," GEMMA SAID meekly.

Although her voice sounded small, it struck him with the force of a smith's hammer, bringing him out of his foul mood. "What?" His grim countenance faded with confusion.

"I said I'm sorry," she repeated a bit stronger.

Tobler's face set into full confusion. "For what, pray tell?"

Gemma bit her lower lip. "For all of *that* back there. For you getting upset and angry. I didn't mean to cause any trouble. I shouldn't have..." She wasn't sure what to say.

He stared at her as if she had been speaking in tongues, searching her emotions. "You think I'm mad at you?"

She gave a guilty shrug, causing him to pull her over to a quiet part of the street, shaking his head.

"Tobler, I—" Gemma began, about to apologize more as panic began to well.

"No," he held up a hand, cutting her off, "you don't talk for a moment, just listen. *You* have no reason to be sorry. Quinn is a slimy shitbag for how he was making you feel, and I know he was doing it on purpose. He was getting off on making you uncomfortable. That was wrong, and there was nothing you could have done to stop him. It was no reflection on you, or anything you did." He stopped a moment, waiting for her to look back at him. "I'm glad I was there. I was all too glad to make him leave you alone, you hear me?"

She nodded, relieved that it wasn't her he was upset with.

His expression lightened, but he felt guilty she perceived his unpleasant mood to be a reflection of herself. "Good, now we better hurry before the old worry wart comes looking for us."

He offered her his arm, his natural charisma drawing her in. They walked a few more streets to their meeting place, where Orianna and Zavier awaited.

"We should probably get going if we're to make it back before it gets too dark." Zavier said.

"Yes, rather not get stuck in the woods at night if we can avoid it." Orianna agreed.

Overall, the shopping excursion was a success. Gemma acquired a few nice dresses, a wonderful perfume, and a new love for Goblidet. She realized this was what hope must feel like, knowing that you belonged somewhere that didn't make you feel like an outcast. Sure, there were a few bumpy introductions, but all in all, it was an amazing experience—a strange feeling she hadn't known in The Echo.

As she climbed up into the wagon, she placed her things down neatly on the floor, making sure not to bump into the sack from the apothecary. Zavier commanded the horses to go, starting their journey back. Looking behind at Goblidet , she felt a strange pull of melancholy for having to leave it all so soon.

"We can come back again, you know," he said without preamble.

"Huh?" She snapped back to where she sat in the wagon.

"We can come back sometime. If you want to, that is. I mean, it seems like you do the way you're staring." He shrugged to hide the fact that he'd been watching her.

"How often do you guys come back?"

"Once a week or so, unless there is an event happening." He reassured her with, "You can't see it all in one shot. It's better a second or third time around."

"I'd love to come back. There's just so much more I want to see." She paused thoughtfully. "I worry sometimes that I'll wake up in my room by the lake, rub my eyes, and want to go back to sleep. That this is all a dream, and I'm still left in the dark in my narrow world. No Orianna, or Goblidet, or magic." Her face fell into a frown.

"It's all real." He leaned in, ready to pull her mood back from the abyss. "You don't have to worry about any of that. We're all real, all of it—especially Orianna. She's been looking for a long time, and when she finally found you... I've never seen that woman so happy. You're very loved here." He spoke the words plainly, but they carried a hefty weight intertwined with an unspoken plea.

All she could manage was a faint smile. "I bank on that every day."

"Then every day it will be here waiting for you."

Gemma took advantage of the time to take in the setting sun, absorbing every pink, yellow, and orange into her memory.

"How long are you gracing us with your presence today?" Tobler broke the silence.

"I'm not sure. We didn't set a time to go back, why?"

Back at the house, everyone began unloading the items they purchased. Zavier helped Orianna carry the bundles of food, clothes, and ingredients. He carried it all with such ease, as if the bundles were filled with feathers instead of heavy supplies. He had the strength of three men—three very strong men.

Gemma managed most of her of her things alone, but the dresses were proving to be more than she could handle. She gathered it all up, steadied herself, and started walking. After a couple of steps, she started to teeter.

Tobler happened to be walking out of the barn and rushed over just as her foot twisted on a rock she couldn't see. She fell backwards, but he caught her.

"Black Hells, woman! Do you have feet or pegs to walk on?"

Her back was against his chest and he held her, steadying her further. He shifted her as if she were weightless, and her head fell naturally back on his shoulder. The undeniable electricity returned, but instead of pulling away, they stayed a moment...consumed by it, savoring the feeling as they tried to pin it down. Tobler was on overload between her emotions and his own. The feelings muddled together, and he couldn't separate them.

She felt his heart thudding, quickening the longer he held on. He had the most striking blue eyes she's ever seen. She'd never seen his face this close before, and she couldn't help but notice the hard set of his jaw. Every one of his features held an endless appeal to her.

The smell of her soft black hair intoxicated him, and her dark eyes held him captive. So close to her, he noticed her lips were fuller, a more dangerous red than he remembered whenever he'd watched her from a distance. But he couldn't lose control over himself—not now, not here.

He helped her stand. As Gemma felt the ground beneath her feet, something in her dimmed with disappointment. But why was she disappointed? She barely knew Tobler. Perchance, she was confusing it with embarrassment over her clumsiness and his misfortune of having to always save her from herself. But there was something else, something more.

"Thank you."

Tobler nodded politely and took some of her things. They walked towards the house. From the corner of her eye, she glanced at him but his face gave away nothing at all.

Inside the house, Orianna continued pulling things from the counter to put them away in cabinets and cubbies. She turned to see Flip still perched at her side, looking tattered and tired; she gently took him from the air and placed him in his cubbie on the counter. The little notepad seemed to fluff itself and relax against the cool box, preparing to rest.

"Want some help?" Zavier offered.

"From you?" she laughed. "That's sweet, dear, but you know how I am. I like things put away in a certain way." She kissed him, then shooed him off. "Why don't you go relax a bit?"

His mouth quirked to the side with no real response other than a shrug. He resigned himself to the sitting area with his pipe. He lit it up and relaxed as a sweet, licorice aroma began filled the air.

"Where should I put my things, Aunt Orianna?" Gemma asked.

"Yeah, I'd like to quit my duties as part-time pack mule." Tobler interjected.

"Part time? Now Tobler, I thought being an ass was your full-time job?" Orianna flung flippantly back at him. "My mistake. You can put them in the other bedroom for now, until you're ready to sort and organize all of it. Oh, and would you mind taking the apothecary and this other sack to my workroom, please? Thank you," she said to the pile in Tobler's arms.

He mocked her while her back was turned but headed up the stairs with all of Gemma's things. Taking each step with careful grace before turning to Gemma. "Do you need to go first?"

"No, why?" she said, curious at his odd question.

"Well, if your inept feet fail you again, I might need to try and catch you. But then, you will most likely burn down the house in the process with concoctions in this sack," he said full of sarcastic playfulness.

She huffed at him, "Oh, stop braying and move your big ass before I push you."

"Whole family thinks they're full of jokes."

She followed him up to a door she hadn't noticed before. Inside was a decent sized room, but it was far too dark to make out much else. Tobler cleared his throat.

"Would you mind?" He gestured to some large candles on the wall that she could just barely see. "Without setting us all on fire, preferably."

She sighed heavily and concentrated; within seconds, they flicked to life along with some other candles she hadn't noticed before. "Set your pants on fire one time, and that's all you remember."

Instead of lighting the space, the candles only made the room dreary. There wasn't much to be seen in it except a bed against the wall with one end table, a closet, and a vanity on the opposite wall. She plopped her things onto the bed and noticed a black drapery. She walked over, hooking the drape to the side and revealing an arched stone window. She left it open to make the room less gloomy and more open.

"Is this where you sleep?" she asked.

"Most of the time. I usually stay here, but sometimes I go out with friends or wherever."

"So this is your home, too?"

"Eh, I guess so."

"Do you have family living around here?" The words fell out before she could catch them.

"Well," he rubbed the back of his neck, "no, I don't. Truth is, I don't know any of my family. Zavier found me wondering the streets when I was very young, never found out what happened to them. He took me in and raised me like his own son. They've both have, and I do what I can to pay them back."

"I'm so sorry, Tobler. I had no idea." All she could picture was a poor, sad little boy wandering the streets of Goblidet, dirty and hungry with no place to go; the image broke her heart. She never would've imagined he'd struggled, given his carefree and laidback attitude.

"It's no big deal, really. I'm fine now. I have a nice place to live, and they don't charge me for staying."

He didn't want the pity he felt trickling from her. He stopped feeling sorry for himself a long time ago and didn't want her to keep searching for the right words; the past was immaterial to him now.

"Gemma!" Orianna called, as usual, interrupting whatever moment they might have had. "Would you mind helping me get things together down here?"

"Just a minute!" she called back to her from the doorway.

"That's alright, just set them in my room. You should probably change while you're up there."

"Okay, good idea. I'll be down soon." She turned back into the room to see Tobler sitting on the bed with his arms crossed.

"Well, you heard her," he said with a mocking smile. "Get changed into something more comfortable."

Gemma grabbed the cushion from the vanity chair and threw it at him. "Get out, you dog, before I sick Aunt O on you."

Tobler put on a fictitious expression full of terror. "Oh no, not her!" Laughter rippled through his belly. "I'm quaking in my boots."

She almost started laughing but grabbed his arm instead, proceeding to drag him out the door. "Come on now, out." She tossed him out the door and shut it quickly behind him.

"Tobler, I need you to get more wood!"

Although muffled from the other side of the thick wood door, it was undeniably Orianna's loud voice. Gemma laughed as she heard a heavy groan before Tobler trudged down the stairs. She grabbed the sacks of bottles and headed over to Orianna's room after changing into one of the more casual dresses she'd gotten. A nice blue and white dress, pretty but more fit for everyday use. She headed downstairs to see what peculiarity Orianna had cooking for her.

They ate a hearty meal that Orianna skillfully prepared. Having control over fire was a big help with cooking. When the meal had ended, Gemma stretched her levitation abilities some more, hoping to impress Orianna. She concentrated, and to her surprise, the plates levitated much easier than before—steady, right into the sink. A glow emerged from her small triumph, making her feel as if she was finally getting a grip on her powers.

"Great job, dear! You're a quick study, just like your mom and I," Orianna said, placing a hand on her shoulder. "I'm proud of you. You must've practiced at home. It's harder to use magic on that side of the portal, sort of like running through water. When you use your powers here, you'll find there is less resistance."

"Thanks," Gemma said, swelling with pride. She couldn't recall the last time someone had been proud of her; but she hadn't done much to earn it, either. "That would have helped the other night when I almost took my eye out with a pencil. Shot right for me. I had to duck, and I think it's still stuck in the wall." Her expression turned to concern at the thought of explaining that one to her mother.

"Ah well, be careful. We don't want any spontaneous fires or lost eyeballs, especially yours. You have such a nice set. Why don't you relax in the other room? You've had a long day."

"Thanks, but I should finish putting away those clothes first so Tobler has a place to sleep tonight," Gemma said.

"You're a sweet girl. I guess he does need to sleep at some point," Orianna teased.

Gemma started up the stairs, gasped, and almost jumped out of her skin at the sight of Tobler waiting for her. He hid in the shadows, almost indistinguishable, but she noticed the shape of him.

"Shhh!" he hissed, placing a finger to his lips before motioning for her to keep walking.

"Gemma? What's wrong?" Orianna called, having heard her gasp mid-climb.

"Oh! Yes, sorry—it was just a spider, but it's gone now. Scared me, is all."

"Ah, I hate those bastards. Be sure to kill it if you see it again." Disgust radiated from Orianna's voice before she carried on with her activities.

"Okay, will do." Gemma shot Tobler a shocked look, then walked the rest of the way up.

"Come on," Tobler whispered.

"Where—"

"Shhh! Quiet," he said, even more hushed than before. "Woman has ears like a damn deer in a meadow."

Gemma looked behind her to make sure all was still quiet downstairs, then matched his tone. "Sorry."

"Follow me. Don't make another sound," he warned.

"You could have started with that."

He cocked an eyebrow, exasperated by her unbelievable defiance. He led her down to the end of the hallway under a door in the ceiling, then carefully pulled it down. An old ladder of stairs lowered, and he stepped aside.

"Ladies first." He bowed gracefully.

"I'm in a dress, and I'm not running a peep show. I know what you're doing." She glared at him, her hands on her hips.

Tobler's face looked like he was at a loss for words. "Me?" He feigned offense and spoke in an overly proper accent. "I'll have you know, madam, I am a perfect gentleman."

Gemma swatted him hard. "Get up there."

"Ouch! Just like your damn aunt. *Crab* apple doesn't fall far from the tree, does it?" He stealthily made his way up the ladder, then motioned to Gemma.

She climbed up and he extended a hand to help her. They were both careful not to take a tumble for fear of having to explain themselves. Puffs of dust rose beside the well-walked trail, lined with cobwebs that glistened in the moonlight.

"What are we doing up here?"

"You'll see," he said, tiptoeing to a large octagon window on the ceiling. "Come on."

"What—on the roof? Are you crazy?"

"Trust me, you'll be fine." He hopped out the window and onto the roof, extending his hand. "I promise nothing will happen to you."

She watched him incredulously, scanning his face and locking eyes with him. After a moment of thought, she gave him her hand. "You better hope not."

He hoisted her up onto the roof and took a few steps away to sit down. He looked back to see she hadn't moved. "You can come sit, you know? I don't bite...at least, not today."

Her stomach sunk as she peeked over the edge. "Um... I'll just stay here, thanks. Did the house get taller since this morning?" Sweat formed on her brow as her hands grew clammy.

Tobler got to his feet, forgetting about her fear of heights. "Hey." She was frozen at the sight of the ground, so very far below. "Hey, it's okay. Look at me. Come here and sit with me. With your track record, standing isn't safe." Carefully he took her hand and a chill shivered up his arm. "Come on, just go slow, one foot in front of the other. I won't let you fall." Tobler kept his eyes on her, watching as she walked, until they stopped in a safe spot. "See, that wasn't so bad."

She swallowed, trying to relax. If it wasn't for the moon, it would have been pitch black on the roof. "No, it could have been worse, though I worry about getting down. What are we doing up here, anyway, Tobler?"

He put on his most charming half-smile. "I wanted to show you what Goblidet nights are like and to answer your questions you had earlier at the market. But first, look up."

She looked up, immediately awestruck. The sky was black as pitch with the exception for the billions of twinkling, silvery stars. She had never seen such a vast display of night sky. Her family had always lived in cities where the brightness drowned out the stars; but here, there was no competition to rival the sky. Night was not choked off in smog blankets. The moon hung perfect and full, glowing like a mother to the stars. It made her feel small but in a peaceful way, like a baby safe in the womb.

"Wow... It's so beautiful. You get to see this every night?" She couldn't turn her eyes from it.

"Most nights, unless it's cloudy." He stared at the collection of stars overhead, his face childlike and grinning. "This is where I go to be alone. It's the only way I can get away." He waved his arms at the expanse of sky. "No one else's emotional litter, or bullshit, but my own. Except for tonight, of course, since I feel your worry of splatting against the ground like an ant."

Her mouth quirked up, half embarrassed and half laughing, eyes still on the sky. "Shut up. And to think, I almost felt bad for you."

Tobler gazed at her; moonlight filled her eyes and glinted off her black hair. She looked like a child seeing the ocean for the first time, amazed by the immense beauty. She was even more beautiful than when he saw her in the dress shop, sitting there on a roof being herself. He was no stranger to attractive woman, but no other eyes spoke to him like hers. Of all the people he'd met in their large, eccentric realm, no one tugged at him the way she did. Other woman wouldn't have been able to appreciate such a simple moment; that, in itself, was magical to him. Looking at her, he felt as if he gazed upon the bigger picture of life; something deeper inside of him called out, and his heart recognized her.

"You like it up here?"

"Very much so." She looked over at him then. His eyes were a vibrant blue against the night. When she realizes she stared too long, she bit her lip and glanced away.

"It's quiet here. Helps me remember that I'm a person and not just a receptacle full of other's emotions. Allows me to sort myself out, remember where I start and other people begin." He looked more in his element silhouetted against the sky.

"So...your spot, huh?"

"Yeah, I'll spend a few nights a week up here typically. I get overloaded sometimes with everyone's gobbledygook so I come here to replenish. I mean, I can block most but having your guard up like that takes its toll." He sounded uncomfortable as he spoke, as if he hadn't talked to anyone about the issue before.

"Thanks for sharing your spot."

"You're welcome. Thought you'd like it with the moon how it is tonight." He continued to stare into the sky. "And I thought you'd want to unwind, yourself. I'm impressed at your calm in all of this: new places, new dangerous power, crazy sorcerer out there plotting against you, creepy watchers spying. Yet, you stay calm and unmoved—wonderstruck still and not giving up."

She was silent a moment. The serious undertones lingered as the heaviness of the situation hadn't fully sunk in, but his words began to crack the glass wall she hid behind. All at once, her stomach dropped as her barrier crashed down. Her heart sank, but he pulled her mind back from the fearful edge.

"I'm sorry. I didn't mean to push that on you so hard. Shitty timing on my end." His words were soaked with regret.

Gemma searched his eyes, and he looked sorry enough—worried, even. She sensed that, in some small corner of him, he cared for her. "It's okay. I let my inner peace fall away. Sorry you had to feel that. I could have used a reminder of reality. I'm sure I overreacted slightly."

His face stayed regretful. She hadn't overreacted—at least, not in his eyes. In truth, not enough...but he wasn't going to tell her that and frighten her more. "What did you want to say, anyway?"

"What?"

"That's also why you brought me up here, remember? To finish our talk from earlier."

"Oh right," He ran his fingers through his hair, settling them on the back of his neck. "I believe you asked me why my powers are considered dangerous?" She nodded in remembrance. "I can feel emotions—you know that. That's more of a personal issue, a nonthreatening gift if all I could do was feel them. But I can manipulate them, as well." He paused as he watched her expression.

"I'm sorry, Tobler, but I'm failing to see the danger."

"I can change another person's emotions for good or bad. I can make someone feel blissful happiness or deep depression—suicide, even. I could leave someone in a state of angst that might make them lose their mind. I have the power of ultimate control over anyone I choose. That's what makes my powers so dangerous, their intensity." He tried to hide his shame of the ability that cursed him since birth, forcing him to walk a knife's edge his whole life.

Gemma's eyes widened with understanding; that wasn't what she had expected at all. His carefree face creased with a sadness that broke her heart. This laidback guy she was getting to know and befriend now looked older, stuck in the trenches of his turmoil. "But you wouldn't," she bent to catch his eye like he had done for her, "right?"

"Of course not. I live by a code as to not interfere unless asked to. It's not ethical to do such things. That's how magic is run around here—everyone's basic ethics. I could never hurt someone like that."

"Then why do you look so upset?" Now it was her turn to appear concerned.

"Because it's a dark gift." His somber eyes turned away, trying to feel her out.

"Tobler you're not evil, at least from what I can tell."

"But if magic is cut in either black and light, then I must be. You said so yourself."

Gemma scooted closer, placing a hand on his arm in reassurance. He turned to look at her, and she was surprised by how close he was. "I'm sorry, you're right. Evil isn't black and white, there are gray areas. I think..."

"What do you think?" He searched her eyes, big and soft, as he moved closer to her.

"I think your heart is good." She was drawn to him. Silence enveloped them like a heavy blanket on a winter's night. Everything else fell away into the darkness, disappearing from sight until all they saw was each other. They were the realm.

"What do you know about my heart?" he whispered against her lips, dizzying her.

"Just a feeling," She got the words out just he stole her breath away.

The gap closed between them in a gentle kiss. Something more powerful coursed through them at the touch of their lips; it raced beneath every inch of their skin, leaving gooseflesh in its wake. A humming thrummed through their hearts, reverberating like a plucked harp string. The world stood still in such soft silence that even the rushing wind was inaudible.

Tobler pulled away from her with a gasp. "You're something else, Gemma."

She looked back at him, bewildered. "What do you mean?"

"Special." He brushed his fingers against her knuckles before folding her hand into his. "You—" Tobler was cut off by a muffled, yet still loud, voice ringing inside. "Devil woman."

They were still intimately close and unmoving, the moon tethering them the same way it guided the ocean.

"I don't want to go back down," she said hoarsely.

"I know, me either. But dealing with an ignored Orianna is far worse. Trust me."

He pulled away with great effort, allowing his hand to fall from hers. Gemma made the mistake of looking down, panic cutting through with a sudden gasp. Tobler took her arm again, lining her hand with his.

"It's okay. I won't let you fall, ever." Tobler led her back to the window. "Just take your time, slowly now." He watched, hawk-eyed, as she stepped inside, then slid in after her. Orianna's voice carried through that house again. "Damn woman, louder than a screech owl after a shrew." His annoyance was palpable as he eased his way down the ladder.

They hurried to Tobler's room, where Gemma was supposed to be putting away her clothes in the closet and changing. Without giving it any thought, Gemma flicked her hand and the clothes flew neatly inside onto the hangers. Footsteps came from the stairs and the two of them casually began strolling out of the room as Orianna was just coming atop the stairs.

"You're getting good at that," Tobler whispered.

"Where have you been?" Orianna said, putting her hands on her hips. "I've been calling you. Was getting worried someone may have broken in or you were in trouble."

"Someone break in, with all of the protection spells you've casts on this house. Impossible. They wouldn't be able to tunnel in, at this rate. How in ten hells would anyone break in?"

She pursed her lips, annoyed at his outburst. "If anyone wanted to badly enough, they might find a way. Slim chances, I agree, but I wouldn't rule anything out. Don't fool yourself about the lengths some might go to, Tobler. You'd be surprised what evil is capable of." Tobler was gearing up to throw more back at her, but she cut him off. "Wait a minute. What *were* you two doing in there?" Her annoyance now turned to suspicion.

"Not what you thought. Honestly Orianna, you should know me better by now. I'm not an animal and neither is she." Tobler didn't have to pretend to be offended because this time he genuinely was insulted.

"Nothing happened in there, I promise." Gemma reassured in nicer tones, giving Tobler a big of a glare. She wasn't sure why he was trying to protect her honor from her aunt, of all people; she wasn't *that* unreasonable.

"Okay," she sighed, resigning her thoughts. She really did know better, but it came with the territory of aunt/mother figure.

Orianna had to look out for her niece's best interests, after all. "So what were you doing?"

"I was practicing my levitation to put my clothes away. Tobler was only here for support in case I needed some pointers," Gemma said.

"Oh? Good, the more practice the better. I'm pleased you're taking it so seriously."

"She's much like you in that department, Orianna," Tobler said. Orianna smiled sweetly until he finished the sentence. "Stubborn."

She swatted him. "Go do something with yourself. Gemma, dear, is it time for you to head back? I'm not sure how late it could be getting in the human realm." Orianna tried to hide her sadness at her own question, but a sliver of it stayed on her face.

Tobler turned to her from behind Orianna, curiosity gnawing at him as he mocked Orianna's mannerisms. Gemma narrowed her eyes at him while holding back a chuckle.

Go back. Gemma had forgotten that she had to go back to The Echo, her time spent on the roof still clung to her like a dream. With each day spent in the realm, she had less reason to want to return through the portal.

"I guess it's that time..."

"You don't have to leave if you don't want to." Orianna stepped closer, taking her hands. "Gemma, this is your home, too. I don't want you to go, but I don't want to sway you with my selfish reasons. I understand that you have a life in The Echo, but I'll never make you leave."

Her mother loved her very much, but there was something missing. After the divorce, her mother closed part of herself off to her. But she was her mother, and she should see her. "Thanks, Aunt O."

"That's no problem. I'll meet you in the other room to open the portal." Orianna gave her hands a last squeeze, then turned to leave them.

"So," Tobler spoke first, "the roof. What, um..."

"It wasn't good for you, was it?" she blurted out.

"What? No, but I mean if you didn't like—"

"Oh no! I did. I really, really did. It was very good and nice," she stammered. *Nice?* She thought, chastising herself for such an insufficient description.

"Good," he said firmly.

His palms began to sweat, which wasn't like him at all. He was smoother than this and usually more charming. He took a deep breath to center himself—in through the mouth, out through the nose. "Should we start this over again?"

She nodded, not wanting to open her mouth just yet at fear of what could spill out next.

Anticipation tingled in the air now with the new beginning, "We should probably talk about that kiss, right?"

"Yes, I agree. You go first."

"I thought," he took a deep breath, pausing as his eyes turned down, "it was really...great."

"I thought so, too." She tried to hold back and play it cool.

"Good, I'm glad." He stepped a little closer, heart leaping in his throat in anticipation. "What if I wanted to kiss you again? Would that be okay?"

She was trapped beneath that stare, but his eyes didn't make her wriggle in her skin like Quinn's. No, Tobler's eyes were kind and curious, soft and searching—patient, with no sign of ill intent, making her feel safe. "I certainly wouldn't stop you if you tried." She flirted back, inching a step in his direction, encouraging a pull neither of them could refuse.

"Gemma, you ready?" An impatient Orianna called loudly.

"Why am I not surprised," he sighed dramatically. "Impeccable timing, that one." He turned back, running the tips of his fingers down her arm and taking her hand. A shiver pleasantly spread over her skin.

"So what now? What is this?"

"I don't know." He took a moment to search her face carefully. "It can be whatever you'd like it to be." He could feel the pressure starting to build in her chest, tightening. "You don't have to answer right now. Sleep on it, take your time. I'm not going anywhere, okay?" He looked her in the eyes to reassure her. He understood her life was changing fast, and he didn't want to spook her; such matters took time. She nodded as her tensions eased. "Okay, then. Now let's get you going before Orianna loses her tits."

Gemma laughed, but swatted him for his comment.

"Damn," he laughed, "like aunt like niece, always abusing me. May I walk you to your portal?"

She took his hand and he escorted her to the other room, letting go just as they were in her sight.

"Are ready to go back?" Orianna asked, holding up a vial.

"I guess so." She shrugged, sneaking a sideways glace at Tobler, who appeared to ignore her.

Orianna frowned, hating to see her leave. "Alright then, how about you open the portal this time?"

Gemma perked up at the offer. "Are you sure? What if I open it to the wrong place?"

"Nonsense, don't worry about that. Concentrate, show your mind's eye where you want to go, then throw the vial. Simple as that." Orianna pressed the glass tube into Gemma's hand.

The vial felt cool against her now-sweating palm and she nodded, finding her confidence. She took a deep breath, closing her eyes as she cleared her mind like Orianna taught her. She envisioned the perfect picture of Orianna's shop in the human realm, down to the most minute of details. The creaky wood floors, weathered by the many feet that've walked them. Dark beams and crowded shelves, both clingy with the dust of the ages. The hearth with its stone face, the spot that started this disarray of wonder.

Once it was all clear, Gemma opened her eyes and threw the vial at the base of the wall where the portal opened. The glass broke, pouring smoke and a wall of reddish-orange fire that shot to the ceiling in a pillar before disappearing, leaving a smattering of flames licking at the floor. Tobler quickly ran over to each one, stomping them out with his boots.

Gemma's hands flew to her mouth. She looked at Orianna—waiting to see her reaction, waiting for her to be angry—but Orianna was nothing of the sort, mouth hung open in shock.

"That...has never happened. In all of my years of practicing the craft—" now speechless, she walked over to Gemma—who was still in her own shock—and unhooked her necklace. "Promise me that you won't wear this here. When you're over *there,* sure, but it's magnifying your powers too much in this realm." Orianna took one of Gemma's hands from her mouth and put the necklace in her hand, closing it firmly. "Understand? I can't have you setting the house or my shop on fire."

Gemma cleared her throat, "I pr-promise."

"Or the entire realm, for that matter." Tobler snickered.

Orianna grimaced at him, "However, you can practice setting his pants on fire anytime you want."

"Hey!"

"Will do. It'll be nice to have a live target." Gemma laughed, giving him a teasing look.

"Hey now," he pointed a finger at her, "remember I can put out the fires. Therefore, I'm useful."

Orianna began to step through, "Well, the objective was open it and you did. I'll see you on this side when you're ready, but don't dawdle. Portals shouldn't stay open for too long. Never know what could sneak through and wreak havoc." She disappeared completely this time.

They were alone again, but this time Gemma felt more sadness pooling inside her.

"Well then," Tobler cleared his throat, "until next time, I guess...whenever that might be."

"Tomorrow," she said, stepping closer to him.

He smiled his sweet, crooked smile. "Tomorrow, then." Gently he touched her face before giving her a quick kiss. "Good night, Gemma." He inhaled, slightly winded by the small kiss.

"Good night, Tobler." Reluctantly, she left his side and stepped through the portal without looking back, afraid she might want more of his affection.

Gemma reveled in the parting smile that reached from ear to ear, up until she locked eyes with a stunned Orianna. Gemma froze, at a loss for words as the portal closed behind her; too late to turn and escape the awkward situation.

"I can see you." Amused by her niece's silence, Orianna considered what more to say. She hadn't any children of her own and was unsure what proper parenting protocol was for seeing things she wished she hadn't.

"Sorry, Aunt Orianna, I didn't know. I..." Gemma's face slackened, unsure what trouble she must be in. Orianna was silent, which didn't seem to be a frequent occurrence.

"It's okay, dear," she sighed in understanding. "I can't say I'm all that surprised. He's a nice enough boy—and handsome,

I guess. That's all I'll say about the subject, though. Our hearts are the ultimate unexplained mysteries." She hugged her tight. "I see you as being so young, like you still need me around. Time, however, had other plans. You're older now and—well, we should get back. Enough of my blubbering."

"Thank you. But of course I still need you." Gemma said, hugging Orianna tighter.

"Anytime, my dear. I love you and want to see you happy." She kissed her on the cheek, giving her one last squeeze before letting her go. "We'd best start moving. It's getting late."

CHAPTER FIFTEEN

THE DRIVE DID LITTLE to clear Goblidet from her mind as she settled back into The Echo. Her skin still buzzed from magic and the bustle of the market. The intimacy of the rooftop kiss lingered on her lips along with his hand on her cheek.

"So, did you have a good time?" Orianna broke the silent madness.

Gemma was so deep in her thoughts she'd forgotten Orianna was in the car with her. "I did. The market was incredible. I've never seen anything like it."

"Good, I'm glad you enjoyed it. We'll be going back again, of course—sooner, if you're interested in doing more sightseeing."

"I'd like that very much! I saw some interesting places that we didn't have time to stop into, and I'd love to wander." She paused before saying, "Can I ask you something?"

"Of course, what is it?" Orianna held her breath, fearing what it might be.

"Would it be possible for me to stay longer? Like a few days or so? If that's alright with you and Uncle Zavier, of course. I don't want to put you out."

Orianna, however, was doing her very best not to let her excitement show. "I don't see why not. How long of a stay did you have in mind?"

"A few days would be fine—a week, even, if that's alright."

"That sounds reasonable. How about we tell your mother I need help shopping for more antiques? We can say there is a special expo to buy us a few days or weeks, whichever you chose. How's that sound?"

"Sounds perfect. You're good at this. Thanks so much. When can we do it?"

"Whenever you want, you let me know." Orianna's heart soared at the thought of having Gemma with her. It meant so much that she liked Goblidet and the magical realm of her birth; most importantly, it meant Orianna was finally rebuilding her family.

"Can we do it tomorrow?"

"Sure, I don't see why not. We'll just have to let your mother know, and hopefully she'll okay with it. You need to tell her, at least. I don't want any bad blood," she said, wagging a motherly finger.

"Yes, ma'am." Gemma teased.

Orianna snorted, shifting in her seat as a sudden dread took root inside. Discomfort lurched across her previously snickering face; something wasn't right, but she couldn't place her finger on the reason for the abrupt change.

Gemma grew nervous at the sudden change. "What's wrong? Was it something I said?"

"No, no, don't be silly. It's something else." Orianna paused. "Something feels...out of place. The atmosphere is wrong. Call it a witch's intuition."

"I don't see anything strange." They pulled into the driveway, and instant gooseflesh spread across Gemma's skin. There, in the driveway, an unfamiliar car blocked her mother's vehicle.

A red flag waved in Orianna's mind. "I'm going inside with you," she began unbuckling her seatbelt, not waiting for a rebuttal. "If anything, it will put you mom's mind at ease to see you're traveling with me, while adding more weight to your story. Humans love their evidence."

"Aunt Orianna, would The Eyes come this far? Could they cross a portal here?" She paled at the thought of a coven of soulless witches inside with her mother.

Orianna weighed the possibilities as her every muscle tightened. "I can't say for certain. Anything is possible when magic is involved. Portal magic isn't exactly restricted, but they would need to have seen your face or where you lived—a trail of some sort. You haven't been in Goblidet long enough for Leo to know to come here."

"We have to get to my mom." Gemma undid her seatbelt, jumping out of the car.

Orianna was faster, catching her before she could barge through the door. She held her by the shoulders, forcing her to look at her. "Gemma, what are you doing? We can't raise suspicion. If The Eyes are in there, that will only make matters worse, do you understand?" Her voice was a whisper but held the force of a hurricane. Gemma gave a silent nod as fear gripped her. "I'll go in first. Put your necklace on to help channel your powers. If we have to fight, that should help. Remember to concentrate."

She did as Orianna said, digging the necklace from her pocket and slipping it over her head. Orianna approached the door with caution, but she noticed the door was already ajar. Carefully, they stepped inside and heard two voices traveling from the dining room. Alongside the trill of her mother's voice came a deeper, masculine tone.

"Do you recognize that man's voice?" Orianna whispered, frowning when Gemma shook her head. She conjured a fireball in her palm, carrying it into the house.

They crept in further to peek in on them. At the small table with her mother sat a man of average build with reddish-brown hair and a clean-shaven face. He was laughing with her about something, a smile on his face from ear to ear. Friendly, but Orianna was not entirely sold and continued forward. Gemma sneezed, mouthing a silent apology to her aunt.

"Gemma, you're home! I didn't even hear you come in," her mother said through her laughter.

They stepped into the open space in front of the dining room as Orianna hid her fire-filled hand behind her back. She kept it lit for a little longer until she understood what was happening here.

"Yup, I'm back." Gemma fidgeted before gesturing to the strange man, "The door was open. What's going on?"

"Huh? Oh, right, this is Frank. I met him at the annual farmer's market in Ledgeport—you know, the one we usually go to about this time? Anyway, we got to talking at the apple stand, and we just really hit it off. I invited him for coffee, and here we are." She looked just beyond Gemma's shoulder, noticing Orianna behind her. "I'm sorry, who's your friend? Wait, you're the lady from the antique store. I thought you looked familiar. Olivia, right?"

"Orianna." She stiffened, replying, "Nice to see you again."

"Nice to see you, too, and thanks for offering Gemma the job. It'll be good for her to have some extra cash for college. What brings you here?" her mother said pleasantly.

"She just gave me a lift home." Gemma fidgeted beneath Orianna's watchful eyes. "Actually, I wanted to let you know I'll be going on a business trip soon."

"Oh really?"

"Yes, I have to acquire some new pieces for my shop. I'll need some extra help with it all. Gemma offered to help out—

sweet girl you raised and a hard worker. Catches on quickly. You should be proud." Orianna's face lit with a sincere smile.

"I certainly am, thank you. So, where are you going on this trip?" Her mother tried to keep the crease of a smile on her face.

"Four hours north of here, along the border and into Canada. Should take us about a week, give or take—depending how busy it is," Orianna lied.

Gemma was unnerved by the way Orianna could lie at the drop of a hat, but it also sounded incredibly convincing. Her mother look like she was thinking too long about the proposition, the gears turning too long in the soon-to-be awkward silence.

"I just wanted to let you know," Gemma interjected politely so her mother didn't think she was asking permission. "And I wanted you to meet my au—boss to ease your worries, let you know I'll be fine."

"It does seem like you are. I guess I can't argue the matter much," Her tone remained neutral, but the look she gave Orianna contradicted her words. "Have a safe trip, and I hope you have fun."

Orianna nodded, reinforcing her good intentions; she recognized the difference between disdain for herself and a mother's concern. From her peripheral view, she caught the stranger's heavy gaze watching her. She turned to him, "I'm sorry, have we met before?"

Frank shook his head, "Don't believe so."

"Hmm, are you sure?" Orianna took a step closer to him. "You just seem, so familiar." She leaned in, feeling out the stranger. "I own the antique stop a few miles from here, Oliver's Antiques. Perhaps that's where I've seen you before."

"Don't have an interest in old things so I doubt that." An odd flicker crossed Frank's face, too fast for Orianna to see what it was; she didn't want to cause a scene over a mere shadow.

"I see." Orianna gave a taciturn nod Frank's way. "Gemma, that painting your mom bought from me, where is it? I have another frame from the era that you'd like better. I just need to get the exact measurements to be sure it's a proper fit. Excuse us," Orianna politely excused them from the room, not taking her eyes off of Frank.

They made their way into the living room as Orianna slung different ideas around her mind. She had been on edge lately trying her best to keep Gemma safe, but even the safest of measures weren't always full proof. Loopholes were always a possibility in magic, if one was clever enough to find one; even a small detail might undermine the strongest armor.

"Oh my god!" Gemma studied the large painting on the wall, her mouth agape. "That's Goblidet!"

"Shh! Ophelia's Arms, lower your voice," Orianna hissed at her niece.

"It didn't look like that when I left the house this morning!" Gemma hissed back.

"Well, of course not. That's because you'd hadn't been there. This is no ordinary painting or portal, Gemma. It's a morph."

"A what?"

"A morph," Orianna said, walking closer to it. "It's an undefined object that changes to be something you need or allows you to see something you desire. In this case, it seems you want to go back." Orianna examined it, examining and touching various parts of the morph.

Gemma waited, but her patience thinned. "Are we the only ones who can see its changes?"

"Yes, it's strictly seen by magical folk only. Black Hands, nothing!"

"What are you looking for?" The suspense blistered beneath her skin.

She cocked an eyebrow at Gemma's tone, but didn't look at her. "I'm looking for any sign of tampering—a rip, discoloration, a strange stitch, warping—anything hinting at the possibility of another witch altering my magic." She paused, only continuing her explanation when she sensed her niece's eyes boring into her back. "See, the important thing about this morph is you can turn it into a portal with the proper potions. I've had it hidden away in the shop."

"You mean, I could have been using this the whole time instead of walking to the shop every day?" she demanded, growing more agitated.

"Now," Orianna finally faced her, "since the time is right. You might need to use it sooner than I expected."

"Why now?"

"Because there's something off around here." Orianna dug in her purse, pulling out two small black vials. "Here, just in case you need to leave and find me. You'll only need one vial to open the portal. The second is if it doesn't open the first time. Remember not to leave the portal open for too long. We don't want any unwelcomed guests coming through. If you miss, just pour baking soda on the liquid but don't wipe it up—it'll dissolve on its own."

"What? Why? Is it toxic or something?"

"No, it just takes away the stains it leaves behind."

Gemma rubbed her forehead, weary of her aunt's jabbering. "Is my mother safe? Should I do something magical? If I leave with you, will he leave her alone? These are all more important questions than stain removal."

"Shhh!" she hissed again. "No, we can't alarm him. If he really is some dark wizard—or worse, a member of The Eyes—he could retaliate. We have to be one hundred percent sure before we do *anything*. Do you understand?"

Gemma nodded.

"Here," Orianna handed her a small notepad, similar to Flip, and a small hexagon-shaped compact mirror. "Keep this with you at all times. If you need me, write in it. The message will transfer to Flip, then I'll write you back. If things become urgent, open the mirror and speak into it. I'll hear its sister mirror on the other side. Got it?"

"Yes, I got it." Gemma's stomach twisted.

"Notify me as quick as you can, and I promise everything will be alright. I'll be back as soon as possible if you need me." Orianna heard chairs stirring in the kitchen. "I better get going before we draw too much attention." She placed a hand on Gemma's shoulder, giving her a firm squeeze; she hated letting her go.

Gemma watched her aunt leave, and a wicked loneliness slithered under her skin. Her heart raced as the icy fear shot across her body and mind, an assault of questions springing from the sour nest in her stomach. She heard Orianna bidding farewell to her mother and guest, wondering how fast she could get back if the need arose.

A muffled voice carried shortly after, which she assumed to be Frank, followed by footsteps heading her way. She darted away from the painting. If he could see it change, he'd know for sure who she was; that was a disaster she wasn't ready for. They caught each other just at the entrance of the living room. He met her with an artful smile, showing just a tad too many teeth.

"Nice to meet you." Frank paused, in a blank fog as if he'd forgotten her name.

"Gemma." Her mother called from the kitchen, eavesdropping as she cleaned up.

Gemma held back an eye-roll.

"Right... *Gemma*, pretty name." His eyes fell to her neck, and he took a step closer. "Interesting necklace you've got there. Mind if I have a look?"

"I do." She kept her answer short, maintaining her distance, unnerved by his reptilian gaze.

"I have a good friend who would be interested in something like that. Looks old enough to be a family heirloom."

"No," she lied, but struggled as he waited for more, "I bought it at some random flea market my mother dragged me to." He began to reload another question, but she stopped him. "Leaving so soon?"

"Your mother offered to show me around. I was lucky to find such nice neighbors." His mouth lingered on "nice" in a way that chilled her, his sly confidence setting set her teeth on edge.

Her mother popped her head into the room. "Ready, Frank? Be back soon Gemma, okay? Dinner is in the fridge, just heat it up." She smiled, touching Frank's shoulder playfully and heading for the front door.

Frank watched her leave before turning back to Gemma. "Goodnight, Gemma. I'm sure you and I will be seeing more of each other." His bold green eyes seared into her mind as he slithered away.

Gemma's senses flared to attention, and the room shrank. She had been warned of possible danger but foolishly never considered what to do when the danger came to her doorstep. She had to trust they'd been careful enough; after all, no one recognized her true identity in the magical realm. The glass of the black vial cooled in her hand, shaking her from her thoughts.

She turned her attention back to the painting, a spirited Goblidet shining back at her. She remembered it was always there, waiting for her return—a comfort. She was finally getting what she wanted, a home where she belonged, but all too soon, it seemed to slip away from her. She wouldn't—no, *couldn't*—let that happen. There must be something she could do, some kind of magic protection spell to assure a defense against them.

Gemma paced, brainstorming what she had learned so far, but she didn't have a book of spells or raven bones lying around. What if Orianna sent her some glyphs to place on the doorways, similar to what they had done earlier? Quickly she headed to her room, sat at her desk, and flipped open the notebook to scribble a message.

What protection spells will work here to ward off danger?

She waited what seemed like an eternity, only to realize she wasn't sure when Orianna would get her message. What was the proper response time for an archaic form of texting? The waiting dragged as she kept an eye out the window for any return of unwanted company; suddenly, the book flashed a golden light signaling a response.

The Echo requires different glyphs than the ones we use here, more complicated. You'll need a pointed, gold end and soot. Blood can be used in place of soot but makes for very tricky magic. Scratch the glyph into the door, starting with the gold, and then trace over it with soot. It will disappear, but don't be alarmed. That means it worked. Be safe.

Gemma wrote back a quick reply and closed the notebook. Scanning the room, she spotted a pair of gold stud earrings on the night table, picked them up, and examined the back. Her next problem was she needed soot. She wished desperately for a fireplace. The thought of using her own blood was not enticing, and she hoped to avoid it. She looked around, finding the used candle on the dresser; maybe the burned wick would yield enough soot. Grabbing the supplies, she hurried to her mother's bedroom door.

Orianna had told her multiple times that magic worked differently here, but no one had ever explained what that meant. There was less of it here in The Echo. She would need every inch of her concentration, keeping a clear mind—no exceptions. Gemma inhaled deeply through her nose, pausing, then slowly released the air and unnecessary thoughts.

She placed the candles on the floor, lighting them in turn so she would have fresh soot. With one of the earrings and the book as a guide, she scratched the glyph into the rough wooden door. Done, she stepped back to check that she included every detail—no missing pieces, or else it wouldn't work. When she was satisfied, she blew out the candles and rolled the wicks between her index finger and thumb until they were black. With care, she traced the image. Despite her caution, two large slivers of wood pierced her finger. She flinched, pulling her hand back in pain. She pulled them out and resumed tracing the symbols.

The sound of gravel under tires sent her into a panic. She attempted to trace faster. Gemma's haste left soot and blood mixed in the image, fading just as her mother came through the door.

"I'm home," her mother announced.

Gemma cursed under her breath, "Back so soon? I thought you were having a good time?" She scrambled to a nearby hall table, shoving the candles in the drawer.

"Yeah," her dejected tone mixed with the sound of keys on the table. "Just got," a yawn escaped, "so tired all of a sudden."

Footsteps thudded up the stairs and she cursed, trying to shove the rest of her things away but the drawer was full. She started to panic, dropping the earrings into a nearby antique vase as her mother cleared the landing. Gemma stuffed the notebook into her back pocket; it just fit.

"What's going on up there, Gemma?"

"Nothing, Mom. A spider startled me, but I couldn't kill it in time so...look out, it's roaming free." Gemma gave a nervous chuckle. She needed to learn to be a better liar.

"I see. Well, I'm sure you scared it enough it won't be bothering us tonight." She set down her purse. "Oh Gemma, you're bleeding. Are you alright?"

Blood droplets welling from her finger before dripping to the floor. "Oh, I just had a splinter. Strange, thought it finished bleeding." She put her finger in her mouth, cleaning the blood with a pucker. "See, I'm fine."

"Long as you're sure." Her mother gave a second tired yawn. "Are you excited for your trip tomorrow?"

"Yeah, it'll be interesting." A strained pause stretched between them. She had been too concerned with her mother's safety to work out any particulars for a false story. "I'll miss you."

Her mother smiled, "I'll miss you, too." She came in closer, wrapping Gemma in a snug embrace. "I forget sometimes how grown up you are. I still think of you as the little girl hosting tea parties with her stuffed animals and imaginary friends. Look at you now, all grown up headed to college. How did the time fly so fast?"

Gemma wrapped her arms tighter. "I don't know. Everything seems to happen so fast these days..."

"I know, honey, but it'll all be okay. Everything has a way of working out, just take it day by day and—" she yawned a third time, a deep and sleep-filled yawn, before pulling away. "That's enough of that, I suppose. Ugh, so tired from doing the simplest things. Never get old, kid. Good night, I'll see you in the morning," she teased, kissing her daughter on the cheek.

"Yup, good night."

Gemma smiled as she watched her mother retire to her bedroom for the night, heading to her own room. She laid on the bed, staring at the ceiling and at a loss. What was one supposed to do while waiting for the dark forces to attack? But soon, a yawn of her own fled from her chest, and her eyes drifted shut.

CHAPTER SIXTEEN

"WE HAVE A PROBLEM." Orianna hurried to a shelf by the window, without explanation, frantically searching as Zavier and Tobler stood by the fireplace.

"What's going on?" Zavier demanded.

"It looks like they might have found her. Dammit, where is it?"

"What are you talking about?" Zavier strode over, turning her to face him. "Who has found her?"

"The Eyes, Zavier! There was a stranger in her house tonight, and I have no exact proof other than he felt cold and familiar. His face was—wrong. But I can't figure out why."

Tobler felt his skin blister.

"He could have been a wayward portal traveler, or an inhabitant of The Echo—doesn't mean he's one of them. Don't get hot before the fire is lit. We need to know for sure before we start burning bridges and brandishing pitchforks," Zavier said.

"But what if—"

A deadened thud sounded on the other side of the door. It came again, this time shaking the house like the quiver that ran up Orianna's spine. Someone was battering the defensive shield—blow after blow, in blinding flashes of gray light—causing more shaking inside the house. They wore dark robes with hoods pulled up, a unifying symbol embroidered on the front marking them as members of The Eyes. A burning rage uncoiled inside Orianna, fueling her decision to burst out the door after the hooded figures.

"Orianna, no!" Zavier lurched to stop her but was too late.

She flung open the door, and he made it just in time— slipping through before it slammed shut. Barring Tobler, who pounded his fist against the door in a futile attempt to get out, forced to watch helplessly from the window. Deep in his bones, he felt something more dangerous afoot this night but he couldn't place where it would strike. He pounded his fist again.

Two witches in dark robes assaulted the home's protective barrier with plasma balls, each hit illuminating the strong protective shield. One was small and blonde with harsh blue eyes that darkened with every strike against the barrier. The witch beside her had hair the color of flames; her feline green eyes narrowed at the sight of Orianna, mouth splaying into a predatory grin.

"Hello, Orianna," the red head purred. "It's been so long."

* * *

GLASS SHATTERED DOWNSTAIRS. GEMMA'S heart thumped at the telltale baritone of a man's voice, rising up the stairs.

Gemma rushed to the enchanted stationary, scribbling for help. She tried to wait, but he grew closer every second. With quiet speed, she placed a protection glyph on her own door even though it was too late for her to grab the candles for soot. She found her earring in the vase, promptly stabbing her finger and scratching the glyph on her door with her blood.

He was closer. Panic shot through her as she heard him coming up the stairs. Frank's mouth twisted into a grin as the light shone off the patches of green scales on his face. His eyes were slitted like a snake, tinged yellow.

"There you are," he said, a forked tongue passing over his lips. "I thought I sensed you."

Gemma ducked into her room, slamming the door and locking it as he slithered down the hallway.

"Come out, come out, little girl. You can't hide from me now that I have your scent," he hissed, tasting the air before turning his attention toward her mother's door. "Ahhh, I'll bet your sweet mother is passed out, safe and sound in her bed thanks to those herbs that I added to her tea. I'll check in on her for you."

"No! You leave her alone. She's got nothing to do with this!" Gemma yelled, grabbing the doorknob but stopping when she remembered the glyphs. She hoped it would be enough to protect her mother.

Frank walked over to the door, and she held her breath. He slammed a hand against the door to knock it down, only to find the glyph appear and engulf his arm in flames.

"Aaaahhhhhh!" he cried out, violently swinging his arm to put out the fire. He looked down at his singed scales, taking a deep breath as they grew back in place. "Clever little witch, aren't you?" He stalked to her door, wiser now, grazing a finger over the wood to reveal the crude glyph.

Gemma took a huge breath but realized she was trapped. She grabbed the compact mirror from the desk and opened it, but a low chuckle from the other side of the door stopped her cold.

"Tisssk, tisssk, young witch. You can keep *me* out, sure, but I see you haven't protected againssst my children." He held his hands at his sides as two venomous cobras materialized from his arms and slid across the floor. They faced their master, bobbing in place, black scales shining as they waited for their command. "Go," he commanded. They slithered beneath the door and into Gemma's room.

She screamed at the sight of the two snakes with their blood-red eyes fixed on her. She outstretched her palm to burn them, but nothing came. Again she tried, but the panic consumed her concentration. All that emerged were the slightest of sparks.

"Help!" she shrieked into the mirror, realizing how defenseless she was. "ORIANNA! HELP!" She ripped down the curtain rod in an attempt to fight off the snakes, but they were too fast and dodged her every move.

From beyond the portal into Orianna's house, Gemma's scream echoed off the walls.

Tobler ran for the sister mirror, discovering Gemma's terrified face. "Gemma! What's going on?"

"Tobler, help! He's here, and these things are trying to attack me! They're too fast!"

"Stand back!"

"What?"

"NOW!" His voice deepened as he recited a spell that pulled him through the mirror and into Gemma's room, shattering the compact.

"How..." she started, but the hissing of the snakes snapped her back.

"Give up, and I might let you live long enough to see me rip your mother's head off," Frank instigated from behind the door.

Waves of Gemma's terror burned Tobler from within. "We need to get you to safety. I'll deal with him."

"How? There's no way out."

"There's always a way out." Tobler stepped in front of Gemma, focusing all of his energy on the two snakes blocking their path. The snakes turned toward each other; then, in a flash of motion, the reptiles lurched to attack each other. They rolled, biting and hissing, in an elaborate dance. With an outstretched hand, Tobler bewitched Gemma's tall standing mirror; the glass rippled and part of it shattered to the floor. The break was so forceful, a shard impaled his forearm, cutting deep to the bone.

"Dammit!" he exclaimed through gritted teeth. A large piece remained intact, reflecting an image of Orianna's living room. "Gemma, go through the glass—now!"

"No, I'm not leaving you here. It's not safe!" She tried to take his wounded arm, but he pulled away from her.

"I'll be fine. Step into the glass. There's no time for arguing, just trust me!"

"But you're hurt!"

"Do it now! I'll be better off knowing you're safe." He took the curtain rod from her as he ushered her toward the glass.

Reluctantly, Gemma did as Tobler instructed, vanishing in a flurry of blue light. Seeing her safe on the other side, he turned his attention back to the beast who had tried to harm her.

Tobler felt something sick and twisted from the other side of that door, reaching out to enter his mind. His heart galloped, his eyes grew colder, his expression turned callous. He focused on the snakes again, dooming them to a painful fate, but the flurry of blows, swearing, and pounding at the door jerked his attention away.

He thought of a bigger plan for his new hand puppets, a way of killing one pest with two others. Focusing on the cobras, they stopped their mock attacks and slithered back under the door. The lethal pair struck Frank multiple times on the legs and feet until he thudded to the floor. Tobler knew a single bite from the black snakes would stun their prey, the venom spreading rapidly enough to kill in hours. He commanded them to attack until Frank was dead.

He waited in patient darkness, enjoying the sounds of his enemy's last breaths; when the poison choked him out of existence, the cobras withered along with him. Once the deed was done, Tobler turned his attention to the mirror shard sticking out of his arm and ripped it from his flesh, walking through the jagged slice.

He searched for Gemma, sensing her terror. He found her in a corner with her knees to her chest, trembling as tears streamed down her cheeks. Within seconds, he was by her side, arms wrapped around her as he pressed her rigid body against his.

"It's okay, you're okay," he reassured her, stroking her face. "I've got you. You're safe." He calmed her enough to stop the trembling, not bothering to ask permission.

"Gemma, how did you get here?" Orianna demanded, back in the house. Her eyes were hot with anger as she hurried over.

"Some psychopath tried to kill her!" Tobler exclaimed.

"Frank..." Orianna whispered under her breath, "I knew I shouldn't have left you alone."

Tobler turned to Orianna in outrage. "You knew? You knew, and you left her there anyway? Ophelia's Tits, where is your crazy mind when it's needed? You stupid—"

"Watch your tongue, boy! I wouldn't have left her if I was sure there was danger." Orianna's anger reached a boil. "Why didn't you use the portal and glyphs I gave you?"

Gemma whispered, "I didn't have time to finish it all before he showed up—"

"Then why didn't you use your powers? You could have easily set him on fire!" Orianna interrupted.

"I tried, but—" Gemma tried to defend herself, but Orianna was a train derailed.

"But what? You—"

"Let her speak, Orianna." Zavier's voice boomed against the walls of the house.

"I tried to use my fire, but nothing happened. All I could manager were some sparks. I tried to clear my head, but I was too scared to think straight."

"Well, of course you were scared! That's an appropriate response to an intruder, but you have to fight past that. Dammit, child!" She struck the floor with her fist. "Have I taught you nothing? Weren't you paying attention?"

"I have been. I made a damn mistake!" Gemma snarled, eyes hardening under Orianna's verbal assault.

"Mistake? That's not an excuse! How could you be so stupid as to let your fears control you?" Orianna's face reddened as her voice raised.

"Do *not* yell at me!" Gemma attempted to shout through a web of tears in her throat.

"Orianna, I wouldn't—" Tobler attempted to warn her.

"Shut up, boy!" Orianna hissed, "What were you thinking? Answer me, then?"

"I wasn't, at least nothing past 'I'm going to die!' And I would have if it wasn't for Tobler!" Something snapped inside of Gemma, teeth clenching as she stood, causing the fireplace to burst into flames. "Where were you?"

"I was pulled away by an issue outside—" Orianna said.

"What could have been so important that you left me stranded like that?" Barbed malice lashed out from her voice, striking her aunt.

"*They* were at our door, Gemma! I had to do something! Why didn't you call me like we discussed?" Now Orianna had to defend herself with nothing but her stubbornness.

"I did call! You said you'd be there for me, but you were nowhere to be found. You abandoned me, *again*!" Every candle in the house shot a long plume of flame.

"Horse shit! I never abandoned you. I've been doing *everything* I can for you. *Everything* I've done has been for *you*! You were aware there were risks," she emphasized with such effort that Orianna couldn't tell if it was Gemma or herself that she was trying to convince.

"I never asked for this! For *any* of this!" The hearth fire burned hotter, unrestrained emotion turning the colors vibrant shades of red and orange. A furious calm shadowed Gemma's features. "You were there for me? Is that how you were there for my mother? *Is that* how it really happened?" Before the heavy accusations landed, Gemma already regretted losing control.

"How dare you?" Orianna slapped her hard, clear across her cheek and the corner of her mouth. As if she could hit the words instead of her niece. Orianna's face fell; it was not what she'd intended.

Tears filled Gemma's eyes, hand holding her cheek with embarrassed hurt. She stormed to the door only to be stopped as Zavier, towering and firm, his burly face thick with disappointment. He placed a caress against her wounded cheek.

"No." Zavier's tone was gentle, but Gemma heard it as a soft command. She allowed him to turn her back like a small doll. "Orianna," he called, but she ignored him. "Orianna," he commanded again. "You should *both* be ashamed of your behavior. This is not the time to act like a pair of rabid foxes. We need to work together, fix this now. Right now." He gave each of them a firm, fatherly look.

Gemma and Orianna rolled their eyes in sync at the thought of apologizing.

"Nooo, the two of you aren't related in the slightest," Tobler chimed.

"Shut up," the pair said in unison, causing a tiny smirk on their faces followed by silence.

Orianna broke first. "Are you okay?"

Gemma nodded.

"I'm sorry. I lose my temper when it comes to your mother, but that's more my problem than yours. It's also not an excuse for what I did." Orianna moved closer. "Let me see your cheek."

"I'm sorry for what I said. I was out of line. I didn't mean—"

"Shh. I know. I'm sorry for jumping on you. You're new, and I shouldn't have left you alone like that. If I had known for sure, I wouldn't have left you there—" Orianna choked, and she couldn't continue.

"I know." Gemma's eyes filled again.

"I'm just so relieved you're safe." Orianna enveloped Gemma in a tight hug.

Zavier smiled, knowing his stubborn girls just needed a nudge. "Now that's settled, I believe Tobler and I have some business to attend to on the other side of the portal." He lowered his gaze to the sandy-haired boy and began heading for the stairs.

Tobler paled; he had almost forgotten about the body he'd left behind in the house. "Yes, well, there are some things we should discuss—"

Zavier stopped on the stairs, stiffly turning to Tobler. "What kind of some things?"

"It's complicated."

"Define complicated."

Tobler took a breath, "Gemma was in grave danger. I had to take drastic measures."

"Speak plainly, dammit, before my balls sag from old age!"

Tobler cleared his throat of his nerves. "On second thought, it's better for you to see for yourself the severity of his injuries."

"Come on," he continued warily. "We shouldn't wait on it."

Color came back to Tobler's face as he hurried up the stairs after him.

"Will you be needing my help, Zavier?" Orianna asked.

"No, no, we should be able to manage," he replied, turning to Tobler with a raised brow, "Right?"

"Right," he said, swallowing dryly. They continued up the stairs once more.

Gemma watched Tobler leave and couldn't help but feel deep inside that something was not quite right with him. His carefree face was now tight and expressionless; although she'd only known him for a short while, something was amiss. As she began to wonder how bad things could have gotten in her room, a shiver ran down her spine. Before she could fathom the worst, Orianna pulled her away for some tea.

Tobler reached the wall for the portal and felt a shiver run down his spine; except it wasn't his shiver. It was from Gemma. He felt her angst and apprehension and something else...worry? For him? He wasn't in a good situation. Things had been bad in her bedroom, but he'd acted in self-defense. He lost his temper, yes, but it was all for her, to keep her safe. And yet, she was worried. Was she afraid *of him* or afraid *for him?* He couldn't pinpoint the emotions...

"Alright, you'll have to open the portal," Zavier said.

"Why me?"

"I haven't been to Gemma's bedroom so you will have to open it." Zavier handed the vials to Tobler, chiding him. "We should stick only to the portals. You know mirror jumping is frowned upon."

"I know, I know," Tobler huffed, "but I had to. Zavier, she was in trouble. We both know I can't brew up a portal potion in that time. Plus, Orianna keeps that stuff strapped tight and in short supply. Was I just supposed to let her die while I waited for Orianna to finish waging war in the front yard?"

"Listen, boy," Zavier looked over his shoulder quickly to assure they were alone. "I know why you did it. Personally, it seems you did the right thing. If something happened to Gemma, it would destroy Orianna. But she strictly forbids the use of Black Magic under her roof. Now, I'll make sure she forgives you this time, but don't you dare make do of it a second time. Understand?"

"Understood." Taking the vials, Tobler brought the bedroom into his mind and threw them, causing a swirl to appear. They crossed in silence, cleaning up the dead body of their enemy.

CHAPTER SEVENTEEN

BACK IN GOBLIDET, ORIANNA poured tea into two cups and brought them over to the table. A wool blanket sneaked from its corner, wrapping itself around Gemma's shoulders. She was surprised but grateful for the sudden warmth, pulling the corners closer.

"Enchanted linens?"

"Nope, all me. You look chilled, figured the blanket would help," Orianna said. "Although, enchanted blankets would be a fun idea." She gave it some thought, adding, "The mechanics of it might be dicey, though. Wouldn't want them to go rogue."

Gemma sipped her tea, the mint and honey making her tongue tingle. "It's very good, thank you."

"You're welcome." Orianna tried a smile, but it didn't fit on her face.

There was a discomfort held thickly together by all the things they weren't saying. Even though their heated words had come and gone, they could never truly be removed; like a nail pulled from a wall, words had their way of leaving irreparable marks on the soul.

"Oh," Orianna got up from the table, walking into the living room to fetch a thick red book, "I meant to look through this before all hell hit the ceiling."

After plopping it on the table, Gemma studied the title and tattered edged pages. "*Book of Demons*? What is it, a dictionary?"

"Yup. We have a book for everything around here. We don't run on internets like you guys do in The Echo. We're more civilized than that." Orianna flipped through page after page. "He must be in here somewhere, the slimy beast. How did he attack you?"

"He couldn't. The glyph I managed to get on the door didn't let him in, but it didn't guard against the snakes he sent under the door. Why were they able to get through? Did I etch it wrong or something?" she asked, confused.

"Not exactly. If it kept him out, then you did the evil part right. But if the snakes made it through, you forgot a symbol."

"But the snakes *were* evil. They had thick black scales and pointed red eyes, and they tried to attack me as he commanded."

"The snakes weren't evil. They behaved as snakes. Also, you can't go off of how they looked, my dear. That's not fair to any species. The glyph wouldn't keep them out without the animal symbol because animals aren't evil, especially ones that are conjured. They are only doing as they are told. If we mistreat them, or trick them to obey our own evil actions, that makes them unknowing bystanders—innocents, perverted by our sick human whims." Orianna said as she flipped some more.

"Oh, I never thought of it that way." Gemma sipped more tea, chewing on the thought.

"Snakes, reptiles, dangerous..." Orianna flipped faster until she landed on the exact page she was looking for. "Ah ha! Found him! Festae, demon of venomous creatures. Akin to snakes, which he created as children of his image—oh, who'd have thought," she mocked, causing Gemma to grin. "Banished to the underworld at the dawn of time, never to be unleashed due to his creation of poisonous creatures he spreads across the realm."

"So if we kill him, will all of those creatures disappear?" Gemma wondered.

"Well, that's a nice thought, but that's another problem," Orianna said, looking up from the book, "demons can't be killed. They can only be sent back to the underworld. You can kill their processed bodies, maybe wound the demon's true form, but they can't be killed. Banishing works fairly well, but from time to time some dunderhead will break the spells, and they slither back into present."

Gemma's face dropped at her aunt's words. "So there's no hope. We'll never be able to stop them, any of them... I can't stay here." She stared into her teacup, as if the solution hid at the bottom, until a hand clasped over hers.

"No, that's not true," Orianna said, leaning closer. "There is always hope, Gemma, always hope. How do you think I found you? By *never* losing hope that I'd see you again. We will find a way to fix this together. I'm not sending you away." She jumped up, squeezing her tight. "I will never lose you again, not ever. I'd die first before anything ever happened to you. I promise."

Gemma squeezed her aunt back harder, holding back the tears and swallowing the golf ball in her throat until a pair of loud footsteps broke them apart. "Let's both just try to stay alive."

Across the room, Tobler and Zavier descended the stairs with something large slumped in their arms.

"Zavier, what is that?" Orianna asked.

"Not a what, more like a who." Zavier hurled the lump onto the floor, its back making a solid thud against the wood.

Frank was riddled with multiple puncture marks on his face, neck, and arms from the snakes' fangs. His eyes were frozen wide open in what could've been either terror or agony, pale white with a webby red mucus splotched across them. What was left of his skin had turned deathly gray, veins visible in the purplish-blue bruises—all signs of what seemed to be an utterly painful death.

Gemma drew back at the sight of the stiff body on the floor.

Tobler went to her, putting both hands on her shoulders, "It's okay. He's long dead."

"I'd say by the looks of your face, this is the repulsive sod that attacked you in your room." Zavier spit on the corpse. "Looks like he got what he deserved, then. Orianna, how do you want to get rid of him?"

But Orianna did not answer, too astonished at the ghastly sight splayed on her dining room floor.

"Orianna? We can't leave him here for much longer. What do you want to do?" Zavier prompted.

"Who killed him?" she asked in a cold tone.

"I did," Tobler spoke up, and he felt Gemma's eyes on him— not to mention, the minor shocks that rippled from her.

"How did you—" Orianna looked from Tobler to the deformed body, speechless.

"I did what I had to do to keep Gemma safe. He would not back down without a fight, and that's what he got. He was out for blood, and the only blood I'd allow to spill was his own. I'd do anything to protect her, as I'm sure you would do the same." Tobler put an arm around Gemma to emphasize his point; much to his surprise, she did not shy away from him.

"I would, that's true. I can see you'll do *anything*, too, and— I'll be honest—I'm not sure if I like that. Doesn't say much for your mental state, but at least she's safe and unharmed."

Tobler nodded, knowing better than to keep talking and incriminate himself.

"Again, what do you want us to do with him?" Zavier prompted once more.

"There isn't a whole lot we can do, Zavier. Our options are to either burn him, or twine him up with magic and bury him deep."

"We'll burn him. Can't afford the risk of the demon coming back for him." He sighed, "Alright come on, Tobler. Let's get this over with."

"Me?"

"Oh yes, you. Your efforts were noble, and you were obviously brave, but that doesn't exclude you from clean-up duty. Grab his feet and we'll drag him back upstairs into the tub. Best way to dispose of him. Be sure to crack the window first."

Zavier grabbed the dead man under the arms, hauling him up effortlessly and motioning for Tobler to hurry. Tobler grabbed the dead man's ankles, finding him to be heavier than he'd thought, then they continued up the stairs. Another thud sounded, followed by a frustrated, "Pick him back up and move!"

Gemma chuckled at the ridiculousness, her head still gently spinning. "This isn't a regular event, right? Burning someone in the tub."

"Of course not. That only happens on Tuesdays. So yes, this is highly unusual," Orianna gave her a teasing wink. "Come on, let's finish up our tea, and then we'll get ourselves off to bed. It has been a day."

They sat, drinking their tea and softly sharing conversation until the familiar sound of footsteps echoed among them again.

Tobler appeared, face screwed up. "That was the vilest thing I've ever done. Ugh, and the smell," he said, gagging, "it's stuck in my nose."

"Wimp," Zavier taunted. "Remember all that the next time want to kill someone. It is done."

"Good." Orianna pushed away from the table, "Alright then, I'd say it's time to get ourselves off to bed. Tomorrow will be grueling if we don't get some solid sleep."

"Who the hell can sleep after that?" Tobler said under his breath.

"Gemma, you'll take the bedroom upstairs. Tobler, you'll sleep down here on the sofa." Orianna said as a blanket slipped itself into Tobler his arms.

"Oh no, I can sleep down here. I don't mind," Gemma offered.

"No, it's fine. I'll sleep down here, unless you're still scared. I can always share—umph!" His sentence was interrupted by a hurled pillow, hitting his head with an audible impact. "I was only joking."

"I'm sure," said a glaring Orianna. "Don't worry, dear, he'll be just fine down here. Come on, we'll get you something to sleep in." She guided them up the stairs.

Once she was certain Gemma was comfortable, Orianna kissed her niece good night and walked to her own room. Reaching into a drawer, she pulled out an older white nightgown from her wardrobe, reveling in the warm softness as it slid across her skin. Flipping down the cover of their bed, she caught Zavier eying her and a sense of deja vu enveloped them.

"Why are you looking at me like that?"

"Just looking at you. I've earned that much, I believe, over the many years," he said lightly. "Are you okay?"

Orianna sat on the bed, looking away from him. "Of course I am. Why wouldn't I be?" she said picking up the brush from the end table.

"You can't fool me," he said, moving closer and holding her. "I remember this night dress. It's the same one I bought for you the night you ripped my head off for the first time."

"Yes, it is." Orianna said dreamily, chuckling to herself. She recalled how he'd made her so furious. Now look where they stood.

"You only wear this when you are in need of some comfort. Don't tell me nothing is the matter." He kissed her neck.

Her tension dissipated, and a sigh escaped her lips; he was right. "Why can't they just let me have her for a while longer before waging a war?" Lowering her brush to her lap, she appeared defeated.

"I don't know, my love. But we knew there was a chance he'd return. After all, we suspected he wasn't really rotting in the pit cells."

Her throat thickened.

"No, Orianna." He turned her face to his. "Whatever you're thinking in that head of yours, no. The house is safe, and I'm here to protect you and Gemma—clearly, she also has Tobler trained for backup. Do not worry."

"Zavier, I can't stay cooped up in here forever. Eventually they'll all come, and then what? I risk Gemma's life again. She lost her mother because of me. I can't destroy her life more—"

"Your sister's death was not your fault. We've been through this."

"But what if—"

"What if bullfrogs had wings? They'd fly instead of getting crushed under cartwheels. It is poisonous to dwell on uncertainties. You'll go mad with regret."

"I know, I know." Orianna resigned to nuzzling the silken crook of Zavier's neck.

He fell back backward onto the bed, pulling her on top of him and causing her to laugh in surprise. "There's that radiance I love so much, my starlight."

"I love you, too." She smiled back at his old pet name. He'd always called her his starlight because of her bright smile; he also said her temper burned as hot as a star. The memory made her feel more at ease. "I just hope history doesn't repeat itself."

With that, she drifted softly into sleep.

* * *

DOWN THE HALL FROM Orianna and Zavier's room, Gemma lay in bed, tossing and turning in a restless struggle with sleep. She flipped on her back and closed her eyes, hoping the darkness would release her, but it only left her a victim to her imagination.

In a fit of frustration, she turned to her side and looked out the window with its view of the stars. She tried to focus as her mind drifted to the earlier moment on the roof, leaving the worst of her worries behind. Sighing heavily, she wiggled her toes, fidgeting and tapping them against the blanket. The door creaked softly open, causing her to bolt upright.

"Shhh," Tobler walked in with a hushed finger to his lips.

Her shoulders relaxed, and she whispered in exasperation, "What are you doing up here? Orianna will kill you."

"Well if *someone* didn't feel so loudly, I wouldn't be here."

"Sorry, I tried to keep them to a minimum."

He sat at the edge of the bed, facing her. "I know you did, and you almost got them under control. What were you doing that calmed you down?"

"Just was looking at the stars. I tried counting them."

"Ah, I see—the stars." His tone seemed suspiciously calm, as he must've felt her butterflies swarm in her gut. "They are lovely, aren't they? We could go onto the roof, if you'd like, to get a more accurate count. Seems to help."

"Won't The Eyes see us on the roof?" Gemma asked.

"Not really. But it would suck to run into them, that's for sure. I'd keep you safe, though, you know that." He smiled at her.

"Like in my room. I'm so sorry, I forgot to thank you for that." Gemma shook her head, chastising herself.

He waved her off, playfully downplaying the murder. "Don't worry about it. It was nothing." Except he started to fidget with a crease in the sheets.

Her nerves scurried inside of her again. "Tobler?"

"You can ask me anything Gemma, no need to be nervous."

"Right. So what happened back there?" She kicked herself for being so transparent.

He knew she'd be asking about it, sooner or later, but he still wasn't ready to explain what had happened. Her eyes compelled the truth, like salve to draw out a splinter. Averting his eyes back to the crease in the sheet, he answered.

"I commanded the snakes. I turned them against Frank. He died almost instantly," he said, gauging her reaction before continuing, but her face was unreadable. Her emotions scattered between fear, worry, and nervous. His next words surprised him, a plea meant to convince the silent girl. "You don't need to fear me Gemma. I'm not a monster, I swear it."

She put a hand on his fidgeting fingers. "I know."

"Why are you still afraid then? I guess you're a bit torn."

"I'm worried, yes, but not about you—well, not in the sense that you're dangerous. I'm worried about how you're feeling, and if protecting me might have hurt you."

"What do you mean? I'm fine."

"Have you killed someone before, then? Did you feel nothing?" She was slightly alarmed.

"What? No, no, this was the first time. It doesn't feel good—not now, anyway—but I did it to save you and your mother. That eases my thoughts."

"What do you mean?" she asked, now confused.

"I don't know, never mind. It's nothing." He tried to brush it off, but she wasn't about to give up. He felt the weight of her care, the generous emotion changing him.

"Please, tell me." She gave his hand a willing squeeze.

"It—I didn't feel much at all when it was happening. I was just so angry he had tried to hurt you... I lost myself in the anger, the redness of it..." He looked down, feeling ashamed. He wasn't used to being the vulnerable one. "I've never felt anger like that before. It was as if he set my nerves on fire, and I just couldn't stand it...a pain-riddled anger."

Gemma listened, her heart aching from his hurt expression. "I'm sorry, Tobler. If I hadn't come back, this never would have happened. This is all my fault..." She hung her head for being the nuisance her new family never asked for—a plague, sweeping in without invitation.

"Don't say that, Gemma. Don't you wallow in those false feelings. Yeah, I can feel those new ones, too. Listen, from what I can decipher, this storm has been brewing before you came back. Orianna and Zavier are happier than two pigs in shit that you've come back in their lives. *I'm* happier." He squeezed her hand back. "You coming to the realm, I already know, is the best thing to happen to me in a long while. I know it's soon, but I just know. You do things to me."

She felt the slow surge of electricity from his hand to her chin as he slowly turned it, cupping her cheek. He felt the surge too, a force unlike anything he'd experienced before.

"Do you feel it? This electric sensation?" she asked, hushed, comforted as he stroked his thumb against her cheek.

"Yes," he said, losing himself in her eyes.

"What is it?" she asked, dazed as the world fell away again.

"I'm not sure. It might be what we in this realm call kismet, but...I've never felt it before," he murmured, trying to focus on the feeling, but his attention was thrown off by the creaking of the house. "I better get back downstairs just in case they wake up. Are you sure you're okay? If you're not, I'll stay a bit longer."

"The edge has worn off. Thank you for coming up here. Good night."

He leaned in and kissed her gently, "Goodnight, Gemma."

He made his way back down the stairs with mouse-like reflexes to avoid creaky steps. Once at the bottom, he exhaled with relief at having made it without Orianna ripping his guts out. He laid himself back down onto the couch. It wasn't the most comfortable, but it was warm. She was comfortable, that was all that mattered. Tobler would not have slept easily, otherwise. There was something else he could do to help, but it would take him someplace dark.

* * *

UNBEKNOWNST TO THEM ALl—somewhere far away, in the sharpest teeth of the night—the diabolical festered, growing like a grotesque sore on an otherwise pristine world. Morning would dawn too soon, delivering new troubles for all of Goblidet.

CHAPTER EIGHTEEN

THE BACKROOM OF THE apothecary boiled hot as Quinn stirred the contents of the large cauldron. He brooded over the steam and smoke, whipping sweat from his brow, choking and miserable. His entire life he'd worked in the apothecary under Finn's mastery—grossly underappreciated, putting in long hours ladling up liquids and concocting sticky salves all while facing scrutiny from his snooty boss. And for what? A small room for sleeping and meager pay that barely supported his lustful addictions.

Madam Poochette ordered another overzealous amount of elixirs and ointments to help her cling to her withering beauty, all resulting in a foul-tempered Quinn slaving in sweat while Finn slept warm in bed.

Someday, he thought, *I'll be rid of this stinking shithole.*

He had been trying to save up enough to leave, but with his pathetic pay grade, it wasn't possible. Not unless he gave up spending his coin and free nights in dark taverns, filled to his eyes with rich fae liquors with a host of promiscuous women to warm his bed. His hobbies drove him, filled the emptiness, if only temporarily...until he woke the next morning, covered in a crusty layer of self-loathing, scorning his job, and bitter over the path life pushed him to follow.

Sure, if he cleaned up his act Finn would probably leave him the apothecary when he passed, but how long until that happened? He wanted more out of life—more power, wealth, something larger than the humdrum task of selling piss in jars—far outside of the large, white prison that had been his home for most of his disappointing existence.

Lost in himself, he didn't notice the thin, jet-black fog that slinked beneath the door. It crept behind him before cascading upward into the shape of a man, red eyes flashing before the rest of the body materialized. Quinn paused, sensing a presence; he turned, shocked to see a tall man in a red robe standing behind him.

"Black Hells, where did you come from?" Quinn demanded.

"Now, is that anyway to speak to your new master?" the stranger asked coolly.

"What are you talking about? I have no master. Finn hasn't sold the place, so who are you?"

"Who I am is not important. What you should be asking is what I can do for you?"

Quinn snorted. "You're drunk on too much ale, you old windbag. You'd better leave before I throw you out—or worse. I'm in no mood for raving crackpots."

"I'll go, if that's what you desire, but you'll never get out of here without my help." The stranger walked a half circle in front of Quinn.

"I doubt a crazy old man could help me. You don't even know me. But I have ways to make you leave me alone." Quinn walked to the other end of the room where an old sword leaned against a corner.

"You need me, Quinn," said the stranger, leaning both hands on the edge of the cauldron.

Quinn's stiffened, gripping the hilt, "How do you know my name?"

"Oh, I know more than just your name. I know all about you: how much you hate it here, your boozing, your lust after the brothel woman." The man turned his gaze towards the cauldron and the fire.

"You're a liar! You must've followed me. Probably one of Probust's men looking for the coin I owe him." He flipped the sword up, anger blazing. "I told that slimy cock I would pay him back for the night with the redhead. I don't like this little surprise visit he has you on."

The man's eyes shot up. "I've heard about that infamous temper of yours. Got to say, I'm a big fan of the stories, but I feel like I'm not seeing it. I like a nasty temper—have one, myself, that I'm fairly proud of."

"Is that a threat? Are you threatening me, old man?" Quinn approached the stranger with the sword.

"It's more than a threat, which is more than what you have. I don't think you have the stomach to use that blunt shard you keep waving around, boy."

"Don't. Call me. Boy." Quinn swung the sword in a harsh zip, but missed.

The stranger laughed. "You're so clever aren't you, *boy*. Desperate halfwit, no wonder they abandoned you—your mother could smell the stupid on you. Finn took you in for his own benefit, cheap labor for profit. He mocks you, you know. Looks down on you and tells people the kind of putrid vermin you really are."

Quinn felt the intensity rise through the stranger's babble and took silent aim, cutting through mid-forearm. The limb fell as blood splayed, splashing into his eyes and streaking his clenched teeth. The man clutched his gaping wound. Quinn's face changed from satisfaction to horror as the man gave a low and animalistic laugh, unaffected by the loss. A deep chant came from the stranger's lips, and the arm regenerated from what was a bloody stump only seconds ago.

"Now *that* is the fight I'm looking for!" The stranger smiled.

Quinn looked on, speechless, as his brain tried to make sense of what it was seeing.

"You really don't know who I am, do you?" he said, flexing his newly grown fingers and hand.

Quinn swallowed sawdust lumps. "The Devil comes to mind."

"Close, but still not important. I want you to join me and my army, Quinn," the stranger offered.

"I'm nobody's puppet. I don't see what's in it for me." Quinn turned to leave, only to be standing face-to-face with the stranger.

"I can give you much, Quinn. A place you'll belong, for starters—wealth, power, ways to slake your lust." He lingered in the doorway, watching Quinn but making no effort to leave. "You're destined for far better than this filthy rat's nest. *I'm* how you get there. All you have to do is join my fight. And if you're who I assume you are, you'll rule at my side. Together, we will put all of them in their place—below us, where they belong." He watched the boy's eyes flicker with prospect.

"I want one more thing," Quinn said.

"Name it, and it's yours." He chuckled.

"I want a girl—a particular girl—all for myself, to do with as I please."

"My boy, you will have your pick when I'm done with you. But if that is your wish, I'm good for it. Do we have a deal?" The stranger put out his strong hand, eyes rumbling in anticipation.

Quinn thought a moment, but it wasn't long before he placed his hand in the stranger's binding grip. A solid contract of loyalty.

"Oh, one more small thing you'll need to do to gain admittance. You must prove your loyalty."

"What do you mean?" Quinn asked with lingering distrust.

"Kill Finn, the man who took you in. I want to see blood on your hands, by my orders. Do this, and you'll gain your power. It's that simple." The stranger disappeared in a fog, his eyes the last to go.

Quinn was alone, contemplating his next step into his dark future...eyeing the contents of the room with new purpose.

* * *

LEO LANDED ON THE on the border of a property in Goblidet. A sneer marred his face as he walked closer to the house but was met with an invisible, but solid, barrier. He pushed his hand against it, eventually pushing through. In seconds, his skin began to smoke. Despite his persistence and success in penetrating the wall, he could not withstand the scalding and pulled back his blistered appendage. He cursed and spat at the protected ground, then watched as the skin grew back.

"Clever, my wayward witch, but there is one thing you did not account for." Leo uncorked the black bottle he kept in a deep pocket and took a long sip. It tasted of sour milk and burnt rat's skins. He kept it down as his eyes rolled back in his head, all-white, and leaving him in a trance. From there, he began his mental assault deep into Orianna's unsuspecting mind.

He threw her like a ragged doll. She flew through the air, her heart tumbling in her chest, and collided with the door without time to brace for the impact. When she met the stone, it was hard enough to make pain blossomed up her spine. She fought to take in air that wouldn't come. The beating left her in a haze of confusion. Her head filled with lead and her bruised skin felt like someone else's.

The new assault, however, jolted her senses as she fought against unconsciousness. Digging deep for strength, she propped herself on her elbows, tasting the fear and blood in her mouth. The room was damp, rain falling in drips and spurts from the roof, the humidity enhancing the wretched smell of sulfur.

The looming silhouette of the man she once loved stood in the doorway. That was all he was to her now—an empty memory, a shadow. The ghost of the man she had once shared her time with, an intangible wisp of a former life. He crossed the floor with heavy feet. She scrambled away, every move sending screams through her beaten flesh, the unexpected assault rendering her powerless. The pain drained her of the focus she needed to defend herself.

Lightning struck across the sky, filling the room with a blaze of light; it was then she saw him. The eyes that she once gazed into on sleepy afternoons now filled her with an icy terror. They were tinged red, filled with the rage a storm would envy. His once-handsome features contorted in an evil stranger's scowl.

He closed the gap between them as she struggled to get up, but there was nowhere for her to go. She was trapped in too many ways: fear, pain, space. But she had to try. She had to keep fighting back. She was nothing if not stubborn, and would be until her dying breath, which she feared would be soon.

Sluggishly raising a heavy arm, she attempted to focus. Heat rose to her palm, but the feeling left as fast as it came. She was still too disoriented to focus.

He grabbed her by the wrist, pulling her to her feet, and slamming her to the wall. Her back crushed against the wet brick as the impact stole her breath away once more. His laughter boomed into the room, vibrating through the walls she huddled against. Sickness roiled in her stomach as he placed a firm hand on her throat.

"Leo, please..." her voice was thin as paper as she struggled.

He snorted. "Begging? All of your fight gone so soon? What happened to that moxie of yours? All that power you wield, where is it?" Leo's grip tightened as panic consumed her.

"Leo, no, this isn't you..." she managed to croak as he loosened his grip. He was toying with her, a cat with a mouse.

"I can't just let you go, and I won't let anyone else have you." A thick smoke churned around her, hissing and winding up her body. It curled around her neck, replacing his hands as she choked in terror. The room faded to black.

* * *

LEO FELT HER AWAKEN abruptly as his eyes rolled back into place. Satisfied with the terror he sowed, he vanished in a wisp of black smoke.

Orianna was left behind, shaken and awake, lost in the darkness of her mind.

CHAPTER NINETEEN

TOBLER LAID SILENTLY, EYES closed on the couch, enduring the clamorous clatter of pans being pulled from cupboards. It was early morning, but Tobler felt like he had just closed his eyes. He sensed only one person in the kitchen, and from the prickly heat, it had to be Orianna. What had her up at this unsocial hour? She had never been a morning person, and her emotions gave off strange readings. There was a new anxiety inside of her with old frayed edges, like a cast-aside cloth meant to be forgotten.

A tea kettle gave a faint whistle followed by the scrape of it being taken from the flame. A mug clanked onto the wooden table, water rushing into it; the scent of flowers and black tea leaves permeated the air, followed by the sound of a creaking chair. Abruptly, there was no sound but the stirring of her emotions that began to make him feel nauseous.

Orianna drank the tea, and he felt her calm down. She was afraid, more afraid then he had ever felt from her—an old fear missed with fresh guilt, metallic and burning. The tea had something medicinal mixed in which he attributed to the strange, overly sweet smell. All around her, she radiated scandal, pain, and fatigue.

"I know you're awake, Tobler," Orianna said, breaking his reverie. "No use faking it, boy. Come and have tea with me." She levitated another mug to the table, along with the kettle of water.

Tobler groaned. "How did you know I was awake?"

"You stopped snoring like a damn bear and weren't flailing, as usual," she said, unamused.

"I don't snore," he refuted, pulling a chair back to sit down. "I might flail, but I don't snore."

Lifting the mug, he sniffed the tea and found it didn't have the sweet smell like Orianna's. Closer now, he recognized it as Lougrous root, an unorthodox way of quelling pain both emotional and physical. Lougrous root was not in the common repertoire of Light Magic herbs.

"I couldn't sleep last night. I imagine you didn't, either?" she asked uncomfortably.

"I feel like I had just drifted off when I heard you creeping about down here." Tobler yawned.

"It's not creeping when it's my kitchen."

"Are you alright, Orianna? You just seem off."

"I had to confront The Eyes at my door last night so yes, I'm off." But she didn't look at him, just spoke into her tea mug.

He wanted to push her on, weed out what she was hiding, but she would just push back harder. Erratic emotions were the dangerous kind, and he'd rather not tangle with a nest of that magnitude. He waited.

Orianna looked up at him, strangely fragile as weariness rimmed her reddened eyes. Her mouth opened as if she was ready to confess, but Zavier's advance down the stairs stopped her.

"Ophelia's Eyes, there you are. Dammit woman! You near scared me to death by not being in bed this morning." He moved to her side, kissing the top of her head.

Orianna covered the cup with her palm, steaming the water to burn away the Lougrous root before Zavier could smell it. Tobler saw but said nothing.

"Sorry, I just couldn't sleep. Thought it better to come down here than to wake you." Orianna smiled up at him. She never kept secrets from Zavier, and it put Tobler's mind on edge.

Then, as if it were just another normal morning, Orianna pushed up from the table. She started taking out mixing bowls and heated the cast-iron pan, moving about the counter beating batter. Soon, there were fresh hot cakes and bacon for their breakfast. She flicked her fingers, causing coffee to brew in the old pot over the fire. Within moments, the sweet fragrance of the Lougrous root was lost in smells of strong coffee, butter, and the beginnings of the day.

Orianna placed a stack of hot cakes in front of Tobler, topping it with a dollop of soft butter and strawberry syrup—his favorite. Her wide brown eyes beseeched him, and he gave a discrete nod to ease her worries. Considering his own plans, he picked up a fork and cut into the hot cakes, tasting every bit like a delicious bribe.

Halfway through breakfast, Gemma made her way down the stairs. Her hair was in disarray, clothes tossed on in a rush, and eyes still carried traces of sleep.

"Good morning, dear," Orianna said, and the table echoed her.

"Good morning, everyone." Gemma took a seat at the end of the table. "Smells delicious in here."

"Should have smelled it earlier." Tobler grumbled under his breath when Orianna kicked him square in the shin.

Orianna was about to offer her breakfast as a plate came forward, a few hot cakes jumped on it, then rested in front of her. Seconds later, coffee, cream, and sugar swirled before the handle of the stone mug landed in her hand.

"Oh, that's perfect." Gemma looked up to find the table staring at her. "What? I've been practicing."

"Looks like she's a switch off the ol' family tree, huh?" Zavier nudged Orianna with pride.

"I agree, but that doesn't mean you should stop practicing. We need you to be strong while under pressure." She gave a firm nod. "Did you sleep okay? The bed wasn't too lumpy, was it?"

"Hey," Tobler whined. "You never cared if it was too lumpy for me."

"Oh hush, you can deal just fine. And if it was, you wouldn't have been quiet about it. Eat your breakfast," Orianna said.

"I slept okay, no lumps. But it wasn't easy to fall asleep. Probably just nerves and things." Gemma took a long sip of coffee.

"I imagine that would be enough to rattle anyone—wouldn't you say so, Orianna?" Tobler asked, and she shifted.

"Of course, perfectly normal considering recent events." She smiled at him with a daggered look over her coffee mug.

Gemma sighed, missing the tension, and took a bite of her hot cakes. "Hopefully today..." she paused, at a loss. "What are we supposed to do now, anyway?"

Everyone at the table silenced as the mood changed, none of them wanting to be the first to speak about the topic they'd been evading all morning.

Zavier spoke first, being head of the house. "I'm not sure what the standard procedure is, but Gemma and Orianna, you guys should stay put. Tobler and I can scout around, see if there is anyone suspicious loitering."

"I can't just stay cooped up in here. Zavier, there's more I need to do than ever before. I'll need more supplies and advice," Orianna said.

Gemma stayed quiet, unsure of what was customary in the family households of this realm. She longed to explore more, despite the countless risks outside of the protection perimeter.

"We should all stay together and carry on about our business? Search out suspicions together." Tobler managed in between squabbles.

"Possibly, but I don't think it wise to have the ladies traipsing about since they're the targets. May as well have them carry giant beacons," Zavier replied with exhaustion.

"True, but," Tobler stopped, hoping to gather everyone's attention, "if we leave them here and those things come back, then they're on their own."

"I'm sure between the two of us we could hold them off. We're not helpless." Orianna huffed.

"I'm sure you can, but they'll find a loophole to get through the perimeter. You can't account for everything, and there's no such thing as airtight. Eventually they'll find a weakness, and then what? We'll be left with nothing but our skin, which may work against a couple of them, but if they come in a horde?" Tobler paused, shaking his head. "The two of you couldn't possibly handle that. We need to stick together."

He knew Orianna was proud, but the odds weren't in their favor; he couldn't stand the thought of Gemma being at risk again. Pissing off the scariest creature in the realm was the smallest price he was willing to pay for Gemma's safety, but Orianna did not jump into a pool of rage with him. Emotions could betray the most stoic of people, and she was no different.

"I agree with Tobler." She almost choked on the words.

"What?" Zavier asked, eyes wide. "You never agree with him."

"I know, I know, but he has a point. We'll be stronger together." She fiddled with her mug, unhappy with her own choice.

Before Zavier could speak again, Gemma piped in with a raise of her hand. "Uncle Zavier?"

"You don't need to raise your hand, dear. What is it?" he asked.

"Oh, sorry. I agree with us all sticking together and going about like normal." Her heart gave a thud. She was not big on speaking up in disagreements. "If we alter our daily routines, we could look vulnerable to The Eyes."

Zavier sighed as he looked at the people who sat around the table, each imploring and outnumbering him. The Eyes didn't scare him, and though wanting to protect them, he couldn't keep everyone locked up. Eventually they would have to leave—if not to gather supplies, then to keep them from going stark mad.

"It's settled, then. We'll all head out together to make sure we have things we need and to keep up appearances. Get yourselves together. We'll be leaving soon." Zavier pushed back from the table.

"What do we need?" Gemma asked.

"Potential allies, and I'll need to speak with Maggie if I stand any chance of figuring things out around here," Orianna said as she cleaned the table.

"Why allies?" Tobler inquired.

"As pointed out before, we'll need help," she stated, as if having explained it already a hundred times. "We could try to handle it all ourselves, but we don't know how much he's infiltrated Goblidet." She washed the table, then paused to say, "Gemma, go upstairs and straighten yourself up. Can't have you being labeled sloppy."

Gemma looked down at her ruffled dress, not realizing pre-coffee how disheveled she appeared. Tobler felt her self-consciousness as she left, annoyed by Orianna's chiding.

On his way out, Tobler eyed Orianna. She returned his stare until he was through the door.

She contemplated her nightmare, worrying about the strange bruises she thought she saw on her neck; instead, she shifted her focus to scrubbing the dishes to stay calm. The marks matched where Leo strangled her, a flashback of the real bruises from the past when nightmares of him plagued her...but this was different. She still felt his hands on her throat, his breath on her face, rage-filled eyes boring into her. The plate slipped from Orianna's grip.

* * *

OUTSIDE, TOBLER WAS BRUSHING one of the large black horses, readying her for their trip, while Zavier hooked the first horse to the carriage.

"Don't get too used to that," Zavier said, fastening a strap.

"Used to what?" Tobler was confused.

"Her agreeing with you. I wouldn't wager my ale against it."

"I'm sure that is a once-in-my-lifetime experience. Not getting cozy with it, trust me, especially with how it is between Gemma and I." He stroked the large animal, and she nuzzled him back. He liked being around animals; they were simple and kind, incapable of ill manners—except when it came to survival. They made sense.

Zavier gave a deep chuckle. "True, you've better chance betting on lightning strikes."

Tobler brought the other horse over for Zavier to harness up.

"Did she seem a little stiff this morning?" Zavier asked, taking the horse from him.

"No, she seems to be getting around just fine. Just needed a good brushing, a little walk will warm her up."

"No, not the horse. I'm talking about Orianna. You were giving a good poke at her today, and she didn't rip your tongue out. Bit unusual for her." Zavier frowned.

"I didn't notice, probably just residual shit from last night." Tobler lied through the guilt, but he couldn't alarm Zavier, not yet.

"Hmm, I don't like it, regardless."

"Well, I'm sorry she didn't rip out my tongue for your enjoyment," Tobler said lightly, leaning against the carriage.

"That's not what I'm saying. Although, I wouldn't have been able to stop her, so you ought to count your blessings." He paused. "She just—I guess I'm just worried about her. Sure, she'll come around." He shrugged it off, rubbing the large mare's face.

The women came outside, and Zavier helped Orianna into her seat with the boisterousness characteristic of their relationship. Tobler grinned slyly at the spectacle, but when he looked at Gemma, he put away the grin. He aided her in a more gentlemanly manner. Then, it dawned on him: she hadn't given him an answer last night. The carriage began to roll, and he soon left the notion behind him. Her answer wouldn't change how he felt about her.

Gemma committed the surroundings to memory, down to the last branch or blade of grass. She appeared to glow in the morning sun as they rode.

"Your spirits are singing a new tune this morning."

She turned to find Tobler observing her. "I decided I should be thankful. Take it day by day and hopefully stay alive through it all."

"That would be most appreciated," he said with a grin, taking her hand for reassurance. "Stop worrying, I won't let anything happen to you."

"You can't always save me." She smiled back, but he noticed the strain. "I have to find ways to protect myself."

"You'll get stronger, I have no doubt about that. You're an Oliver witch, so it'll come easy enough. But you have me while you get stronger—and after."

She watched the trail behind them disappear. "I don't want to be your burden, Tobler."

"Hey," he pulled her attention back to him, "you're never a burden to me, ever, remember that. I'm doing this because I want to."

Her brow knitted. "Doing what?"

There was an icy squeeze in his chest. "Telling you that I'm going to protect you, silly. Keep up."

Tobler moved next to her, and she leaned her head on his shoulder as the weight of the realm leaned on them. Tobler laced his fingers in Gemma's, and she felt something inside her change. The weight of his hand pulled away the things that scared her. Their touch became alive. She grew accustomed to the power of it, the foreign sensations were more comfortable and familiar.

They pulled up to the barn as the same old man came out to greet them with a new farmhand in tow. A man with a face that encapsulated spending long days in the sun, eyeing Gemma with a glint and a foxlike grin. Protectively, Tobler took her by the elbow while giving the new hand a stiff look; she stared at him, confused.

"You don't want to know," he whispered to her.

With that, Tobler and Gemma walked with Zavier and Orianna up the short path into the heart of Goblidet. They stopped at a nearby fruit stand to discuss their options.

"Right, so now what?" Tobler asked.

"We're suppose stick together, remember?" Gemma added.

He then realized the fault in his plan. What he needed to do couldn't be under the eyes of his family, especially not Gemma's.

"Yes, but we could look more suspicious if we clustered together," Orianna interjected.

"I only agreed to this because you insisted that we stick together. What's changed?" Zavier's patience wore thin.

"Yes, but I realize now that the four of us in one shop won't be helpful." She rolled her eyes at him. "I still think we should stick together, but perhaps we should pair off and go about our business. We could meet back here in about a couple of hours. That doesn't sound so bad, does it?"

Zavier sighed. "No, I suppose not. We'll meet back here in *one* hour. No exceptions." He eyed Tobler specifically.

"Why are you looking at me?"

"You're not the most reliable when it comes to being punctual. You have a horrible habit of 'losing time,' and with Gemma around, you might push that even further."

"Which is exactly why he'll be coming with me, and you'll go with Gemma," Orianna said.

They all looked at her as if she'd started pissing in the street.

"I didn't stutter, did I?" Orianna put her fists on her hips, "Zavier, you'll go with Gemma. Tobler, with me—that way we'll know we will all be back on time."

Zavier shrugged, frustrated. "Alright, let's get going before the sun comes down on us. Gemma, we'll rummage through a few places. Let me know if you want to stop anywhere."

She gave Tobler a fleeting look as she followed Zavier. Tobler and Orianna walked their way down the street, neither amused. He would have to find a way to lose Orianna to carry out his plans. An unwinnable situation that he hoped would unfold well. Worse yet, Orianna's emotions were starting to annoy him, turbulent and teetering in her mind. If she insisted on being so aggravating, he really wished she would just spit out what was bothering her.

"How are you doing?" he asked dryly.

"I'm fine."

"Really? For someone who is fine, you're emanating a lot of shit emotions."

She glanced in the shop windows, avoiding eye contact with him. "I don't know what you're talking about."

"Yes, you do. You can't lie to me, but—Ophelia's Ass—I wish you could. It feels like you're up to something. If you keep this shit up, you'd better let us in on your plans." The hypocrisy laid thick on his tongue.

"I don't appreciate what you are insinuating, Tobler."

"Well then, fess up. If something scares *you,* then open up about it. Our lives are in danger here. *Gemma's* life is in danger."

"You don't think I know that?" Orianna hissed back, her voice low and pointed. "You think that's not in the forefront of my mind? I'm more worried than you could imagine."

"Oh, I doubt that," he said, face darkening. "But there is something you're not telling me. I want to help you, Orianna, so tell me. You were about to ask it of me this morning."

"I'm done talking." She stopped outside of The Floating Toad.

"What are we doing here?"

Orianna ignored him and walked in through the door, a chime and a gust of wind blowing past her fluttering hair. Maggie emerged from the back room, color draining from her face at the sight of Orianna.

"Back so soon?" Maggie asked.

"Just can't stay away lately, I suppose." Orianna smiled.

Tobler felt her weight lessen, wondering if she had been telling the truth before.

"Tobler," Maggie said in greeting.

"Maggie," he matched her icy indifference until the hair at the back of his neck stood up. Tobler turned in Maggie's direction and there was an unsettling absence that lingered around her, solid nothingness from Maggie's emotional fields. It didn't make any sense. Everyone always had emotions running through.

Orianna was babbling on about the situation, but something distracted Maggie. From just beyond Orianna's shoulder, Maggie could see the way Tobler was looking at her.

"We should be talking about these things in private, don't you think?" Maggie nodded gently behind Orianna.

Orianna waved him away. "Tobler, you can go now. I'll be fine here."

"You know I can't just leave you. If anything happens, Zavier will kill me." Tobler was suddenly torn.

"I know, but I'm not alone if I'm here with Maggie. She is just as powerful as I am. I'll be fine." She didn't need him around, breathing down her neck while she discussed her personal matters.

Tobler wavered. It was true, Orianna would not be alone, but he didn't like what he felt. He had his own agenda to enact, but leaving the shifty pair together didn't feel right either.

"Alright," he took a deep breath, "I'll leave, but you can't leave this shop without me. When should I come back for you?"

"Come back in about two hours," Maggie stated.

"Can't—we have to check in in an hour. Tobler, come back in forty-five minutes." Orianna turned back to Maggie. "We'll have to talk fast, is all."

Tobler's mouth thinned. "Fine, but be ready when I get back. Don't let anything happen to her."

"Yes—now leave us, boy." Maggie spun and walked away, seemingly hurried to be rid of him.

* * *

TOBLER WALKED OUT OF the shop, fists balled in his pockets. He hoped he was doing the right thing.

He meandered, making a point of looking into random shops and examining their contents. He passed a fae creature playing a lively song on the violin, more beautiful than any he'd ever heard and tossed a silver vellum into the player's case. She gave him a suggestive wink and played faster, flirting through her music and causing him to come close to blushing. Jostling some coins, he took a turn here and there, seeming carefree as he took a shortcut he'd known for many years down a narrow alleyway.

His conscious weighed heavier and heavier with every step. He didn't want to keep secrets from Zavier and Orianna, but they would never allow his plan to see light. Guilt did sad things to the mind, bending and twisting reality from its truths, making him wonder if they would disown him if they found out. He saw her through a shop window, as if knowing he needed her.

Gemma stood in front of a large bookcase, nimble fingers plucking books from shelves, eyes glittering as she touched the rough leathers—a rare excitement that he'd never seen yet on her lovely face. He could feel her through the thick glass pane, fuzzy and happy as if she'd discovered a new world in the bindings. Tobler felt all of the guilt melt away the longer he looked at her, all doubt racing from him.

Tobler took another series of turns, peeking on either side to ensure he wasn't being watched. He quickly walked into Ophelia Black Street. He passed several deplorable witches and scraggly creatures along the grubby streets.

Cobblestones were worn with age, foul smells pocketed the air, and hunched witches rolled bones on one side of the alley while a wealthy landlord demanded rent from a lackluster tenant. Everyone radiated ill will, flecked with evil or lust, or appeared inundated with rivulets of despair. He hated coming here. Shielding himself helped keep him upright, but this took much of his energy; some always slipped through, regardless. It was enough to turn his stomach into sick knots. The sooner he got what he needed, the sooner he could get out.

When he reached The Emporium, he flitted in to escape the surrounding abuses. Shutting the heavy glass door behind him, the overwhelming filth dissolved and returned his insides back to normal.

"Well, well," said a strongly accented voice.

It made him jump, proving his nerves hadn't lost their earlier edge.

"Yer new to here." She was portly and squat with unkempt white and red hair, framing a face screwed into a lemon-puckered pout.

"No, I'm not. I've lived here all my life."

"Not down this way, ya don't. Can smell it on ya," she sniffed, moving closer to him, "Fresh and new, but yer a little like us and not like us, all at the same time. Makes ya new 'round *here*." A grin swallowed her face, showing off yellowed teeth.

"You always sniff your customers? Could be why no one new comes around here much," he said, trying to lean away from her.

"Nah," she spat, backing a step away from him. "Enough small talk, though. I'm Fiona. What brings ya all way here to my neck of the woods? I've got spells a plenty, jars of all sorts ya won't find from wholesome Floatin' Toad. Special thrills in all forms." She wagged her eyebrows provocatively at him.

Tobler cringed but tried to maintain his composure. "No issues *there,* I can assure you. I'm looking for a particular repertoire of spells, a bit of tough magic. I'm not sure if you'd even have it." He gestured to the messy shop.

The old woman smiled and clapped her hands, "OH! I love a challenge. What is it?"

"I'm looking for something to ward off death or harm from someone."

Fiona's face fell into a pout. "Ain't no magic that can ward off death. Only fools think they can stop death. Such magic is impossible. Even we lower dwellers have our limits, ya know."

"But you must have something similar, then—a book of spells that I can buy off of you, bewitched animal bones—anything at all. Just name you price. I'm good for it."

She eyed him with beady eyes. "And what would a young man like yerself need with somethin' like that?"

Tobler paused. "It's for...a friend. I'm just trying to protect her and—"

"Aaah ha! Yer in love with her!" she exclaimed.

"I never said—"

"Don't have to. It's all on yer face, thick in yer words an' speech. Is it the kismet?" She sounded almost fervent in an eccentric grandmother way, squeezing his arm with both hands.

Tobler sighed, "Listen, I don't know. All I know is I don't want anything bad to happening to her. What can you give me for *that*?"

"Oh, we always know. It's deep down in our skin, written on the insides of our bones. Turns yer life on new ends, and ya ain't ever the same again." A thought came to her, and she looked over her shoulder to a darkened room off the main shop floor. Tapping a finger to her lips as if something tickled her mind. She turned back to Tobler, and her eyes sparkled with longing or loss—perhaps both, but he noticed the change. "Say it."

"Say what?" He squinted in confusion.

"Admit yer love fer her, do it now. If you mean it, I'll help you. And I'll know if yer lying to me. I can tell these things." The old woman stood straighter, waiting.

Tobler stared at her trying to see what she might be playing at. She didn't seem malicious, but he felt sadness and deep-seated regret. He looked to her hands to see her fidget with a tarnished silver band, a widow.

"I love her." It felt good to say the words. "I love her more than I love myself. I can't bear to have anything happen to her. I'm just trying to protect her, so please, if you can help me, I'd—"

Fiona held up a hand. "Thas enough, dear. Don't spoil it now with false pleas. Follow me this way, watch yer feet."

She made her way toward the dark room, picking up a lantern from a desk to light the way. A sliver of light shined through, cutting a sharp wedge into the darkness. They moved past tables with strange jars of things he didn't want to know about, into a corner of bookcases brimming with scrolls of parchment in the nooks and crannies. She studied them.

"Nah. No. Nope. Uh ah. Wait, wait, ah!" She reached up a wrinkled pale hand, trying to grab a tattered roll of parchment. "Well, don't just stand there. Help an old lady out."

Tobler reached up quickly as if scolded by his mother, trying not to snicker at her feistiness.

Setting her lantern on a shelf, she unrolled it, nodding as she read the page. "Yes, this is it. Now listen, boy, this is some pretty powerful magic. You'll need a room where you can conjure it alone, but it's what yer lookin' fer alright." She handed him the parchment. "Oh! And this." Fiona removed a slender black box and handed it to him.

He unrolled the scroll with care as Fiona had, scrutinizing the ingredients and trying to remember the bottles on the shelf at home. He then shifted the lid on the box, examining the contents. "Seems simple enough, but what is it?"

"It's an old piece of long-forgotten magic. Considered to be the blackest magic in 1503—horse shite, iffin ya ask me. That there is the recipe for an Apparatus, known also as The Orb of Last Breath. It's only good for one use, so use 'er wisely. But it comes with a heavy price," she warned with a raised finger. For the first time, he saw her eyes were the color of emeralds.

"How much?"

"No, not monetary weight. It cost the maker's body a great deal, though," she said gravely.

"I don't follow." He was starting to get frustrated with her.

"Whatever yer trying to save yer beloved from will transfer to you. Ya will absorb their harm and they will be healed immediately." Her face was still, except for her eyes. "It's the price ya pay to keep a loved one safe. How far are ya willing te go, lad?"

He studied the parchment as he thought of Gemma. "Whatever it takes." There was an assurance he'd never felt before, and it surprised his mind but not his heart.

The old woman nodded. "'Tis yers, then, take it. Use it wisely. Just remember what yer leaving her with, and be sure she's strong enough to burden yer sacrifice."

"What do you want for it? I'm sure you don't give these things away for nothing."

"You will pay enough on yer own," she said, shaking her head. "Go now, do not say where ya got it from. It's the only one in existence, I'll have ya know, so don't go losin' it. Go befer I change ma mind." She shooed him away with a frantic wave, then turned her back.

As he walked away, he felt a rushing of emotion from her crashing down on him. It was in that moment Tobler puzzled out the fate of her late husband, that she was widowed by his sacrifice; now his loss plagued her the rest of her days. He stopped at Fiona's desk before leaving and placed a gold vellum down.

Stepping out into the dirty street, he adjusted the items in his pocket—oblivious to the set of pale eyes that followed him.

CHAPTER TWENTY

BACK AT THE DOOR of The Floating Toad, Tobler heard muffled voices and paused.

No such magic exists anymore.

...so real

...nightmares...more Lougrous root.

None of it made any sense, and he quietly entered. Maggie pushed something wrapped in cloth into Orianna's hand, and she moved it to her pockets. Both were wide-eyed and circumspect at his silent appearance into the shop.

"Are you ready to go?"

"Yes, we better get going. I'll see you later, Maggie." She embraced her friend.

"You just come back if you need anything else, okay?" Maggie squeezed her tighter, opening her eyes to see Tobler staring. "Hit the street before Zavier gathers a posse to find you."

Tobler's eyes swept the shop before leaving.

"You find what you were looking for?" Orianna asked.

"I wasn't looking for anything." His face remained impassive.

"Why else would you be so willing to leave me alone? I expected more of a fight."

The scroll and box seemed to bear the weight of a sun. "Just choosing to pick my battles with you, is all."

"There you two are! We've been waiting so long." Gemma sighed.

Although she sounded happy and excited, he felt her worry and longed to have her return to the carefree girl in the bookshop. The urge to help curb her feelings was tempting.

"So much for one hour." Zavier's disapproval settled on his face.

"We turned up just fine, didn't we?" Orianna said, fumbling with her ring before wrapping her arms around his neck. "I'm sorry it took longer than I thought. I got so caught up with Maggie, and it felt good to get my mind off of things."

"Don't do it again. You had me worried."

"I'm sorry. It won't happen again."

"What else were we supposed to do?" Zavier left the question open to the group, gently removing Orianna's arms.

"It wouldn't be a bad idea to stop at Zinnia's shop to speak with her for a bit. See if she knows of anything suspicious going around town," Orianna offered.

"Demonic witches or warlocks are going to be skulking around a perfume shop?" Gemma asked, perplexed, as Tobler choked back a laugh.

"Zinnia hears a lot of gossip, and she may have heard something useful." Zavier was also holding back laughter. Orianna shot him a look of disapproval. "Don't look at me. She has your sarcastic wit."

"Come on, let's not dilly dally."

Tobler held Gemma's hand as they walked to in the street. She couldn't help noticing a few of the local woman staring, except they weren't looking at the two of them. They were ogling Tobler, some more undignified than others.

"Tobler!" A girl called from a nearby shop door, waving coyly at him.

"Hello, Gwen," he said with a smile. "How's business?"

"Well enough, I suppose. When will you by for some sweets? I made baked almond cakes today." Gwen fluttered her long lashes, carrying on as if Gemma didn't exist.

"Sorry, can't today. Another time, though," he said as Gemma jealously pulled at him.

Zavier noticed what was happening, and despite his efforts, couldn't grab Tobler's attention.

As they approached the shop, there was a new face in the window, a blonde woman watering plants. Gemma stepped inside, breathing deeply the sweet smells of earth and honey. Zinnia's shop would certainly be one of her favorite places.

"Orianna," Zinnia enveloped her in a gentle embrace. "How are you?"

"It's nice to see you, Zinnia. What's new in the shop?"

Zinnia shrugged. "This and that." The woman began chattering of small things and missed time.

"You better watch yourself, boy. You're treading on dangerous waters," Zavier whispered to Tobler.

"What did I do now?"

"You can't be flirty with town woman if you have something going with Gemma. If she's anything like her aunt, you'll find yourself in a hot spot," Zavier warned. "I like you, kid. Just trying to keep you around a while."

Zavier left it there for him to digest, joining the conversation at Orianna's side. Tobler eavesdropped.

"What brings you my way? Something for the wedding, perhaps?" Zinnia's excitement was overflowing.

"I wish that was the case, but I'm afraid I'm here on more urgent matters. May we request a private audience?" Orianna lowered her voice.

"Of course. Megan, please watch the shop for me while I attend to some business in the back," Zinnia instructed, guiding Zavier and Orianna into the backroom.

"Yes, ma'am," Megan said, smiling with white perfect teeth.

She had a dainty frame, displaying well-shaped legs with the help of a short black dress. Her face resembled a masterfully chiseled statue with sapphire eyes. Megan continued to water the plants while sneaking glances at Tobler.

"Tobler?" she called. "Could you help me water the buttercups? They're just too high for me to reach."

"Yeah, I can reach it." Tobler walked over, taking the watering can from her; he was just able to reach the plants on tiptoe.

Gemma watched Megan gawk at the muscles in his back and arms as he struggled to reach, all while twirling a piece of corn-blonde hair. Gemma took a deep breath, turning away to suppress her feelings of discontent.

"Thank you." She set the can on a nearby stand. "It's been so long since you've been by, Tobler. What's kept you?" Her mouth sunk into a full, red pout.

"Oh, I don't know. Just been busy, I guess. This and that, you know." He scratched his head.

"Always so busy," she sighed. "Well, while you've been off doing this and that, I've landed a leading role in a local play. I was wondering if I can count on seeing you out in the crowd."

"What play?" he asked, crossing his arms.

"It's an original by a promising playwright in town. I'll be playing a wealthy queen who mourns the loss of her late husband before being auctioned off for a better alliance. We're performing it tomorrow night. You can always join me in the tavern for the after party." Megan looked at him from under thick lashes.

Suddenly, Tobler was hit with a physical shock—hard enough that it knocked some of the air out of him. He drowned in a pungent mix of envy, insecurities, and jealously. He tracked the rogue wave, spotting Gemma as she browsed bottles on the shelf.

"Excuse me."

He walked over to Gemma, who pretended to not notice him. "Everything okay over here?" He inhaled easier now, the air returning to his lungs.

"Everything is fine. Why do you ask?" She took a pink bottle from the shelf.

"Well," he started, "because while I was over there talking to Megan, someone clobbered me with their emotions—rather literally knocked the damn wind out of me."

Gemma's eyes widened, and her cheeks warmed. "You felt that?"

"As if you ran over and sucker punched me."

"Sorry." She bit her lip to keep from laughing.

He felt more at ease now. "It's okay, but should I take your little show of jealousy as a yes?"

"I was not jealous," she refuted.

A look of sheer amazement came across his face. "Remember who you're talking to."

"Alright, maybe a little."

"If you say so." He smirked, waiting for her to answer his question.

"My answer is yes." She was attracted to him from the moment they met. He stole her heart on a moonlit rooftop, but her nerves kept her from moving more decisively.

Tobler was silent.

"Well? Aren't you going to say something?" she probed, wondering what was going through his head that he wasn't sharing.

"I can manage the lifestyle of a taken man." Tobler, now unabashed by his feelings, gave her his customary wink.

He walked back to where Megan waited, posing to show off her best features, assured she'd be adding him as one more notch in her belt.

"Sorry, Megan, but my lady and I won't be able to make the show. Next time, though— no hard feelings?"

Megan's face deflated, falling even further when she glanced at Gemma. "No problem. I'll let you know when another one comes around." She walked off, dragging her wounded pride, to help another customer.

By now, the shop filled with admiring customers sniffing the different scents on display. Gemma resumed her browsing, particularly interested in a few new bottles, when someone in a black robe bumped into her. The push coming on so suddenly that it almost knocked her over. She grabbed a shelf for balance near Tobler.

"Falling all over me already?" he teased.

"Shut up. I was pushed."

"You alright?" He craned his neck to get a look at the mysterious person, but they had disappeared.

"Yeah, I'm alright. Just startled me, is all."

She straightened up, noticing a small gray book wrapped with a leather string and a strange coin attached to its end. Tobler picked it up and handed it to her.

"That's not mine. I thought it was yours?" she said, taking it.

"It's not mine, but it doesn't seem like anyone is missing it. Sure you didn't buy it while you were at Page & Candle?"

"How did you know I was there?" She looked at him, confused.

"You told me about it when I met you at the checkpoint, remember?" Tobler said.

"No, I never mentioned it."

"I must have just assumed it when I saw your books, best bookstore in town. I figured Zavier would take you there. Speaking of Zavier, I wonder what's taking them so long." He looked to the backroom entrance.

"I don't know." She tried to remember their conversation at the checkpoint.

Tobler was at a loss why he couldn't detect the robed figure now. Nothing sinister piqued his attention, but he also sensed the stranger entering the shop. Any other time, this would have made him happy; during such bleak times, it disturbed him. He was relying on his power to keep them safe. If he didn't have that, how was he to help Gemma?

The tree woman emerged from the curtain of vines, solemn and still speaking in whispers. Zinnia hugged Orianna, handing her a small brown bottle capped with an eye dropper.

"Here, this helps me when I need to unwind. It's just some essential oils from my home, but sometimes the simplest things are the strongest." Zinnia stood proud, more like a ruler than a shopkeeper.

"Thank you. We will keep in touch."

"Visit again soon. I always have time for you. But now, I must tend to business. Take care, my friends." Zinnia began tending to her many plants.

"Are you finished?" Zavier looked for a clock. "What time is it, anyway?"

"There is a sundial outside. Zinnia doesn't use clocks, remember? Said it puts too much pressure on the plants to grow," Orianna said as she ushered them outside, passing a pouty Megan. "What's her problem?" she asked Gemma.

"I have no idea," Gemma said as Tobler bit his tongue.

Zavier stood in front of the sundial and moved from side to side of it, still in deep contemplation.

"Well?" Orianna stood next to him, staring at it as well.

"Um, well..."

"You don't know how to read it, do you?"

"Not very well, no," he admitted.

"It's a little before one o'clock. We have some time for a quick lunch," Orianna stated. "Are you guys hungry?"

"Starving!" Tobler said.

"I could eat." Zavier shrugged. "What were you craving? Ole Sam's Pub has a pretty good fry going today."

"Fry it is. Come on, kids!"

The tavern wasn't terribly far from the perfumery, but there were plenty of wandering eyes as they walked. Folk turned to whisper as they eyed Gemma, heightening her paranoia.

Gemma's blood ran cold, causing Tobler to be at attention, as they saw Quinn walk by; he appeared carefree but vicious. He made sure to give Gemma a wolfish grin, and Tobler felt her stomach churn. But quickly as he appeared, he was gone again.

"One day soon, I'll make sure he doesn't look at you like that again," Tobler said, just loud enough for her to hear.

She held onto him a little tighter. Faint music played in the distance before she saw the sign for Ole Sam's Pub. Outside the door, she inhaled the dense aroma of beef stew and beer, causing her stomach to grumble.

Inside, it was everything one imagined in an Irish pub, adorned with the craftsmanship of old, hand-carved wood, a fireplace roaring in the corner, and a polished mahogany bar. People were strewn about, eating and drinking, with faces full of rounded laughter as a woman played a rib-tickling song about an old drunkard and his tight-faced wife. A redheaded man with a full beard greeted them.

"Aye, Zavier!" He set down the pint he was drying. "How ya been? See you brought the clan in with ya. Hello ladies, anything I can start ya off with?"

"I'll take a pint of your best ale, oh and a plate of your fish fry," Orianna smiled.

"Alright then, how's bout you Zavier? A pint of the usual?"

"That'll do just fine, Dolan, thank you. Fry as well."

"How about you darlin'? Don't think I've seen a sweet face like you 'round these parts before. Passing through, are ya?" Dolan spotted her interlocked with Tobler's. "Aaah, see you've caught our young Tobler's attention. You let me know if he gives you any trouble. I'll give him a good thumpin' for ya."

Gemma blushed as Tobler feigned outrage. "Seven damns, Dolan! Is that what my customer loyalty gets me?"

Dolan chuckled, "Usual for you, too, I presume? With stew? What about you dear?"

"I'll have whatever he's having." Gemma shrugged.

"Comin' right up. I'll have Diana bring em o'er to yer tables." Dolan disappeared to the backroom. They took a table in the corner near the fireplace.

"So where do we stand with alliances?" Gemma spoke up, tired of being the last one to get input.

"Zinnia agreed to keep an eye out for suspicious gossip and swore to help however she can. Doesn't take much to convince a Nature Walker to join a good cause. But book hermits," he snorted, "they take some warming up to ideas that aren't their own."

"Weldon? I thought you guys were old buddies?" Orianna asked.

"Oh, we are. But over the years, he's drawn more and more into the comforts of his stuffy bookstore. Claiming it was all conspiracy theory and practical jokes, even tried to suggest money lenders coming after Tobler." Zavier gave him a look.

"Hey, I don't owe anyone any coin right now. I can't promise for the future, but I'm squared up," Tobler said in his defense.

"Hmm." Zavier grunted. "Bottom line with Weldon is he's willing to believe anything that will allow him to ignore the shit on the wall. However, he'll keep an ear to the ground and order anything we may need. How far did you guys get at Maggie's?"

Orianna hesitated, buying some time as Dianna showed up at their table. The busty bar maid carried their drinks, two per delicate hand, setting them down with a speed that didn't allow even a soft thud.

"Here you go." She smelt of food and ale, tucking a strand of blue hair behind her ear and exposing her slender neck. "Anything else I could get you all? Your food should be out soon."

"We're okay for now, thanks," Orianna answered as the men sipped their beers.

"Very well. Be back soon." Dianna scampered off to server the other customers.

"So, you were saying?" Zavier pushed, gazing at the group.

"She agrees to help us fight however she can, of course. Endless tab for any ingredients and she offered to make whatever we need." She sipped quickly, leaving foam upon her upper lip.

"That's it?" Zavier looked to both of them dubiously. "It was that simple?" This time he directed his question to Tobler, who felt weighed down by Zavier's eyes.

"Those two are thicker than flies on fresh shit. Would not take much convincing one as long as the other was part." Tobler shrugged, his stomach turning.

He sensed Zavier's growing apprehension, but before he could rectify it, something crashed through the front door. One guy tumbled onto the floor as the other one behind him could hardly contain his laughter.

"Come on, you tit monger. Up you go," said the one standing—loud-mouthed and rowdy—as he pulled the guy on the floor up by his coat and ear.

"Ugh! Piss off, Dutch, ya damn near ripped my ear off!" Having already had a few, the clumsy one dusted himself off.

Dolan cleared his throat loudly, looking like a father about to spank his kids. They straightened right up and attempted to be proper gentlemen.

"Sir," they both said.

"Don't you 'sir' me! The two of you come stumbling in here looking like a couple of bulldogs that chewed a wasp's nest, causin' a ruckus, making spectacles of yer selves. Why, I have a right mind throw you back on yer arses."

The pair swayed, looking down at their feet. "Aw come on, Dolan. We didn't mean nothin' bad. Just being a couple of fellas, is all," the clumsy one said, rubbing his red ear.

"Yeah, we'll keep it down. Fella's honor." Dutch held his hand up in all seriousness.

Dolan took a deep breath. "Fine, but break anything, and I'll take it out of yer arse." The two scurried away before he could change his mind, already bickering. "Eejits." Dolan went back about his business.

Tobler saw them coming toward them as he turned his back to the bar room. He was mid-sip of his ale as someone grabbed him by the shoulders, spilling it down the front of him.

"Tobler! Where ya been hiding yourself? Up under Molly Pickins' skirts?" Dutch managed as the two roared out in laughter.

Tobler was mortified. "Very funny, you two." He wiped his chin with the back of his hand. "I haven't seen hide nor hair of Molly Pickins for the better part of six months or so. There's nothing going on there," he whispered the last part to Gemma.

Dutch caught sight of Gemma, his face turning into a toothy grin. "Well then, looks like you found a prettier lass to keep time with." He gave them a wink. "I wanna hear more about this."

"Yeah, Tobler. Shit, where'd you find her hiding?" They began pulling up some chairs, stopping when they caught Zavier's eyes.

"Oh, sorry sir. Didn't see you there," Dutch said, then bumped the other one's arm. "Say you're sorry, dick."

"That's not my name! Very sorry to have disturbed you sir," Angus said, now holding his breath.

"Cause I'm such a little guy," Zavier huffed.

"May we join you for lunch?" Dutch asked, sounding every bit the polite young man.

"No, you may not." Orianna said, poking her head out from behind Zavier. Dutch and Angus tripped over their feet standing up. "Nothing personal, boys, just trying to have a quiet get together. You understand, don't you?" She gave them a smile that was neither friendly nor unfriendly.

"No problem, Ms. Oliver, we completely understand," Dutch said, putting the chair back.

"Y-yeah we didn't mean anything—didn't mean to disrupt your lunch," Angus stuttered.

"We actually better get going, or we'll be late to that thing we had to take care of for your mother, Angus. Nice meeting and seeing you all again." Dutch bid them well as they fell through the door.

"Boisterous bunch you run with, Tobler. Can't say I approve, but you seem to be doing better than they are." Orianna sipped her beer.

"Why were they so afraid of you?" Gemma asked.

"Oh?" Zavier said, "You don't think it had anything to do with that *talk* you had with them last year? She caught them all passed out drunk in our stables one morning. Place was a mess when she found them. She went out there and flipped their worlds upside down, made sure they didn't forget it—also left some mysterious char marks on the floor." He turned his attention to his fiancée. "You never did tell me what you did to them?"

Orianna was smug, "And I never will."

Dianna came out with their food, passing out each plate to the wrong person. "There we go. Here's some bread and butter. Anything else you'd like me to grab you?"

"No, that should be all. Thank you, Dianna," Zavier said. They waited for her to leave and switched their plates to the correct orders.

"Sweet girl but can't remember anything worth a damn. Think Dolan keeps her because she's a little fae around the edges. He likes that sort of thing," Orianna said.

"Fae? What do you mean?" Gemma asked, blowing on her stew.

"Fae around the edges, meaning she has fairy blood in her. Didn't you notice?"

"I wouldn't know where to look. Didn't know they were real."

"They're different than The Echo's perception of them. They're just like you and me, but they have a special look to them. When she comes back, you might notice her ears have a slight point and her cheekbones a little higher. Plus, her skin is creamy white and flawless," Orianna said in between bites.

Gemma looked back at Dianna, seeing her ears. "I wouldn't have ever noticed."

"That's because she's only part fae. The pure-blooded fae look similar to Dianna, but their eyes change color—sometimes glow. Mischievous, at times, but great business partners. They've a real knack for making deals. You could say that's their affinity."

"Staring here makes people edgy," Tobler whispered to Gemma. "You don't have to be so hard on yourself. You're new to this world, it's understandable you'd be curious. No need to feel embarrassed."

"It just feels like every time I turn around there is something new, like your friends." She stirred her stew.

Tobler took a breath. "Yeah, I wouldn't exactly call them friends anymore—more like acquaintances. I used to drink a lot to push out all the unwanted baggage from my affinity, but after a stern conversation with Orianna, I promised to control myself. I'm getting too old for that shit. The thought of rinsing out my tankard has crossed my mind—time to settle a bit."

"You sure you're ready to stop chasing those skirts and the woman in them? Molly Pickins will be crushed," she half teased him.

"Molly Pickins will be fine. Wouldn't be that hard to give up—especially their skirts." He smiled at her, then stopped. "Why, are you still unsure?"

"I'm not unsure..." She desperately tried to change her emotions, which proved to be harder the more she concentrated on it.

"There's just something about you I can't shake off, no matter how hard I try to ignore it. Whatever I'm thinking about, it always comes back to you somehow." His whispering became gentler, and she could almost feel his words touching her.

"Why is that?"

"There's just something about you. All these people here? I've felt what they're made of—every wanton, sad, excited emotion. But they can't grab my attention the way you do."

She felt a surge of power, but she wasn't sure if it was him or the beer that was making her fuzzy. All she knew was she had an overwhelming desire to kiss him.

"I've had a lot of adventures these days." Gemma paused, not needing empathic powers to understand how that statement struck him. "But I could squeeze one more in for you."

"Are you teasing me?" He brightened from his worried frown. "I'll remember that."

She gave him a flirty wink, reveling in newfound courage. He made her feel like the only person in the room, the way he looked at her, as if nothing else mattered.

There was the sound of someone clearing their throat; Zavier and Orianna stared at them with disapproval. Gemma wanted to crawl under the floorboards when she realized how close they were—in public, at that. She moved away to a more respectable distance.

"How is your lunch?" Orianna asked dryly, giving Tobler a sideways glare.

"Really good, thanks. How's yours?" Gemma glugged a big swallow of beer as her knee bounced under the table. Tobler placed his hand on one, and she began to relax.

"It's good. Dolan has a knack for cooking."

A chorus of men's voices and instruments broke out without warning as the crowd joined in. Gemma turned to watch them gather in a half circle: guitar, drummer, and spoons all coming together in an incredible melody. She was transfixed as the crowd began to clap in beat. Someone grabbed a woman and gave her a twirl around the dance floor. He had one of the best voices she'd ever heard.

"Dolan has a knack for talented musicians, too. He always has a good show, 'specially later on in the night—now there's a sight. You remember those days don't you, Orianna?" He tapped a large hand on her knee.

Her eyes cast downward. "I believe we had a drink here a once or twice."

"Once or twice? You should have seen her back in those days. All prettied up, dancing the night away with no shoes, lips painted redder than roses." He looked at her lovingly, lost in the memory as Orianna blushed. "All she'd need was a few drinks to get dancing. Gave me blisters, and I almost couldn't keep poor Dolan off her for a time there. I tell ya, the men I had to beat away from you kept me on my toes."

Gemma gasped, "Aunt Orianna! You? Out late dancing all night!"

"And drinking?" Tobler mocked.

"Oh, hush. It was only a little dance and perhaps two drinks!" Orianna tried to hide a grin.

Zavier scoffed, "Oh no, not you...except when she'd get up on the bar after going shot for shot with Dolan and Hiemz. You had a real wild streak in you, only way I could get you to loosen up—but I never imagined you'd let that loose." A deep guffaw rumbled from his belly.

"Tisk, tisk! Orianna, the almighty responsible one, having a good time. You savage!" Tobler laughed until tears rolled down his face.

"I *was* responsible. I had Zavier there to look out for me, always have."

A heavy weight pulled her back, guilt from her dishonesty...but no, she had things under control. After all, dreams were only dreams and nobody dreamwalked anymore. That was an old barbaric magic, long forgotten. Maggie had said so, herself, back in the shop and she'd never steer her wrong.

"Alright then, enough of that. We should be going soon." Zavier kissed her. "I'll settle up the tab and meet you all outside."

Zavier left to pay for their meal as they took their last bites. Tobler's eyes widened when he saw who walked in wearing a green cloak and an easy smile.

"Orianna, perhaps we should stay here a bit. Tell me more about those wilder days." Tobler tried to distract her.

"Why would we do that?"

She turned before Tobler could stop her from seeing Jane standing next to Zavier. Flirting with him, her big eyes flitting as she chatted, the final straw crashing down when she laid a small hand on his arm. Orianna's eyes flashed and her face reddened.

"Now, now, Orianna let's not be too hasty, I—" Tobler tried to reason with her, but before he could say much, she was already halfway to the bar. He let out a sigh.

"What's going on? Why is she so upset?" Gemma asked.

"Jane Coffers walked in. They've had a blood feud going for years now."

"Oh! She's the lady from the Dainty Pincushion, unpleasant woman. Over Uncle Zavier?"

The two became agitated, then calmed as Orianna linked an arm with Zavier. But the argument flared again, and Orianna stiffened her posture.

"Yup. That's it, we better hurry. She's getting pissed, and I don't want to spend the rest of my week in here cleaning up the charred rubble," Tobler said, making his way swiftly to the bar with Gemma in tow.

"I have a new line of men's shirts that'll look perfect on you. I can help," Jane said to Zavier.

"I don't think we're in the market to be shopping with you anytime soon, Jane." Orianna's smile became a snarl.

"Goodness, pretty sure he already has a mother. He needs a woman, not a caretaker." Jane looked him up and down, sending Orianna spiraling into a hot rage.

"Ready to go?" Tobler put a hand on Orianna's back, and she started to relax herself. He looked to Zavier, who gave him a quick nod of approval. "Come on, ladies, no loitering."

Tobler calmed them both down. Once relaxed, Jane continued on her way through the pub, and Orianna surrendered quietly while waiting for Zavier. Tobler kept her calm until Zavier came through the doors, releasing her from his mental grip.

"You bastard! Where do you get off making me a puppet? I have a mind to blister you—" Orianna lit a fireball.

"Orianna, enough!" Zavier scolded her, and she put it out reluctantly. "I gave him permission to calm you down before you turned Dolan's pub into a blood bath. Why you let her get under your skin like that is beyond me."

"Well, if it was one of my old boyfriends trying to flip my skirt while you weren't looking, you'd create your own blood bath," Orianna spat back.

"She's got the hots for Uncle Zavier?" Gemma said.

"She used to burn a candle for me, if that's what you mean," Zavier clarified, not hip on Gemma's lingo. "But that was a long time ago. We had a run-in once, years ago. Neither of them was

very sober, then it escalated from there. Now, I'm a battlefield."
He shrugged.

"Oh, I get it now. I can't say I blame you, Aunt Orianna," Gemma said plainly.

"What?" Tobler looked at her in disbelief.

"Yeah, she would have deserved it. I would have done the same thing."

Orianna took Gemma by the arm and walked down the road with her, "You were always my favorite."

"Psh! I'm the only niece you've got."

They giggled as Zavier and Tobler stared at them in surprise, watching them go. "Oh, you're in for one hell of a ride." Zavier patted Tobler on the back, and they followed after them.

They passed the apothecary on their way back to the stables. The lights were out behind a "closed" sign during viable work hours. Might've been suspicious, but Finn sometimes had blackout days. Days he would shut down to gather more ingredients for his medicines and remedies, a sign business was thriving—or so it would have seemed.

A pair of pale eyes peeked from the window as they walked by.

CHAPTER TWENTY-ONE

AT THE STABLES, THE old man argued with Zavier, demanding he should be paid extra because one of the horses kicked his new hired hand. The old man was red-faced, wagging a finger in Zavier's direction. Gemma thought him to be daft for picking a fight with him.

Zavier towered over the old man, not getting angry until he insulted his horse. His booming voice raised, but the rest of them remained quiet as the argument raged on.

"Why isn't Aunt Orianna saying anything?" Gemma whispered to Tobler.

"Zavier never gets this angry. Orianna might be thickheaded, but she knows to just let him run himself down," he whispered.

"I heard that," Orianna said, glaring.

"Goblidet merchants don't believe in 'the customer is always right'?" Gemma asked, confused by the display.

"Ophelia's Heart, no! That's a terrible way to run a business. Sometimes the customer is just a grimy shit. You can't please everyone," Orianna answered.

They watched until Zavier had enough of the old man's outlandish argument and reached into his coin bag, handing over a silver vellum. The old man snatched it up and walked off, cursing under his breath. Zavier rejoined them, flushed as if he were still boiling just under the surface.

"Vindictive little gnome," he muttered, reattaching his coin bag.

"I know, dear, but at least you didn't lose your temper." Orianna ran a hand over his arm, and he nodded in frustration.

"Yeah, you could have pounded him into the ground with one shot. What happened?"

"Violence is not always the answer, Tobler. I could have knocked him around like a petulant child, but I'm more civilized."

"Pleasure doing business with ya." The old man handed Zavier the reins and returned his barn.

Zavier muttered more profanities, some so heinous that Orianna swatted him for it as the other two laughed. Zavier and Tobler loaded their purchases and were on their way.

Tobler sat next to Gemma, boldly putting his arm around her shoulder; she leaned her head on him in reciprocation. Tobler kissed the top of her head, reflecting on what Fiona had said. *Is it the kismet?* He patted his pocket, remembering the sacrifice, and looked down at Gemma. Love. What else could it be?

When they were just on the outskirts of their home, the carriage hit a bump, jostling Gemma awake.

"Good morning. Nice of you to join the living." Tobler rubbed her shoulder.

"We're back already?" She yawned, giving a small stretch.

"Might be 'already' for you, but the rest of us had to put up with Zavier's off-tune humming," he snickered.

"You're no troubadour, either," Zavier teased. They pulled into the drive, stopping at the barn.

"Come, Gemma, there aren't too many bags. We can handle it. I have some new techniques we should practice." Orianna began grabbing bag after bag.

"What new techniques?"

"We're going to see if we can hone your strength, learn a few spells and charms, the usual stuff. Let's not burn up too much time out there."

Orianna was already halfway to the house as Gemma hurried after her. Orianna slowed her pace when crossing the perimeter charms, as if worried they would be watching. Gemma found the behavior rather peculiar, even for Orianna and her paranoia, but kept it to herself. They set the bags on the table, and Gemma started to empty hers out.

"No, don't worry about that right now." Orianna gestured, then took one bag in particular. "We're just going to jump right into lessons. Those can wait but you can put your things upstairs, if you want."

"Okay, I'll be right back." Gemma grabbed her few parcels, heading to her room.

Gemma put the sack onto her bed but not before looking at the mysterious book. She turned it over, admiring the gray color. The cover's title was composed of strange runes, and the inner pages were a dull parchment yellow with tattered edges. It had seen better times with its battered cover and weathered spots on the edges, but it was not in horrible shape. Some of the ripped parts had been repaired and the spine replaced with new strings. She examined the coin hanging from the leather strips that held it shut, marked with more runes she could not decipher.

Unwrapping the leather strip, she gave the coin one last look over before placing in her pocket. She opened the book, but the first page was blank. She flipped through the pages, but those too were blank. She frowned, thumbing a page too quick and slicing the pad of her finger; blood welled and dripped onto the page.

Before she could wipe it away with the skirt of her dress, the blood absorbed and disappeared. Within seconds, the book began to vibrate with life. Dust floated from the pages, which now appeared to be full of words from cover to cover. When the book finished revealing all of its contents, it lay still again.

You need a blood sacrifice. I guess that's not too strange considering where I've found myself, Gemma told herself, unnerved as she turned the pages to a diagram of the coin.

"Gemma? What's taking so long?" Orianna yelled from the kitchen.

She quickly rewrapped the leather strap around the book, assuming the safeguard was of some importance. Looking back at the cover, she saw the runes had changed to English. Orianna yelled for her before she could investigate. She shoved it under the mattress and hurried down the hall, the gray book taking up considerable space in the forefront of her mind.

Downstairs, Orianna was pushing the couch toward the window. The entire center of the living room had been cleared, creating a wide-open practice ground.

"Let's get started."

Orianna walked to the kitchen counter where a thick book lay on the table. Gemma recognized it as the one from the potions room, watching as Orianna flipped through. She winced at the cut on her finger that still stung, rubbing it with her thumb.

"Defensive magic." Orianna trailed a finger down the page, nodding as she skimmed. "Yes, this will work perfectly. Alright, there are a few things I want to teach you. First, I want to work on your affinity skills. We need to make them stronger." She walked back over to the cleared space, beckoning Gemma to follow her.

"We'll start with some light dueling and work from there. You need to know how to shield and deflect, like this." Orianna turned her body slightly, raising her arm with a closed fist, then twisting it to an open palm and pushing away.

"It's that simple?" Gemma asked.

"You have to be in the correct mindset, summoning all of your will and power. Now, hurl something at me—go on. That bookshelf over there will do fine." Orianna pointed to the shelf behind her.

Gemma stared at the tall shelf, thick as a young tree's trunk and heavier than a lost soul. "Are you sure you don't want me to try something a little lighter?"

"No, it's perfect! Don't worry, you won't hurt me. Come on, give it your best hurl!" Orianna stood with her hands at her sides, poised and ready.

Gemma concentrated, clearing her mind. She gave the shelf a toss, but it stopped just short of Orianna.

"You can do better than that. Pick it back up and try again—with feeling this time." Orianna resumed her position.

Gemma tried again, harder. The shelf skidded across the room, stopping in midair. Orianna sighed, running a hand through her hair.

"I guess this will be harder than I pictured it." She paced a small section of the floor, contemplating how to make Gemma more motivated. "Try thinking of something that makes you angry. What's something that really gets under your skin?"

"I don't know."

"There must have been something in your life that's ticked you off. Think harder—none of us are happy all of the time."

"Well, I mean, I don't get angry all that much." Gemma shrugged, trying to dig deeper for an angry moment.

"I can think of at least three things today that chapped my ass. Can't imagine what it'd be like otherwise."

Tobler and Zavier came through the door. Gemma thought of the long-legged blonde from Zinnia's shop. She felt something hot churn inside her stomach, recognizing it for the exact thing she had been digging deep for.

"Okay, I've got something. Are you ready?"

Orianna nodded. Gemma centered herself, hurling harder than before. Orianna deflected the shelf towards the stairs, a bang ringing out at the sudden move. Tobler dodged the heavy projectile, hair ruffled by the air as it zoomed by.

"Shit, I guess I'll stay down here a while," Tobler said, putting his hands in his pockets.

"That was very good, Gemma!" Orianna chimed, pleased with the result. She turned to see what had changed her niece's mind. "Ah, you. Well, I guess if I were dating you, your face would make me angry too."

"What?" He looked at Gemma, confused.

"No, I'm not mad at him," Gemma explained, focusing on her aunt.

"Really?" Orianna folded her arms. "Then why did you change when he came into the room? What about him made you angry?"

"Oh, I know what came into your mind." Tobler perked up.

Gemma blushed through hot annoyance. "I'm not sure what you're talking about."

"You don't? You weren't thinking about how Megan got you all flustered?" Tobler raised an eyebrow.

"I wasn't flustered." She crossed her arms. "She just made me a *little* jealous, is all—but only a little."

Tobler snorted. "Hate to see you what you're like full-on jealous. Damn near knocked a lung out of me." Before he could see it, a smaller book from the shelf fell and hit him. "Hey!"

"You didn't shield and deflect." Orianna sniffed. "See, this is why we learn to keep on our toes and protect ourselves so we don't find ourselves ambushed."

"In your own house, even," Tobler grumbled, rubbing the side of his head.

"You never know when, or where, your enemy will strike," Zavier said, then whispered. "Especially when you're prone to putting your foot in your mouth—dammit, boy. You're better off running through the woods with raw mutton strapped to your leg than bringing that up again."

"I was only teasing," Tobler whispered back.

Zavier just shook his head at Tobler's ignorance. Plopping himself down and resting his feet on the table, he took out his pipe and lit up.

"I know you don't have your filthy feet on my table," Orianna huffed.

Zavier promptly took his feet down. "No, of course not, darling."

The stairs creaked as Tobler tried to make a run for it to the work room—better to do it now while everyone was well occupied. But the steps were old, willing to betray anyone who tried to skulk away.

"Where is it you're going?" Orianna accused.

"I was going upstairs to take a nap for a bit."

"You don't have a room, remember? Gemma is sleeping in there, which means you're not," Orianna said.

"But she's not in there."

"That's irrelevant. We should all take this time to brush up on our defense. Get back down here and take a seat." She gestured to the table, and Zavier nodded his head in agreement.

Tobler walked back down the stairs, sending Orianna a cross look. He seated himself heavily onto the wooden chair. He missed the days when he could fiddle with different magics without being under the prying eyes of a certain opinionated witch. It was easier to focus when someone else's emotions weren't clogging your energy fields. He needed to be alone so he could begin his project with the orb. Tobler already felt bad about sneaking around, but everyone being so close made it worse.

The men watched as the woman volleyed between attack and defense. It hadn't taken Gemma very long to get a firm grip on her shield, but learning to deflect objects in a more controlled manner was proving to be a challenge. Many times, Zavier and Tobler found themselves ducking or even mending a few windows. When Orianna suggested moving on to deflecting real weapons, both men grew forthright and suggested that they hold off.

"Let's work on duress, then," Orianna said plainly.

"What do you mean by duress?"

"I mean, how well you handle your powers under pressure—like when you couldn't conjure your fire because you were scared."

"Oh, that."

"How do you propose to do that?" Zavier asked. "Going to invite a demon or Eye into the house?"

"No, no, she's not quite ready for that. I'm going to just conjure up a little something semi-dangerous for you to destroy." Orianna thought for a moment, then rolled up her sleeves. With a flick of both wrists, two snakes shot from her palms onto the floor—exact replicas of the cobras. Gemma's eyes widened as terror flooded her body.

"You can't be serious." Tobler jumped up from his chair.

"Sit back down, and don't interfere," Orianna said.

"Best do as she says, boy." Zavier nodded, watching close to reassure him.

Tobler sat down, knowing it to be unnecessary. Orianna turned her attention back to Gemma.

"Burn them up. Do it fast before they roam about the house," Orianna instructed.

Gemma felt cold and scared, which made centering herself almost impossible. They slithered toward her, hissing. A drop of venom fell onto the wooden floor, causing the wood to instantly rot and leave behind a hole. Trying to take deep breaths that wouldn't come, Gemma held out her hands but only produced flickering flames.

There needed to be more motivation. Orianna debated internally, deciding a change of pace was in order. She whistled and the snakes turned to face her, awaiting commands. She flicked a finger in Tobler's direction, causing the snakes to focus on their new target. They slithered quickly, making way to attack his legs and feet. Tobler cursed and hollered for Orianna to stop.

"If you won't save yourself, maybe you'll save him! Tick tock, Gemma, come on!" Orianna shouted, growing more frustrated.

Gemma was appalled. "No! Turn them back to me. Stop this!"

Tobler stood on his chair, trying to get away from them. Fangs, at the ready, dripped with toxic venom; he dodged enough for the one to miss him, but the other snapped in warning.

"Save him, Gemma! Focus your power!"

Infuriated by Orianna's belligerence, Gemma sensed the heat of her buried temper surfacing in her palms. She focused all her energy on the slithering creatures, sending two streams of fire at the snakes before one pierced Tobler's leg. The floor scorched where they fell.

"Ophelia's Tits, Orianna! The hell do you call that shit?" Tobler hollered.

"Motivation. Very good, Gemma! Well done."

"That was bullshit! How could you do that? You could have killed him!" Gemma looked at her aunt in horror.

"Nonsense, we all knew you wouldn't let that happen."

"I didn't!" Tobler said.

"You were fine, sit back down," Orianna commanded, and Tobler did as she said.

"Love is a great motivator, but that doesn't mean you should prey on it, Orianna," Zavier criticized, looking up from his pipe as he took a deep toke.

"I did nothing of the sort. I gave her the nudge." She turned back to Gemma, resting her hands on the girl's arms.

"I agree with Uncle Zavier. No life-or-death situations."

"But how else are you going to learn to use your powers under pressure?"

"Gemma can figure out on her own to summon her powers. No need to push the issue. Don't you agree, Zavier?" Tobler suggested.

"Orianna, the boy has a point, Gemma now knows what it's like to work through fear and recreate that when needed. We shouldn't be putting Tobler in danger, anyway. Who's going to help me outside if something happens to him?" Zavier teased.

"Yeah, you have to keep me alive or poor old Zavier here will die of exhaustion," Tobler said, reclining in his chair.

"Who the hell are you calling old?" Zavier's brow knitted, insulted.

"Fine, no more dangerous situations." Orianna wagged her finger at Gemma. "Just remember to focus and not lose yourself to fear. Let's hope there won't be a next time."

A growl sounded from the kitchen table.

"You two are hungry already?" Orianna said.

"Already? It's been hours since we ate at the pub. Look," Tobler pointed to the window, "it's almost dark out."

"Yeah, old woman, where's our dinner?" Zavier winked at Orianna.

"On the bottom of your shoes if you call me that again," Orianna warned.

Gemma let out a yawn, "Would you mind if I sit this one out?"

"I don't mind, dear. Go relax on the couch a bit."

The men had already put the living room back in order, avoiding the burned floorboards. Tobler stacked wood in the hearth.

"Would you mind?" he asked. With a flick Gemma brought the hearth roaring to life, causing Tobler to stumble back a bit.

"You should lower the heat a bit, dear," Zavier said, smiling.

"Oh, sorry."

"Much better, thank you."

Zavier rested his head on the back of the couch with the ease of a lounging cat. Tobler took a seat on the opposite couch next to Gemma, putting an arm around her shoulder as he settled in. She rested against him, watching the fire flicker and lick at the wood and stones. It felt good to take a break, to find peace and relaxation. Her eyes grew heavier. Soon, the sounds of Orianna's chopping and the crackling flames lulled her to sleep.

She dreamed of strange things happening as she walked the streets of Goblidet, pulled back by the vibrations of Tobler's voice. He was whispering, and she remembered they were in the living room when she must have nodded off.

"I'm just saying be careful," Zavier replied softly. "These women will tear you to pieces if you're not."

"I know." Tobler stroked the top of Gemma's head, her eyes closed in what he thought was peaceful slumber. "You don't have to worry. I won't do anything to hurt her, and I've learned about the jealousy issues the hard way."

"Is it serious?" Zavier asked.

"Us? We just started to be an us, but I can't deny strange things have happened. There's an emotional charge when we're together that I haven't seen before," Tobler said, trailing off.

"Do you love her?" Zavier asked.

The point-blank question took Tobler off-guard. He understood Zavier's concern, with Gemma being his niece-to-be, but there seemed to something deeper than sheer curiosity. Tobler searched within himself for an answer.

"I do."

"Does she know?"

"No, I haven't told her. There hasn't been a time—*somebody* keeps barging in."

"You can't blame her much. She just wants what's best for her, even though she can go over the top." Zavier puffed his pipe again, before asking a softer question. "Is it kismet, Tobler?"

"I'm not sure, not having felt it for myself...but it could be. In this short time, I already know I can't live without her. It pulls at me in ways I can't put into words." For a moment, Tobler considered telling Zavier about his visit to The Emporium but thought better of it.

"Tobler, it sounds like kismet. I know from my own run-in with it. I don't think there is much you need to worry about. Just keep doing what you've been doing but smarter."

"Pretty sure my life will depend on it. She'll burn me to bacon, otherwise."

"Right you are on that," Zavier agreed. "Much like her aunt but more powerful."

"More powerful?" Tobler asked.

"Dinner is ready," Orianna announced from the kitchen.

Zavier stood up from the couch. "Best keep that one between us for now, huh?"

"Agreed—all of it, if you don't mind." Tobler gestured toward the kitchen.

"Yes, but you should tell her soon."

Tobler nodded back and brought his face closer to Gemma's. "Hey," he gently shook shoulder, "wake up. Time to eat."

Gemma slowly opened her eyes, releasing a faint groan. "What time is it?"

"Time to eat, come on." He squeezed her shoulder. "You were snoring like an old bear."

She rubbed her eyes before sitting up. "I was not."

"You were worse than Zavier," he laughed. "I pity your future husband for all of his sleepless nights."

"Oh, shut up."

Gemma took his hand, following him to the dinner table as she rolled around their words in her head. Tobler loved her, but she didn't understand what kismet was supposed to mean. From the way they talked, it was hard to decipher if it was a good or bad thing, but it didn't sound like the type of thing to ask about over a family dinner.

CHAPTER TWENTY-TWO

DOWN A DARK, TWISTING alley, shrunken heads with tight smiles swayed in the window of Pinsworth. Dry ears opened as a feminine voice chanted. Living potions trembled on the shelves at Cat's Tails, scandalized by the words spoken aloud. The black creatures of The Emporium huddled before her intentions. Beyond the dingy cobbles lined by dim green-fire torches, she concocted her spell behind a bend of crumbling barrels beneath a flicker of red flame.

Behind a weathered door guarded by powerful glyphs, a pair of pale eyes gazed into darkness, invoking her will over a silver bowl filled with disturbing contents. Raising the bowl above her head, the contents stirred as the candle blazed high, settling when she brought the bowl down onto the altar. She looked into the mirror above the altar, dipping a finger into the bowl and drawing symbols on the glass surface. She spoke again in a lost tongue until the mess inside the bowl began to smoke, oily tendrils curling against the mirror. The smoke conjured an ominous face from the other side.

"Why have you woken me?" commanded the face in the mirror.

"I have information about the fire witch and the young woman she now has with her."

The face in the mirror split into three. "We're listening."

CHAPTER TWENTY-THREE

ZINNIA PLUCKED A STRAY flower off a nearby plant; it lay in her palm, shrunken and dull, until it regained its color and reeled back to life from her touch. With a sweet smile, she tucked the flower's stem back into the dirt until she felt it reroot itself. Satisfied, she walked to the back of her shop and raised her hand, signaling her owl. He flew down and perched on her finger, yawning as it settled in comfort.

"Aw, my sweet dear, have you had a tiring day?" She brought him closer, and he nuzzled her cheek. "Perhaps it's time we both recharge on our home soil. Things this far from Westwood Forest are too exhausting. We'll take our leave, as it has been too long."

Scops made a small, purrlike noise in response, disapproving.

"Yes, we have to work in the morning, but folk can wait a little. You underestimate them, our loyal customers." With her words, a slender vine twisted on the sign's hours and changed the time of opening.

Zinnia walked through a curtain of leafy vines into her backroom, similar to a greenhouse. Each exotic plant had its own clay pot or plot of dirt, growing with a flourish, vast and strong. The floor was made of up wild grasses, cut short at the brick wall where a tree branch jutted out. Zinnia caressed the bare limb with her finger, admiring her work as fresh, green leaves sprouted from each tiny branch. The leaves spread from the tree to touch the wall, shaking as they formed a circle. From the leaves, green-gold light swirled into existence, expanding until in engulfed the entire wall.

Zinnia stepped across the threshold into a sunny forest of trees and soft grass. The aroma of the countless flowers occupied the air, and she breathed them all in deeply. Her owl pet fidgeted on her finger in anticipation; she stretched her hand, encouraging him to take flight.

"Go on, enjoy it my darling." At her words, the young bird took off in merriment; he flew high, making small loops then zipping through the trees.

A path of her own manifested, meandering through the forest until she reached a shimmering pool basking in the golden twilight. She kneeled, picking up a floating leaf and dipping it before taking a drink. Quenched of her thirst, she dug into the supple dirt, her whole-body recharging from the rich nutrients. The starchiness of Goblidet fell from her skin as she rooted in the ground, a tree being replanted. Her eyes flared emerald green as the charge of magic coursed through her, the pure touch of nature seeping into her essence.

While in her trance, she didn't see the peculiar vine creeping closer, shooting up from the ground and wrapping tight around her wrists, feet, and legs. She toppled to the side, her connection to the earth breaking as she wriggled against the thick restraints. Her vision clouded, and her mind became disoriented after being violently uprooted.

"I'm sorry," said a gruff male voice. "Did I interrupt you?"

Through her foggy eyes, Zinnia couldn't see more than a shadowy figure walking toward her. She slurred, almost drunkenly, her head spinning from the effort.

The shadow figure circled her, a predator examining its prey. "I've heard so much about you, Nature Walker, but you're more than that aren't you? Lady of the Forest, such an honor."

He came into focus as the fog dissipated from her mind. "How do you know me? Who are you?"

"That's privileged information you have not yet earned. I have been sent to you to make a special offer. I have a master with certain interests in your domain. He would like your cooperation." His voice was both sharp yet velvety. He snapped a branch from a tree.

"Cooperation in what? No one controls the Westwood Forest. It has caretakers not owners." She was regaining some of her speech.

"That's exactly what he needs, ownership. That, and your affinity for nature to help build a kingdom of sorts." He whipped the branch around, resting it beneath her chin. "How about it, sapling? When the world is upturned, don't you want to be on the winning side?"

Zinnia shook her head in protest. "I don't know who you're working with, but I will never betray my homeland!"

"Foolish bark lover. Leo does not take kindly to rejection."

She could almost see him. A tall man with dark hair, almost as dark as his complexion. His eyes were brown and bloodshot, and his breath could've felled an ox. The sight of him brought the taste of fear to her mouth.

"You lie! Leo was banished into exile long ago for his treachery. He rots in the pit cells. It is impossible!" Zinnia felt sick, struggling to break free but the vines squeezed harder.

"Such things do not keep away the lawless." He threw his head back in a deep chuckle. "You're all so funny with your High Authority. They have not been useful for many years. They're tax collectors with delusions of power." The stranger moved closer, speaking in a hushed whisper. "He is stronger now, and soon, all will know his power. He will reign supreme, and this place will know him down to the last blade of grass—with or without you."

Her soul quivered at the thought of Leo coming back as ruler of the realm, even more dangerous than before.

"So I ask you again, worm-wood, will you join us or not?" He reached into his coat pocket, clutching something she could not see.

Her face set into a fierce storm. "I will never join you and sacrifice the sanctity of my forest. I'm true to my vow."

His lips twisted, seemingly just as satisfied by her refusal. "Then I must honor mine. Goodbye, Lady of the Forest." He opened up his hand, blowing the dusty contents into Zinnia's face.

It crawled through her airways, leaving trails of fire and ice. She gasped for breath, coughing and fighting against the spores, giving up when something black poured from her mouth. Dark splotches appeared on the bark along her face and body, a rot sinking in.

"What have you done to me?" she asked as more black splattered from her mouth.

"Like it? My special concoction of black spores, fire insects, and molds. You'll rot from the inside out. I can't wait to watch my work." He smiled as her face became grayer, the black ooze seeping down her lips. "By the looks of it, you don't have much longer. I must have gotten a potent batch from—well, you're not privileged to that information."

Zinnia opened her mouth again, trying to speak, but the rot in her throat suffocated her voice along with the never-ending river of sludge. Her body grew brittle and weaker with each passing second; finally, she succumbed, falling back onto the ground. The black ooze trickled from her ears as the light was snuffed from her eyes. The grayness took over, but not before he vanished in a cloud of black smoke.

CHAPTER TWENTY-FOUR

TOBLER TOOK OUT A soundproof charm and hung it on the doorknob. Nothing would wake them now—not from that room, anyway. He set the instructions on the worktable and hurried to begin his project.

He retrieved three black, corked bottles from his pocket, placing them gently on the table along with a piece of broken glass from Gemma's mirror and a slim blow pipe. With a hand on the rim of the cauldron, he shrank it down to a more manageable size and lit the fire beneath. Giving the fire time to get hot enough, he carefully read the parchment again to ensure he understood the process fully. He'd only have one chance.

He picked up the first black bottle and opened it—Oil of a Dead Man—and watched as it dripped onto the glass, its foul fumes wafting into his face. Then he grabbed the second bottle, smaller than the others, Black Sea Water. Once it touched the glass, it hissed wildly as it squirmed. He was thankful for the silencer charm. When the sizzling subsided, he opened the last bottle with extra care—Lizard Venom. Its viscous ink dripped slowly and smoked when it made contact with the mixture, reminding him of the cobras.

It all melted into a lump of goo, but it was only almost complete; there was still one ingredient left. He took the knife from the wall and cut the tip of his finger. He let three drops fall onto the molten concoction.

Tobler took the blow pipe from the table, a relic covered in ancient etchings. He brought the tip of the blow stick to the hot glass and watched as it fused together, emitting a golden glow. He set the orb into the burning hearth. The flame turned black, screeching in pain. When the screech diminished, he pulled the orb from the fire and blew through the other end of the pipe—long, deep breaths as the parchment had instructed.

After he finished, he held a flawless glass orb, tinged with red and gray. He cut a small circle off the top. The job was almost done. There was no turning back now, he had to follow through.

Tobler quickly cleaned up Orianna's workshop, putting everything back where he'd found it. He crossed the hall and opened the door, peering inside; she was sound asleep. He needed one last ingredient for the orb to be effective—Gemma's breath.

Her face was bathed in beams of moonlight coming through the window. His breath stilled as he inched closer. She made a distraught moan in her sleep; something in her dream was disturbing her. He eased her fear, kneeling beside the bed before focusing on the task at hand.

Tobler took the orb and placed it close to her mouth and nose, nearly grazing her skin. She released three long breaths into the orb before he swiftly closed the lid, sealing it with a ring of light. He watched her breath swirl inside the glass container; artful work but it was dangerous—an intrepid secret he could not impart to a single soul.

Tobler made his way back downstairs, slipping the orb into a black velvet bag. The orb had to be kept out of sunlight until it was broken, releasing the person's breath and essences.

The hard part was over, and now his life ticked on borrowed seconds. He'd save her life, no matter the cost.

CHAPTER TWENTY-FIVE

"You're late." Griselda said.

"It was a long journey getting here."

Griselda snorted, moving aside so the woman might enter. "His mood is sour. For your sake, you'd better have good news."

She took graceful strides down the hall as the tired woman attempted to keep up. They passed some seedy witches and wizards, staring with eyes that held their own agendas. Their faces appeared almost inhuman, boasting monstrous features that didn't belong on this side of the ground. Others lacked the demonic luster of their fellow counterparts but reeked with a mix of rotten flesh and sulfur—the stench of evil.

Turning down another corridor, they came to a heavy wooden door. Griselda pushed it open to reveal Leo, seated beside a lit fireplace. The room resembled a study with packed bookcases and stacks of papers strewn about. The fire barely singed the room's dampness despite its fierce crackles. Leo swirled amber liquid in a glass as he gazed into the flames.

"She's here," Griselda announced. "What do you—"

"Leave us."

Griselda arched like an offended cat. "As you wish." She glared at Leo, then at the woman in the scarlet robe, before slamming the door with a thunderous crack.

"So, what do you have for me?"

"Well—"

"Keep it short. Don't bore me. I've a lot to do." Leo shot back before she could start.

The woman swallowed. "It worked. You successfully infiltrated her mind."

"Does she suspect anything?"

"She suspects, but her uncertainty keeps her at bay. She doesn't have a way of guarding against it, either."

"And what of the girl's powers?" He remained facing the fireplace.

"Her magic is very potent—possibly the most powerful of the bloodline—but she has much to learn still. There is no doubt the girl would make a good addition to your ranks. You could do much with her."

Leo nodded, swirling his drink again as if bored by her presence. "Any way of sneaking into the house or luring Gemma out?"

"No, the house is locked tight—except from dreamwalking. As far as Gemma is concerned, I can't find a way to pull her out from under Orianna's thumb. She never leaves her alone. They have her paired with family everywhere she goes." She began to sweat beneath her hood.

"Such a shame." He finished his drink.

"Sir?"

"I had such high hopes for you." Leo threw the glass into the fire. "What use are you to me if you can't give me what I need?" He raised his hands and black smoke poured from his palms.

"I *can!* I can get you what you need. I'm the only one who can get close enough to get information to you." She quivered beneath her robe.

"And what makes you different from other in my ranks?" he demanded as the smoke coiled around the woman's feet.

"They trust me! Ahhh!" One of the smoke coils touched her foot, burning and digging into her flesh. "How many of your legion are in my position?"

Leo paused, pulling the black coils back into his palms. He took a few steps closer. "I'm not big on second chances." They stood, nose to nose, and he gripped her throat. She choked, unable to breathe. "But perhaps you aren't useless to me just yet. There may be something I can squeeze out of you. Leave now, before I change my mind."

Leo released her, returning to his contemplation by the fire. The woman darted for the door as Griselda reentered.

"Where are you going?" Griselda said.

"Let her go, Griselda. I presume she can find her way out by now," Leo commanded, and the woman in the robe swiftly exited.

She pushed past Griselda, bumping her shoulder as lightning flashed beyond the window. Griselda's glare, sharp as a chef's knife, followed the woman down the hall.

"You let her go?" she asked, outraged.

"Do not question me. Do you have the potion?" Leo snapped.

Griselda slammed the door, setting a black bottle down next to him.

Outside, it rained in sheets as the woman raced through the downpour.

CHAPTER TWENTY-SIX

ORIANNA STOOD AT THE mouth of a wooded grove in a flowing, white gown. She held a bouquet of white flowers bound by white ribbons. The white popped against the greenness of grove, lush with its soft grasses and ancient trees abloom with leaves. A violin sprang to life from an unseen corner.

She strolled down the grassy path to a white, wooden altar with fabric woven into the branches above. Her heart fluttered as members of their families stood and watched her. Ahead, she saw a tall man dressed in all black; from the set of his shoulders and his height, she recognized Zavier. She smiled, thinking how dapper he would look when she reached the top of the aisle.

A cool breeze rolled through the grove, rustling her hair until it blocked her view, but the breeze carried the smell of something rotting. Clearing hair from her eyes, the man at the altar turned. Blue eyes froze the blood in the veins, her knees giving into a threatening wobble. A sharp smile split the man's face, both handsome and menacing, as he looked hungrily at her...

Her groom, but not the one she wanted.

She held something wet and hot. The once-lovely white bouquet dripped thick blood down the petals and onto her hands. A gasp flew from her throat as she dropped the flowers, turning around in a grove that was now dead—the grass black and dried, trees blazing with red flames that crackled in the breeze. Charred remains laid at the base of trees, mounds of once-happy wedding guests.

She screamed as she backed away from the sight, stopping when someone from behind wrapped thick arms around her shoulders and chest. His breath warmed her neck as he squeezed.

"What's wrong, my love? Lost your taste for blood?" Leo's lips grazed her ear, sending an unpleasant shiver down her spine.

"You killed them." Her heart pounded against her chest.

"Oh no, I didn't do this." Leo moved Orianna back down the aisle. She saw a womanly figure dressed in black, matching her raven-feathered hair. She had Gemma's face, but her eyes were darker; malice dripped from her as if she were the embodiment of pure evil.

Orianna's breathing hitched. "What did you do to her? That's not Gemma, it can't be."

"But it will be. So much potential, so much power. She just needs our help to get there." He turned her towards him, placing a hand on her face. "Come back to me. Rule by my side. Together, we will own the realm. All will worship us or crumble at our feet."

"I never lusted for power. That was all you!"

"Oh, I remember something else you lusted for." There was a wolfishness in his face as he pulled her tighter against him, "You could have all of that back, every inch."

"I'd rather drop dead!" Orianna fought against him, watching his face contort into something familiar, hitting him until she was free of his grasp.

She tried to make a run for it, but Leo pinned her—face first—against a charred tree. Her breathe wheezed from her lungs after the collision. A stinging developed in her temple as he pushed *her head against the bark, cutting into her skin. His hands gripped her arms, twisting one behind her back until she cried out.*

"You will join me, or the girl dies." With an outstretched palm, Leo released one of the black smoke coils. It headed straight for Gemma, who made no move against the attack. She stood still as it curled up around her feet...until she screamed in pain.

"No! Leave her alone!" She watched helplessly as her niece was devoured by the black smoke, reduced to nothing but ash and bone. Orianna's screaming turned to weeping; she rested her forehead against the tree trunk.

"You don't have long. Make your choice or everyone dies!" he bellowed from behind her.

Orianna's eyes ripped open as she tried to catch her breath. There was an aching in her temple and a sharp twinge in her shoulder. She sat up, cringing at the soreness in her chest, panicked by the eerie reoccurrence of aches and pains. Breathing deep, she tried to tell herself that it was only a dream. She recalled Maggie saying there was nothing to worry about, that this sort of magic didn't exist anymore.

Careful not to disturb Zavier, she made her way to the standing mirror. There was just enough light from the rising sun to reveal dried blood and scratches on her temple. Fingerprints bruised the arm that Leo twisted behind her back. She pulled down her nightgown and saw deep, splotchy bruises blossoming in the center of her chest. Hot tears stung her eyes as her hands shook. She grabbed a robe, seizing the small bottle of powdered Lougrous root from the vanity drawer.

Leo's warning sounded in her ears, and the hairs on the back of her neck stood. She jumped when the kettle whistled.

Pouring the water into the mug, her body felt numb. She dumped the powered Lougrous root into the mug as it stirred itself. She breathed in the sweet scent and drank fast, its warm tingle sliding down her throat and insides. The tremors eased; palms to forehead, she stared into the tea and tried to formulate a plan.

"Orianna?" a voice whispered.

Tobler. His face held traces of her own emotions and nausea. She had a bad habit of forgetting that he often ended up tangled in her emotions.

"Orianna, what is going on? Are you crying?" Now filled with his own concerns, Tobler took a seat across from her.

"N-no, I'm not c-crying," she lied, eyes red and swollen.

"You can't lie to me. It's written all over your insides and your... Your face, what happened?" He stood, reaching to touch her temple, but she shrugged away. "Black Hells, Orianna! If you tell me what's going on, I can help."

She hung her head, staring into her mug again, out of options. The future grew bleaker as the terrible images of Gemma returned. She moved her hair over the scab on her temple.

"Orianna, please." Tobler put a hand on hers, his skin warm against the flesh on the backs of her hands. "There's more at stake here than you and me."

Orianna swallowed dryly. "I've been having some nightmares..." she started, trailing off as she her words failed.

"And?" Tobler pushed gently. "Feels like more than just nightmares."

"I think he's...dreamwalking through my mind."

Tobler's face turned grave. "Is he making contact with you? Physical contact?"

Orianna pulled up on sleeve to show the marks. "I'm afraid so. Here," she said pointing to her wounds, "and some other places I won't show the likes of you."

"Thank Ophelia for *that*, rather too intimate." Tobler rubbed his face. "What does Zavier say about this?"

"Zavier doesn't know." She placed a palm flat over its top and burned the Lougrous root away from her tea.

"You have to tell him. We can't keep this secret from him any longer."

Without any notice, Tobler found himself thrown high and hard against a wall, nose to nose with an infuriated Zavier.

"Tell me what? What have you been doing with my wife? I suspected something foul happening, but I never would have thought this from *you*!" Zavier rattled him again until Tobler's head bounced back from the wall.

"Are you crazy? I don't want that lunatic! I'm more of a long-lost relative type!" Tobler fumbled against the clenched fists, a hiss releasing from his chest as Zavier threw him a third time. "Orianna, tell him!"

"Speak, woman! As if I didn't hear enough from the stairs."

"You heard nothing, you ass!" Orianna moved to Zavier's side. "Put him down! How dare you pin me to something so scandalous. Shame on you!"

Zavier looked back at her, confused. "You're not sleeping with him?"

"No!" they said, both aghast.

Zavier allowed the air back into Tobler's chest before he turned blue but still didn't let go. "What is it he wants you to tell me?"

"I might be afflicted by a dreamwalker." She fiddled her fingers, looking almost embarrassed.

"What do you mean? By who?" Zavier turned to Tobler, jostling him.

"Not by me!" He braced himself for another impact.

Exasperated, she sighed, "No, not by *him*, Zavier. Leo has been haunting my dreams."

"When did you plan on tell me this?" He faced Tobler, anger receding to annoyance. "And *you*... You knew about this?"

"No! I detected she was upset, but I never would've guessed it would be this."

"Are we positive it's dreamwalking?" Zavier asked.

They began speaking over each other, bickering back and forth at a dizzying speed. "No—one at a time, dammit. You, shut up," he told Tobler. "You," he turned back to Orianna, "start talking."

"I asked Maggie about it yesterday. She says is an old and *dead* magic," she explained.

Zavier looked to Tobler.

"That's true, it's an old magic—ancient, even—but these are not ordinary times. Who's to say Leo didn't come back with this? They have demons, why not dead magics?" He breathed deep through his aching chest.

Darkness brought darkness, that much was true. "Boy has a point. It is possible."

"Thanks. Can I come down now?" Tobler kicked his feet, desperate for ground.

"Oh, right." Zavier dropped him to his feet. "Sorry 'bout that." He extended a hand.

"No harm done, I'm sure." He shook his hand, rubbing the back of his sore head.

Zavier's expression hardened. "I want to see them. Show me what he's done."

Orianna hesitated before moving her hair aside. He touched the side of her face gently. She winced then pulled up her sleeve to show him the purple and yellow against her otherwise flawless skin.

"Is there more?" His anger simmered that Leo had the audacity to lay hands on her.

Orianna lowered her head, parting the top of her dress to show him the bruises on her chest.

"No! Nine hells, not down here! You take your tits upstairs, or anywhere else but here." Tobler protested, head turned and hands up.

"That's enough." Zavier said, eyes steeling. "Orianna we can't ignore this. Something has to be done."

"Like what?" Orianna crossed her arms in frustration. "I already talked to Maggie. If this is dreamwalking, there isn't a way to stop it anymore."

"It *is* dreamwaking, and you know it," Tobler grumbled. "No magic is irreversible."

"Are you listening? It's too old of a magic. No one has a way to ward if off because nobody thought it could come back."

"What does he want with you, anyway?" Tobler asked.

"I can only imagine," Zavier snorted.

Orianna shot him a nervous look. Tobler gauged her emotions and became confused. It left his stomach unsettled.

"He wants me in his ranks. Whatever it is he's planning, he needs my powers."

"That's not happening." Zavier shot back.

"That's not all..." Orianna paused. "He wants Gemma."

"He can't have her," Tobler growled.

"Clearly!" Orianna snapped.

"I swear, Orianna, I'll—" He stepped closer to her.

"You'll what? And pick your words carefully or I'll rip your tongue out, charbroil it, and feed it back to you. How dare you insinuate I'd give her up?"

Neither backed down until Zavier placed a hand between them. "That's enough." They glared but backed down as the anger faded. "There's a lot of tempers flying but no solutions. That's not going to do us any good."

Tobler had a good idea who could help them, but not without raising suspicions.

Orianna broke the silence. "I could ward off sleep for a while until we find a solution. I think there is a spell upstairs for that."

"You can't never sleep again, you'll go mad." Zavier rubbed his face. "What if you only sleep in short spurts? We can watch in shifts to make sure you're okay."

"Sounds simple enough, could work." Tobler said hopeful.

"That won't work. All he'd have to do is fatally wound me once, then waking me won't do any good." Orianna sighed at the ignorance. "Coffee?" With a flick, she commanded the grinds, water, and pot to work together.

"What if we got a second opinion?" Tobler spoke up, watching as they gave him the exact reaction he suspected.

"What do you mean?" Zavier asked, curious, while Orianna bristled with offense.

"Maggie is a good resource, but what if we asked an older witch. One just as powerful, and in the same line of work, to get their perspective. She might have a way to fix it."

"Like who?" Zavier asked.

"Okay, I need you both to be open-minded and—"

"No, I don't like this already. The answer is no." Orianna sat up, the very picture of concentrated stubbornness.

Zavier exhaled, trying to hold his words back. "Orianna, let him speak."

He hurried, cutting to the meat of his idea. "There's an old woman by the name of Fiona who owns The Emporium down Ophelia Black—"

"Absolutely not!"

Zavier rubbed his forehead. "And you're saying this Fiona can help us?"

"Word is, she has magic of all kinds in her shop. I'd bet gold she would have something that could help us with this."

"I doubt it. If Maggie doesn't have it, then I doubt anyone would."

They ignored her ridiculous claim, as the facts did not stack in her favor. Maggie was a good friend, and it felt like a betrayal to look elsewhere for advice; but with such a serious matter, consulting an older witch wasn't a bad idea. Someone older could have been around when dreamwalking was in full use, making it easier to remember the proper warding.

Zavier stroked his dark beard. "You're talking about Black Magic. I don't know if I like it, Tobler."

"What other options do we have? All of the old magics are considered 'Black' now. They may not actually be all that bad," he said, thick with angst. Zavier remained impassive, but Tobler could sense his emotions wavering emotions and added, "We need an equally potent magic if we stand a chance in keeping *any* of us safe."

Tobler was half tempted to give their minds a gentle nudge when he suddenly felt Orianna's mind shifting, but it was Zavier who caved first.

"It's worth looking into since our prime source is out of ideas." He sounded a little defeated, unable to find moral high ground.

Orianna leaned in. "How do you know about this Fiona?"

Tobler sighed, "I just told you, word of mouth." He was becoming increasingly frustrated with her, but he felt another change; something had slipped through the cracks of her best mental armor. "Why don't you tell us a little more about your connection to Leo? What secrets are you keeping?"

Orianna began to sink like a stone. "I'm not keeping any secrets."

Zavier leaned over to Tobler and whispered, "Don't."

Tobler wasn't backing down. He searched deeper as she attempted to stop him. "You had sentiments for him? Black Hands, Orianna, no wonder he pushed through like a nib through paper!" He could not hold back his outrage, shocked by the weight of that hidden emotional baggage. He pulled away from her. "You...you loved him!"

"Loved who?" Gemma said from the stair landing. "What's he talking about, Aunt Orianna?"

Zavier gave Tobler a glare. "Jackass."

"You knew." The words fell from Tobler in a whisper.

Orianna cradled her head with her hands; when she looked up, her face was milk pale. She hoped to never have to tell the whole story, to never have to air out the past which their tragedies were built upon. Outrunning one's past wasn't a real-life expectation.

Gemma walked to the table, and sat across from her aunt. "I'm done being left in the dark. Tell me what's going on."

"Orianna, I don't want to open old wounds, but it's time. There isn't getting around it anymore." He gave Tobler a stern look, disappointed at his inability to let matters go.

Orianna wiped away a tear but couldn't stop them from watering further as she looked at Gemma. She deserved the truth.

"You have to understand, it was a very long time ago. I was younger and stupid. Love can make you do foolish things." She squeezed Zavier's hand, still resting on her shoulder. "That's what I thought it was, anyway, when Leo and I were together. I travelled down a dangerous path then."

"You were in love with the man who killed my parents?" Gemma did nothing to conceal her shock.

"It was a long time ago, I—"

Gemma attempted to jump in again, but Zavier interjected. "Gemma, let your aunt finish her side of the story."

"We were together since our teenage years, but Leo changed. He became obsessed with Black Magic. There was a small group of friends we shared, and we all practiced together. But it was different then."

"*You* practiced Black Magic?" Tobler asked.

"Yes," she snapped back at him, "but Leo turned into a stranger. I wanted no further part of any of it—not him or our friends." She sipped her coffee, hands clasping the cup for warmth, and paused her speech.

"You tried to leave," Gemma prompted.

Orianna nodded. "Of course I did. I broke things off with Leo, refusing to see all those 'friends' we made and the magic we shared. But he wouldn't let me go so easily. He sent gifts to beg for my forgiveness. He visited the house many times, despite my rejection, but he never offered to leave the darkness behind. It consumed him. I believe he started talking to it and was convinced that power was the answer to everything."

Zavier carried on for her. "He kidnapped Orianna, tried to bring her back to their side. When she refused, he tried to kill her. He would have if it wasn't for your grandfather. He beat Leo back long enough for her to escape, but he was cut by a poisoned dagger. Your aunt lost everyone that day."

Orianna said, "The High Authority wouldn't have done anything if he had left my father, a leader in The Guard, alive. After he and his friends tried to burn down the town and killed your mother and father, they took an interest. It was considered as an act of treason since their goal was to take the realm for themselves. When they seized Leo, the law sentenced him to be banished for eternity to the High Authority Pit Cells. They compensated me for what they thought was a suitable price for my family's lives. That's what they do here, use coin to counterweigh the value of your lost loved ones."

"What about your mother?" Tobler blurted.

"Gemma's grandmother vanished after they refused to banish me with him. To her, I was the bad omen that brought it all upon them in the first place. I haven't heard from her since. She left without a trace." The memory left a bad taste in her mouth.

The pain of it all caused Tobler to wince as it seeped outward like a busted blood vessel. He backed down.

Tears pricked behind Gemma's eyes. "How could you? You lied to me."

"I'm sorry." Her words threatened to choke her. "Gemma...I never meant for anything to happen to your mother and father."

"I don't want your apologies. It won't bring them back." Gemma snapped like a wounded stray.

Tobler put a hand on Gemma's knee. "She is sorry. You need to give her some slack here—"

"Why should I? Whose side are you on, anyway?" Gemma moved her knee.

"I understand you're angry, but she really is sorry for all of this. Trust me, I've been around, and she has always blamed herself for your parent's deaths. You have a right to be angry.

She should have told you the whole story, but she's not the enemy here."

Gemma huffed, still angry, but knowing he spoke the truth. "So I'm just supposed to forgive her? Just like that?"

"No, I wouldn't expect you to so quickly. But you need to at least acknowledge she wasn't at fault. You wouldn't be here if it wasn't for her." Tobler nudged.

When Gemma looked back up, she noticed the lines of sadness creasing Orianna's face and diluting her spirit. Gemma reached across the table, taking one of her aunt's hands.

"It's okay, I forgive you. I'm sorry for what I said." With that, both started to tear up and Gemma noticed the marks on Orianna's arm. "What happened to you?"

"I've become the target of a dreamwalking."

"Dreamwalking?" Gemma ran her fingers over the marks.

"It's when someone maliciously enters your mind through dreams, unauthorized, and interacts with you," Zavier said.

"They hurt you in dreams, and it passes into real life?"

"Yes." Orianna said. "Leo ripped a path into my dreams and attacked me. I just thought I was having nightmares, but this is much worse."

"How bad can he hurt you?"

"Bad enough." Orianna tone spelled her fate.

"No, that can't happen. There has to be something we can do—anything at all." Panic slipped into her voice.

"Tobler thinks we should try talking to a lady down Ophelia Black Street, and Orianna is resistant," Zavier explained.

Gemma turned to him. "Down the place you warned me about? You've been there before?" Now it was his turn to face her scrutiny.

"I've wandered, in my time. But this was through word of mouth. There's this woman who owns a shop called The

Emporium, and she could be helpful. The place is a trove of magics that many of us wouldn't have thought of."

"And you think she can help?"

"What do we have to lose? If she can't help us, she'll know of someone who can." Tobler rationalized. "But Her Stubborn Highness won't go because it's Black Magic."

"Please, Aunt O, I don't want to lose you."

"You won't lose me."

"I want to be sure."

"It's not just her he's after, dear. It's you, too," Zavier said.

"Why me?"

"Because he wants your power to add to his army," Tobler said.

"That makes me more directly involved, and I say we should go."

Orianna looked into Gemma's face, the determined expression changing her mind. "Okay, we'll give this woman a try, but I don't want to make this a habit." She wagged a finger at Gemma and Tobler. "I still don't condone dabbling, and it's still not allowed under this roof—got it?"

"Yes, of course." Gemma agreed, elbowing Tobler who was too silent for her liking.

"Yes." Tobler cleared his throat, though it was his conscience that needed the real clearing.

"Go on and wear something dark and indistinguishable, the less flesh the better!"

The pair ran upstairs as Orianna hung her head in her hands; it was far too heavy with sorrow for her neck to hold.

"It will be alright." Zavier reassured, as much for himself as for her.

CHAPTER TWENTY-SEVEN

THE ALLEY THRIVED IN the morning light with magic folk popping in and out of every doorway. The group of visitors blended in, unseen in their black cloaks. Gemma was surprised by the diversity of those living in this part of town, each appearing stranger than the next—wild-eyed and afflicted. She took Tobler's hand so as not to get lost in the busting throng. It made her more stable while surrounded by their darkness.

He was equally thankful for her hand, steadying himself amongst the putrid atmosphere. "You're okay. They won't hurt you," he reassured her. "They aren't the most moral bunch, but they're more afraid of you than you are of them."

"How much further? I don't like being down here so long." Orianna pulled the hood of her cloak closer to her face.

"Why? Worried someone might recognize you?" Tobler shot back. He was growing woozy as his patience ran thin.

"It's possible." Orianna's examined the crowded space, missing the pale set of eyes that found them some paces ago.

Tobler pulled open the large glass door. Fiona moved about the shop, customer-hopping in a way that seemed to suit her unorthodox self. Fiona sniffled as she went, stopping at a taller customer and taking a deep whiff. Tobler grinned in amusement.

"Is she...sniffing them?" Zavier asked.

"Yup, she is."

Zavier gave him a weary glance, concerned anew by Tobler's judgment.

"I said she was good, not sane. You can't always have both, and we should probable try to mingle." His suggestion met with silent dissatisfaction as they split up. Tobler took the chance to speak with the old witch. "Fiona, nice to see you again."

"Well, look what the rats scrounged up. Were ya not jus' here the other day? Ya come to return the orb?" Fiona inquired.

"No, no, I—"

"'Tis fine, boy." Fiona clapped him hard on the shoulder. "No cowardice in returning it—smart of ya, really—but all sales are final, mind."

"No, I'm not here to return it. I made the orb." He rubbed at his shoulder. "I'm here with some people, family kind of people. They're looking for a rare magic, but it needs to be kept a secret. Also, please don't mention my coming here the other day."

Fiona put a finger to her lips, eyes gleaming in excitement. "Hmm, a secret within a secret. Ya got yerself a deal. Now wait 'til these folks are gone, and we'll talk about this further."

"We need more privacy than that. Could you close the shop temporarily?"

"Hmm...I s'pose I could, but it'll cost you extra." She held out a wrinkled hand.

Tobler opened his coin purse, groaning at the sight of how low it had become. "How much?"

"Silver vellum'll do for today," Fiona said.

Tobler dropped a silver piece into her hand. She held it close to one eye, examining its color, then bit it before putting it into her pocket. "Methinks you and I shall become pretty good acquaintances."

"I don't think my pockets could handle that."

She gave him a wink before plodding along, helping another by customer showing them the door. Tobler was beginning to like the crazy old bat.

Customers gone, she tapped the sign and changed the words to "Go Away." She rubbed her hands together, taking a deep and excited breath.

"Now then, what can I do ya for?"

Zavier stepped forward, "We have a challenging matter of utmost importance. It must be kept in secrecy."

Fiona waved him off. "Ya, speak plainly already." She gave him a sniff, wagging her eyebrows. "Ye have a soldier's heart. Get on wit' it, handsome."

Zavier cleared his throat, taken back by her remark.

Orianna spoke up, displeased. "I'm being attacked by an old magic no one thought existed."

"Pah! No such thing as not existin'—either it be, or it ain't be." Fiona crossed her arms as she circled Orianna, sniffing about her left shoulder.

"Hmm, got a bit of darkness in yerself. Interesting, but yer not so bad...just a bit dimmed. I know the smell of ya, but ma finger can't seem to touch it." Fiona eyeballed her fiercely. "How're ya being attacked?"

"Dreamwalking."

Fiona stood by Orianna, grabbed her shoulders, bringing her close to her beady eyes. "Say it again." This time her face scrunched, deeply perplexed, as her lips thinned.

"Dreamwalking. You heard me the first time, old woman." Fiona let her go, turning around to pace while scratching her chin. "Not so simple now, is it?"

Fiona whipped around with daggered eyes. "Quick of tongue but slow of wit. Don't give me your snippy tits, sweety. I has things for such a problems as this, but 'tis risky fer business. Must be certain yer worth it."

"We will make it worth your while, Madame. We can pay." Zavier reached into his coin purse.

"No, no. It ain't gold n' silver I'm concerned wit'—although, I ain't saying no. Dreamwalking remedies are dangerous as the actual act itself. Dealin' with blood magic can be fatal if ya ain't experienced. Simple dangers abound, also—might lose a limb, skin ya nose, liver shrinkage." She eyed Orianna as she spoke. Pondering. Trying to gauge her strength. "I see yer more than willin' to do such things so long as yer the one to die. Noble, but it's still ill-advised."

Orianna became uncomfortable. "Enough of your gimmicks. Get on with it, woman."

"Prissy witch," Fiona snorted, brushing at a moving speck on her dress. "Well then, ya follow me. Need to do some diggin' about, but they're somewhere."

Fiona brought out a lamp, guiding them into the back of the shop—a dark space that seemed to swallow the faint lamp light. Stopping in front of a box, Fiona took out four candles, then craned her head toward Gemma.

"Girl? Come here. What's yer name?" Fiona asked, giving Gemma the same scrutiny she'd given the others.

"Ash—"

"No, no, that ain't yer born name."

"Her name isn't important!" Orianna huffed like a puffed-up turkey.

"Who pissed in her gruel? I ain't no secrets peddler. What's yer born name?"

"Gemma."

She sniffed. "Yes, you smells like a Gemma." She sniffed more in Gemma's direction, then stopped. "Come closer, child. There's something peculiar about you."

Gemma hesitated, her stance stiff with caution.

"Come now, I don't bite—witch's honor."

Gemma moved forward. Fiona circled her, sniffing about like she did with the others. She jumped when Fiona's head poked out almost on top of her right shoulder then her left, sniffing all the while.

"An Oliver witch. Funny ya come back to these parts." Fiona whispered, loud enough for only the two of them to hear.

"I'm sorry. I don't understand what you mean." Gemma was unsure why she was playing along with the old woman's antics.

"Ya will, but you must look into yer family's history to understand. There were once Black Bloodlines in the hearts of the Oliver's. I tell ya this as a friend." Her tone wavered between urgency and gentleness as she placed a finger to her lips.

Gemma nodded halfheartedly. Fiona held a candle out to her, expectant. "Well?"

"Well, what?"

"Light it up," Fiona demanded.

Gemma concentrated, staring hard at the candlestick.

"Any day now, sweet-cheeks. I ain't gettin' younger."

Gemma's temper flared, inspiring her to try harder.

"Damn girl, are ya a witch or ain't ya? Pretty sure I grew another gray," Fiona instigated further.

The heat rose from Gemma's chest, increasing to unnatural temperatures which weren't unpleasant. The candle burst into flame, accompanied by fire from the box. Fiona jumped back, flustered by the blaze. She pushed her candle into Gemma's free hand before swooping a hand, floating them about the room.

"Ya better heed what I told ya. Look at the Black lines and Oliver bloods." Fiona warned just loud enough before addressing the rest of them. "This way."

They continued to walk further into the dark, on their toes after the fiery display. Tobler admired the size of the back room, which was bigger than it appeared at first.

Fiona halted, causing Gemma to run into her. "Pay attention."

She took Gemma's candle and touched it to a peculiarly dark part of the wall. Bright white flames rolled upwards and out, making a perfect square from floor to ceiling. With the crackling came strange shrieks of pain before it reduced to dead embers. An open doorway gaped, leading to a set of crumbled stone stairs. It was a different kind of dark, inky spots that seemed to shimmer and crawl. Tobler reached out, sensing their vibrations, before having his hand smacked away.

"No touchin'. I ain't liable for them bitin' a finger off. Can never tell what mood they're in."

Tobler stared back in mixed confusion. "What are they?"

"None of yer business. Don't touch or get out." Fiona pointed to the exit.

"Alright." He walked back the group.

Fiona led them down the stairs, past damp walls until the air grew thick and humid further inside. Orianna gasped and spat curses as a step gave way beneath her foot, crumbling and tumbling to the lower steps.

"Shh! Black Damns ya, wench! Have you no mind? Quit yer yellin', or you'll spoil somethin'!"

"Wench?" Orianna's eyes went wild at the insult. "I nearly fell to my death. Fix your damn stairs! How could sound possibly ruin anything?"

Fiona whirled around, shining lamplight into Orianna's face. "There are ancient magics down here that've been steeping in power before you were a tinge in the womb. Too much noise can drain their power. They're very, very delicate." An exasperated sigh left her before they continued down.

Zavier gave Orianna a tight-lipped warning glance.

The chamber resembled an old dungeon. On each side of the hallway sat a series of sunken rooms; the doors were barred and stone carvings were imbedded above, one-word descriptions of what forgotten magics laid within. In the chamber's center sat jars filled with parts the group would rather not have examined too closely, old wooden and metal trunks, strange books with locks, and unlit candles of various sizes and colors.

Fiona stopped in front of a particularly rusted-over gate. She peered through the keyhole then held her ear to it, nodded, and whispered something inaudible through the keyhole. The gears turned, creaking open with a rusty groan.

"Just need to know how ta talk to 'em, is all." Fiona waved Gemma inside with her, pointing at a row of purple candles. "Oh-kay, girl. Light them up but wait a moment. Yer strong, but ya need refinin' before ya blow yerself up—or worse, me. All ya need is what's in here." Fiona put a finger to Gemma's heart, eyes twinkling. "It all comes from here. When yer open to what's in here, then yer powers will merge."

"How?"

"Ya clear yer mind to do magic? Do the same with the heart. Mull it over, and ya'll feel it." Fiona patted Gemma's arm. "Go on now, and easy goes it."

Gemma turned to look back at Orianna.

"No, no," Fiona turned her face back to her, "this ain't somethin' anyone else can help with. It's just a bit o' confidence yer needin'. Let me explain: yer mind is strong, powers be strong, but it needs the heart to be complete."

A fog was pulled from Gemma's vision, allowing her to see through to the logic of it all, but it slid back a little further as if to draw her in.

"Deep cleansin'...close yer eyes. I find that can help." Fiona stepped outside the room, waving the others to do the same. "Give 'er some room. We ain't sardines, now."

She searched inside herself for an opening that felt right, wrestling with her mind and heart. Time ticked, encouraging Gemma to center herself beyond its distracting beat. A quick tingle flashed across her skin.

"Fiona, it's not working."

A cackle rippled gently toward her. "Open yer eyes, silly girl."

She opened her eyes, blinking against the light. All of the candles in the room lit in a lovely soft flame, no stray fires.

"I did it," she whispered as a hand touched her shoulder.

"That ya did, Gemma. Good job, I'm proud of ya." Fiona beamed.

Orianna stood in shock, amazed at the ease with which Gemma controlled her magic.

"So much for crazy old bat that can't possibly know anything." Tobler jabbed.

A small fireball grew in Orianna's hand.

"Ey! None of that shite here!" Fiona spat. They would have been nose-to-nose if it wasn't for her slight stature. "Ya listen here, Oliver witch, I won't be havin' ya blow up my magics here. We may be in the dark side of town, but we do have some values we live by. One being we respect our elder witches. Ya hear?"

She nodded in apology, realizing the old witch had merit. "I'm sorry."

"'Tis fine, but don't try me again." She waddled off into the dungeon room.

Zavier and Tobler stood back, staring at Orianna, both with faces dying to split into grins.

"Shut up."

The room was lined with many drawers, some mash-up between old library filing systems and bedroom dressers, which covered two walls. Thick, dusty books were suspended in midair, some with locks thick as human thumbs and other wrapped in heavy black chains. Gemma jumped back at a jar that looked to have human fingers inside it, coated in some strange gray liquid.

"Are those," Gemma swallowed, "*real* fingers?"

"Where? Oh yes, pickled witch's fingers. Not easy to come by nowadays."

Gemma curled her own fingers, wincing at the thought of ever losing any of them.

"Oh, not to worry, dear—removed postmortem. Good for givin' yer potions a nice boost—and the fertility nuts swear by em. But we won't be getting' into those details." She continued to rummage along before unlocking a trunk, opening it, and releasing a plume of dust.

"Would you like a hand?" Zavier offered.

"Nah dearie, it should be right about...here!" Fiona whipped out a thick book, opening to its middle, and releasing a silvery moth that trailed dust; she sneezed directly into the pages. Tobler winced, wondering how long it had actually been since Fiona had to use social etiquettes. She flipped wildly before stopping and dragging a long finger down a few more pages, skimming its contents at a dizzying speed.

Orianna huffed. "Well, do you—"

"Okay, alright." Fiona sighed with a force that made her bones creak. "Ya have a few options. First, and easiest, is killing the one affected to void all power of the dreamwalker."

"Absolutely not!" Zavier said.

"Worth a try." Fiona shrugged, turning back to the book. "Secondly, he can be stopped and rendered powerless with a simple potion. It will require three drops of the walker's blood, a piece of flesh from the afflicted, a witch's finger—see, told ya so—and five drops of poison toad oil."

"It'll be impossible to get his blood," Tobler croaked.

"Not to mention, I'm not about to flay off pieces of my skin." Orianna pointed out.

"May as well. You'd have to cram it down his throat, bottle and all." She looked back down at the book. "Another option here is to cut the ties by cutting the walker. This requires one other than the afflicted to walk in the same dream and wound the dreamwalker with a knife of dragonbone. Dragonbone severs the connection between the dreamwalker and the afflicted. He could attach to another still, but not the one who wields the knife."

"How does one become a dreamwalker?" Gemma was the first to speak.

"Well, I'd have to brew up a potion to grant the power. Takes a few hours, and a bit of blood."

"Blood magic?" Orianna said.

Fiona shrugged. "Better than what ya came in with."

Zavier moved closer to Orianna. "It's not a bad option. Better than the first two. I'll be the one to do it."

"Not that simple, handsome. Says here it has to be blood-of-blood to save the afflicted. I don't peg ya two for brother an' sister." Fiona looked over to Gemma.

"Me?" Gemma said, her throat a desert.

"No, absolutely not." Orianna's face fell as a knot turned over in her stomach.

"There must be another way," Tobler interjected.

"Ya still have the first choice." Fiona flipped another page.

"We're not killing her." Zavier scratched the back of his neck, weighing the options while studying Gemma. "No, it's too dangerous a task."

Fiona looked about as their voices rumbled into murmured conversations, all but Gemma. She could see it all burning just above the surface.

"Why not ask the girl what she wants to do?" Fiona spoke up.

"What?" Orianna asked.

"Shouldn't I have a say in this?" Gemma asked.

"Haven't you been listening? It's much too dangerous," Orianna insisted.

"But it's our only real option, and I can speak for myself."

"Don't be so stupid. He'd kill you. It's my job to protect you." Orianna raised her voice.

"Shhh!" Fiona hissed at them.

"I'm doing this, no matter what any of you say. I'm tired of being the helpless onlooker while everything falls apart. If I'm supposed to be a powerful witch, then YOU need to treat me like one."

"She's right, you know," Zavier said.

Orianna walked up to Gemma, placing a hand on each of her shoulders. "You're sure about this? Because there is no turning back once it's started."

"I'm sure." Gemma turned to Fiona. "What do I need to do?"

Fiona nodded. "I make the potion. You wear the knife to bed tonight, then drink the potion. While she's asleep, you go from here to inside the dream. Simple enough—hard part is inside."

Gemma nodded again. Fiona loaded the men up like mules with the ingredients she needed, then led them back upstairs. They laid out every jar and plate along a wooden slab in the dark room as she stood poised in front of her iron cauldron.

"Now, give me time. It'll be ready soon, and we'll settle up," Fiona said, eying each of them.

They nodded silently and turned to leave the old woman be. Before leaving, Tobler pulled Fiona aside.

"You're supposed to be keeping her safe, not putting her directly in danger."

"The young woman must learn to defend herself. Ya cannot expect to be available at every turn of danger's crossroads." Fiona looked across the room to Gemma and back as she chewed her tongue. "There is a darkness upon her soul, Tobler, though it be dormant. It is unknown to her. Wise to be careful."

Tobler stiffened. "Shouldn't she know?"

"Knowing a thing can be worse than not knowing. Watch out for her, boy. There is more than meets the eye with this one." Fiona dropped a few fleshy pieces into the cauldron.

His brow knit together. "Are you saying she's evil?"

"No, not quite evil—not yet, anyway—but there is something there." She grabbed a pinch of dirt, tossing it with some gusto inside the brew. The mixture began to steam, spewing thick smoke from its mouth. "Go now. There is much to be done in this short time."

When he was far enough away, Tobler looked back to see pieces of the inky black things crawling from the walls and shooting toward her. He turned with a shudder when they seemed to have swallowed her whole. He followed the group, leaving Fiona to concoct whatever she may in the silence of her shop.

CHAPTER TWENTY-EIGHT

BACK OUT ON THE street Gemma, Orianna, and Zavier argued in muted tones, volleying back and forth until their voices became a frenzy.

Tobler was just about add more input when something distracted him. There was no change to the hustle and bustle of the people. He listened closer to their emotions, realizing what it was: the people of Ophelia Black Street were panicking. The panic was out of place for their kind, an emotion that crept along like slick mercury spilling across table...rejoicing. Even worse, some of the passing people were proud—a strange sense of elation they did not openly display but harbored inside their dark hearts like a triumphant secret.

"Shhh!" Orianna hushed them. "What's wrong? Tobler? What's wrong?"

He glanced over, foggy as if he couldn't remember her face from mud. "You don't feel that?" His voice felt thick in his mouth, slipping out in a dreamlike whisper.

"I don't feel it, but I see it." Orianna looked up and down the street.

Zavier grabbed a passerby's cloak. "You. What's happening here?"

The witch bore an uncanny resemblance to a rat with her pointy nose and buck teeth. "Powers are shifting! Haven't you heard?"

Zavier shook his head.

She made a strange clicking sound with her mouth. "Deep in the Westwood Forest they found her. Dead! She's dead! She's dead!" She cowered, then added, "No one attacks the Nature Walkers in their sanctuaries. Nobody ever! Powers are shifting—beware!" She broke loose of his grip and ran down the street.

The fearful words chilled Zavier. His brave face paled; for the first time, he appeared truly frightened. "No one attacks the Nature Walkers."

"What do you mean?" Gemma asked, not following.

"The Westwood Forest is a sanctuary for all magic-practicing types, a healing place. Nobody spills blood on their soils. It is strictly forbidden," Tobler replied.

"They're afraid of murder? They don't look like they care for the law." Gemma shifted her weight.

"What the immoral fear should make us all uneasy. Zinnia?" Orianna put a hand to her mouth. "You don't..."

Zavier nodded. "We should go to her and see if she can shed light on this oddity."

"You think she'll be at Phlox and Thistle?"

"I'm not sure, but we need to get in touch with her. She's the only Nature Walker we know," Zavier said, resolute.

"You guys go. We'll stay here to wait for Fiona's potion and see what we can puzzle out," Tobler said.

Orianna stilled, thick with hesitation. "This is no place for a green witch like you."

"I know the difference between right and wrong, Aunt O," Gemma slung back, face hardened as if with insult.

An icy prickle crossed Tobler's skin at Gemma's words.

Orianna set her shoulders. "Fine, but be safe. We shouldn't be long."

"Meet us back here, *inside* The Emporium," Zavier said sternly.

"Understood," Tobler agreed.

Zavier led Orianna out; she turned to gaze at them once more, then disappeared amongst the throng. Gemma stared at the crowd, a sinking sensation filling her stomach.

"We better move." Tobler took her hand.

"Where are we going?"

"I don't know, but we can't stand here. It'll draw too much attention."

He guided them down the street, going further into Ophelia Black Street. The stores melded together the more she looked at them, each painted either gray or black with generic wooden signs hung on or above the doors. Gemma noticed Tobler paled, sweat beaded his temple, and his expression teetered.

"Are you okay? You look sick."

"I'm fine, it will pass." He waved off her concerns. "What were you thinking?"

Her brow furrowed at the sudden question.

"What were you doing back there agreeing to dreamwalk? It's dangerous."

The muscles between Gemma's shoulders tightened. "What else was I supposed to do? I'm the only one who can stop it, remember?"

"We could have searched for other options. It's reckless and foolish to send *you* inside of a dream state with Leo." His voice edged on anger.

"You heard Fiona. We have no other option, unless you have some miraculous way to get his blood. What's your problem?"

He halted abruptly by the corner of a shop, whipping around to face her. His eyes were harder now, his jaw set firm. "My problem? You! You're not ready to stand against one of the strongest sorcerers ever who also wiped out your entire family!"

"I already told you I never wanted to be your burden!" It was her turn to raise her voice. "I'm well-aware what he's done, but I will not stand by and watch this monster attack her, Tobler!"

"You're not, I just don't want you to get yourself killed! I'm trying to protect you. They died for her, but that doesn't mean you have to." He reached for her hand, but she tugged away from him.

"I'm not stupid, and I'm not changing my mind. Family sticks together, not that you'd understand." The last words were sharp enough to cut, but she continued anyway. "I never asked you to protect me."

"I'm in love with you. Of course I want to protect you!" Hard lines disappeared from his face the moment he realized what he had said. Too late now to barricade that truth.

Her expression softened. "Tobler—"

"Shh!" He looked through the window of the shop he was standing in front of and saw Quinn talking to the shopkeeper. A dusty looking warlock, who appeared to be babbling, jumped as a fierce woman smacked both hands onto the counter. Her red hair swished as if a breeze had passed through, but he didn't see any of the doors or windows open. It was clear they were arguing, and the shopkeeper was losing.

"What's happening?" Gemma asked.

"Shh!" He had a finger to his lips and lowered his eyes and voice before answering her. "Something is very wrong here. There's all kinds of bad energy, and Quinn seems to be involved." Gemma moved toward the window, but he stopped her. "Stay back, these are not the sort we want to get involved with." He motioned for her to move deeper into the darkness of the nearby alley.

Gemma fled, all but disappearing into the shadows.

From behind the counter, a new man walked out from a hidden doorway. His face was the epitome of arrogance; the slicked-back hair and fancy, black attire made him look like old money. Tobler tried to make out what he was saying. He fumbled with something, flicking the object into the air with a glint of light—a gold vellum. Catching it in shaking hands, the shopkeeper pocketed the coin and escorted Quinn and the woman to the back of the shop.

Tobler was so fixated on the pair vanishing that he hasn't noticed the well-dressed man exiting until the bell on the door caught his attention. He looked down his nose at Tobler. The man's eyes were dark as extinguished lumps of coal, dead and cold, sending iciness trailing from his throat to his stomach.

"Window shopping?" The man's voice fell like a marble slab.

"Just wandering." Tobler tried to remain unnerved. He'd seen him before, recognized him as a powerful warlock but couldn't think of from where. Tobler concentrated on him, but nothing happened—not one flicker of emotion.

The man took a breath; it was then Tobler noticed a slight bulge just below the collar of the man's shirt. Tobler wouldn't have ever noticed it if it wasn't for the man's proximity.

"What is it you're doing?" The man inquired, sharpening his gaze and taking a step closer.

Tobler felt the bottom of his stomach drop out.

"I suggest you wander on and not speak of this to anyone, before you lose something of value." He looked him up and down scathingly. "On second thought, I don't see that being possible. Better run along all the same."

The man was about to take his leave of Tobler until he caught movement in his peripheral. He turned slowly, gazing toward Gemma's direction in the alley.

Desperate for a place to hide, she'd searched the alley before remembering something she'd read the night before in the gray book. If she could pull pieces of the alley shadows to and around herself, perhaps it'd be dark enough to conceal herself. She held out her hands, muttering an incantation. A shadow quivered, and she pulled back her hand but it slipped. She tried again. This time the shadow flew into her hand, laying itself along the left side of her body and covering her from head to feet. She matched the motions with her right hand, seamlessly meshing both halves over her face.

They felt cool against her skin but not uncomfortable. Similar to when people sat in the shade—was it a lack of sun or the cool touch of the shadows themselves? The texture was similar to tulle, resembling a widow's veil—a rough surface, but also slippery. It didn't help that her palms were sweaty, making her hold on too tight; she kept having to readjust her grip.

The man scowled back at Tobler, straightened his stance before walking away. He pondered on what was around the man's neck; something tugged from the back of his mind, but he couldn't place the information that danced just out of his reach. Before giving it more thought, someone bumped into him—hard. It brought him back to his surroundings, but when he looked in the person's direction, there was nobody near him.

The shadows fell from her, enough to give Tobler a peek before they sank into to their original positions. He nodded for her to come out.

"What was that all about?" she asked.

"I'm not sure, but he's someone we should try to stay clear of." The man's unease and foulness clung to him as if he'd walked into a sticky spider's web.

Abruptly, the crowd swelled with a roar as people flooded the street in sheer, frantic terror. It was then Tobler smelled the black smoke clinging to them. People bumped into them harder now. Smoke billowed high above the line of buildings, catching Gemma's eye; her body flooded with dread.

She tried to yell above the throng to Tobler. "We have to do something!"

"What are we supposed to do? It's a fire!" he shouted back.

"I don't know...anything! We have to try, at least!" Another person bumped against her, pushing so hard that she lost her grip on his hand. She regained her footing and charged forward.

"Dammit, Gemma!"

Tobler did his best to keep up as she raced ahead. The crowd continued to batter them, spitting curses to escape the mysterious threat. Before long, the heat hit them in a rush. They were getting closer. They reached a building, rolling in a blaze of angry flames. Its destruction was audible in the cracking wood, thrashing against fiery tongues.

There was crying from a nearby corner. Gemma moved hurriedly, choking against smoke, to find a small girl crouched on the side of the street. She was covered in soot with burns scattered on her arms, sobbing on the ground. Instinctively, she gathered up the small girl and tried to soothe her.

"It's okay. You're okay." She looked for Tobler, who was stunned by the pillaring inferno before him. "Tobler! Tobler, I need you!"

He ran to her side. "We need to get her out of here before she's trampled."

"No! I can't go!" The girl choked between sobs. "My mother is inside still!"

Flames reflected in Gemma's eyes, a dissonant chord striking deep within at the thought of the little girl becoming motherless...just like her. "Watch her!"

Tobler caught her by the elbow, pulling her back slightly. "Gemma, no! Are you insane? It's not safe! You can't go in there!"

"I'm not going inside!" She broke his grip in one thrashing motion.

"Gemma—"

"I have to try!"

She stood amidst the blaze. Gemma stretched her hands out; closing her eyes, she took a deep breath and cleared her mind, concentrating on putting out the fire.

"What are you doing?" Tobler shouted over the roar, scooping the child in his arms.

"I'm trying to put it out!"

"You can't! Even an experienced witch couldn't put this blaze out."

Her expression was fierce as her stubbornness burned even hotter. The flats of her hands turned a dangerous shade of red, causing her to yelp in pain. Tobler knocked down her hands, severing the connection between her and the fire. Gemma's temper flared as she tried to move her finger. She studied the blaze again, noticing the fire grew then faded to a translucent green.

Tobler's face fell. "Cursed fire..." He saw Gemma put her hands back up to reestablish the connection. "No, stop! You can't put this out. It's cursed fire! It's made to destroy its mark, and it will burn you with it."

Her heart sank like a stone in her chest, and she grimaced. "We can't just leave her in there to die, Tobler! There must be something—"

"Black Hells, Gemma, there is nothing we can do!" His face hardened into a mask she did not like.

The longer she looked on, the more useless she felt. She tried to think through her pounding heart and stinging hands when an idea came to her.

"Tobler, what if we didn't try to kill the fire?"

"People die."

A woman's face flickered in a window.

"No, listen: what if instead of putting it out, I just move it?"

"Move it where, to another building? You need to let this go, Gemma we can't—"

"NO!" Gemma spat in exasperation. "I can try to move it around the building, clear a path for her to get out."

"It might work, but you still have to be stronger than the spell, or whoever cast it. The building is too damaged for a safe way out. It's risky, at best."

"Mommy!" the little girl cried out, thrashing against Tobler's arms as if seeking to run into the building herself.

Gemma clenched her teeth and moved closer to the building. The green flames sputtered and spat at her advance. She resumed her connection, closing her eyes to block everything out: the crackling, the girl's sobs, Tobler's angry shouts of angst. Focusing on her racing heartbeat, she slowed it down to gentle thuds. She breathed, raising her hands, and forced the fire upward.

Inside the room where the woman stood, the fire rose to the ceiling; when her eyes discovered Gemma, she understood. The woman darted through the opening and to the door.

Sweat beaded Gemma's brow and temples. The fire felt heavier in her hands as her muscles strained to hold onto it longer; the heat against her palms became more painful. A faint image of blisters crossed her mind, taking her concentration away long enough for a spasm which caused her arm to twitch. Her control stumbled as the flames jerked down, followed by a scream from inside.

Gemma struggled to maintain control. She was just about to lose her hold on the fire as her arms faltered under the weight; the rest of her body became hotter, unbearable.

"Gemma!"

"I've got it!" she growled back.

From the set of her eyes, Tobler knew there was no turning back. "Okay, just a little longer. You can do this. I think she's almost out," he encouraged.

Gemma regained her control and strength. There was a loud crack of wood as the roof fell in on itself. The girl screamed, burying her face into Tobler's shoulder. The rest of the structure crumbled to cinders. Glass shattered as the front breams of the house splintered. Tears poured down Gemma's cheeks as she froze in her control stance.

"You can let go now, Gemma," Tobler said softly, but she didn't move. "Come on, let it go."

She tried to swallow past the massive lump in her throat. "No."

Tobler looked down, noticing her hands were blistered and bleeding. "Gemma, let it go now!"

Before Tobler could stop her, a woman stumbled out of the doorway moments before it fell into fiery heaps. The girl burst from Tobler's arms, running to her mother who scooped her up into her arms.

"Thank you both so much." The woman's eyes glistened with tears as she buried her face into her daughter's hair.

"She did it. She saved you." Tobler eased some of the woman's anxiety. "Could you tell us happened here?"

"They trapped me inside the building," she spoke quickly.

"Who did?" Tobler pushed.

The child shook her head and her mother held her tight to her breast. "We dare not say."

"You don't have to tell us." Gemma crouched down next them, about to place a hand on the woman's arm before the pain stuck her.

The woman looked down at her trembling, soot-smeared child, and Tobler felt her gain the strength to speak. "I denied him."

"Who?"

"I've said too much already." She scrambled to her feet, gripping her daughter. "I'm sorry."

Gemma stopped her. "Where will you go?"

"I don't know, but we can't stay here. He cannot know I survived."

"Come back with us," Tobler offered. "We can keep you safe."

"I can't impose on you more than we already have. You've done so much."

"Please, at least consider it." Gemma pleaded, putting her hands on the woman's shoulders then jerking away in pain.

"Gemma, your hands! We have to tend to them before they become infected." Tobler urged.

The woman gently touched the back of Gemma's hand, turning it over to examine the palm. Her face dropped at the extent of her burns. "I can help with these. I'll need a few things. Do you have healing supplies?"

Tobler nodded. "We do back at the house. Does that mean you'll come with us? To fix her hands?"

Her eyes darted about their surroundings again. "Yes, I will. It's the least I can do after you saved me. Where should I find you?"

CHAPTER TWENTY-NINE

THE STREETS FILLED WITH a strange variety of peddlers as Orianna and Zavier made their way to Phlox and Thistle. They walked closer to the end of the ally, stopping as a man in stood in front of them. He smoked a fat cigar, his mouth buried within a straggly beard, and long hair pulled back into a rough ponytail.

Blowing a cloud of smoke, he took the cigar out of his mouth and eyed Orianna. "Good looking woman, how much?" He spoke to Zavier in a thick accent.

"You bastard!" Orianna protested. "I'm not a whore!"

The man gave a deep chuckle. "She talks out of turn. I like fiery woman. Everyone has a price." He spit to the side then crossed his arms. "How much for some quick time?"

The man reached out a rough hand to touch her waist, but not before Zavier grabbed hold of his arm.

"Keep your hands off her." Zavier stepped forward. "The lady isn't for sale."

The man pulled away. "Pity. She could turn you a few silver 'round here. How 'bout you just turn your head?"

"I'm sure you heard me the first time," Zavier said, squaring up with the man. "Touch her, and I'll rip off your limbs and beat you to a bloody heap."

Zavier's face boasted a scowl anyone in Ophelia Black Alley would have envied. It transformed him into someone Orianna had never seen before, but the smile that followed was chilling.

"It's been a while since I've given a good thrashing. I won't bore too quickly."

The man held his composure for the span of a breath before backing down from their standoff, but not before he gave Orianna one last hungry look.

"I wouldn't exactly call that low-key," Orianna said.

"I could have made it so," he said with a superior confidence she forgot he possessed. "I could not have anyone harm my greatest treasure." He rested a hand on her lower back, guiding her to the end of the alley; not man nor beast dared approach them after Zavier's public decree for bloodshed.

Walking back in the main streets of Goblidet felt like the first breaths of clean, country air after visiting a smog-covered city. As they treaded toward Phlox & Thistle, their ears picked up dropped pieces of conversation that slithered like blown leaves.

Westwood Forest...black...

...dead.

Murdered...poisonous...

They quickened their pace, fearing the worst.

After almost knocking over a group of small witches, they arrived at the shop. Bobbing between heads, they saw the sign on the door reading "Closed: Restricted Ingress." Somewhere near them, a woman gasped.

"Zavier, we have to get in there. It's the only way we'll see what really happened," she murmured.

"There's no way—it's impossible." Zavier nodded toward the storefront. "You see those guards? They're not just drunkards looking for work or farm boys drumming up coin. Those are High Authority sentries. Ruthless, loyal bastards brainwashed into doing everything the members they're protecting ask of them."

She scowled inwardly, craning around the crowd, scanning for a way to get closer to figure out what was going on inside. She spotted the alley between Phlox and Thistle and Cups of Plenty, a store that sold some of the finest pottery in the realm. A memory flooded back to her. When they were children, Zinnia and Orianna used to hide behind the shop, using the angled alley to play hide-and-seek from the Strutson sisters. In their efforts to win, they'd cheat by running to the shop's back door just before they were caught, tricking the sisters into going the other way around and back again.

"I have an idea," she said to Zavier.

"No—" Before he could continue, she was on the move— halfway to the alleyway without him. He grumbled, striding to catch up while not looking too conspicuous.

Turning the corner, he saw Orianna squatting against the rough wooden door connected to the back of the building. With a finger to her mouth, she motioned for him to take the same stance. He grunted, sinking into position beside her.

"What in the Blackest Hell makes you think I can get up from this position?"

"You'll be fine. I won't leave you behind, old man." she teased.

"You're not going to hear shit through this door."

"Sshhh!" She cut him off, placing an ear to the door. He followed her lead, careful not to end up with ear splinters.

The voices were too quiet—further away from the door than they had hoped—but loud enough to make out pieces. One was pitched sharp in a woman's tone, while the other sounded more like a man's pompous tenor.

"POISONED?" the woman continued to shout. "Poisoned?"

"My dear..." the man started, but the rest of his words were muddled.

"A Lady of the Forest does not poison herself by mistake!" the woman shot back.

Another hum of sentences rattled to the door, most of it lost, until more came out just loud enough to hear.

"Zinnia would never take her own life."

Footsteps grew louder as he walked to the door, causing Orianna and Zavier to lean away and against the brick wall in fear they'd open the door.

"The appraisal is more than fair compensation—always is, unless it's suicide. So, watch what you say. We've neither ruled it suicide nor slaughter, therefore your lump sum will arrive to you within days. Your sister's situation is closed."

He started walking away. The ground and the door trembled, followed by a sudden scraping, a metal clatter, and the shuffle of rushing feet. They assumed it was the sentries seizing Zinnia's sister after attempting to assault the man. The woman shrieked and cried out like a kicked dog, either in pain from a physical restraint or the emotional wounds of loss. Orianna couldn't tell for sure, but she recognized the echoes inside the cries.

* * *

WITH A PROTECTIVE ARM around Gemma, Tobler navigated their way through the busy crooked streets and back to The Emporium. Gemma held her hands limply to her chest as her palms throbbed.

"That was stupid what you did—brave, but still stupid."

She cringed at a sharp throb. "Cowardly thing to leave her to die."

"A coward wouldn't have scorched hands," he snapped back with irritation. "You can't do things like that!"

"You'd just hold that child while her mother burned in the flames?"

"If it meant making sure I got back safely to you—I don't know. That's not the point! You can't do things like this. I won't allow it." Tobler almost regretted the words as soon as they came out of his mouth, but he stood unwavering.

"You won't allow it?" she spat. "Who do you think you are? Things work differently in this realm, but I won't be treated like some witless moron!"

"I'm looking out for you!" Tobler raised his voice as he took her wrists, making her see the injuries. "I'll be held responsible for this! I'm supposed to protect you, but I can't if you insist on being some damn fairytale hero!"

She tried her best to swallow back tears. "I don't need you protecting me. I don't want to be your responsibility."

"You know what I meant," Tobler said, struck by her words. "I have to—"

"Enough of this." Gemma broke away from him, darting down the street.

Tobler did his best to catch up, and when he did, he was wise to keep his distance. He stayed close enough to stop anyone from bothering her but far enough not to touch her. He had heard of cursed fire, baffled that she could control it. She was oblivious of the powerful, inexplicable magic that she shouldn't be able to possess.

Gemma reached to open the door, causing her to yelp like a kicked dog. Tobler shielded her from the throng and opened the door for her; wounded animals didn't stand a chance around here, even worse for wounded people.

He put a hand on her back. "It's okay. We're going to fix this."

It was darker inside the shop than when they had left. Fiona needed ambiance to stop the dreamwalking disaster in progress. A strange new scent wafted about the room, acidic fat mixed with wet dirt and cinnamon.

"Ah, back a bit earlier than I expected. Still got a few minutes for simmer, but ya can stay I suppose." Fiona's voice floated from deep within the room.

They found her working over a grungy black cauldron in a dark corner of the shop. She wiped her hands on a raggedly towel as she came around the pot to them.

"Takes me back to my greener years, when I—what in Black's Name happened to you?"

Gemma cringed at Fiona's rush, turning her body away from her. "No, please! They hurt so much."

"Shh, I'll be gentle. Let me get a little look." Fiona took hold of Gemma by the forearms just above the wrists, careful to put distance between her and the burned flesh. "How did this happen? Someone start explainin'."

"It's my fault. I rescued a woman from a burning building. Tobler tried to warn me about the cursed fire—"

"Where the bloody damned hell did you come across cursed fire?" She addressed Tobler directly this time.

"Building back on Vortens Divide was hit with cursed fire. Gemma saved the woman inside but not without consequence."

"That woman's damned lucky, and so are you—that was reckless, child. Yer lucky this all ya got, but never mind that now." Fiona gave her forearms a gentle rub. "Lemme see what I can do here."

Fiona led Gemma toward the back of the shop when the door opened. Zavier and Orianna stepped in, morose, until Orianna caught sight of Gemma's hands.

"Oh, for Ophelia's sakes, 'ere we go. Hold onto yer skirts, child, there's a wild hair crawling up her bum," Fiona cautioned, rolling her eyes.

"Who did this to you?"

"Calm yer britches. No need gettin' yer fiery tits in an uproar," Fiona slung back.

"Fiery tits—look at her! She's severely burned."

"Yer arse is burned! This ain't severe, either, since it can be fixed up. No need gettin' the dear all scared-eyed over it."

Orianna opened her mouth, but Fiona held up a hand.

"My damn shop, my damn rules. End of it," Fiona said, turning back to Gemma. "Now, let's see." Fiona muttered to herself as she made mental notes of measurements while using her own hands as rulers.

"You were supposed to protect her out there." Orianna snapped at Tobler. Zavier put a hand on her shoulder in an attempted to stop her, but she shrugged him off.

"I was protecting her, but we came across a situation." Tobler tried to keep his voice calm, fighting off his temper.

"That doesn't matter! Your sole job was to keep her safe, *unharmed*, and you couldn't even do that!"

"Aunt O, that's not fair. He—"

"You know, it wouldn't have mattered what I could have done. She was doing the right—"

"You're right, it doesn't—she's hurt! Scorched on your watch, but I see *you* are without scratch!" Orianna spat.

Rage began to take hold of Tobler. "You old b—"

"Oye! That's enough!" Fiona commanded, wagging a finger at the two of them as she faced Orianna. "Shut. Yer. Face."

Gemma took a deep breath. "Tobler's right, Aunt O, it was the right thing to do. There was this little girl crying in the street, her mother was trapped inside the burning building."

"It wasn't your problem. She would have gotten out without you putting yourself in danger," Orianna said.

"She didn't—" Tobler started to interject when Fiona gave him a quick cuff to the back of the head.

"'Tis not yer fight." Fiona whispered, leaving him rubbing the back of his head.

"I didn't go inside the building. I did my best to control the fire from the street, but I couldn't get a good grip on it," Gemma said.

"It was your fear again, wasn't it?" Orianna said back sharply. "This just proves you cannot go against him tonight."

"NO! Just, shut up for five seconds!" Gemma was at her breaking point. Orianna's face hardened as her nostrils flared. "I didn't get burned because I was afraid. I had a good grip, felt it like rope in my hands. I didn't know it was cursed fire, that's all."

Orianna's face changed from patronizing anger to horrified. "You didn't stop her?"

"Trust me, I tried but she's more stubborn that you are," Tobler snorted.

"Aunt O, if it wasn't for Tobler, I'd be worse—hell, I might not have hands at all!"

"That's all very well, but it wasn't your job to save that woman. I don't care what you say. There is no excuse for you to put yourself in danger like that," Orianna lectured. "Especially if it was cursed fire! It was stupid to put yourself in reach of harmful Black Magic."

"Stupid? Why, because I didn't run? Because I held my ground?" Gemma spoke in a conversational tone that carried a heavy slap. "Stupid, because I didn't orphan a little girl and then forget about her like you?"

Orianna steeled her face against anguish. Gemma should've felt terrible. Instead, a part of her felt vindicated for taking a stand for herself. But in that small corner of vindication lurked the blackened spots of change—a tarnish wrought in toxic roots, defining the difference between taking a stand and belittling another.

Their attention whipped to the other room where footsteps sounded and a voice called out.

"Did any of ya invite someone here?" she asked quietly.

"We might have..." Tobler began.

"Might've? Or did? Pick one, ya can't be both," Fiona shot back.

"We did. The woman and child we helped. We mentioned them coming back here for safety."

"I ain't running a harbor house." She shook a fist at him.

"No, we only wanted them to meet us. They're coming back home with us." Gemma winced at a throb of pain.

Fiona nodded. "Very well. Just make sure not to forget them when ya go. Back here, dearies! Come on through!"

With footsteps like mice, the mother and daughter joined them in the back of the shop. The young girl clung to her mother's skirt. The woman carried a large sack on her shoulder and the little girl a smaller, matching one.

"Are you okay?" Tobler asked, walking closer to them.

The mother eyed the strangers around the room before nodding. Tobler sensed her fear and smelled the lingering odor of smoke. He rested a hand at her elbow.

"You're safe here. This is Gemma's aunt and uncle, and Fiona owns this place. You don't need to be afraid."

"Thank you again, Gemma. If it hadn't been for you—I just don't know what would have happened..." She patted the child's hair. The child turned a blue eye from behind her mother's side to stare up at the people around her.

"The important thing is that you're safe." Gemma said and gave the little girl a smile. "You were very brave, too, you know. We wouldn't have known your mom was in there without you. You're a hero."

The little girl peeked out, tilting her head at Gemma's praise. Fiona pulled a slender, rectangular box from a low cabinet and brought it over. When she opened it, Gemma smelled the faint scent of fish and river water.

"Okay, no more dawdling.'" Fiona pulled out two translucent strips.

"What is that?"

Fiona lifted up one of the delicate skins, thin as paper, iridescent in the candlelight. "This is how we fixin' yer hands. Put yer palms out an' close to me. Spread them flat as you can get 'em."

Gemma did the best she could, biting her cheek at the pain as Fiona put the chilly things on her hands.

"It's wart-fish skins. There well known for healing, best with a bit of—"

"Festor's oil? I have some here in my bag." The mother rummaged around in her sack.

"Why, yes! Now where did ya come across this? Couldn't get me hands on it for months!" Fiona took the oil with enthusiasm, drizzling it on the fish skins; then, as careful as she could, she rubbed the oils in.

"I know it hurts, dear, but I have to make sure it's in there."

"How fast will this heal my hands?" Gemma asked through clenched teeth.

"Hard to say." Fiona said still rubbing her hands. "Skin alone would have been about halfway set, but with the black root oil yer about fully healed—maybe a day or so more."

"That won't work." Gemma's angst agitated inside her. She had to go against Leo tonight with her aunt. Entering the battle with half-healed hands she could barely move was less than optimal. "The plan is for tonight. It can't wait."

"You can't go into this wounded, Gemma," Orianna piped in, her face still an expressionless mask. "I won't allow it. Yes, you can make your own choices, but it is my dream. I won't send you in to get killed."

"I agree with Orianna." Tobler put a hand in his pocket, fingering the orb still inside the case. "You can't go in there hurt. It's not safe."

Gemma's guilt hit her all at once, causing Tobler to wince. She had been so awful, yet here they were fighting for her safety. She looked to Zavier for something to say, but he put an arm around Orianna's shoulder. Desperate, Gemma turned her attention back to Fiona, who was muttering a pile of words she couldn't make out. Her skin began to tingle, which turned to intense itchiness like bugs crawling over her hands. Fiona stopped her muttering.

"Fiona, you're all about me standing on my own two feet. Tell them I'll be fine, and that this is my choice," she pleaded.

Fiona peeled back the fish skins to reveal red, blistered palms. A series of gruesome scars were left behind, thick lines like wadded bed sheets. Tears pooled in Gemma's eyes at the sight, causing something heavy to plummet inside of her chest.

"I'm sorry, dear, this is the best I can do," Fiona said. "Truth is, ya can't go into battle like this. There needs to be healing and then, after that, who knows if you'll be able to use them like ya had before."

No one had words to say that could console her. Tears streamed down her cheeks until someone tugged her dress. Looking down, Gemma saw the little red-headed girl staring up at her. Her eyes were the most magnificent light blue she'd ever seen, and a smile cracked through her sadness. The little girl motioned for her mother as Fiona took in a deep sniff. Something in the air made Fiona give the girl a wink and nod, crossing the room to give giving them space.

Puzzled, Gemma squatted down best she could to meet the little girl's eyes. Her sweet face still spotted with soot, she appeared so young but her eyes were older. Though they were clear and spry, they held a depth of knowledge that would have required many years of living.

"Would you do it again?" the little girl whispered gravely. "Do you regret saving my mom?"

"No, I don't regret it. This is a small price to pay to keep you with your mom." More tears fell down Gemma's cheeks even as her heart lifted, knowing the little girl wouldn't be an orphan. "I'd do it again."

"What is happening?" Orianna asked and received a swift swat as Fiona shushed her.

The little girl took the backs of Gemma's hands. Gemma eyed the girl as a new fear of being touched rose in her throat.

"Trust me like I trusted you to save my mom."

The little girl assessed the scars and warped skin. She looked to her mother, as if asking permission, then closed her eyes. The little girl's face grew peaceful as a soothing chill filled Gemma's palms. A gentle light beamed from the little girl's hands. The little girl straightened her back, turning her face upward as a flash of heat rippled across her skin. The light retracted back inside; weary, but she still managed a tiny smile that widened when she looked down at Gemma's hands.

"Look," she said with a child's wonder.

Gemma's hands were healed. She was shocked a child did what a seasoned witch couldn't. The little girl smiled at her accomplishment, the way most children did when trying what others considered normal for the first time. Doll-like and excited, she clasped her hands beneath her chin.

"Move them!" she demanded, earning a gentle shush from her mother. The little girl whispered instead. "Move them, please."

Trying not to laugh, Gemma closed her hands and wiggled her fingers; there was no pain. She took the little girl in her arms, whispering, "Thank you."

The little girl squeezed harder before whispering back, "Thank you for saving my mom."

There were no dry eyes in The Emporium; even Zavier had to take a few sharp sniffles to maintain his composure. Tobler smacked him on the back as he wiped at a tear on his cheek.

"It's okay to cry, man," Tobler said.

Zavier returned the clap on the back, sending Tobler stumbling to the floor.

The two women wept without concern. Fiona pulled a handkerchief from her pocket and blew her nose with a honk, which caused the little girl to giggle.

"The most beautiful magic I've ever seen." Fiona smiled at the girl.

Orianna and the red-headed woman exchanged meaningful nods, and she hugged the woman in a silent thank you. The little girl ran over to her mother, expectant and wide eyed.

"Did I do good, Mommy?"

"You did very good, baby." She hugged the child tight to her chest and kissed the top of her head.

Zavier was astonished. "The small child is a healer?"

The red-headed woman nodded. "A rare gift, I know. It skips a few generations before resurfacing."

"It makes sense, pure soul."

"What do you mean?" Gemma asked.

"Healers have the purest souls, which is why they're gifted with the power to heal," Tobler said.

"Is this a common gift?" Gemma asked.

"No, it is one of the rarest affinities. Healers and Seers are the least common affinities in any realm," the woman answered. "There are only ever a handful around at a time—a coveted power, like Empaths. My Lydia is the youngest in existence, so she can replenish faster."

"What do you know about Empaths?" Tobler asked quietly.

"They're cunning people. It's not pure hearts that gain the affinity. Takes great control—unless they go mad first, but those tend to be of the darker sorts. However, it is possible for them to hold onto their humanity if they are gifted. It is not our power, but how we use it that defines us," she reassured him. "Anyone willing to hold a crying child and help save her mother can't be all that bad, you know."

Tobler nodded. "At least we hope so, right?"

She put a hand on his shoulder. "All any of us can do is try."

"Right, let's get movin'. Ya need a bone knife and skin, the knife laid on the forearm of the person who will wield it." She handed over a clear jar with a rolled-up piece of skin, gray and pickled in an alcohol liquid.

Gemma's face contorted in disgust at the slimy film on the inside of the bottle.

"Cover it up with the skin, stitched to yer body or not. The watchers, you boys, have to make sure it doesn't fall off her arm or else she she'll lose her weapon."

"Let's go with not stitched." Gemma suppressed a gag.

Fiona shrugged. "Yer pickins, not mine. The two of ya lay down beside one another and drink this potion in proper order. Order is very important. First, the rescuer with the dark potion of dreamwalker essence. The afflicted should sleep first, then the rescuer. You'll both be transported to Orianna's dream where the shite will be waiting fer ya, no doubt of it. That is when you attack. Best do it as a surprise—don't give him time. After ya get into the dream, it's out of my hands. I can get ya there, but that's all."

"We appreciate it, Fiona. Thank you for all of your help," Gemma said, giving Orianna a prompting look.

"Yes, thank you." She folded her hands. "Let us know if there is anything we can do for you. We owe you a great favor."

Old Fiona smiled another crazy smile. "Really burnt yer ass sayin that ta me, huh, Oliver witch? I accept and take you up on that favor. 'Til then, no worries. It's been a pleasure doing business wit' ya."

"Despite your crockery," Orianna stated, "I feel we possibly made a good team."

"Aahhh," Fiona's expression went sly, "'tis possible."

"I'm glad you two are playing nice, but it's getting later than I care to be traveling," Zavier said, giving Tobler a hefty clap on the back that swayed him on his feet.

"Yeah, we should probably head back before you fall asleep on the ponies, old man."

"We probably should be going too, Lydia," the red-headed woman said.

"Would you like to come back with us?" Gemma asked.

"No, you've done so much already. We'll find an inn somewhere close."

"What will ya do when they're all full?" Fiona asked. "Lot of people without beds tonight. I doubt there's space this late."

The red-headed woman nodded, not surprised. "I half expect there won't be anything open, but I'll settle for a spot on a tavern floor or a secluded alleyway. I'm not too proud."

"Ta hell ya will," Fiona said. "Ya not be wanderin' through the blustery nights wit' the poor little child. Ya both staying here wit' me. I have plenty of room and warm places for ya both to get some good rest and figure out what you'll be doing next."

Lydia pulled at her mom's skirt, looking up at her.

"Okay, fine. We'll stay, but only until we figure something out. Don't get too cozy." She tousled Lydia's hair.

"What's yer name, deary? Need to know since ya be stayin'"

"Cora."

They exchanged heartfelt hugs before respectfully departing. Orianna gave one last look and something surprising happened. Cora joined Fiona, both fussing over little Lydia. The girl beamed in the glow of their attention, comfortable with the new dynamic. Then, Orianna saw it. The change worked its way through until they transformed; the trio became a family, one to replace what they'd all lost and sorely needed. A miracle. She joined arms with Zavier, ready to go home.

Ophelia Black Street was more daunting in the dark, the shadows more menacing than before. Gemma locked eyes with a man in a doorway, taking all of her courage not to shriek out as his eyes smoldered red. Tobler stepped up next to her, putting himself between her and the man who growled before closing the door.

"What was that?" Gemma whispered.

"Could be a werewolf. Didn't think there were any left."

"Werewolf?" she gasped.

"Oh? You've seen flesh-targeting fire, creepy skin in a bottle, a child healer, but a werewolf seems unbelievable?" He chuckled low in his throat.

She shrugged.

"There are all sorts of folk here. You haven't met them all yet." He smiled at her, his same easy smile, and rested a hand on her lower back.

Back in Goblidet Center, they felt like they could breathe; even then, Gemma found shifty characters skulking about. She kept close to Tobler when she glimpsed a hooded figured watching them from a street corner. She made out part of the figure's face, enough to see a pair of pale blue eyes. Gemma felt an icy coldness spike inside her body. But the woman did not move, simply watched them go with her face set in a smirk.

Tobler could not get a solid read on her. She was something dark, but there was a gray area that he had never felt before. "It's okay. I don't think she'll hurt us."

"What is she?" Gemma asked.

Tobler gave some thought to her question. "I don't know, but hopefully she's on the right side. I don't think I'd want her to go up against us."

They walked down the street with a little less fear than before, but the pale eyes watched even after they disappeared from sight.

CHAPTER THIRTY

It was cold inside the house, coating Gemma's skin like a thin frost. She shivered in the darkness that didn't allow her to see far, paralyzed until her eyes adjusted. With care, she navigated the faint shadows. Orianna asked her to start a fire while she lit candles. Once the first candle was lit, Gemma moved with more confidence as her field of vision illuminated.

In the hearth, a scant number of wood pieces rested in the ashes; holding out her hands, Gemma ignited them with effortless will. She found controlling normal, everyday fire to be much easier after her encounter with the obstinate cursed fire, plopping on the couch in relief. Tobler fed the fire and took a seat next to her, resting his arm on the back of the couch.

Zavier helped Orianna scrape together something for them to eat, slicing bread while she cut up some raw chicken for frying. He watched both of the women carrying on with their activities, making a point not to look at one another. The tension between them carried in the air like sour milk; if they intended to pull off tonight's stunt, there needed to be mending. They had to trust each other again and strengthen their bond or else the plan would end in disaster. Zavier shifted from foot to foot as he pretended to stretch his lower back, giving a groan of discomfort.

"Are you alright?" Orianna asked, taking the bait.

"I don't know. I think all of that riding and crouching around today pulled something."

"Poor thing, you're getting old," she teased him. "You should go sit down."

"No, you need help. Unless someone else would like to step in," he said and looked over at Gemma, who was not taking the cue. "Gemma, would you mind helping your aunt cook?"

Zavier walked over and sat down beside her, groaning about his back. Gemma sympathized, walking over to the counter with apprehension. Things had been heated with her aunt, which made talking so soon uncomfortable. Tobler watched them, seeing right through Zavier's plan.

"I hope you have enough medical supplies for the cat fight you just instigated," Tobler said.

Zavier waved him off. "They'll be fine after they talk it out. Besides, they need to be on the same side when Gemma dreamwalks tonight. Things could go south fast, especially with Gemma being new to the craft."

Tobler stared at the pair of silent ladies. "I see your point, but forcing them to work it out might backfire on you. I hope for their sakes it's not, but they're just so—"

"Alike," Zavier said. "Yes, almost exactly alike—two halves of a double-headed coin, and one side more bull-headed than the other. They'll come to a compromise."

Tobler, not persuaded, questioned Zavier's thought. "The queen of bull-headedness and Gemma, the ever-stubborn creature, coming to a compromise. Meaning one of them has to say sorry. You think we'll live to see that happen?"

Zavier shrugged. "I don't see what other choice they have."

They watched as the two bumped against one another to get to the opposite ends of the counter, trying to cook without speaking. "What's going on over there?"

Tobler shrugged. "I'm not supposed to meddle in their emotions without permission, you know that."

"You don't have to meddle, just see if they're getting any closer to patching it up."

"That sounds an awful lot like meddling. Orianna would string me up, right here in the living room, if she caught me."

"Yes, yes, and you'll make a lovely ornament. I'm sure if you're quick about it she won't catch you." Zavier prompted, "Don't change anything. Observe their emotions and get out of there quickly."

Tobler sighed, rolling his eyes. "Fine, just stop talking."

Zavier waited as Tobler closed his eyes to isolate the others in the room. After a few minutes, Zavier whispered but Tobler did not answer. He tried again a couple more times with no response. This time, he kicked Tobler's foot.

"Ouch," he said through his teeth. "What the hell?"

"I said in and out, don't linger. You're bound to get caught that way."

"I'm sure I would have been fine without you breaking my foot," Tobler exaggerated.

"Well? What did you find out?"

"They're both a pain in the ass, that's what." He crossed his arms. "Neither one is budging. But if I had to bet money on it, I'd say Gemma will crack first."

"That's possible, but Orianna has a soft spot for the girl. She could back down first," Zavier countered.

Tobler raised an eyebrow. "Do I hear a bet?"

Zavier looked back at the women, at their stiff postures and tight lips, and nodded. "You do. I bet you Orianna will crack first."

"And I bet Gemma will cave and apologize. One gold vellum—deal?" Tobler put out his hand.

"Deal, and you'd better actually have that gold vellum," Zavier said as they shook on it, watching as if the scene was a story put on by a company of players.

The time passed between them like sludge through a keyhole. Both women resigned themselves to not saying much of anything, which made preparing dinner a challenge.

Gemma decided she'd start small, gauge Orianna's attitude, before diving right into an apology; the carrots would be a good icebreaker.

She cleared her throat. "Do you have another peeler?"

Orianna looked up at her, startled. "What?"

"For the carrots." She said again, "Do you have another peeler I can use?"

"Oh, of course." Orianna said absently, digging through a drawer and passing her the peeler. "Here you go."

"Thank you."

"You're welcome."

Short and curt, but Gemma decided to continue trying to make conversation. Her aunt didn't seem angry, but wounded; she was hard-pressed to pinpoint which played on her guilt more. She peeled the carrots; the more she thought, the harder she peeled until her mind took over and she wasn't paying attention to the blade. Gemma dragged the blade back in a stroke, stinging her finger. She yelped, jarring Orianna's attention.

"What happened? Did you skin yourself?"

She held up the side of her finger. "Maybe a little."

Orianna stepped closer, taking her niece's hand with care as she watched small beads of blood well up from her skin.

"Not too bad, just a little blood. Here, run that under the cold water a minute while I get you a cloth." Orianna instructed before rummaging through another drawer.

Gemma did as she was told. The cold water felt good against her hot skin. She hadn't realized how warm she had been running, wondering if it was a side effect of the healing Lydia had done. Orianna returned with small round tin, a strip of cloth, and a clean towel.

"Here, give me your hand."

Gemma complied, watching as she patted down her wound and opened the small tin. Inside, there was a green paste that reminded her of lip balm, smelling of aloe and leaves. Orianna scooped some out onto her finger, with sticky strings clinging to the substance; she swirled to attach the strings to the wound and not herself. To Gemma's surprise, it did not sting. The paste was soothing, and the blood stopped welling up.

"What is that stuff?" she asked.

"It's a salve made with particular medicinal plants. It will help heal and keep it from getting infected." Orianna continued to spread a generous glob across the cut.

"Oh." She watched as her aunt fastened the cloth around her finger, and the guilt came back in a crashing wave. "I'm sorry."

The words were so soft Orianna wasn't sure she heard them.

"I'm sorry, Aunt O," Gemma said again. Without meaning to, a tear fell down her cheek as a dam broke inside of her. "I didn't mean what I said back in Fiona's shop. It was wrong, and I don't know what came over me."

Orianna threw her arms around her niece, hugging her tight to her breast. She felt a shudder run through Gemma's body as she stroked the girl's hair.

"Shh...it's okay, Gemma," Orianna said in a hushed tone. "It's okay, you were in pain. You didn't really know what you were saying."

Gemma choked back a sob. "I didn't. I didn't mean to hurt you, but you just wouldn't listen. I just—I was so scared."

"I know. I was, too. I'm sorry I yelled at you. In truth, it was a wonderful thing you did. You were so courageous." Orianna pulled away from Gemma, holding her face between her hands.

Gemma shook her head in protest.

"I know you were scared, and that's okay. When you're scared, that is the only time that you can be brave." Orianna cracked a forlorn smile. "I was just so afraid of losing you that I overreacted. You're an amazing young woman, and I will start trusting you more."

Gemma wiped away her tears and took a deep breath. In a low voice she whispered. "Like tonight?"

Orianna's face fell a little. She gave Gemma's hands a squeeze. "Yes, like tonight."

Gemma said with determination, "I won't let him hurt you. We're going to stop this tonight."

Orianna's pride stirred. "So long as we try our best, I believe we will manage—no matter what the outcome. I will keep you safe, too."

Tobler held out a hand to Zavier, grinning like a school child. "Pay up."

Zavier released a long string of inaudible grumbles as he fished in his pocket for a gold vellum piece. He put it into Tobler's hand with a less-than-amused expression.

Orianna and Gemma prepared the rest of the meal, chattering away like two hens. Orianna taught her some cooking tricks and the importance of proper seasoning; though it went unnoticed, there were hints of despair in her lesson. Teaching the young woman life tidbits that would be useful in case Orianna didn't make it through tonight. Gemma learned where she kept her recipes, simple tips to run a household, favorite meals, how to feed a fire for cooking, and she somehow slipped into a conversation about where she hid the important documents. The last perked Gemma's suspicions, but she soon forgot the notion once charged with setting the table, calmed by Tobler's touch as he helped her with the task.

He wrapped his arms around her waist, hugging her from behind—which was seen by all, but no one objected. To Gemma's surprise, she didn't care that his advances were in eye-shot of her family, either, as she worried more for the coming events. Dinner was filled with brief touches or caresses that went unnoticed by her aunt and uncle, who were also in their own world. Each couple grew lost in the other's eyes, sealing precious moments of warmth and love while they could.

Once dinner had ended, Zavier offered to help Orianna clean. Tobler took it as an opportunity to steal Gemma away for a few moments alone.

"I think I'll step outside for some fresh air." He extended a hand. "Gemma?"

"Do you think it's—"

"Go ahead, dear. Some fresh air will probably do you some good," Orianna interrupted. "It'll clear the mind, and the moon is lovely. Just stay within the charmed barriers."

Gemma smiled, giving Tobler a nod of approval. He took her hand and led her out the door.

Zavier entwined his arms around her waist. "That was awfully generous of you. What happened to that domineering, control freak I've been engaged to all of these years?"

"Oh, hush." She swatted him. "She's taking a break for tonight. It's been too stressful a day to try and control it anymore."

Orianna turned around, kissing her fiancé with the passion of a new lover and the knowledge of an old soul.

* * *

TOBLER LED GEMMA TO the back half of the house. He turned her around, pulling her against him. She settled in, pleased that she fit perfectly against his body. She rested against his shoulder and entwined her fingers with his, which already rested on her hips.

With his arms around her, the tensions in Gemma's body dissolved. Whether the sudden relaxation was from his powers or not, Gemma didn't care; it made her feel safe instead of standing in the shadows of dread. He hugged her tighter, and she savored the sense of being whole and loved.

The moon shone brighter and higher than their rooftop rendezvous. Their view of the woods was not a bad one, either. They watched the wind sway the trees back and forth, accompanied by the melodic rustle of their leaves. High grasses danced to the rhythm, scenting the air. Gemma took a deep breath, easing into euphoria.

"This is perfect," she said with closed eyes.

He rested a foot against the wall. "That's only because you're here, otherwise it would be just an ordinary night amongst the sky and trees."

She smiled, not knowing what to say back. They listened to the woods a while longer.

"I'm glad you came here."

"Are you sure you don't miss normal?" she asked.

Tobler chuckled. "Days filled with gambling, drinking, bearing the full wrath of Orianna's scorn until I got myself together, grabbing a tall tankard with friends from time to time," he paused. "Emptiness, I know that now—lonesome pieces of a life I wasn't happy living."

"What do you mean? What made you so lonely? There were tons of women falling at your feet. I mean, hell, I see at least two or three whenever we go out."

He nodded. "This is true, but none that sparked any interest. No one who wanted to hold my company for anything more than my looks, or to make someone else jealous, or break in their bed for the night. I've had some fun times, enjoyed a bit of attention, but that's all it was. Nothing more than blank pages in the wind."

He turned Gemma around to face him. "Then you come, and the world has color. You offered more than daydreams and idleness. You gave reasons to my days, warmth to my nights, and anticipation of the future."

Gemma, stunned into silence, stared back as if seeing him from beyond a veil.

"You don't have to say anything. I just want you to know how I feel. I just—need you to know..." Tobler trailed off as he felt the edges of desperation come upon him.

Gemma's heart quickened. "Know what, Tobler?"

"You remember the conversation we were trying to have the other day?"

She giggled. "We're interrupted an awful lot—which time?"

"True." He snorted as lighter tones filtered in. "The time we were talking about fate."

Gemma nodded.

"We have two kinds of that here." Tobler started. "The first is about life and what you're meant to do. The second is a little more complex. It involves who you are fated to be with in terms of love. We call this kismet. Legend says that when you find your kismet you just *know*—no explanations, just a heightened sense of befuddlement. They say your soul searches for this person, knowing who to look for." Gemma looked intrigued, so he continued. "Some older believers say it can change a person's life, rescuing them from an evil path. They believe this type of love could save lives, Gemma."

"That's a beautiful belief, but what do you believe?" she said, avoiding his eyes, unsure if she wanted to know the answer.

Tobler lifted her face so they might hold each other's gazes. "I believe, deep in my heart, that *you* are my kismet; my fated other half. The soul that my soul has been searching for my entire life. I love you, Gemma."

Tears welled in her eyes. "I love you, too, Tobler."

They sealed their words with a passionate kiss, a gesture that would've stirred the envy of any who saw it. When he pulled away, he felt something troubling streak crossed her.

"What is it, Gemma? Did I say something wrong?" he asked, full of concern.

Gemma shook her head but remained silent.

"Come on, you can tell me anything. None of this 'nothing' shit—remember, I can sense it too." He gave her a half smile.

His smiles were infectious, causing a small one to cross then wither on her mouth. "What if you don't really mean it?"

Tobler prepared a counter argument, but she stopped him.

"I mean, what if the stress of things is making you think you're feeling this way? What if I make it back—"

"When you make it back," he corrected.

"*If* I make it back and realize it wasn't true? High-stress situations can make people do crazy things. It's why they tell you not to do anything rash when something bad happens to you, like chop your hair short after a breakup," she said, every word dripping venom that seared Tobler's heart.

Tobler held her face in his hands. "I've never meant anything more, in my whole life, than what I just said to you. I will not wake up with regret. I wouldn't say it if it wasn't true, you silly, stubborn girl."

While her mind clung to some doubt, a deeper part of Gemma wholeheartedly believed he was telling the truth. She worried as she prepared to enter battle; the thought of not coming back trumped her fear of him being insincere.

She lowered her head. "It's important we tell each other the truth tonight, especially with how we feel..."

He caressed her cheek with his thumb. "You will survive this."

"You can't know that for sure. This could be out last night together." The bottom of her stomach fell at the thought. Her chest compressed in pain at the thought of never seeing his face again.

Tobler shook his head. "I know for a fact you will be okay, I promise."

"I'm trying to accept this, Tobler. Don't give me false hopes." She sighed, adding, "It will be okay. I'm glad that I'm spending this time with you."

His face hardened as his brow furrowed, waging an internal battle over telling her the truth about his plans. But there was a chance she'd have him destroy the orb, and he could not risk that.

"Do you trust me?" he asked.

"Of course I do."

"Believe me, then. No matter what, you will see me again on this side. Do everything you can to keep safe, but if anything happens, you will come back."

There was something in his tone that Gemma didn't like. Something camouflaged beneath the surface, making gooseflesh prickle over her arms and the fine hair on the back of her neck raise in alarm.

"Tobler, what are you planning?"

"What makes you think I'm planning something?"

"How else would you be so sure that I'd have a guaranteed safe way back?" Suspicion formed with the frown on her lips.

That's when he gave her his most disarming smile. "Well, there is such a thing as an affinity for premonition." He stopped Gemma mid-rebuttal with a finger on her lips. "I never guaranteed you safety, simply said you'd be coming back. Don't read more into it. I don't want to fight with you, not tonight."

Her face relaxed, placated by his explanation, but something still nagged at her. "Okay. But you'd tell me if it was dangerous?"

Tobler swallowed against the tightness in his throat and kissed her. "Of course, don't worry so much. Let's stay in the moment, just us for a while. I don't want to think about anything else. I love you, Gemma."

"I love you too, Tobler."

Gemma settled against Tobler with her head on his chest, taking comfort in the rhythm of his beating heart.

CHAPTER THIRTY-ONE

GEMMA AND TOBLER PASSED the time holding each other and talking. He compared her to the stars and moon, making her blush a gentle pink as he whispered things, his breath suggestive and warm against her ear and neck. He entertained her with old stories and legends of creatures beyond the trees, waiting and watching in the boughs of trees or hunkered behind bushes. It sent a shiver up her spine, the thought of being watched from afar by a stalking beast. Tobler squeezed her closer to dispel her fears. Their kisses grew more heated. When he made further advances, she swatted him. He stopped with a grin but respected her boundaries. Her emotions gave away, anyway—she didn't mind his hands lingering, but feared being caught by Orianna. This sobering thought snapped Tobler out of his dream world, tossing him back into the fires of reality.

"Tobler..."

"I know." He pulled her back against him. "I don't like it, but we should probably head back inside. It's almost midnight."

They stayed a few minutes longer, basking in their precious second, but Gemma's angst nudged him to get moving.

"Okay, let's head inside." He rubbed the sides of her arms, trying to keep the warmth of the moment.

They paused by the window before entering, staring at Zavier and Orianna who rested on the couch in front of the crackling fire. They both looked so cozy. Zavier held her from behind, and Orianna nestled in the crook of his arm; in this pose, they appeared as young as Tobler and Gemma. In turn, the younger couple both hoped deep down that they would end up like this years from now. Tobler pulled her close to him again, deciding they should give their older counterparts some extra time alone.

"They're so perfect together," Gemma commented, her voice a gentle marvel.

"They've earned it," he remarked. "Or they perfected it over nineteen years of being together? Who knows."

"Such a long time to wait."

"Zavier has inexhaustible patience."

"They say love is patient. I'd never thought that patient, but it must be true."

Tobler snorted. "I guess... A bit ridiculous."

Gemma looked up at him. "Are you saying you wouldn't wait nineteen years for me?"

"Why in Ophelia's Name would I do a thing like that?"

Gemma gasped in mild outrage, then giggled when he mocked her gasp with a dramatic flourish. Oh, how good it felt for her muscles to pull up a smile so wide. He grew serious, and she stopped, allowing her smile to lurk under the surface.

"I've waited my whole life for you. I think that's long enough, don't you?"

She leaned a little closer to him. "Maybe."

He met her the rest of the way with a kiss. In all of the worlds, he never imagined he'd be so lucky. He hoped he'd have the pleasure of spending more time with her; hoping the universe would be on their side for a night.

Gemma turned back to the view through the window of her aunt and uncle—in love, oblivious to the rest of the world.

"I don't want to bother them," she said in a dreamy tone. "They just look so peaceful."

"They do, but Orianna will be incredibly un-peaceful if we do not get started in the appropriate timeframe. As sweet as she looks now, she'll rain blackened hell on us—actually, me—for delaying things."

Gemma trailed Tobler, taking in every drop of the night, clinging to the last pieces of the moment—all together, unharmed and happy. Watching, as the world seemed to hold its breath before witnessing the ripples in time that would forever disturb their perfection.

***

UPSTAIRS, THE BUSYING SOUNDS of preparation felt insignificant and isolated as the house let its ominous presence be known to them. Cloaked in a different veil, the house appeared like a whole new place near midnight, bearing its own set of rules it was not willing to share. The floorboards creaked, groaning beneath passing feet. Gemma sensed the house's defenses whipping around corners before eventually settling. The emptiness in the halls was thick with their whispers, demanding silence. Obeying this need, none of them spoke unless it was necessary; they grabbed jars, cleared the bedroom, and never said a word even when laying the cadaver skin on Gemma's arm.

Tobler gained the courage to break the silence. "You're still sure you want to do this?"

"Yes, I have to do this. It's too late to back out now," Gemma replied.

"No, it's not," Tobler said.

"He's right, Gemma. It's not too late to back out," Orianna interjected, recognizing the worry in Tobler's voice; understanding, because she still didn't want Gemma to go through with the plan.

"Aunt Orianna, you know this is the only way." Gemma's voice was more confident than she felt.

"Who cares what that old bat said? I can find ways, brew potions to stay awake. He can't get to me if I'm not asleep."

"That's crazy, you can't do that. Besides, this could end all of our problems." Gemma's chest tightened at the thought of everything resting on her, but it disappeared as quickly in the midst of the painstaking preparations. She shot a skeptical look over at Tobler, who looked the guiltiest she'd ever seen him.

"You're not wrong," Orianna paused, "but it's not the only thing that matters. Your life matters more to me than some sleep, or even banishing this evil."

"It shouldn't—" Gemma stopped herself, not wanting to incite another heated argument. She took a breath to collect herself, then held her aunt's hand. "Aunt O, I want to do this. I can do this. Everything will be fine."

Orianna studied her niece—so grown up, there was no point in arguing further. She would have to stop thinking of Gemma as the baby. She had to let go of the past and acknowledge the strong, young woman standing before her—a young woman ready to shoulder the weight of responsibility, of family duty. Her heart ached at the missed time, tears filled her eyes, but there was no time for that now. No time to dwell on all the things she wished were different. No time to think of the mistakes she'd made over the course of her life. Orianna squeezed Gemma's hand back in unspoken understanding, vowing she would keep Gemma safe...even if it cost her soul.

"Let's review the plan one last time," Zavier suggested.

"Yes, good idea," Tobler said.

"Right—so skin has to be intact." Gemma evaluated the skin. It was slimy and slippery, but some of the edges had dried out and peeled away from her arm; there was a possibility it could fall off.

"It does look a little flimsy." Tobler eyeing the skin with distrust.

"Do we have any glue?" Gemma asked Orianna.

"I don't believe so, but I have some gut to attach it." Orianna watched as Gemma's face went whiter. "It's okay, a couple here and there."

Gemma mustered up a nod and watched as Orianna left to get the gut. Tobler tried his best to stick the edges back against her skin, but as one piece stuck down another rolled right back up again.

"It's okay, Tobler. Thanks for trying." She gave a faint smile that faded when Orianna returned with a few strings of gut and a rounded, fine needle.

Orianna knelt down beside the bed where Gemma was sitting and began threading the needle. Watching the look in Gemma's eyes, Tobler took the needle from Orianna in an unspoken offer to do the stitching. He put a hand on her leg, easing her tension and fear. Gemma didn't object to his emotional intrusions as a knot set deep in her stomach. With nimble fingers, Tobler stitched the cadaver skin and soothed away the pain for Gemma.

"Do you have the potions, Orianna?" Zavier asked.

"Yes, all three vials." She held them out for all to see before placing them on the nightstand next to Zavier.

Zavier nodded as he searched his mind for anything he had missed, looking about the room and making mental notes until he was satisfied.

"How's it goin' over there, Tobler? Just about ready?" Zavier craned his neck to get a better look.

The skin over Gemma's forearm was stitched every few inches, simple knots pulled taut over the bone knife—a perfect outline jutting from the skin, which still sickened her. Tobler was tying off the last stitch, but the particular edge he was stitching was thicker than he expected. After apologizing to Gemma for how long it was taking and promising he was nearly done, she helped wriggle the needle through.

"Done," he said with the last twist and pull. "That should keep in place, and they're simple enough to undo once you come back."

Gemma studied his handiwork, something she would have admired had it been anyone else's arm he had stitched pickled flesh to. "How'd you learn to do this?" she asked, trying to take her mind off the smell.

Tobler shrugged. "Eh, I was a stupid kid and required some skin stitched back together here and there. I watched enough to do it myself, so as not to alert anyone of anything stupid I'd done as I got older."

"Is that so?" Zavier cocked an eyebrow at him. "What have you been hiding?"

"What I've seen, I'll never tell." Tobler gave Gemma a wink and changed the subject to get things moving. "Okay, what's next?"

"Just getting in position and drinking the potions, I believe," Orianna said. The heavy words fell off her tongue, reluctant but knowing it was time.

With deep breaths and a burst of adrenaline, Orianna and Gemma both sat on the bed next to each other. Zavier took a seat at Orianna's side, giving out the appropriate potions. Orianna hesitated as she took hers, studying Zavier. His cool exterior was no match for her; she sensed his angst underneath, and spoke truths they needed to hear.

"Zavier, you need to promise you won't wake us up."

He nodded, still wearing his stone mask. "I can't promise that. You can't expect me to sit here and do nothing."

"You must, my love. You can't wake either of us too early."

"Do you understand what you're asking me? You're asking me to let you die." Zavier's face hardened further. "I won't sit here and watch you die, Orianna. If you're in danger—"

"We can't waste this attempt, Zavier. We will be fine. He won't expect two of us to show up, and you can't stop it until we finished."

Tobler and Gemma held their tongues like children when their parents squabbled, knowing better than to interrupt. Gemma watched the weight settle on her uncle's shoulders, sympathizing with the unfairness of what her aunt asked of him. Her mind turned to Tobler, looking older than his years and graver than a tomb. Zavier took a hard, ragged breath before speaking.

"I promise." He took her hand in his and kissed it. "Come back to me. Promise me."

"I promise." As she said it, she shouldered a mutual weight.

"Are you ready?" Zavier asked, turning to Gemma.

She nodded, uncorking the first vial. Gemma paused as the odor hit her; she gazed into the blue eyes by her side, which seemed to read the plea hiding in the darkest part of hers. Tobler put a hand on her leg and took away her fear.

"Go ahead, one quick gulp. No worries." He whispered, "I'll be here the whole time. I'm not leaving you."

Feeling more confident, Gemma tipped her head back and allowed gravity to work the thick concoction down her throat. It had the consistency of cod liver oil with a taste even more unpleasant; her contorted expression summed it up for all of them. She suppressed a dry heave as the vile liquid threatened to come back up.

"Taste like chicken?" Tobler teased, trying to make light of the situation.

"Oh, of course," Gemma joked, her face still scrunched and battling her body's reaction. Giving them all one last laugh before the real work began.

Orianna took her vial, swallowing the contents with more ease, and laid down. She drifted off to sleep. Gemma's eyes underwent a strange change as she gulped the second vial fast, stretching out beside Orianna. Tobler jumped as he saw her eyes turn white before they closed for sleep.

Without preamble, they slipped from the waking world. Their counterparts watched, helpless, searching for clues of a safe departure and awaiting a return.

CHAPTER THIRTY-TWO

GEMMA FOUND HERSELF IN a vast wooded area she had never seen before. Tall trees, thick with dark bark, surrounded her and grass layered beneath her feet. Ferns and wildflowers of all colors scattered as far as she could see. The mixed scents of floral and pine lingered in the air, generating a sense of peace. A rustling came from behind her, but it was only leaves rattled by the wind.

Gemma looked, but there was no one else around. Everything appeared as it would in the waking world. She wondered if she had even crossed over into the dream. She took a step forward, but the motion made her fuzzy. Ignoring the feeling, she took another a step—a move which was faster than normal. Unsure what to make of this bizarreness, Gemma moved on and hoped that once she found Orianna things would make sense.

The more she walked, the fuzziness increased, and her movements surged ahead. She slowed down, which helped the fuzziness go away; she wondered how she'd feel if she needed to run. Would it be possible, or would she topple over as numbness overtook her body? She would find out soon enough, she feared.

She continued her walk through brushes, ducking beneath branches. Small creatures scurried through treetops and the tall ferns, causing her to jump when they sounded too close. As she was about to duck under another branch, she found herself eye to eye with a fluffy animal about the size of a squirrel except it had longer fur and shorter ears. They stood still for a minute, the creature tilting its head, left to right, until it ran up the branch to disappear among the leaves.

Gemma continued on for a while, dodging plants and creatures, until she came to a small clearing. Although she would have liked to have remained in the protection of the thick woods, she'd have to step out to enact the plan. From where she stood, Gemma was behind an altar—a wooden arch full of white flowers, crawling up each side and meeting in the middle. This was flanked by two thick rows of log benches with an aisle between them.

The closer Gemma got, the more she recognized it as an empty wedding ceremony. The bile in her stomach churned, making her queasy as she considered what the scene implied. From off to the far side of the clearing, something white caught the corner of her eye. It was Orianna, motioning for Gemma to come toward her. No sign of Leo yet in the quiet clearing.

Gemma walked with care, trying not to raise suspicion in case they were being watched. The fuzzy numbness came back, but not in such a force as it had before. She thanked her lucky stars it was dissolving from her limbs the more she moved.

Orianna folded Gemma into a strong embrace. "Where did you end up? I was so worried when you didn't enter alongside of me."

"I was dropped off somewhere in the woods back there. I wasn't too far," she said, hugging her back.

"Thank goodness for that." Orianna held Gemma out at arm's length. "Are you okay? You're not hurt?"

"No, no I'm fine." Gemma studied her aunt, her confusion thickening. "Aunt O, what on earth are you wearing? Is that a wedding dress?"

Orianna looked down to see she was indeed dressed in a long, white gown; icy horror spiked through her stomach. She had not intended to show up in the wedding dress from her prior dream.

"Well, this won't do! Of all the nerve." Orianna flattened her palms above her waist and slid them down her torso, all the while muttering to herself. She changed the white wedding dress to her typical black dress. "Bastard. That's better."

"Why would you show up here in a wedding dress?" Gemma asked, looking back at the setup in the clearing; something cold ran over her skin. "You're not going to marry him, are you? Aunt O, please tell me you won't marry this guy?"

"No! Of course I'm not!" she said, her hands on her hips. "That's what he proposed in the last dream, but I won't do it. I'd rather rot from the inside out than marry that man."

"He wants to marry you? I don't understand."

"Leo wants me to join his army. Part of that includes taking my hand in marriage." Orianna's face went grave. "That is not happening. No one can ever force me to marry. Now Gemma, we have to hide you somewhere and fast."

"Why am I hiding? I thought we were doing this together?"

"We are, but he can't see you too soon. If he does, he'll try to use you as leverage against me. He's already tried it once. If he sees you here, it's over."

The ground started to spin under her feet. She forgot how involved she was in Leo's plans. "Why me?"

Orianna shrugged. "He believes you are one of the more powerful members of our family's bloodline, the alpha affinity. He wants access to your power so he can control it. I won't let that happen. No one will touch you."

"Aunt O, you can't always protect me. Let me stand by your side and fight him with you."

"No, that's out of the question. I won't let you put yourself in danger like that. It's not necessary."

"But we can take him! If we work together, we can bring him down! Don't you see? We need to do this together." Gemma began to raise her voice.

"Keep your voice down, girl!" Orianna scanned over Gemma's shoulder again in fear of what she might see. "I said no."

Gemma geared up to argue again, but Orianna stopped her. A quick anger burned through her veins at the sight of Orianna's flat palm, stopping her as if she were a child to be seen and not heard. As it faded Gemma tried to hold onto that anger, attempting to weaponize it—after all, it would be effective to use against Leo. She thought of the book she kept secret in her room, studying night after night, and reached deep in her mind for any other possible tools.

Her thoughts were interrupted by the sudden shift in the air that vibrated through the clearing, reaching the edge of the woods where they stood. It rattled on top of her skin before burrowing deeper. Orianna's eyes widened and she directed Gemma toward the trees to take cover.

Gemma listened, despite herself; it might be better to catch him by surprise. She pulled the shadows toward her for cover, finding they obeyed her much easier than in the alleyway when she first attempted it. Their silky essence slid into her palms and she disappeared, blending in perfectly.

Beneath her cloaked vision, Gemma watched as a tall man in a dark robe approached Orianna. He was tall and imposing, with a handsomeness that was undeniable. He reminded her of someone else, but who it might've been escaped her. The image intensified as she watched his approach, the coolness in his stride and a lustful spark gleaming in his green eyes. Her aunt stood still and straight, answering his lustful look with a stoic stare and the collected calm of a coiled snake.

"Ah, there you are," he said in greeting. "A vision, as always. How I've missed your beauty, among other things." He reached out to put a hand on Orianna's waist, but she stepped to the side.

"Hello, Leo." Her mouth felt like thick wool when she said his name, and her palms prickled with sweat.

"Such a cold welcome for your future husband, and you're so underdressed for the occasion." He appeared displeased as her expression slackened.

Orianna adjusted to appear more neutral. "I haven't fully decided if that's what you'll be. I have some reservations."

"I've given you enough time. What are your reservations?" He stepped closer. "Or perhaps you need a different kind of convincing."

She put a hand up, and he stopped. "That isn't necessary. It's only time I need."

Their words balanced along a knife's edge, daring an argument to break out into something more dangerous—a possibility which Leo somehow seemed to enjoy. Orianna dragged out the conversation with short responses, keeping him where she wanted him. The interaction aligned more with something sick and twisted, as opposed to how she and Zavier interacted with care and understanding.

Gemma waited for the right moment as Orianna gained momentum with her disturbing dance. The shadows start to fall apart in her hands, turning against her. They were no longer like taut silk sheets, dematerializing where she touched them. Her finger slipped through a hole on the right shadow, pulling it up to avoid exposure and regain her camouflage.

Orianna was stunned by Gemma's ability to manipulate shadows. It was not something she had ever taught her; that skill was considered Black Magic. Pondering briefly where she could have learned such a thing, her heart jumped in her throat when she witnessed her niece's near-exposure.

"I have my reservations," she cooed seductively, bracing herself for her next sentence. "But perhaps you need to persuade me some more."

His face relaxed into a grin. "I remember the kind of persuasion you liked, and despite how your interests have matured, I'm sure I can offer a few things you've missed." He ran a hand down the side of her body. "You may find some new points of interest."

Gemma fixed her grip on the larger of the shadows when she saw Leo turn and lead Orianna away. Orianna stopped him, grabbing his shoulder and locking him in with a kiss. The familiar shape of his lips reminded her of their youth, spending so much of their time like this...but instead of longing, she felt dread. A coldness filled the hollow spaces she hadn't thought of in years. His arms wrapped around her waist and his hands scrabbled like filthy paws up her back, causing her to push him back.

Leo's face lowered, inches from her, his hot breath on her skin. "I have missed you."

Orianna shivered like the mouse trapped in the lion's den. When she opened her mouth to return his affections, his eyes reflected a sixth sense. She tried to pull him back and distract him, but he put a hand on her chest and pushed her backward. Orianna almost lost her balance but caught her footing.

Leo turned as Gemma charged, knife swinging to plunge into his chest. With a flick of his hand, he threw the knife from her. He grabbed her by the wrist, squeezing until the small bones crunched with agonizing closeness. She feared he'd break it, the pain causing her knees to go weak. She struggled to recover the knife, but it was nowhere to be found; a cold sweat washed over her whole body as she feared the worst. She saw his cold eyes change from blue to full black to blue again. She tried to summon fire, but couldn't concentrate.

"You little—" His words were cut short by a groan as something struck him hard on the back. Still holding Gemma's wrist and twisting it, he turned around. "You bitch!"

"Let her go!" Orianna said, her hand covered in flames and coiled for another strike.

"You tried to have me killed after everything—" An unnerving calm overtook his expression, and without warning, he dropped Gemma's wrist. "*This* is what you really came here to do!" He stalked her, each step making her sicker.

Orianna threw the fireball, but he stretched and extinguished it his palm. She tried again and again, with no success. She tried to call out for Gemma to run, then he threw into a tree. Before she could regain her bearings, he stood before her with his hand gripping her throat. He slammed the back of her head against the rough bark.

"You reject my proposal for some lazy, noble-born son with almost no power of his own. Did he buy your love, you money-hungry whore?" As rage consumed him, the black tendrils uncoiled from his hands, sneaking their way around Orianna and the tree.

Orianna cried out as they burned her skin, her pain echoing through the woods. Gemma scrambled, desperate to find the knife; when she turned, she saw it tucked behind some brush. She grabbed it and tried to stab him again, but he caught sight of her from the corner of his eye. As he faced her, Gemma's eyes locked on. His eyes were full of cold callousness, freezing her to the ground. He appeared calm as the black fog, which paused its assault but never released Orianna.

"Stab me, and she dies."

"Kill him!" Orianna shouted, writhing in pain as the black fog burned her for talking out of turn.

"You could kill me. You're in the right position to do so, but that'll mean you aunt dies." He watched Gemma's unmoved expression, smiling as she struggled with her dilemma. "Once I die, there will be no stopping it from consuming her whole, ensuring her a most painful death. But of course, that choice is yours."

"Why should I trust you?" Gemma said with steel in her voice, her hand gripping the hilt of the bone knife tighter.

"Well," he grinned, "you should never trust anyone. There is no trust, only gambles. So here is your gamble—kill me, right here and now. Perhaps she lives or perhaps she dies. Or come with me, and we'll talk. If you agree, Gemma, I won't harm her."

She felt an icy chill layer over her skin at the sound of him saying her name. "How do you know who I am?"

A deep chuckle echoed from inside his chest. "How could I not?" With a snap of his fingers, Orianna was restrained to the tree as he walked towards Gemma. "Look at you—night-pitch hair, dark eyes, all leading toward those full red lips. You're an Oliver witch, alright." He glanced back at Orianna before moving closer, stopping an uncomfortable distance near Gemma. "So beautiful...perhaps I should trade up for the younger, more beautiful Oliver witch. You could be more like your aunt than you realize. I could give you so much power and more, things you couldn't imagine."

Gemma was paralyzed, unsure if it was from fear or her resolve to appear brave and in control. Leo traced the side of her face with his fingers, causing a strange slithering inside—something she did not understand, inspiring her disgust.

A series of words mumbled from a distance before Leo arched his back in agony, and Gemma's paralysis slid away from her. A string of loud cracks erupted from his body, like bones breaking and resetting as he made his way back to Orianna.

With each step closer, she struggled to loosen the magic bonds. She was free for a few seconds before he struck again, slamming her into the tree; this time, she couldn't move anything, and the white dress reappeared.

"Looks like you haven't forgotten the old tricks, after all. You should have agreed to come back to me," he growled.

The black fog appeared, thicker and angrier to reflect Leo's mood, binding her with a searing heat. Their hot tendrils circled her neck, threatening a blistering death if she dared to move again.

"No!" Gemma screamed, charging. As she about reached him, she was thrown into the air and slammed into the ground. A storm darkened, overtaking over the clearing.

"Enough of your games. Make your choice, girl!" His eyes pulsed a bright green, along with a thick vein in his neck. "You will agree to my terms or history will repeat. You will be at my side for it all, I swear."

"Let's talk!" Gemma called, collapsed on the broken ground where she was thrown. "I'll hear you out, just let her go."

Leo turned to study Gemma. He released her aunt, seeming pleased. He nodded as Orianna shook her head.

"Gemma, no, don't—" Orianna's words were cut short by another painful tug.

"You said you wouldn't hurt her. Stop it!" Gemma scowled.

"I believe what I said was, I wouldn't kill her," he said, walking over and extending a hand. "Take it. We're not talking here since the two of you cannot be trusted."

"I won't leave the dreamscape with you." Gemma said with her mouth in a firm line. "I'm young, not stupid."

Leo nodded in understanding. "Very well, take my hand and we'll go to a different part of this dreamscape—one where I can ensure no further ambushes."

Gemma took a deep breath and placed her hand in Leo's before they disappeared.

CHAPTER THIRTY-THREE

THE HOUSE ECHOED WITH recurring footsteps, back and forth and back again, across the wooden planks of the upstairs bedroom. An unusual chill clung to the air around the master bedroom, growing more frigid if either of them stood too close to women on the bed.

Tobler's pacing gave his muscles some heat as he tried to take his mind off of what could be happening inside the dreamworld. Trying to avoid imagining what Gemma faced in a place he could not reach her, wondering whether Leo appeared to kick off what was sure to be something nasty. With each turn down the room, his blood turned angrier—worse, as he caught sight of Zavier. Although he was supposed to be the counterpart in this scheme, he felt anything but.

Zavier sat by Orianna's side in an old wooden rocking chair, creaking with each steady movement. His face was the epitome of patience; he took the pipe from an inside pocket of his shirt and set it between his lips, not ready to light it yet. He pulled open a drawer in the nightstand, poking and prodding until he found his matches. Minutes ticked away, and with each expelled breath, the orb grew heavier in Tobler's pocket. The delicate business sparked a pressurized turmoil he'd never experienced. Tension built within, greater the more he witnessed Zavier's detachment, tighter until Tobler snapped.

"How are you calm right now? They could die in there!"

"I'm calm because losing my mind won't help anything. You'd do well to remain calm, yourself—if you're smart." Zavier, striking a match, lit his pipe. The air filled with notes of tobacco and dark fruits. Tobler's footsteps resumed their rhythm: forward, back track, forward, back track, forward, back track. "And stop your incessant pacing. You're making me nuts."

Tobler's fists clenched. "At least I'm *concerned*. I'm not indifferent and smoking my pipe like it's any other night while— ugh, Black sodding Hells. She could *die* in there, damn you! Do you understand what that *means*?"

Zavier sat up and took another pull off his pipe, staring at Tobler before speaking. "I'm aware that they *both* could, but not staying calm will make us no use to them at all. You'd do well to listen to your elders, boy."

Blistered at being told how to behave like some child, Tobler mumbled a string of words under his breath. Zavier caught the ramblings, mostly insults toward his parentage. No longer the face of calm, Zavier stood from the creaking rocking chair and towered over Tobler—even from the opposite side of the bed.

"Watch yourself, boy. I've snapped larger men than you before. Now is not the time to test my patience."

Intimidation striking the proper nerve, Tobler backed down. Zavier took his seat, signaling for Tobler to do the same next to Gemma. They were quiet for a few minutes, and the restlessness on Tobler's face shone through, causing Zavier's angry eyes to soften as he remembered the earlier years of his own relationship.

He let out a blustery sigh, heavy with stress, and ran a hand over his face. "I know your heart is deep in this, Tobler—fresh love, and all—but you've got to get your head on straight."

"I'm trying to." Tobler fidgeted with a pebble on the floor, not making eye contact. "It's not as easy as you make it look."

Zavier nodded, lost to memories, but his heart sympathized. He was not the only one going stir crazy; although Zavier did not show it, he was wracked with turmoil over both women being in the direct line of fire. "I understand, son, really I do. But—"

"Shit, Zavier, look." Tobler interrupted, looking like he'd seen the Devil himself.

Zavier followed his eyes to see purple and blue splotches emerge against the delicate skin around Gemma's wrist. Her body remained still, as if nothing happened, illustrating the injuries originated in the dreamworld.

Tobler paused, his posture stiffening as he scowled. "Looks like he found them."

Zavier reflected Tobler's disposition, illuminating the primal protective instincts buried within the heart and blood of every man. "Now. We watch. We'll wake them if we decide this gets carried away."

Tobler looked at Zavier, unsure if he had heard him right. "But you promised Orianna we wouldn't wake them, no matter what happened."

A loud, sickening crack came from Orianna, the unmistakable sound of ribs breaking. It resonated in the quiet room, striking Zavier hard in the chest as he stomach turned.

"I lied," he said, gruff and angry as he leaned in to jostle Orianna awake.

Tobler reached out in reflex, stopping Zavier's hand. "Wait! Not yet! We should wait until something worse happens." He attempted to push Zavier's large hand away, but he wouldn't budge. He was treading on dangerous ground. "This could be our only chance. I understand you're angry—trust me, I want to stop this, too—but if we don't wait, it'll be worse. I can't afford...

I don't want Gemma to have to do this again. We've only got one shot at this."

"How far do we let this go? More broken bones? Blood from their ears?" Zavier spoke through gritted teeth. "Where do you propose we draw the line?"

The question hung between them as Tobler didn't have a good answer. There was no winning in this situation; if he tried to force-calm Zavier, then he would become enraged. Honesty was the only option.

"I don't know. If there is any *serious* damage happening, we stop it." He tried to think quicker. "Blood—we'll draw the line at possibly fatal bleeding and try our best to wake them. Deal?"

"Fine," Zavier shook off his grip and Tobler felt the full weight of the large man's scrutiny, "we'll wait."

Tobler waited until the angry man sat back down before lowering himself into his own seat. An abundance of air returned to his lungs, making him aware that he had been holding his breath while he waited for Zavier to reach a resolution.

The minutes ticked through the sluggish night.

CHAPTER THIRTY-FOUR

THE CYCLONE OF BLACK smoke faded, and Gemma found herself in a less pleasing part of the dreamscape. They were still in the same woods, except this section appeared run down. Leo walked across dead grass, and Gemma followed him along the black path. Leo's arm brushed against hers, sparking a gross hatred deep within her. Surrounding them were broken trees with shattered limbs, black fungus suffocating the bark; the infected trunks showed signs of decay. They stepped through a fog of noxious gas which made her ill, reminding her of rotten eggs. She held her breath until they made it to the edge of woods, free of the fog.

The mouth of the path opened to a weathered stone bridge crossing a sluggish river. Its round, brown stones were slick with dark moss, except where pieces of the stone were broken. The sight of its damage and decay frightened her, but she kept walking. Leo remained silent, which fueled her anxiety, but she attempted to appear composed. The knife was back, hidden in the sheath beneath her skin. It should've made her safer, but instead her heart raced within her chest. She was armed, but what good would it do if she couldn't reach it? Or what if Leo saw the outline—how far would he go to disarm her?

The threat of a storm hovered on the horizon, waiting to release rain from the dark clouds. The smell of a waiting downpour stained the air, and the sky lit from oncoming thunder. The calm before a thunderstorm was an overlooked gem not many appreciated; it was always one of Gemma's favorite moments, but this one filled her with trepidation. She thought of Orianna, still bound to the tree and in pain. She remembered why she was here, why she chose, and pulled courage from her cowardly soul.

"How much further?" she asked, surprised her voice didn't crack.

"We're close," he said, stepping to the side of a hole in the center of the bridge and offering his hand. "Watch your step."

Gemma paused, looking down at the water—not a far drop, but she feared what lived in those murky depths. She wondered briefly if she could cross on her own without falling, preparing to test the surrounding area with the tip of her shoe.

"You don't want to do that." Leo warned, his hand still out.

"Why's that?" As Gemma pushed down, the step crumbled, and she jumped back.

"That's why. It's not worth the risk. But if you take my hand, I'll make sure you cross safely." He watched her, seeing she was not entirely convinced. "Trust me."

"I trust you as much as I trust a cannibal to babysit," she snorted, testing for another way around, but more stones fell beneath under foot.

He chuckled at her struggle. "Such strong wit. Take my hand, or you'll fall—and believe me, you don't want to fall down there. Unless you don't value your skin, then by all means go on ahead and jump in the acid—it'll feel great."

Gemma watched the acid bubble and eat the fallen stones before they sank. Her heart stuttered as she realized he wasn't lying. She accepted his hand, taking a literal leap of faith to the other side.

As Leo promised, he pulled her along and gave her safe crossing...until he swept her into his arms. She cringed from his disgusting appeal, pushing him away but careful not to fall back into the acid. As she brushed herself off, she noticed he eyed her with a salacious grin. She didn't give him the satisfaction of acknowledging it; instead, she walked to the end of the bridge.

Before she could relax, he caught up with her. He was faster and quieter, and her newfound courage foundered.

"I'm not so terrible, after all, now am I?" he asked.

She refused to look, walking farther ahead. "No, you're not—you're worse."

"If I were worse, I would have pushed you off that bridge and watched your body be eaten away by the hungry river. Instead, I chose to save you and keep my side of the bargain."

"How do I know that you're keeping your side? For all I know, you could still have your bloodthirsty...whatever the hell it is, wrapped around her." The thought unsettled Gemma and she grew angry not to have asked for proof of Orianna's safety earlier.

Leo stopped, revealing the black tendrils sliding and coiling around his hands and wrist. "Because I took them with me."

Gemma's mouth went dry, but she nodded. Leo's slithering minions retracted into his wrists and continued walking. He looked back to see Gemma frozen to her spot.

"If I wanted to kill you, you'd be dead already. Come on, almost there." He continued without her, and as she found the strength in her legs to move again.

They were quiet for a few hundred feet until reaching another clearing; this one contained a graveyard instead of a wedding altar. The stones were dirty, obscuring the names. All air left Gemma's lungs at the sight. Leo stopped at the black iron gates guarding the entrance.

He spoke to Gemma in a commanding, yet honey-coated voice. "Let's talk."

* * *

From the other side of the dreamscape, Orianna was still bound to the tree despite Leo taking his black beasts with him. She struggled against the invisible restraints, but the pressure around her limbs and wrists bit into her skin. The more she struggled, the more intense the pain became. Resting her head against the tree trunk, she tried to relax in hope that the invisible attacker would release its grip; she sighed with relief when she realized she was right. Her breathing was ragged until she focused, in through her nose and out her mouth, trying to regain mental clarity.

Orianna thought hard, but the only option was a nasty spell she'd nearly forgotten. She would have to reach back into her dark past with Leo, plucking the strings of the blood magic they had delved into when they were young and naïve. But she had no choice. This was not the place for her ethics.

She took another deep breath, closing her eyes and reaching deep inside; her eyes opened when the spell came to mind. She muttered a foreign language, surprised by how much she remembered; once one touched darkness, there was no forgetting its power. In the middle of a sentence, she bit her tongue and continued the verse as the blood pooled to the side of her mouth. A split second after she finished, she spat the blood at her restraints—or where she thought they were. The bonds cried out, then slackened from around her shoulders. It was working.

She repeated the process—mutter, spit, mutter, spit—until she was freed. Her feet hit the ground. Unchained, she rubbed at her sore wrists, happy to see that there wasn't much bleeding. Now, she had to find them.

Orianna walked to where they disappeared, searching for any evidence of the magic he used, but there was no residue.

Leo had clearly gotten better at hiding his trail. She cursed his name under her breath and a thought came to her, a memory. She couldn't call to Gemma's blood, unwilling to taint her with dark magic, but she could call to Leo's. When they were young and in love they made a blood pact, a form of binding spell, and these things never left. A binding of the blood was unforgiving due to its permanent nature, but that very permanence often drew young lovers to try it.

Curiosity and naïve love drew them to one another, but their toxicity tore them apart.

Walking over to the tree that held her captive, Orianna snapped a branch from one of its limbs and broke it in half. Holding the pointy end, she pressed deep into her palm over the small white scar where she had made her binding with Leo. She dragged it across her skin until dark red beads welled up and pooled in her palm.

With her hand outstretched, palm facing upward, Orianna made a fist and tipped her hand, watching as the blood dripped to the ground. Keeping her arm steady, she turned to make a circle of blood as she muttered the strange language again. She called to Leo's blood in an effort to find where he'd gone. The blood transformed into a crimson flame around her, rising over her head before it disappeared...taking her with it to whatever destination it found.

* * *

"In the right hands, power can be an immense asset. You just need to understand the benefits. We miss out on so much when magic is hoarded from us." Leo droned on, trying to make a self-righteous case for his needs.

"It's hoarded from the likes of you, people who abuse magic. I'd rather cut the magic out of me than give into it with you," Gemma snapped back without thinking.

An inhuman chuckle arose from deep in his chest. "So fiery and vocal. I enjoy such qualities in a woman."

Leo walked closer, and her throat went dry again. She feared he'd lay a hand on her; she froze, unable to put any distance between them. This caused her to wonder if it was by her own choosing that she didn't move or was some strange, powerful force working against her. But he stopped—close, but without doing anything other than making eye contact.

"I'm not the monster you think I am. Your beloved aunt had a desire for power once, too—a lust greater than mine, as it were. I don't deny that it still lurks under her skin, waiting to be stoked back to life." The words dripped from his tongue like honey, and Gemma saw the yearning behind his eyes. "But someone kept talking in her ear, talking down our relationship, our alliance...a mutual need for drunken ecstasy, which came with the darkness of our needs. No loss to me when that meddling bitch burst into flames."

Sparks of rage built inside her, smoldering into a full-fledged fire that threatened to engulf her. He had a lot of nerve to speak that way about her mother, whom she loved but had never met. The knife burned in its hidden sheath. She no longer cared if he saw her rip it from her skin, so long as she could plunge it into his chest.

"Once you touch dark magic, there is a high you crave, Gemma. It invigorates your soul, sets your nerves on edge but makes you more alive than you've ever been. You grow the inability to feel pain, if you do it right. True liberation from this oppressive world, which grows far more tolerable when you're soulless. Truly, it's worth the cost."

"Nothing is worth your soul," she said, unmoving. "Such darkness only brings bad things with it, making people evil. It is morally wrong."

"Is that what you really believe?" He paused, green eyes weighing her down. "What of your aunt, then? She dabbled in dark magic, was very good at it. Is she evil?"

"No, of course not. She gave it up and redeemed herself. She always talks about its evils. She is against Black Magic of any kind."

"Are you sure? Really sure? You know this because of what? It's what she tells you, is that right?"

Gemma nodded, not having a need to explain herself further to the likes of him.

"Ah, I see. Of course, she wouldn't lie to you. Tell me, what Light Magic involves the use of bones?" His face darkened and thunder rumbled beneath their feet.

Gemma hesitated, the bone knife becoming heavier on her arm. "I know nothing of bones used for magic."

"Dark magic, if we follow your train of thought, is wrong no matter what. You would never participate in that—no, not you. Yet, that's what protects you in that house, makes it so no one can see inside the windows—raven's bones, a nice touch. Your aunt was smart with that one." He grinned, making him appear both handsome and dangerous. "What do you know about blood magic?"

Gemma tried to move again, but with no success as sweat beaded her temple. "That it's Black Magic and not to be used. It's forbidden."

"Is that right? So dark and forbidden that you used it to save your mother's life with your little protection glyph?" He watched as the blood drained from Gemma's face. "Worked well, I must say. No one has been able to beat down the doors since. But you'd never use such magic, with it being so dark and all," he scoffed, mocking her as he walked toward the gate.

Gemma's words dried up on her tongue, leaving her motionless; had her aunt been dealing in the dark arts, after all? But that was different. Orianna had used Black Magic to keep Gemma safe. There was a fine line between Black and Light Magic, but Leo was way over the line.

"You see?" A salacious grin formed as he felt the scales tip in his favor. "You've been saved by Black Magic, more than you know. Doesn't seem all that bad, does it? Let's try one more. Your little shadow trick, now where did you learn that? I *almost* couldn't tell you were there. Quite the skill, for an amateur—a spell the average witch struggles to master."

"I-I read about it in a book I found. That can't be evil, it's just a protection spell." And at the word protection, she felt the bottom of her stomach fall out. The other dark spells he had mentioned were also for protection.

A mischievous glint sparked in his eye. "Of course it is—well, not in the *exact* way you used it. For centuries, shadow-cloaking was used in diabolical schemes: robbery, murder, ambush, and more. A way to hide when you're in places you are not supposed to be. Once you've mastered it, you can even take the shadows as ingredients for various poisons and elixirs. That is, once you can get past their screams. After the first one, it's like squashing flies."

"I didn't know they could feel pain. I didn't mean to—"

"Oh, but that's how it starts. You dabble. Try new things, unknowingly or knowingly break a few of the rules. You get your first taste for it, that first caress of," Leo stepped closer to Gemma, so close they were almost touching, "true, unadulterated power. The rawness fresh on your skin, thrumming in your veins with that first high. Eventually, you keep reaching out because it's so good. It's exhilarating! I'd be glad to be the one to teach you how it all works."

Gemma grew breathless in the wake of his offer and his proximity; some part of her was attracted by the notion. Shame flared inside, and she fought the part of her blood singing for his guidance.

He touched her arms, gentle but firm as if reading her body language. "I know that look. You think it shameful. I used to think so, too, once—but it's not. Don't deny your natural instincts. You opened yourself up to the darkness, to me. Let me help you develop your hunger for it. You'd be of much use to me."

Gemma's limbs trembled, unable to comprehend what had come over her. Leo seized the opportunity to take advantage of her state.

"Let me show you what you could be."

With a snap of his fingers, Leo set a dilapidated shrub on fire. In the flames, he conjured an image of Gemma from the last dreamwalk. She recognized herself, but something was different. She wore a fine black dress, hair cascading past her shoulders to reveal a face radiating ethereal beauty. In this image, she appeared powerful and respected. As Gemma peered closer, she grew distracted by a circular column of red fire out of the corner of her eye.

Gemma didn't turn, ignoring her aunt so Leo wouldn't sense her approach, but she found herself captivated by the image of who she could become under Leo's guidance and tutelage. A strange want called to her, awakening something dormant within; it hungered to feed off of Leo's words and promises.

Orianna rolled her hands and produced a ball of black flames; she took aim before hurling, but Leo moved. Moments before he was assaulted by the black flaming ball, Leo attempted to deflect it but the blow held too much force. Instead of flinging it away, it hit him mid-thigh and knocked him back a few steps. He called out in pain, loud enough to pull Gemma from her trance as the images of herself shimmered back into the air.

"I knew you'd come," he said with a wicked grin.

Orianna, too angry to reply, rolled another black fireball. "Get away from her, you bastard."

Leo stepped toward Orianna, his face all-knowing. She realized he was getting what he wanted, but she was too far deep into his plot to stop.

"I always knew how to push to get what I wanted out of you."

Orianna threw her weapon, but he was ready. He deflected her attack, sending the graveyard gate up in flames. Gemma watched for a moment as the iron melted to liquid, pooling onto the ground and evaporating without a trace. She shuddered at the thought of what that heat would've done to a human body. Her mind wondered what sort of magic was capable of such fatal results, but she knew thanks to a nagging tug at the back of her mind.

Leo walked around Orianna, causing her to move away. They circled each other, a predatorial dance that he appeared to enjoy. He held the upper hand, backing her into a corner like a cat. Leo flicked his hand as Orianna recoiled for an attack that never came. Orianna's guts knotted up as she realized he toyed with her, testing her reflexes and paranoia.

"So jumpy! You never had to be mistrustful when we were calling the shots, on our way to rule and ruin," he smiled, but between his teeth laid treachery.

"I never would have stayed if..." she paused, startled by a softness for him she'd thought was gone long ago. "I never intended to go through with the plan. I never wanted the plan."

"No, no, I was always upfront with you, Orianna," he said her name the way he used to, causing the hair on her arms to stand. "I showed you the depths of my heart, sharing all the plans I had for us. The things we suffered...I would've done anything to right those injustices, to change the future in my favor and yours."

"You held secrets you're not talking about! It was selfishness that resided in your heart all those years ago, and it is devilry that lives there now!"

Orianna threw two fireballs this time, but he deflected them both with little effort, sending them into the woods. One whizzed pasted Gemma's head, jarring her wits. She tried to remove the knife from under her skin, but nothing happened. With one hand over her forearm, she tried again to force it through her skin; it sparked a searing pain, burning her arm from the inside out. She began to shake, stopping when she could not take the pain anymore.

"You were always such a good liar, saving face in front of the girl. You Olivers always were all about appearance!"

He pulled a small dagger from his cloak, slicing across his palm. Cupping the blood, he brought it to his lips and whispered; the liquid sputtered and hissed, until he flung it at her. She tried to deflect it, but missed; it hit her face, and she recoiled from the pain.

"You stood at my side, every step together...studying and practicing, savoring every piece of magic we stole. No matter how dark it was, you had your black hands in it just as deep as I did. Conjuring, perfecting, charging—you were there to help me with it all. You can't deny it." Leo stared her down, hungrily awaiting her answer as she fought against the blood spell.

Orianna's face contorted in pain. "I helped you back then, but we were just kids. This wasn't how it was supposed to end. I never wanted to lose my family."

Leo tilted his head to the side. "You liked it though, didn't you? How many times I watched you relish in the rush, in the adrenaline of it all. You lusted after the high ever since it first ran through your veins, just as much as I did. Didn't you? Didn't you! Tell the truth, I'm not the only monster here."

As his blood burned inside of her, Orianna's voice cracked. "I did, and its tantalizing thrum gave me a thrill each time we used it...but it wasn't right. I trusted you."

Gemma's stomach turned at her aunt's words, adding to her panicked failure to free the knife. Desperate, her eyes darted for something that could help her cut the knife from her skin—anything—as she clawed her skin with her fingernails. Orianna hurled a heavy branch across their circle, but before it collided into him, Leo shattered it into large splinters—some of which landed at Gemma's feet. She seizes the largest and dragged it across her skin, cutting her the way to the knife.

"They stood in our way, poisoning your mind!" Leo bellowed; his face masked in anger as he spread his arms wide. A distinct rattle vibrated through the ground, followed by the sound of something bursting from the earth. "Sacrifices were to be made! I never kept that from you. I will take you and the girl back with me!"

He shoved forward, and a tombstone hurled toward Orianna. Distracted by the pain his blood caused her, Orianna was unable to rebound the stone; she tried to evade but it sent her tumbling to the ground. Orianna held her shoulder, crying out as the crippling pain tore through. Leo stormed over to where Orianna laid on the ground and grabbed her by the back of her hair, dragging her to the tombstone. Once her face was over the stone, he pushed her against its smooth surface...engraved with her sister's name. A heart-wrenching sob broke out from Orianna's lips, and tears poured down her cheeks.

"This was not my fault! If you had just stuck to what we agreed! You did this! You—"

His insane rambling was cut short by the knife Gemma plunged into his back, replaced by a deafening silence after his lungs exhaled a sharp gasp. He released Orianna, and she fell onto the headstone. As the blood trickled down her temple, she propped herself up on an elbow to watch him.

Stiff with pain, Leo tried to stand upright but stumbled towards Gemma. Furious and pained, he turned to his attacker but she was ready. His labored breathing empowered her. She squared her shoulders, delivering a forceful blow that threw him far and away from Orianna. Leo landed with a force that shook the ground until he crumbled, motionless in the dirt.

Gemma ran to Orianna, slumped over the headstone, fearing the worst. She touched Orianna's shoulder, causing her to yelp in pain. Somehow, Orianna lifted her torso and muttered in the foreign tongue. The dreamscape flickered like vapor off of hot pavement. Pieces of the setting started to disappear and Orianna sped up. They were starting to awaken. She stopped as a ring of fire surrounded Leo's body.

"What's happening? What are you doing?" Gemma asked, panicked.

"We're waking up. Hold on!" she commanded.

The headstone tumbled back but not before Gemma caught the name engraved across its face. The hair on the back of her neck stood on end before the stone shattered into rubble.

CHAPTER THIRTY-FIVE

ORIANNA AND GEMMA GASPED as they bolted straight up in bed. Orianna let out a wail of pain before falling back, trying to replace the air in her lungs. Zavier and Tobler let out heavy breaths, relieved to see that their watchmen duties were over and both women survived.

Tobler grabbed Gemma, kissing her hard while his heart pounded against his chest. Both were lost to elation as he ran his hand through her hair, holding her even closer. And Gemma reciprocated, all too happy to be free from a dark world where she didn't have him and feared never seeing him again.

Zavier embraced Orianna's battered body, stopping at once as she inhaled sharply. The gasp expanded her chest, sending multiple stings of pain in every line of her cracked ribs. He cradled her with care. She took in more air with careful measure, pushing through and cautiously kissing Zavier back to assure him she was okay.

"I'm sorry, my love."

"It's okay. I didn't realize how bad off I was," Orianna said through clenched teeth, gestured toward the various items of first-aid bottles on the nightstand.

Zavier inspected each label until he found a clear bottle for pain and handed it to Orianna. She took a large swallow, waiting until its heat ran through her chest and over her ribs.

"I'm so relieved you're both alive," Tobler said, resting his forehead against Gemma's.

"Me too," she said, breathing in his scent which calmed her raw nerves. "I was scared we wouldn't make it, that I would never see you again."

"I had my doubts," Zavier said. "If it hadn't been for Tobler, I may have woken you too soon. Thanks, son, you were right."

"Eh, it wasn't anything you wouldn't have done. Although, I may need fresh pants after you standing over me like that," Tobler jested, and their laughs echoed in the room.

Orianna winced as her chuckles reverberated off her ribs, then turned her attention to Zavier. "I had a sneaky feeling that was a fragile promise. Things looked pretty bleak, but Gemma saved us both. Thank you."

Gemma nodded as images and words flooded her mind, leaving her unsettled. She recalled how Orianna trapped Leo in a ring of fire and she won. "We both did what we had to."

Nodding back, Orianna wondered how much Gemma had heard from Leo's insane ramblings, and a fresh fear tinged her skin. "That we did. But it's over now, and we can put it behind us."

Gemma felt a part of her bristle at her aunt's suggestion of forgetting what happened. She had questions that needed answering. She couldn't leave this in a dusty corner of the past.

Sensing the tension, Zavier stood up. "I'll grab a few things to start bandaging you two up. Tobler." He nodded towards the door.

"I don't want to leave you," Tobler said to Gemma. Before he could get a response, Zavier picked him up by the back of the shirt and set him on his feet.

"Come on. You can be all hearts and flowers later," Zavier grumbled, leading Tobler out and closing it behind him.

A pregnant silence hung between the two woman and Orianna waited, not wanting to make the first move.

"I don't know how to ask you so I'm just going to say it. Do you still use Black Magic?"

Orianna took a breath in. "What made you think that?"

"Don't answer me with a question. I want the truth, damn it. Have you been using Black Magic—yes or no?" Gemma crossed her arms over her chest, surprised at the soreness in her wrist. She wondered briefly if Leo had bruised her.

Orianna swallowed, knowing Gemma was right and that she deserved the truth. "Yes, but only certain kinds to help protect you."

"Did you ever stop to think that you not giving up Black Magic is what brought this on to begin with?"

Orianna shook her head. "That has nothing to do with this. I told you before there are bigger things that he is after than some lovers spat from eons ago, Gemma. It doesn't matter—"

"Yes it does, especially when you lecture against dark magic practices and spit in the presence of those who practice it. You're a hypocrite."

"Don't raise your voice at me. You think I'm not ashamed of the things I've done with Black Magic? I've made mistakes in the craft, but that doesn't mean you should dabble in things that shouldn't be touched. I haven't thought about it for years, until now, but it's all been to keep you safe." Orianna tried to sit up but couldn't, settling against the headboard. She gritted her teeth, taking a deeper breath to quell her anger. "So quick you are to point out my shortcomings, yet you seemed to have mastered some rather advanced shadow-cloaking. Where in the Black Hells did you learn that? Certainly not from me."

"Learning from your mistakes means you don't repeat them." Gemma sneered. "I didn't know I was doing Black Magic. It was just something I read about, and it seemed harmless. I only used it to save myself."

"And that's what I did! Yet you seem perfectly fine persecuting me for keeping us all safe. Everything I've done, it's been with your best interest in mind, Gemma. Don't let Leo poison your mind." A memory struck Orianna, and something inside of her twisted. "Unless he already has."

"What is that supposed to mean?"

"What did you discuss when you were alone?"

Their conversation was interrupted as Zavier and Tobler walked back into the room. Each man brandished an assortment of first-aid jars and bandages, resembling makeshift war nurses. The palpable tension faded, calming the heat of the argument from their tongues.

"Alright, that's enough of that." Zavier commanded. "Gemma, you go down the hall to your room, and Tobler will fix you up. No funny business, boy, you hear me?"

Tobler nodded with a mock salute. "Yes, sir. Gemma, let's take care your wounds."

Gemma swung her legs over to the side of her bed; dizzy, at first, she held the sides of the bed to steady herself before moving again. Tobler shifted his supplies to one arm, offering Gemma his free one to keep her balance. She got up, pained in places she didn't recall having injured, and a slight pounding filled her head. Stepping with care across the creaking floor, they continued down the hall to her room. Tobler closed the door behind them.

"Your turn, stubborn woman." Zavier walked over to her side of the bed, stopping her as she tried to sit up further. "I don't think that's a wise idea. I can see you're worse off than the girl. Can't imagine he went easy on you."

"Well, I was the target, after all. I had to keep her safe." Orianna pushed herself upright in a sitting position.

Zavier grunted as he continued to tend to the wounds around her ankles. The sinking hole in her gut foreshadowed another oncoming fight. Patient, she waited as he tended to her cuts, bruises, and burns; soon enough, he'd let her know what was on his mind.

Through the door and down the hall to the bedroom door near the stairs, Tobler and Gemma sat in muted conversation of their own. In the gentle glow of clustered candles, Tobler worked on Gemma's scattered wounds. Although far less extensive than her aunt's, they needed tending all the same. With precision, he altered between cleaning her cuts and scrapes to eradicate any infection that might've lurked inside, apologizing when the solution burned or caused her discomfort.

"You don't have to keep saying you're sorry, Tobler," Gemma told him, wincing at the sting of the alcohol.

"I know, I know, I just feel bad" he gazed up at her, catching her pained expression. "And when you make faces like that, it's impossible not to."

"I know, I'm sorry."

"Now you're the one apologizing," Tobler chuckled. "What a screwed-up mess *we* are."

Gemma tried to chuckle in agreement, its ring lightening the room. Tobler couldn't help but smile back. He had been scared earlier that he might never hear her laugh again; to hear it now was a balm on his raw nerves. The sudden weight that had plagued them all evening drifted away. The thoughts they had both survived clambered onto them, and a moonlight sliver of hope took root. They lived. They were sitting beside each other, eradicating a dreaded threat and escaping death.

In a flurry of movement, Tobler was kissing her and the pain didn't matter to Gemma anymore. The sensation of his lips on hers felt right, and the world fell into place again. No place could've felt more like home because he was her home.

Their souls recognized one another's before they themselves were entirely aware of it.

CHAPTER THIRTY-SIX

LEO GASPED AS HIS eyes opened wide, frightened and still covered in the white dreamwalker's film. His vision clouded, the entire room a foggy screen as his eyes returned to their natural states. He tried to take a deep breath but excruciating pain sprang from his back, forcing him to manage shallow breaths that left him wanting more. He sat up, inflamed with more pain and the stickiness of something wet and warm beneath him; unable to reach behind, he noticed the red massacre on the sheets beneath. A thin sweat of panic covered his body as he realized the severity of his injury, knowing he couldn't reach the wound to tend to it.

He tried to control his groans of pain, making his way to the opposite end of his room. Another failed attempt to breathe threatened to bring him to his knees. He stumbled, catching himself on a chair by his fireplace. Pausing, he gasped and tried to walk again. The more he exerted himself, the more his legs threatened to become a gelatinous mess, hurling him to the floor.

He lasted in time to grab hold of a particular wall panel. There, an intricate carving of a roaring gargoyle was carved into the wall. Leo puts his hand inside of its mouth, pushing on the tongue until he heard a click. Bracing himself against the joining wall, he waited until the pocket door vibrated and slid open to reveal a dark, short hallway.

Leo stepped in, banging on the door as the wall behind him slid closed. Swallowed up by the pure darkness, he continued to bang against the door in front of him. He grew weaker, waiting. The door was cold against his forehead, and he heard a muffled string of curses from the other side. Another familiar click and the door slid open. Unable to hold himself up any longer, he slumped into Griselda's arms.

"Leo? Leo!" Griselda shook him to consciousness, and pain caused him to open his eyes. "What in the Black Hells happened to you?"

He answered her with grunt as she brought him to her bed, sitting him down. Griselda climbed on the bed, her insides gone cold at the sight of the blood at his back. His shirt was saturated with it, and she tore it off his body. Her breath caught in her chest and her heart give a thud at the sight of the deep, bloody wound.

"Leo, what is this?" Griselda asked, paling. "Who did this to you?"

Leo groaned. "I was ambushed trying to recruit some new members."

"What members are capable of getting the jump on you? This is why you have your low-grade minions. They are the expendable ones—that's what they are for." Griselda put pressure on his wound to stop the bleeding.

"Orianna and Gemma... I had them trapped in the dreamscape. Gemma got the upper hand while I was busy persuading Orianna to cross to our side." Leo cried out in pain as Griselda pushed harder on his wound.

Anger and jealousy seethed out of Griselda's every pore; her teeth clenched at the thought of him being alone with his lost flame, and her sympathies waned. "Stupid man. It's a good thing it hadn't hit you a little more to the right or else you'd be dying a slow, painful death in your bed. Choking on your own blood and leaving me with nothing."

"Jealousy doesn't lay well on you, Griselda. Besides, you know where you stand with me. That should be enough."

"So you say, yet I catch you chasing Orianna through your dreams."

Once she was satisfied that his bleeding had slowed down, Griselda got off the bed and headed to a large armoire. He watched as she opened the door, listening to the clinking sounds of her searching for something.

"It is the girl I am after, her and her power. An alliance with Orianna is extra insurance—better to have her on our side than on someone else's." He took another breath in. "But I don't need to explain myself to you, now do I. After all, I am the one in charge here."

Griselda looked over her shoulder with a cocked eyebrow. "Funny, you aren't very in charge from where I'm standing."

She turned back to her mixing and stirring, unaware of Leo's targeted grimace. His patience had been wearing thin with her for some time, each time becoming harder and harder to keep his composure. He ignored her rebellious nature, for the moment. She was capable of both fixing him and keeping quiet about how close he came to death. If the others knew he could bleed or be wounded, they'd never listen to him or his promises of immortality; he'd have an uprising outside of his control.

He ignored her, but she could not keep quiet.

"I remember something about you being able to regrow limbs." She finished pouring and mixing the last ingredients together before walking back to him. "Where is your magical half-immortality now?"

He watched her saunter back and sit behind him, packing his wound with whatever concoction she came up with from the armoire.

"Apparently fatal wounds in other planes aren't something I guarded against."

"Oh? Didn't think to specify that in your dealings with darkness?" Griselda spat. "Good thing for you the apothecary boy works for us now. This would be easier if you'd laid down." She pushed farther into the wound.

"Would it now?" he growled at her order but complied, desperate for relief.

"I can't believe you were so foolish." Griselda pushed more of the medication into the wound.

"I suggest you watch your tongue with me." Through the pain, Leo tossed Griselda onto her back before straddling her. He towered over her as he held her wrists down. "I am not so hurt that I cannot correct your petulant insubordination."

Griselda stared back in defiance, despite the fear creeping inside of her; there was a rush that came from such danger. "You never complained about my tongue before."

The words stirred familiar sensations that dulled his anger, and Griselda watched his gaze grow carnal. "Perhaps that is what saves you. How ironic, the thing that gets you in so much trouble saves you the most."

He kissed her deeply, his familiar lust for her returning. He healed quicker than either of them expected, and once again, she outsmarted his anger.

CHAPTER THIRTY-SEVEN

As he patched her wounds, Zavier brooded without explanation. He helped Orianna change out of her damaged clothes and into her nightgown. He was quiet, distant; his mood left Orianna more unsettled.

"Zavier, please, tell me what's on your mind," she pleaded, unable to recall the last time he was so upset. "I survived. What could you possibly be mad about?"

He stood with his back toward her as tensions pressed against them. "Did you really think I wouldn't notice the scar bleeding? Thought I wouldn't realize what it meant."

Her heart stopped mid-beat, suffocating her lungs. He was right. She didn't think he'd notice the scar bleeding, or even consider he'd know why it was happening, assuming she could chalk it up to battle wounds. All that had mattered in the moment was saving Gemma by invoking the blood binding; in turn, she'd forgotten to craft a lie for Zavier about the scar.

"I...I forgot about it," she stammered, her heart beating too fast for her ribcage to contain it. "I didn't think I'd ever need to call on the binding again, Zavier. It was truly a dire emergency. But I mean, at this stage of our lives what does it matter?"

"You forgot?" He turned to her, his face hardened into exasperation. "That's an exceedingly heavy piece of magic for you to have forgotten about, Orianna. Magic like that doesn't just slip someone's mind! And it matters to me, damn it—isn't that enough of a reason? Or am I not enough for you?"

Orianna adjusted her nightgown, but this did not fix how naked she felt. "No, Zavier, of course you are. You're more than enough!" Regret filled her entrails with greasy clots. "I'm sorry. I never thought—"

"That's just it! You didn't think at all!"

"Don't you raise your voice to me." Orianna spat back as her legs wobbled beneath her.

"I'll do as I damn well please, woman," he growled, shaking the walls.

Orianna took a deep breath and crossed her arms over her chest. "What difference would it have made, whether or not you knew?"

Zavier's face remained unchanged. "That doesn't matter. It was the right thing to do. I had the right to know the truth. You might've told me you cut yourself doing housework and whatever elaborate story came with it."

He stalked off to the other side of the room, hurt and angry. Orianna couldn't tell which, making her feel as if her skin was peeling from her body. She was a stranger to this side of him, being the subject of his anger; her nerves shook as tears stung her eyes.

"I didn't want to lose you." Her voice was a whisper. "Would your love have changed for me if you knew?"

He turned to her, hard-pressed to believe what she said. Shamed as he realized the heat of his temper but unwilling to remain silent.

"You think me so shallow?" He walked closer to see what hid in her eyes. "No, my love wouldn't have changed. But you were the one who insisted this relationship be built on truth and honesty, yet you withheld something like *this*. It's just the same as lying." He put his hands on her shoulders. "My love could never change for you, Orianna, but doesn't mean I'm not hurt."

Orianna sat quietly, staring back at him. "I could perform a cleansing."

He let go, walking away again. "There is no cleansing for something so serious. That's why it's called a binding—it's *binding,* and it's in blood, one of the strongest bindings there is."

"But there is. I know the spell well enough. I considered using it years ago. It is dangerous, but from what I've read, those who survive it say it works."

Zavier turned back to her, his temper quaking. "You weren't going to tell me that, either? Were you just going to do that without saying a word to me?"

Guilt swept back over her as she nodded. "Yes, I was."

"That's just great, almost kill yourself to be rid of him. You almost threw away everything we've built...over him."

Orianna's anger erupted, propelling her across the floor to him. "Make up your mind, Zavier. Are you madder I didn't tell you about the binding, or what *could* have happened if I tried to rid myself of the binding? You *can't* have both ways."

He stayed mute as she stared up with her large, dark eyes, too upset for the words to come. When she spoke again, her voice crackled against the cold silence.

"I would have done it for you." She swallowed hard against the lump in her throat. "To cleanse myself of Leo. To make myself purer for you. To be what you deserved."

The words cut into him and he reached out, cupping her face. "I've never *cared* about how pure your soul was—and you're more than I could deserve." He took a deep breath. "Damn you, Orianna. I love you for the aggravating, obstinate, beautiful woman that you are. The only woman who sets my blood on fire and lightens my stone heart. I've loved you for how you've always made me feel, not for who you try to be. You mean more to me than anything my birthright could have given me."

His words rendered her speechless as large tears fell down her cheeks, which Zavier wiped them away with his thumbs. He pulled her closer, drawing her face towards his.

"Nothing—and I mean, nothing—could ever change that. You hear me? Nothing," he whispered against her lips before kissing her, then resting his forehead against hers. "I love you, my starlight disaster of a woman."

* * *

AS THE WORLD STANDS silent before an approaching dawn, the darkness arises to ripple beneath its skin. In the eaves and shadows of Goblidet, wickedness holds tight—fixed in position, waiting for the command to strike.

However, opposing forces align to counter and find balance. Deep in the hearts of the sleeping members of an undisturbed house beat the demise of an evil that continues to plot against them.

But the paths of good and evil are never so clear cut. A heart that beats in the light may turn dark when crushed by extreme power, tarnished by black spots left unseen, and sometimes in the relentless fight to do what's right it might be lost to malice forever.

ACKNOWLEDGMENTS

Where do I begin? This has been a long time coming and a road I've been lucky enough to travel.

To RhetAskew, the biggest of thank you's for taking a chance on me and giving me a chance to break into the writing world.

To Jennifer Soucy, my creative editor, for all of your help in helping me refine the book and for cheering me on at every corner. I could not have worked through this without you.

To my parents and family, thank you for your support and being examples that nothing is impossible.

ABOUT THE AUTHOR

VINCENZA DI MARTINO is an American author who has a passion for writing fantasy novels and reading. With a talent for tension and comic relief the budding author finds new ways to transfix words into exciting page turners.

Raised most of her life in rural New York, she continues to live there with her husband, Travis, and their dog, Oliver.

46005510R00214